Dear Reader,

Thanks for picking  you enjoy reading ...g it.

About the setting: W... ...ayou Blue is a real town, the fictional Bayou Blue is a composite of several small, lovely towns in southern Louisiana Creole/Cajun country. So, welcome to Louisiana, cher! Sit back and listen to a little zydeco, sip cafe au lait and get a bit of Louisiana lagniappe.

Visit my website at http://*lynnemery.home.mindspring.com* or write to me at P.O. Box 74095, Baton Rouge, LA 70874. Send a SASE for reply.

All the best,

Lynn Emery

LYNN EMERY

GOTTA GET NEXT TO YOU

HarperTorch
An Imprint of HarperCollinsPublishers

This is a work of fiction. Names, characters, places, and incidents are products of the author's imagination or are used fictitiously and are not to be construed as real. Any resemblance to actual events, locales, organizations, or persons, living or dead, is entirely coincidental.

HARPERTORCH
An Imprint of HarperCollins*Publishers*
10 East 53rd Street
New York, New York 10022-5299

Copyright © 2001 by Margaret Hubbard
Excerpt from *Crazy Thing Called Love* copyright © 2001 by Cynthia Louis
ISBN: 0-380-81304-1

First HarperTorch paperback printing: May 2001

HarperCollins ®, HarperTorch™, and ❦ ™ are trademarks of Harper-Collins Publishers Inc.

Printed in the United States of America

Visit HarperTorch on the World Wide Web at www.harpercollins.com

10 9 8 7 6 5 4 3 2 1

Prologue

✳

Charlene Noble glared at the man on the other side of the mahogany desk. Outside the window behind him was an expanse of sky. Blue turned to orange and pink as the sun set in a summer south Louisiana sky. The offices of Gulfco, Inc., were designed to impress, even intimidate. Two things John Mandeville, influential in Louisiana politics, was good at doing. He'd taken over the family business started by his great-grandfather and made his old-money family even richer. His gaze was steady, his bearing straight, as he faced his former lover. At the moment Charlene was neither impressed nor intimidated. Her copper-colored eyes narrowed as she stared him down.

"It's the least you can do for your daughter," she said, her tone cold.

"It's been four years since I've seen you, and you

come in swinging. There's nobody else like you, Charlie." His lips curved up in a slightly flirtatious smile.

"Cut the crap, John. I'm serious."

"I can't just tell the board who to hire."

Charlene wore a tight smile. "Bull! You run this town the same way your father did."

"I'm just part of the advisory council," John said mildly.

Charlene leaned forward. "John Mandeville, you haven't done nearly enough for Andrea."

"I did what I could, given the circumstances," he said in a taut voice. John clenched one hand into a fist.

"What circumstances? The fact that you didn't have the guts to stand up to your mommy and daddy?" Charlene tossed back.

John blew out a gust of air. "Oh hell, here we go again."

"I'm not going to dredge up ancient history, so relax."

John's dark brows came together. "What kind of life would we have had thirty years ago, Charlene? An interracial couple in south Louisiana with no money. None. My father would have seen to that."

"Heaven forbid you would have had to get a job. Too high a price to be with the girl you claimed you loved more than life." Charlene pressed her lips together.

John's face flushed pink. When he spoke his voice was low and husky. "It was more complicated than that, and you know it. Sometimes . . . I wish we could just go back."

Charlene stared into John's eyes without flinching. "But we can't."

"No. We can't," John said, regret making his voice deeper. "So now what?"

"The clinic needs a new director," Charlene answered firmly.

"What makes you think—"

Charlene waved a hand, her crimson fingernails polished to perfection. "I have my sources. I know Bob Billings, the current director, accepted a position in Baton Rouge."

John gave a grunt of exasperation. He did not bother to deny what she obviously knew. "The bum."

"Andrea has the qualifications. She's been the assistant director of a county clinic in Chicago for the past year."

"Really?" John rubbed his chin.

"You've gone through two directors in the last four years, three now," Charlene said.

"Each one was worse than the one before." John frowned.

"Andrea wants to come home." Charlene looked down at the purse in her lap. "If only to be close to her grandmother."

John studied her for a time. "And you want a chance to fix your relationship."

"I'm getting—" Charlene said.

"Older?" John's eyebrows went up.

She ignored him. "The point is, I want her home, too."

"I understand, Charlie. Really I do." John's voice was sympathetic. He glanced away from her stony gaze.

"Don't give me some phony excuse," Charlene said.

"The clinic is going through a rough patch. We need someone seasoned, someone who can stand firm."

"And?"

"I can't push anyone on them. It's got to be done carefully." John toyed with the Mont Blanc ink pen on his desk.

"You mean having *our* daughter put in charge. Don't tell me you're worried about your reputation, or what's left of it after thirty years of raising hell." Charlene's lovely mouth curved up in a sardonic smile.

"Damn it, Charlene, I'm thinking how rough it could be on *her*." John's fingers raked his black hair.

"Andrea is strong willed. She inherited that on both sides," Charlene said promptly. Her expression softened. "Please, John. Do this for me and for her."

The speaker phone on his desk buzzed. John pressed a button. "Yes, Norma?"

"Your appointment is here, Mr. Mandeville." His secretary's voice came through clearly.

"Give me ten minutes." John gazed at Charlene. "Okay, Charlie. Andrea can have the job."

"Good." Charlene sighed.

"You're welcome," John said dryly.

"You're not doing me a favor, you know." Charlene stood.

John shook his head in amazement as he stood. He lifted a hand to touch her hair, but Charlene moved away. "God, you're such a lovely woman. When will I see you again?"

He followed her to the private elevator that would take her from his office to the first-floor lobby without anyone seeing her.

Charlene got on the elevator and punched the button. "Goodbye, John," she said tartly.

Suddenly there was a knock on the door and it opened. Norma entered. "Are you available now?"

"Send him on in." John stood in front of the elevator to block the view when he realized the doors were not completely closed.

"Evening, Mr. Mandeville." The tall, muscular man

strode into the office. He extended a large, dark brown hand even as his gaze flicked to the elevator.

"Mr. Matthews, nice to meet you. What's your first name? We're used to being informal down here," John said.

"LeRoyce, but call me Lee." He let a beat pass. "Good meeting you, *John*." The newcomer did not intend to let the Mandeville mystique affect him either.

John's smile faltered. "Yes, well, sit down." He pointed to the seating area of two chairs and a small sofa near another window. "Would you like a drink?"

"Seven-Up, thanks," Lee said. He folded his six-foot-four frame into the leather wing chair.

John walked over to the small built-in bar. He poured himself a finger of scotch, then poured the soft drink into another glass. "I was sure a two-fisted private eye would want a strong belt."

Lee scanned the office carefully, taking in each detail. "Only in old movies. And you wouldn't want to hire a private investigator who drinks."

"Good point," John said as he walked over to his desk and sat down. He handed Lee the glass of soda and sipped from his drink. "You've read our report about the problems. What do you think?"

"It's tricky." Lee stretched one long leg out.

"What do you suggest?"

"If I worked at the clinic for a few months, it would help." Lee looked at him directly for the first time. "I'm pretty good on a computer and a darn good receptionist."

"Put you inside the clinic." John rocked his chair and wore a thoughtful expression.

"The one they've got now needs a career change. One in a string of bad hiring decisions."

John scowled. "I've heard about her!"

"It's an opening and won't seem strange." Lee sat back as though waiting for John to process his proposal.

"A receptionist built like a linebacker. You don't think that would look strange?"

"With the characters in and out of that place, some of the patients might welcome it," Lee retorted.

John laughed out loud. "Damn it, I like you!" He shook his head. "I'll get that woman out of there and you can start immediately."

Lee stood. "Give me a week to wrap up some other work with my partner, Vince."

"Excellent." John walked him to the door. "Er, we've hired a new director, by the way," he said in a tone meant to be casual.

Lee studied him. "Something special I should know about him?" His full eyebrows went up as John avoided his gaze.

"Her. Andrea Noble. And no, I just wanted you to be fully informed."

Lee's eyes narrowed as he glanced at John. "All right," he said in a voice that implied he'd find out eventually.

John watched the tall man stride off. "Damn place. More trouble than it's worth," he muttered.

One

"Good Lord. What have I gotten myself into?"

Andrea turned around in a circle. A layer of dust filmed every surface. Faded blue plastic chairs were scattered across the floor in an uneven pattern. Patients waiting to be seen looked just as forlorn as the waiting room of the Bayou Blue Public Health Clinic. Her grandmother and Cousin Pam had warned her it might need "a bit of sprucing up." What an understatement.

"Hey, you!" a gruff female voice called out.

A woman with hair piled high and stiff with styling gel looked at her from behind a Plexiglas partition with a small opening. She sat in an office that faced the waiting room. A plastic tag pinned to her chest had the name Shonda etched in white letters. Her wide, light brown face was bored. Her jaws moved as she worked on a lump of chewing gum.

"Are you talking to me, ma'am?" Andrea asked, her tone deliberately measured and polite.

"Yeah. You need to sign in before you sit down. Come here."

Immediately Andrea decided to go with the flow. She walked over to the window. "I left my Medicaid card at home. And I don't have an appointment."

Shonda rolled her eyes and threw down the pencil she was holding. "Then you can't see the doctor."

"They told me you accepted walk-ins." Andrea could see Shonda was losing what little patience she had.

"Well, *they* told you wrong. Dr. Hayes ain't even here. Them people waitin' to see the nurse." Shonda waved a hand at the twelve or so people sitting in faded blue plastic chairs.

"I thought the doctor was in Thursdays." Andrea grimaced and put a hand to her stomach. "I've got a pain that's killing me."

"Look, he ain't here, okay?" Shonda snapped. "How many ways I hafta say it?"

There were a few snickers from several of the women nearby. Andrea ground her teeth. Sally Ranger, the registered nurse who'd recruited her, would definitely get a phone call. So would her mother. To think she'd left Chicago to come home to this.

"Now, what's your name?" Shonda slapped a clipboard down on the desk. A form faded from too much copying had two columns with times, dates, and names.

Andrea ignored her question. "Will the doctor be in at all today?"

"Well, I'll be—" Shonda bit off as she shoved her chair back and stomped through the door.

Andrea heard muffled voices, one of which was Shonda's. After a few moments, a heavyset white woman came out. Nurse Cresson appeared to be in her fifties. Her brunette hair was pulled back. She had on a green scrub suit.

"I'm Nurse Cresson. What's wrong with you, baby?"

"I told her Dr. Hayes ain't here," Shonda muttered over Nurse Cresson's shoulder.

"I'm in pain." Andrea held her stomach again.

"Well, you need to go to the emergency room over in Houma," Nurse Cresson said in a crisp tone. She did not even look at Andrea.

"But I thought Thursday was the day the doctor would handle small emergencies. I don't have a car and—"

"He's not here and he's not coming," Nurse Cresson cut her off sharply. "You can make an appointment for follow-up. But if you in that much pain, go to the hospital."

"Let me tell you—"

"I don't need to hear it." Nurse Cresson turned away from Andrea. "Shonda, give her an appointment. She can't be too bad off if she can stand here arguing."

With a furious frown, Andrea walked around the corner of the office and down the hall that led to the examination rooms. As she passed the public rest rooms, the smell told her they had not been cleaned for some time.

"Hey! You can't come back here without bein' called," Shonda yelled.

Nurse Cresson rushed out into the hall and held up a hand. "You go right back the way you came."

Shonda joined her, looking fierce. "Some people got more nerve than sense!"

"You wanted to know my name earlier. Well, I'm Andrea Noble. Your new clinic director," Andrea said, her voice like a razor. She wore a hard smile and nodded as the expressions on their faces transformed from outrage to shock.

"But you ain't supposed to be here until next week." Shonda's mouth was slack with dismay.

Nurse Cresson's dark eyes flashed with suspicion. "Sally Ranger is supposed to come that day along with some of the health clinic board members for a tour."

"I can show you my driver's license if you don't believe me." Andrea held up her purse.

"No. I'm sorry," Nurse Cresson said, forcing a smile onto her crinkled face. "You just caught us off guard."

"Exactly," Andrea tossed back. "I got home yesterday morning and decided not to wait for the official tour."

"Home?" Shonda blinked at her. "You're from around here?"

"I grew up in Bayou Blue. I've lived in Chicago for nine years." Andrea looked at her. Shonda was no more than twenty and she did not recognize her. "What's your last name?"

Shonda hesitated. "LaMotte. I'm from down on Sweet Road."

Andrea remembered the LaMotte brood. They were a rowdy bunch. She knew several of them. The women liked a good fistfight as much as the men did. "I know Raleene and Wyvonne. Are they your sisters?"

"Cousins."

"The Crazy Dog Bar still there?" Andrea walked past them. She glanced in several rooms as she talked.

"Yeah." Shonda shot a worried glance at Nurse Cresson.

"Uh-huh." Andrea knew she had established herself as a native. No outsider would know about the LaMottes and the Crazy Dog.

"I can see we've got a lot of work to do. We might as well start now." Andrea turned around to face them abruptly. Both women jumped back.

"We was gonna clean up . . . I mean we always keep it clean. But the janitor been sick." Nurse Cresson's gaze darted around the hall.

"Really?" Andrea let skepticism lace her tone. "Well, let's just do a walk-through and see what we have."

For the next two hours she put Nurse Cresson through the wringer. Andrea suspected Thelma Cresson was a nurse with little real skill beyond first aid and not much ambition. She made a mental note to find out what relative had gotten her this job. Equipment at the clinic was in poor condition. There were no real health education programs to help the largely poor, welfare patients. Andrea made it clear to Nurse Cresson and Shonda that things would change. Their morose expressions told her just what they thought. After making a long list of things she wanted done, Andrea headed for home. Once outside, she paused to glance around.

It was a glorious sunny day. The sky was still bright blue, but turning darker with touches of orange as the sun set. Cottony white clouds floated along. Bayou Blue was surrounded by lush prairies and bayous. Her grandmother's house, the house she'd grown up in, was three miles from town. Andrea had not really paid attention to the area on previous visits home. But Gran had told her that a group of businessmen were trying to revive downtown. Having the clinic improved and under new management was part of the initiative.

Being home again was part of Andrea's own five-year plan after her divorce. She'd been eager to come. The concrete and fast pace of Chicago only served to make her feel more disconnected. After a while, Gran's urging that she come back to her roots did not seem like a bad idea. Andrea wanted to get her life on an even keel. The fact that crime and decay threatened Bayou Blue angered her.

She walked halfway down one block and stopped within a few yards of a store. Downtown Bayou Blue needed a face-lift for sure. The shabbiness of abandoned storefronts contrasted with the beautiful rural setting. Still, the Improvement Committee's efforts did show in a few places. Several historic buildings had been attractively restored. Andrea had fond childhood memories of skipping to keep up with her father's long strides as they walked downtown. Andrea mentally identified the old dress shop where her father had bought her first party outfit. Around the corner had been a combination shoe store and shoe repair shop. It wasn't much of a town by big city standards, but it was well worth saving. The sound of footsteps brought her back to the present. Andrea realized she'd wandered a good two blocks from where her car was parked outside the clinic. The area was scattered with shabby vacant storefronts. Trash and weeds filled two empty lots to her left.

"Yeah, man. Them dudes crazy. I—Whoa, looka that." A male voice went from conversational to provocative.

Three men wearing low-slung jeans strolled toward her. They seemed to have appeared out of nowhere. They were young and lanky, their conversation filled with profanity. Andrea looked around, hoping to see someone else on the street. But what few businesses remained were closed and no one was in sight. She turned around and started back to her car.

"Evenin'," a different male voice called out.

"What's up?" A tall man wearing a tank top and jeans

trotted up beside her. He was soon joined by his buddies.

Andrea increased her pace to reach the clinic. "Hi," she said over her shoulder.

"Hey, baby. How ya doin'?" A young man grinned, revealing three gold teeth.

"I'm fine," Andrea said without breaking her stride.

"That ain't no lie." The young man rubbed his chin with one hand.

Andrea glanced at him briefly. She'd worked in a Chicago clinic that saw a lot of troubled kids and adults, even gang members. This young man was more bluster than real menace, but the two men with him were another matter. One had a scar along his left cheek that he rubbed as though proud of it. The other, shorter and the color of ebony, wore a red kerchief around his neck. His muscle shirt was hiked up on one side.

They jumped ahead of her on the sidewalk, blocking her progress, forcing Andrea to stop as well.

The one with the scar spoke first. "My name's Javon, an' I got what you need," he said with a smack of his lips.

Andrea's throat tightened with fear. "Excuse me, but I'm going to my car."

"You outta your league. Classy lady ain't got time for kiddie stuff. I'm Bo, baby." He let his gaze trail over her body suggestively.

"Hi," Andrea said. She tried once more to continue on, but Bo did not move to let her pass.

"You must be new in town, 'cause I know *all* the pretty ladies. And they know me." His buddies guffawed and his grin widened.

Andrea decided to make this her first community outreach effort. She allowed the snickering and sassy comments to die down.

"I'm from here, just been gone a long time. I'm Andrea Noble, the new health clinic director." She pointed toward the Bayou Blue Health Clinic.

"I'm in good health. Strong as can be, baby. Wanna feel?" Bo slapped his chest.

"No, thanks. But we'll have information on good nutrition and exercise, like weight lifting." Andrea made a stab at what might interest them.

"I see something I wanna pick up right here." Bo wet his lips; his eyes narrowed to slits as he stared at her breasts. He took a step closer to her. "Yes indeed."

Andrea frowned in distaste, realizing suddenly that this was a bad idea. "Excuse me." She made another attempt to go around him. When he didn't move, she tried to push her way through.

Bo stopped smiling, his expression turning hard. He glared at his laughing friends and they grew quiet. When he turned back to Andrea, she felt a trickle of fear at the look in his eyes, but she was determined not to let it show. She stared back at him, chin raised.

"Why you in such a hurry? Be friendly." Bo moved closer, until he towered over her. He made a grab for her arm.

Andrea jerked back, avoiding his grasp. "Leave me alone."

Bo grabbed for her again. "That ain't the way to—"

Andrea knocked his hand aside and kicked his shin hard. Bo yelped at the glancing blow, then lunged for her. In a panic, she turned to run and collided with a man's hard chest.

"We got a problem out here?" a deep voice asked.

Shaking with fear at the realization that she was surrounded, Andrea looked up and up. He was at least six feet four, with smooth skin like fine chocolate milk. His eyes were a deep brown, like strong Louisiana dark-roast coffee, as he gazed at them calmly. He wore a light blue cotton Henley shirt and blue jeans that hugged narrow hips. He looked powerful even standing still. Andrea was caught between the aura of masculine strength, as palpable as the musky scent of cologne he wore, and the feeling of fear that made her pulse race. Or was it fear? She stared at the strong line of his jaw. This man inspired something more: exhilaration. He surveyed the group of men calmly, and Andrea felt as though the cavalry had just galloped across the horizon.

"Nah, we just gettin' introduced," Bo said. He glared at Andrea. "Awright?"

"Funny. Looks like the lady is trying to get away. What about it, ma'am?" He glanced at Andrea.

Bo's whole body was tensed for battle. "Stay outta my business."

"I know y'all can't read, so I'll help you out." Wearing a mild expression, the handsome newcomer pointed to a rectangular sign attached to the stone wall of the clinic. " 'No loitering near entrance,' " he read.

Javon's mouth flapped open as he decided to join in. "You can't tell us nothin'—"

"Come on, ma'am. Let's go inside. The air is cooler and better smelling," he said with derision. The man put a hand under her elbow and guided her inside the clinic.

Andrea was through the door before she could protest, but for some reason she did not feel alarmed. This man had a solid, reassuring presence. He radiated confidence, with a dash of boldness thrown in. She looked at him and felt a shock of warmth travel up her spine. When he fully turned to look at her, the warmth turned to a full-blown fire. His full brown lips pulled back in a dazzling smile, revealed gleaming white teeth. This man was more than handsome. The knit shirt seemed to strain across his chest. His muscular arms were even more defined when he put both hands on his waist. His gaze went over her head briefly as he checked to make sure the thugs were gone, then back to her face. He was stunning. A dimple in one cheek made the delectable creature near perfect. He glanced around the waiting room.

"Looks like the roaches scattered." He turned around in a half circle.

Andrea said nothing, still taking him in. His dark brown hair was cut short and the tight curls looked like soft wool loops. She had a crazy urge to reach up and touch them. When he faced her again, Andrea blinked rapidly. She must be losing her mind. She looked away, sure that she was gaping at him like an idiot.

Andrea recovered. "Thanks," she said in a restrained tone.

"You're welcome, I guess."

"I do appreciate your help," Andrea said, "but I've been in tough situations before."

"Sure." Disdain dripped from his voice. He continued to look around.

"I worked in Chicago and dealt with lots of people." Andrea's gratitude was being tested by his know-it-all manner.

"This may not be Chicago, but you obviously don't know how much has changed."

"Thanks again. But I think I do."

"Is that right?" he said.

"Yes, that's right." She decided that what she'd mistaken for charisma was really plain old-fashioned arrogance.

"Well, I'd advise you to stay out of this part of town."

"Decent people should be able to go anywhere they want," Andrea said. "We can't let hoodlums dictate what we do."

"Look, lady, use common sense. Unless you want something to happen, don't strut your stuff around here." He eyed her from head to toe.

"If being free to walk in town is 'strutting my stuff,' as you so crudely put it, then I've got a right to strut my stuff where I please, when I please." Andrea spoke the words in a rapid-fire burst and waved a forefinger at him. "You hear me?"

"Yes, ma'am. Folks for miles around heard you." He nodded his head.

Two patients, apparently the last for the day, stood staring at them in amusement. Several women were nodding. One woman wearing large hoop earrings that touched her shoulders bobbed her head from side to side.

"Tell him 'bout it, baby, that's right."

Andrea lowered her hand quickly. What was wrong with her? Causing big scenes, especially in public, horrified her. And here she was, the instigator. She'd spent years trying not to be like her emotional mother. Charlene could create high drama over a broken fingernail.

"Maybe you *could* have taken care of yourself out there," he said, dark eyebrows raised almost to his hairline. A twinkle of amusement lit his eyes.

Something about this man set off strong reactions in her, first attraction, then wrath. Every hair on her body seemed raised. And worse, she felt strangely elated.

"Just don't make a simple walk into something it's not," she managed to stammer out.

"I was out of line, okay? I'm sorry." His baritone voice was soft.

His apology and the hint of tenderness in his deep voice were like fuel to an already smoldering flame. Andrea gazed up at him. "I owe you an apology, too. Here you help me out and I jump on you with both feet."

He smiled at her warmly. "Now that we've said our pardons, maybe you could tell me your name."

The tingle of desire was pleasurable, and terrifying. She stuck out her hand in a businesslike gesture in an attempt to keep their meeting from becoming too personal.

"Andrea Noble. I'm the new director here."

He shook her hand. "Glad to meet you. I hear they've got plans to fix the place up."

Andrea liked the firm pressure of his handshake. She pulled her hand away quickly, but the warmth of his hand lingered on the soft skin of her palm. She took a deep breath and steadied herself.

"Ahem. Yes, we certainly do," she said.

"Think it could use the improvement."

"The clinic and downtown, too." Andrea nodded. "Lots of shady characters hanging around."

"Hmm."

The man's gaze drifted around again, scanning every inch of the place. He sauntered off and looked down the hall toward the back of the clinic. Andrea's wariness kicked in. Her reaction to his good looks had temporarily blinded her. Something that had led her to ruin before, she thought sourly. Now she really looked at this man. He seemed to be sizing up his surroundings. Andrea thought about the drugs stored in the small clinic pharmacy. She noted every detail of his appearance, in case she had to pick him out of a lineup.

"I didn't get your name," she said.

"Jamal Turner." He spun around and strode to her. "Pleased to meet you."

Andrea fought off the sudden spike of desire when that tall, fine frame loomed over her again. "Mr. Turner."

"Call me Jamal. And I'll call you—"

"Ms. Noble," Andrea cut in. She moved farther from him to avoid more tingling than she needed. "Well, Mr. Turner, what brings you downtown at this hour?"

He smiled at her formality. "Went to pick up my dry cleaning and got there five minutes too late," he said smoothly.

Too smoothly, Andrea thought. "Mr. Peters has closed his store at four on Fridays for twenty years. You must not be from around here."

"Actually I am new to the area. But I'm learning fast." His dazzling smile came back, all charm and sex appeal.

This time Andrea was ready for him and his dimple. His explanation had holes in it, smooth or not. "What were you doing on this street? Clotier's is two blocks around the corner."

"I was at the bank and decided to just walk over. Wouldn't make sense to drive such a short distance. Good legs." Jamal slapped his thighs.

Andrea's gaze settled on the well-developed limbs in question. Her gaze drifted a little higher, then she blushed and turned away. Her knees felt shaky. So this was what the phrase "temporary insanity" meant. She had to get control of herself.

"Thighs—I mean, thanks for helping me." Andrea

wanted to sink into the floor. She prayed he hadn't heard the slip. Good God, she was behaving like a sex-starved idiot!

"No problem," he said in a cheerful voice. "Next time you decide to stroll in a high-crime area, I'm your man."

Andrea whirled around to set him straight with a sour reply. "Very funny, Mr. . . ." Her voice trailed off and she couldn't think of what to say. Instead of being annoyed, he was amused; she noticed the delicious curve of his top lip.

"Cease fire," he quipped. "Just be careful, okay?" He titled his handsome head to one side.

"Okay," was all she could manage to murmur.

"See ya, ma'am." Jamal flipped a wave at her and pushed through the glass door of the clinic.

Andrea stared after him, hypnotized by the graceful, loping stride of impossibly long legs covered by dark blue denim. Despite his size, his body flowed like liquid.

"We lockin' up." Shonda's voice broke into her rather rampant fantasies. Shonda popped her gum three times as though to emphasize her statement.

Andrea snapped out of her daze and back to reality. "Right. I, uh, I'm leaving now. My first full day is a week from Monday, but I'll drop in again for a few hours tomorrow to check on your progress."

"Great," was Shonda's sarcastic response. She clumped over and stood at the front door, jingling the large ring of keys impatiently.

"I look forward to it as much as you," Andrea replied with a tight smile. "Good-bye."

She left and heard the click of door locks behind her. Andrea walked the short distance to her car, keys in her hand. When she turned for one last look at the clinic, Shonda and Thelma Cresson stood staring at her with rancorous expressions. She looked forward to setting those two straight.

She sighed. It was obvious she had a lot of work ahead of her. She was living with Gran until she could find an apartment of her own. Between clearing up the problems at the clinic and apartment hunting, she had no time to fantasize about a handsome player like Jamal Turner. She'd had her fill of that kind of trouble.

Andrea needed to feel success, if only professionally. Her marriage had ended with a bang and work in the inner-city clinic had overwhelmed her. Here she could make a difference. She would put her focus on the clinic, and no smiling tower of testosterone would distract her.

TWO

Andrea and Gran walked into the municipal building, where both the city aldermen and the school board met. Rows of stadium-style seats faced the raised dais where city leaders sat. One long curved table faced the audience. Atop the table were microphones. Tonight the aldermen, along with the health clinic's board of directors, would hear progress reports. Introducing her as the new director of the clinic would be part of a report. Andrea took a deep breath to steady her nerves. More than anything, she wanted to make a good first impression. Community cooperation was vital, and the local leaders could help the clinic or hurt it. She glanced at the agenda she'd been handed as they walked in.

"At least I'm not first," Andrea said.

"You gonna do fine, cher." Gran pinched her cheek. She glanced around and waved at friends. "Good turnout."

"Then again, it would be nice to get this over with," Andrea said with a grimace.

"Stop worrying your nerves, girl. All those years of school, you're used to getting up in front of folks. Just look at it like that."

"This is ten times harder than grad school," Andrea said as she gazed around the room.

Small-town judgments could be harsh. Already, talk of how she felt about changes needed at the clinic had caused a stir. Andrea now remembered the part of small-town life she'd never missed, lightning-quick word of mouth. Some on the board had not been pleased with her candid assessment. They would be only too happy to sabotage her efforts to bring in more funding and expand the clinic. Bob Billings, the director leaving, worked part-time in a transitional capacity until Andrea could come aboard. The board had instructed him to make whatever changes he saw fit to make her first few weeks easier. Andrea was relieved and encouraged by this show of support. Yet dealing with the board was far less stressful than facing what looked to be one third of Bayou Blue.

Andrea scanned the audience, her gaze stopping at Shonda. From the venom in her eyes, Andrea could guess what she'd heard. Thelma Cresson sat four rows behind Shonda. She cast hostile glances at Andrea and whispered to a group of heavyset women surrounding her. They took turns scowling at Andrea. It was then that Andrea remembered that two of the aldermen were Thelma's cousins and three members of the board were friends of hers.

"I guess I shouldn't expect a round of applause when I stand up," Andrea muttered quietly.

"What, baby?" Gran paused in the act of exchanging

a new recipe with a lady who lived down the road from her.

"Nothing, nothing." Andrea took another deep breath.

Gran gave her arm a nudge. "Look, Cousin Esme. Always bragging 'bout her son the chiropractor. Boy ain't even a real doctor."

"Gran, be nice," Andrea mumbled close to her ear. She smiled at the approaching woman. "Hi, Cousin Esme."

"Hello, Esme," Gran said. She wore a restrained smile. "Nice crowd. Guess everybody wants to hear what's going on."

Esme held her head high. Her hair was pulled back in a bun. "Guess so. My Charles and his family said they would be here. Of course, being in his position, he's interested in these things."

"What position?" Gran raised one eyebrow.

"He's givin' consultation to the Health Clinic Board, of course. He *is* a medical professional," Esme said.

Gran pursed her lips. "Crackin' bones ain't—"

"That's wonderful, Cousin Esme," Andrea said loudly, drowning out Gran. "So Charles is doing good?"

"Yes. His little girl is a straight-A student and Charles Jr. is a whiz on the xylophone." Esme glared at Andrea spitefully. "You got any children yet?"

"No." Andrea shot a sideways glance at Gran, who was having the human equivalent of a nuclear meltdown.

"Andrea is on the agenda. She's head of the clinic, you know." Gran's voice was tight with suppressed ire.

"That's nice, sweetie." Esme gave them both a condescending smile. "Here's Charles."

"Hi, Andrea. Glad to see you home," Charles said as he joined them with his wife, Janice, a good-natured, plump woman expecting their third child. "I've got a few ideas for the clinic. I'll be talking to you."

"All suggestions are welcome," Andrea replied. She ignored Gran huffing with indignation beside her.

"Big head, that's his problem. Just like his momma," Gran muttered when they left to find their seats.

"Hush. Let's sit down," Andrea whispered.

Having been so long in Chicago, she'd forgotten about the forced intimacy of small-town life. What others thought of you was very important. Alienating your neighbors would seriously limit your social life and even hurt a business. Not to mention how hard it was when most of them were relatives. So for years there might never be an open battle, just a simmering feud. Andrea felt a renewed dread when she glanced around.

"Hello again, Ms. Noble." A deep voice broke through her thoughts.

Andrea looked up. The dark eyes and dimple were familiar. His smile made her feel special, like she was the only woman he saw in the crowd. But it was his eyes that drew her in most of all. She was momentarily lost in the smoky depths that invited her into a sensuous other world. Andrea's practical, cynical side fought hard to pull her from the edge.

Andrea's gaze took in all of him. He was wearing an olive green and navy blue striped polo shirt open at the collar. His pants were navy also. A leather belt the color of dark wine coordinated with his loafers. The cologne he wore was a spicy, warm scent. He seemed oblivious to the stir he was causing. In fact, women all around the auditorium were staring at him in avid curiosity.

Gran glanced from Andrea to the man. "Guess I better introduce myself, since my granddaughter's been struck dumb. I'm Mavis Ricard."

Embarrassed and suddenly irritated, Andrea snapped out of her stupor. Exactly what she needed tonight, to make a fool of herself, especially in front of this man. His knowing smile grated even more.

"I would, Gran, except I can't quite recall his name," Andrea said, lifting her nose and glancing away.

"Jamal Turner. Nice to meet you, Mrs. Ricard." He dipped his head to her in a courtly bow.

"Baby, everybody calls me Miz Mavis. You can, too." Gran grinned at him widely. "Such a polite young fella. Not like some of these other rascals."

"Thank you, ma'am," Jamal said.

"Who are your people? You from around here? Don't sound like it. I'll bet you from up north or something." Gran went into full investigation mode. "Don't you think, Andrea?"

"Hmm," Andrea said in what she hoped was a disinterested voice. Still her heartbeat picked up speed when he spoke.

"I'm from Los Angeles actually. Born and raised there." Jamal seemed more than willing to answer her questions. "My grandmother lives in Lafayette."

"Well, then you're as good as a Louisiana child," Gran declared. She nodded with approval, then leaned toward him. "Got a good job?"

"Gran, really!" Andrea wanted to sink under the gray-tiled floor.

"Just got a pretty good one right here in town," Jamal answered smoothly as though not the least bit put out.

"That sure is nice. Isn't it, Andrea?" Gran's eyes twinkled.

"Right." Andrea laced her answer with doubt. "So what are you doing here?"

"I'm part of the effort to make Bayou Blue a better place to live," he said. "I'm helping the local Improvement Committee."

"What?" Andrea was no less astonished than if he'd announced he was from another planet.

"And I'm committed to improving the quality of life." He squared his shoulders.

"Exactly what we need," Gran put in with enthusiasm. "A talented young man with a good heart. And strong arms, too. Don't you think he's built real strong, Andrea?" She nudged Andrea with her elbow.

"Oh, please!" Andrea hissed in a low voice. She was mortified to find him watching her with an amused expression.

"Thank you, ma'am. I try to work out three times a week. And I eat all my vegetables."

"Your mamma raised a fine son." Gran patted his arm and glanced at Andrea. *"Real fine."*

"The meeting is about to start. Let's sit down." Andrea pushed Gran toward empty seats in the second row from the front. "Excuse us."

"Come on, baby." Gran snagged Jamal's hand before she could be hauled off. "There's plenty seats."

He glanced at Andrea, pressing his lips together, apparently to keep from laughing. Andrea ground her teeth in frustration. Gran's blatant matchmaking was galling. Yet the only thing she could do was follow them. With the grace of a ballet dancer, Gran maneuvered herself so that he was placed between them.

"Perfect," he said, grinning at her.

Andrea's stomach fluttered. Somehow she'd become susceptible to that darn dimple! She did her best to ignore him. Her heart had only just healed from the bruising Ellis had inflicted. He, too, had a smile that could melt icebergs, the liar. Andrea had gone back to using her maiden name before the ink was dry on the divorce decree. One whole week had been devoted to changing her credit cards and driver's license. It was a move to obliterate Ellis Reeves from her life. Andrea vowed to be in total control the next time, if there was a next time. Jamal Turner was not going to change her mind. Neither would her crafty grandmother.

As though reading her mind, he turned to look at her again. Some kind of force snatched away her thought of resistance. His gaze traveled down her face to her neck and beyond. Andrea's breathing now matched her increased heart rate. There was no denying the raw sexual energy this man could put into a simple glance. Andrea squirmed in her seat as a pleasant aching need stabbed her pelvis. When he looked up into her eyes again, she felt pure desire. She glanced at his hands. A vivid picture of him reaching up to unbutton her blouse popped into her head. Her head was swimming at the thought of his fingers on her bare skin. Andrea looked from his hands back to his face and swallowed hard. She put a shaky hand to her forehead and rubbed hard to break this disquieting spell he had woven.

She was obscenely happy to be introduced by the time she was called. When asked to give a statement, she did not mind at all. Anything to distract her from the way her body kept responding to Jamal. She was brief. Andrea made broad mention of problems, but did not spend much time on them.

"I look forward to working with everyone to make the clinic one we can be proud of." Andrea said.

"Thank you. I'm sure you're going to do a fine job."

Fred Hilliard, the president of the board, looked at the other officials. "Y'all got any questions?" When no one spoke, he moved on to other business.

"You did great," Jamal said when she slipped back into her seat.

Andrea let out a long breath. "Thanks. I need all the support I can get."

"That's what I'm here for." He grinned at her.

"What are you talking about?" she asked, but he put a finger to his lips.

"Listen." He nodded toward the aldermen.

"And, Ms. Noble, we know inventory and the books at the clinic are in a bad way. Mr. Jamal Turner there is going to help you get it all on the new computer." Mr. Hilliard smiled. "He's just what you need."

"Ain't that the truth!" Gran burst out. She clapped her hands with glee.

Andrea stared at Jamal in shock. "But what, how—"

"They interviewed me two weeks ago. The clinic needs my services, I needed a job, and bam! You got me."

"In my office?" Andrea whispered to herself.

He dipped his head in a mock bow. "Jamal Turner, at your service."

Andrea sat stunned. She gazed at Gran and then back at the dimple that kept yanking at her pulse. This was incredible. All her plans to keep out of his line of fire shot down! He'd be within reach. Trouble already. Just the thought of being close to him brought on the urge to feel those muscular arms. Was her armor strong enough?

He tilted his head to one side, an impish glint in his dark eyes. "I look forward to working with you, Nurse Noble."

Three

"No place like home," Andrea murmured.

She stood on the far edge of her grandmother's land and gazed into the distance. Tall grass moved in the muggy breeze of late spring. From a mile away, Andrea could smell the wet earth that surrounded the bayou. Snowy egrets floated in the blue sky gracefully, white wings stretched wide like glider planes. In imitation, Andrea spread her arms and turned in a circle.

She stopped spinning and faced the spacious house where she'd spent so many happy days. The cypress walls were a weathered grayish brown color that blended with the scenery. A porch wrapped around half the house. On it were cane-backed wooden rocking chairs. These had been made by her grandfather and father. She could remember the secure feeling of sitting in her father's lap while he crooned and rocked her. Interspersed between the chairs were several small tables. Of course, potted plants and hanging ferns were plentiful. Gran had to have her greenery. Andrea smiled as she remembered her grandfather teasing Gran that she lived in a jungle. Being with Gran here and now seemed natural, as though she'd never grown up and moved away.

As though she knew Andrea was thinking of her, Gran appeared at the kitchen window and beckoned to her. Andrea waved back as she strolled across the yard. She smiled as she took one last look around her. Even after being here for two weeks, she still could not get over how much the beauty of Bayou Blue cast a spell over her.

Andrea was hardly through the back door when Gran started talking.

"Sit yourself down right here and let me wait on you."

Gran bustled around the kitchen, adjusting the flame underneath pots and stirring. Cousins, uncles, and aunts filled every available space in the wood-frame house on Basin Road. The sound of laughter came from a group of her relatives on the porch. In the living room, another crowd sat in front of the color television, intent on a baseball game. Andrea was still trying to adjust to the constant stream of adults and children. She'd become accustomed to a quiet, almost isolated life with Ellis. One of her young cousins was shooed from her lap by Gran. The sixty-nine-year-old dynamo placed a plate piled with red beans and sausage in front of Andrea.

"Go play outside with the other children, Ché. Andrea's not gonna disappear." Gran patted her head, full of pigtails and colorful barrettes.

"I know you don't want to miss the ball game. Besides, I live here now. I'm not company." Andrea breathed in the smell of red pepper, onions, garlic, and bay leaf.

Gran put a wedge of cornbread on a saucer and placed it next to Andrea's plate. "I'm having more fun in this kitchen, as usual. Hey, Leonard. Get you some more, darlin'." She pinched the cheek of her tall, husky grandson.

"Hey, Drea. Heard you gonna run the clinic. That's great." Leonard grabbed another can of soda, plopped a link of hot sausage on a bun, and winked at her before leaving to go back to the game.

"That Leonard is a mess. Always stuffing himself. Don't know how he stays so thin." Gran chuckled. "You know he worked on fixing the clinic up. He's a master carpenter like his daddy." She looked proud as she always did when talking about her sons.

As though he'd been summoned, the nut brown man came into the kitchen. "Mama, you got some more potato salad? Hey, now, little lady." Uncle Curtis gave Andrea an affectionate pat on the head as though she were still ten years old.

"Yeah, cher. Best slow down, though. You know what the doctor said." Gran did not try to stop him from getting thirds despite her warning.

"I lost seven pounds," Uncle Curtis protested.

"And you gonna put 'em back on in one day," Gran quipped with an indulgent smile.

"This little bit won't hurt. Ain't that right, Drea?" Uncle Curtis leaned against the counter and scooped up some potato salad. He chewed with a look of pure satisfaction. "Hmm, can't nobody cook like Miss Mavis Ricard."

"Go on now." Gran blushed with pleasure.

"I understand the clinic is comin' along great," Uncle Curtis said. "Gonna be like new."

"Just needs a few finishing touches," Andrea said.

"Good thing, too. Folks need a decent clinic around here. Talk was, those folks stole more than they helped the patients." Uncle Curtis shoved more potato salad in his mouth.

"That's right," Gran agreed. "But with Andrea taking over, things gonna turn around. She's got some good new employees. Like that nice young man." She glanced over her shoulder at Andrea.

"For sure." Uncle Curtis nodded and chewed.

"Now that you mention it, I don't appreciate the board hiring staff without my input."

Andrea scowled at the thought of a handsome face wearing a smug expression. Irritation mixed with an odd tingle of attraction.

Gran cleared her throat. "If he's qualified and likable, what's the harm? Besides, I can tell he's the right man for the job."

"From talking to him for five minutes? Sure you can," Andrea said dryly.

"I don't know why you meet a nice, single man and get your back up," Gran said, both hands on her hips.

Andrea pointed a forefinger at her. "Stop right there."

"What?" Gran assumed a look of pure innocence.

"None of your tricks, Gran. I'm not kidding." Andrea scowled at her, hoping to look fierce.

"All I'm saying is, you don't have to give up men forever just because your husband was no good." Gran turned back to the stove.

"I don't want to have this talk again, so let me say this clearly. I'm concentrating on my career for now." Andrea walked over to her and tapped her on the shoulder. "Got it?"

"I saw the way you were looking at him." Gran put the lid on the pot of red beans and faced her again.

"Gran—"

"Fine, be by yourself," Gran grumbled.

"I'm going to enjoy my homecoming and get the clinic in shape. That's more than enough."

"If you say so." Gran lifted a shoulder.

"I do say so," Andrea added firmly.

"But you gotta admit, that Jamal is sure gonna dress the place up. Such a fine-looking young man." Gran's dark eyebrows arched.

"I need competent, qualified staff. Not window dressing." Andrea clenched her teeth. "But I'm stuck with him, I guess."

"He didn't take the job just to get on your nerves. Right, Curtis?" Gran said.

Uncle Curtis choked on a bit of potato salad. He shook his head. "Hmm . . . ahem, dunno," was his garbled answer.

"Don't you think he's a nice young fella?" Gran pressed on.

"Yeah, umm, I, er . . ." Uncle Curtis blinked like a deer caught in headlights.

"Ellis seemed like a nice young fellow, too. So do half the serial killers on death row," Andrea retorted. "The man's got 'player' plastered all over him."

"Now, that's plain silly to judge the boy so fast. Ain't that right, Curtis?" Gran turned to her son for support again.

"I've got tire marks all over me from the last hit-and-run. Trust me, I know the type." Andrea waved a hand.

"Curtis, tell her she's being unreasonable," Gran said. She fixed him with a hard look.

"Leave me outta this. I didn't have nothin' to do with it."

"Nothing to do with what, Uncle Curtis?" Andrea looked from Gran to him.

He shook his head as though warding off danger. "Not me, uh-uh."

"Tell me what—" Before Andrea could finish, her cousin Leonard came in, talking to someone behind him.

"Don't worry. If my grandmama invited you, then you can come in the kitchen with the family." Leonard grinned. "Ain't that right, Gran?"

Jamal strolled in behind him. "Boy, sure smells good in here. Nothing like down-home cooking."

Andrea's mouth dropped open. She gaped at him for five seconds, then turned to Gran with a scowl. The woman had more nerve than ten busybodies put together.

"We're so glad you could come, sugar." Gran pointedly avoided looking at Andrea. She strolled over and took him by the arm. "You have a seat right here."

"Thanks, ma'am." Jamal sat at the kitchen table and beamed at Andrea. "Good to see ya again."

Jamal looked perfectly at home with his elbows propped on the table. Andrea squinted at him. The man was so annoying. She was determined not to be affected by him. Let him parade around in front of her. *So he looks okay. So what?* Andrea lifted her nose in the air and continued to gaze at him.

His broad shoulders were covered by a dark blue cotton knit shirt with a white stripe on the collar and short sleeves. Andrea tried not to notice how his powerful brown arms bulged even at rest on the table. He wore a leather belt the color of dark wine around his trim waist. The shirt was neatly tucked into khaki pants that fit snugly and molded to his thighs. He shifted his legs to get more comfortable, and that one simple motion made her blink. When he rumbled a deep laugh at something her cousin said, Andrea felt heat course through her body. Jamal's voice, rich and melodious, hinted at secret pleasures. His full mouth curved up when he turned to her. An image of his lips against hers blossomed in her mind.

"You excited?"

Andrea drew a ragged breath. "What?" she asked, mortified that he had seen into her thoughts.

"About the clinic, I mean." Jamal wore a half smile. "You must look forward to starting in a few days."

Andrea leaned against the countertop to get her balance. "The clinic, right," she blurted out.

"Right, the clinic," he echoed. His brown eyes glittered with mirth. "You know, that place where you're the boss?"

Jamal wore a sexy smile. Could he see the lusty images that had formed in her mind? Andrea took a deep breath to clear them away. Annoyance took over again at the conceit he seemed to radiate. He was sure of his ability to charm her. His appeal evaporated at that instant. The last thing she would do was give him the satisfaction.

"Yes, I'm the boss. I look forward to setting things straight and keeping them that way." Andrea folded her arms and stared at him.

Jamal did not lose his smile. "I'm with you on that, ma'am."

"Exactly what I was saying just a minute ago," Gran jumped in. "Having good workers is key. Andrea is darned lucky to have a man like you."

Andrea ground her teeth. She tossed a sharp glance at

her grandmother. "Gran . . ." She hoped her tone would say it all.

Gran ignored her attempt and made a show of serving Jamal. "Here you go, darlin'. A nice helping of Louisiana-style red beans."

Andrea moved close to her uncle. "When did he show up?" she mumbled in his ear.

"While you were outside," Uncle Curtis said in a low voice.

Andrea watched Gran's performance and fumed. "Gran is unbelievable." She spoke more to herself than to Uncle Curtis.

"Some of this, Andrea cooked." Gran served him a helping of cornbread. "She's mighty handy in the kitchen when she wants to be."

"Which I rarely do," Andrea called out. "Hate cooking. Eat out every chance I get at the finest restaurants. I don't do windows either."

Gran chuckled. "Lordy, these single girls. Of course, things change once you get to be a couple."

"My grandmother used to say the same thing," Jamal chimed in. He shot a sideways glance at Andrea.

"There now! Didn't I say he had southern roots?" Gran patted his back. "Doesn't matter where you grew up, you're one of us."

"Oh, please," Andrea whispered.

Uncle Curtis cleared his throat. "I'm goin' to go back to the game and give y'all more room." He darted off.

"Me, too," Leonard added. He seemed unaware of anything amiss. "You comin', bro? You can bring your plate. Right, Gran?"

"Nah, I'll stay here and finish. Wouldn't want to make a mess," Jamal said, glancing at Andrea.

"Gran ain't fussy like some. Man, that game is—"

"Don't rush him out, Leonard. We're talking with your cousin," Gran cut in sharply, and tilted her head to Andrea.

The light came on in Leonard's eyes after a few seconds. "Oh, yeah, yeah. Y'all talk." He winked at Andrea, then loped out.

Andrea wanted to scream with frustration. Her uncle had abandoned her, and now Leonard assumed she was a willing participant in this scenario. She could imagine the story that would shortly be told to the rest of the family. By tomorrow morning, all of Bayou Blue would be buzzing about her love life. Andrea's hands formed fists.

"Gran, you have a short memory," Andrea said.

"What, baby?" Gran wore a guileless expression. "Oh, you're right!" She slapped the table. "I forgot to tell your cousin Pam about the church fair."

"I haven't heard anything about a church fair," Andrea said. "Wait a minute."

"You oughta include a booth about the clinic. Great way to tell a whole bunch of folks about all the improvements you're making," Gran said.

Jamal pushed away the now empty plate. He glanced at Andrea, then at Gran. "You know, Miss Mavis, you've got an idea there."

"Good." Gran beamed at him. "Y'all talk about it. Matter of fact, go on outside. It's too nice to be stuck in the kitchen."

"I'm sure Jamal wants to watch the game," Andrea said. "And I'm going to do the dishes."

"That hungry pack in there is gonna dirty up more dishes in a few minutes. Go on out and enjoy the weather."

Gran pulled Andrea by one arm and beckoned to Jamal at the same time. She cut off the exit toward the house and propelled them to the back door. Jamal went willingly.

"Nice breeze blowing today, too. Get Andrea to show you that old oak out there. Planted by her great-great-granddaddy. I don't need y'all in here crowding me when I clean up."

"But you just said there was no point to washing dishes," Andrea protested.

"This is my kitchen and I decide when to clean it. Quit contradicting me, for goodness' sakes! Go on." Gran gave Andrea one last shove onto the back porch.

Jamal followed soon after. "This is a wild guess, but I think she wants you to show me around." He wore a crooked smile as the door shut firmly.

Andrea glared at her grandmother's retreating back. "If she wanted you to take in the sights, she could have done it herself."

"And leave her hostess duties? She obviously takes those seriously." Jamal grinned.

"Yeah, right," Andrea said with a grimace.

"I could wander around the swamp on my own. Just call out the bloodhounds if I'm not back in an hour." Jamal cocked his head to one side and gazed at her.

Andrea looked into a pair of dark eyes deep enough to get lost in. They were the color of strong Louisiana coffee. Andrea tried to remember what it was that irritated her so, but couldn't when he looked at her that way.

"I don't think that will be necessary," she heard herself say.

"Does that mean I'll get the guided tour?" Jamal swept out a muscular arm.

Andrea watched the fluid motion in fascination. She imagined him lifting weights, or wrapping his arms around someone in a solid embrace. Hard muscles, smooth skin. A crazy urge to touch him took hold of her again. She hurried down the steps to put distance between them.

"It won't be much of a tour. Just trees, grass, and muddy water."

"Hey, it beats concrete and traffic jams any day." Jamal caught up to her.

Andrea concentrated on her surroundings and not looking at him again. At least until she'd regain her senses. "So how long have you been in Louisiana?"

"About three years."

"You don't seem like the small-town type." Andrea led him toward the massive oak tree.

"I moved to New Orleans to get away from big cities. I got tired of the crowds and hassle."

"I see. Still, it must have been an adjustment."

"I got used to it. I needed to get away from Los Angeles." There was a hint of tension in his voice.

"Life gets tough sometimes. That's the way it is." Andrea made an opening to find out more about him. He looked pensive for a moment, then smiled.

"You were in the big city, too. What made you come home?" he asked, deftly changing the focus to her again.

"When Gran told me about the clinic, I couldn't resist. This parish has needed preventative health care for poor people since forever," Andrea said. As they approached the wide trunk, she plucked a wisp of Spanish moss from a branch that curved to the ground.

"You didn't have any ties to keep you in Chicago?" Jamal turned to her. The question in his eyes was clear.

"There's nothing in Chicago for me now. I'm divorced," she said. Andrea blushed and looked away.

"I see," he said. "Seems we've got a lot in common."

Andrea looked up at him. He smiled and her breath caught, his smoky eyes pulling her in so deep she felt consumed by their warmth. She wanted to pull back, turn away from that hypnotic gaze. She'd been here before, her mind fogged by romantic fantasy. Then she remembered that pain had followed that particular pleasure. Andrea blinked and pulled herself back from the edge.

"Well, that's about all there is to see," Andrea said, her voice brusque. "Let's go back inside and catch that game."

She spun around and started to march off. He grabbed her arm, and Andrea felt a jolt, as if an electric charge raced up her arm. As she'd imagined only moments before, his skin was warm and a bit rough. She did not pull away. Every muscle vibrated with a hunger for more.

"I'm not into baseball," Jamal said in a quiet voice. "And I expected us to go much farther."

Andrea tugged free of his hold. "We won't," she said, and faced him with a controlled smile.

"Okay, later then." Jamal shrugged casually. He seemed confident there would be a next time.

"I don't think so," Andrea said in a clipped tone. "Let's get something straight. I don't date employees. And I wouldn't date you even if you weren't an employee."

"I was just talking about a walk in the woods, Nurse Noble. You're safe from me." He strolled off with an unhurried stride.

Andrea glared at his back. Okay, so she had jumped all over that conclusion, but he didn't have to gloat about it. Worse, he was walking off with the last word.

Andrea spluttered frantically and searched for a comeback.

"Let's just stay clear of each other as much as possible."

"That will be hard. The clinic isn't all that big." Jamal's mouth lifted at one corner, causing one dimple to appear.

"Then we'll just have to make the best of it. Remember, I'm in charge. Just do your work and we'll get along fine." Andrea brushed back her hair and walked past him.

"I can see we'll have so much fun."

Andrea kept going and did not look back. "You're not there for fun."

"Good thing, too," was his droll response.

She increased her pace and reached the back porch in record time. Andrea stomped cross the wooden planks and through the kitchen door. Gran met her with an expectant smile.

"Bet y'all had a nice walk, eh? That boy is too good to be true." Gran's smile faded when Andrea continued to frown at her.

"Never again," Andrea burst out. "No more trying to fix me up, Gran! I mean it!"

"Some gratitude! Here I give you a perfect chance to be alone with one of the finest young men for two hundred miles and what do you do?" Gran put both fists on her wide hips.

"I didn't ask you to invite him! Jamal Turner is not the kind of man I need right now." Andrea rubbed her forehead in exasperation.

"Don't talk trash, child. He's smart, hardworking, and comes from a good family. Women for miles around want him."

"He's already got a hot love affair going, with himself!" Andrea waved her hand. "The man's got 'dog' written across his forehead. He—"

"Hush," Gran said, waving frantically for her to be quiet. "Here he comes."

"Miss Mavis, that view is everything you said it was." Jamal ignored Andrea and gave Gran his full attention.

"Have some dessert, sugar. Guess you need some refreshment right about now." Gran shot a look of reproach at Andrea. She patted his shoulder as though to comfort him. "Go on in the living room and I'll bring you some pie and cold milk."

"No, thanks, Miss Mavis. I'm full. I'll be going now. Bye-bye." Jamal grinned at Andrea as he headed out.

"Shame on you," Gran said within seconds of him disappearing.

Andrea pushed down another acid comment and counted to ten. "Gran, I know you're trying to help me, but don't. I'm not attracted to that kind of man."

"So you don't like sexy, tall, intelligent men?"

"Looks aren't everything. Besides, I've got my hands full right now. I've got a lot of responsibility."

Gran did not budge from her position. "You need more than a job, Drea."

"I'm not ready. It's too soon. Please try to understand, Granna."

It was the name Andrea had called her grandmother when she was little. It usually melted her grandmother's rock-hard will. Gran's fierce expression eased.

"I know you've been hurt, sugar. I shouldn't be rushing you like this. But I want you to be happy." Gran crossed to Andrea, hugged her, and gave her a kiss on the cheek. "There now, you go on with the rest of 'em and I'll bring you a slice of pie."

Andrea planted a kiss on Gran's plump cheek. "Thanks, Gran. Really."

She went out the door and down the short hall past the formal dining room that led to the den. Andrea knew this wasn't the end of her grandmother's matchmaking efforts. It would take at least three times before Gran would accept that she was not interested in Jamal. Period. No way.

She paused and checked her appearance in a mirror hanging on the wall. The woman who looked back was cool, collected, and definitely not interested in Jamal Turner. Andrea practiced several facial expressions of haughtiness and disdain. Satisfied, Andrea sashayed into the room with her shoulders back and chin up. She would let Mr. Wonderful know he wasn't the center of the universe. However, when she walked into the living room, she found herself glancing around for a glimpse of him. He really wasn't there. She told herself she was glad he was gone as her fingers caressed the arm he had touched.

Four

A musical female laugh accompanied by a lower, deeper one jabbed a hole in Andrea's gratified mood. She rolled her eyes. Jamal again. He caused a minor sensation among female staff and patients just walking down the hall. To Andrea it was a source of constant irritation. Another round of laughter set her teeth on edge. What was so darn funny anyway? There was a knock on her door and Katy came in. As clinic manager, Katy was responsible for the day-to-day operation of the clinic.

"How you doin' in here, boss?" Katy's Cajun accent was slight, but distinct nonetheless. Her long black hair was pulled up in a twist.

"Fine. I'm just finishing up the paperwork for the new nutritional program." Andrea tapped a stack of forms in triplicate. "Between state and federal red tape, it could take another two weeks."

"Yeah, but at least we'll be able to give out those

WIC coupons again." Katy sat down in one of three chairs facing Andrea's desk.

"It took me three hours of hard talking to get us back in. But I can't blame them. Four hundred dollars worth of coupons missing." Andrea shook her head. "Did I say talking? I meant begging!"

"I know. You think they'll do more than question the former employees?" Katy said just above a whisper.

"Probably not. But I'll bet they were either selling those things or giving them to their buddies." Andrea was still angry. Daily she found more evidence that confirmed her decision to fire so many of the former staff and start fresh.

There was now laughter from both of the young student nurses. Andrea frowned at her closed office door.

"Lisa and Troylyn sure don't mind coming to work these days." Katy grinned and winked. "Can't say I blame 'em. Mr. Turner is one good-looking man."

"They'd best keep their minds on why they're here," Andrea said peevishly. "Fortunately he's only hired on a temporary basis."

"Oh, Mr. Turner, you're so funny!" a delighted Lisa giggled.

"That's it!" Andrea said.

She sprang from her chair, marched out of her office and down the hall to the records room. Lisa and Troylyn stood on either side of Jamal. Both batted their eyelashes at him, hanging on every word. Naturally his so-called charm would work on females barely out of their teens. When Lisa giggled and put a hand on his arm, Andrea clenched her teeth.

"Excuse me."

Lisa started. "Oh, Nurse Noble. I was just looking for a file." She darted to the tall metal cabinet.

"Er, I, er . . ." Troylyn was lost for words. The best she could produce was a jittery smile.

"You're supposed to be out front at the reception desk. Right?" Andrea asked with a stony expression.

"Yes, ma'am." Troylyn rushed past Andrea, then turned to smile at Jamal. " 'Bye Mr. Turner." She waved her fingertips at him.

" 'Bye now. And don't worry, you'll do fine on that test." Jamal gave her a thumbs-up sign. Then he aimed his dimpled smile at Andrea. "Hi, boss."

Andrea bit back the urge to toss out something flippant. "How is it going?"

"Well, Sally Ranger wants me to get you guys hooked up to the health department's mainframe. A guy from their information systems unit has already called me." Jamal glanced at her, then down at the computer again. "I'll be around here awhile."

"Great!" Lisa burst out. She turned pink when Andrea looked at her. "I mean, it will really improve how we can serve the patients."

"I'm happy you're so excited about advancing health care." Andrea gave her a pointed look.

"Um, I'll bet Troy needs some help." Lisa made her getaway.

"She's right, you know. You'll be able to access health stats, get E-mail, and communicate faster with the department." Jamal beckoned to her. "Let me show you what I've done so far."

Andrea reluctantly walked over to where he sat. As she leaned down to see the screen, she caught the scent of his cologne. It was a delicate but enticing blend of wood and spice. She had the sudden urge to brush his strong jaw with her own cheek. She froze. *Too many months of celibacy, that's all,* she told herself. A biological itch that had not been scratched in . . . She did not want to think about how long. *Ignore it and it will go away.*

"I should be able to configure this program soon. Then it's on to the big hookup." He looked up at her. "You're not paying attention."

Andrea yanked her attention back to the computer monitor. "Of course I am."

"Pop quiz then. What did I just say?"

"That you're very pleased with yourself, as usual," Andrea retorted, standing up.

"Stop trying so hard not to like me." He tilted his head to one side. "I'm not Jack the Ripper."

Stung by guilt, Andrea relented. "I'm sorry. You've helped us out a lot. Now we can track appointments."

"See, even you think I have a good reason to be conceited." He grinned.

Andrea stepped back. Maybe distance would help clear her head. "I wouldn't go that far."

"Seriously, though, you're the one with a reason to feel proud. The place was a mess. But you cleaned house."

Andrea felt a flush of pleasure at his compliment. "We're taking baby steps in the right direction."

"Lots of rumors about theft." He raised an eyebrow at her.

"Gossip is worth about what you pay for it, nothing." Andrea leaned against a table and crossed her arms. "Record keeping was sloppy, so that could just be it."

"Really? How bad was it?"

"Katy and I had to spend three twelve hour days sifting through files just to make up a patient list. No wonder food coupons went missing without anyone noticing."

"Those things are just like cash, untraceable." Jamal rubbed his chin in thought. "What about the drug stock?"

"I'm looking into an inventory system next."

"No, I mean have you found any missing?" Jamal stared at her intently.

"I'm pretty sure we don't have a problem there. But I've got to go over at least six months of purchase orders to be sure. Which is where that program comes in." Andrea pointed to the computer.

"What about equipment? You've got items around here that could be sold easily."

"Not anymore. Katy and I are on top of it."

"But if you don't have a detailed list . . ." Jamal gazed at her.

"Denny keeps a daily list for me," she said, referring to the young man who functioned as a ward clerk and pharmacy assistant.

"Lotta money at stake." Jamal stared off as though talking to himself. "Bad management is one thing, but—"

Andrea stood straight. "Excuse me, but I have managed a clinic before, thank you."

Jamal glanced at her sharply. "Just a few random thoughts."

Andrea felt a rise of aggravation. She'd had to fight sexism and racism for much of her career. Ellis had second-guessed her decisions, too. Her ex-husband had let Andrea know in subtle ways he didn't think much of her ambitions or abilities. Jamal was behaving like the grand inquisitor. Being a man did not give him the right to assume he could instruct her on management.

"I'll run the clinic. Just take care of the duties I assign to you."

"Sure. You're in charge. I've got it," Jamal said in a curt voice.

Andrea swallowed hard at the tight look on his handsome face. His brows were drawn together, making his handsome face look rugged, dangerous, and seductive at the same time.

"I'll let you know when I select the inventory application we'll use." She gave a crisp nod and walked out on rubbery legs.

Andrea escaped to the safety of her office. Once the door closed, she took a deep breath. Being close to him was dangerous. She had almost given in to a stupid romantic flight of fancy twice in the space of only a few minutes. She'd have to be more careful to guard herself against that sexy smile and those smoky eyes.

Lee sat at the front desk and pretended to be engrossed in the words on the computer screen. He listened to Andrea give instructions to the student nurses in an efficient tone. She seemed to be a very together lady. He smiled, remembering how anger made her eyes flash with fire. She had a habit of pursing her lips before she tossed out a smart answer. The soft rose-colored lipstick she wore most days made him think her lips would taste as sweet as candy. Her voice was like liquid silk. He supposed nurses should have a soothing voice. He wanted to run his fingers through her shoulder-length hair, which was the color of bronze with red highlights. Then his mind formed an image of the rest of her. Andrea's curves—full breasts, firm hips that flared out deliciously—could not be disguised even under the prim outfits she wore. Her walk was smooth motion, a sensuous rhythm that hinted at hidden passion.

As though in tune with his thoughts, Andrea laughed at something Katy said. The sound washed over him in a wave that set off a pulsating hunger that started at the base of his spine then spread to his pelvis.

"You okay, Jamal? You're sitting so quiet."

It was only then that Lee realized he'd closed his eyes, the better to picture Andrea. When he opened them, Troylyn stood only two feet away, going through a file cabinet. Thankful her back was to him, he inhaled and exhaled a few times to recover. It only took an instant to pull himself together, although he still felt a bit off balance. He'd let thoughts of a woman sneak up on him and rattle his concentration. That would not do. This was just another assignment: get the information the client paid him for and get out. He had to remember why he was working here.

"I'm concentrating on all this work the boss lady has given me."

"Miss Noble is not one to mess around, huh? Came right in and took over." Troylyn closed the metal drawer and walked over to him. She leaned against the desk.

"Yep, all business, for sure. She's got a lot to clean up."

"Tell me about it." Troylyn's voice dropped low and she looked around as though to make sure they were alone. "If you ask me, she's riding on a sinking ship."

"What do you mean?" Lee now turned his full attention to her.

"She's still got some of the old staff left, like Miss Cresson." Troylyn nodded when he glanced at her.

Lee thought about the fifty-year-old registered nurse. She'd practically ruled the place before Andrea had come. Andrea had cut her hours until she was only part-time.

"Miss Andrea can handle her, though," Troylyn said.

Lee thought back to his last conversation with Mandeville. As usual with clients who hired a private detective, he'd held back information from Lee. Mandeville had controlled the clinic through the last three directors. Now the board wanted him to clean it up. Despite his wealth and influence, several of the board members were just as powerful. In fact, they were challenging Mandeville's power in other ways. Lee had no doubt there was more Mandeville was hiding. He seemed to get a strained expression whenever Lee probed about Andrea. Six years as a cop and five as a private investigator gave Lee a sixth sense when someone was holding back. Could there be some scam that involved Andrea Noble? If she was involved, then the wrongdoing could be more than petty employee theft. He definitely wanted to know more about her, strictly for purposes of the investigation, of course.

"How long have you known Miss Noble?" Lee said.

Troylyn blinked her wide eyes a few times. "Not long. Just since I came here for my fieldwork." She shrugged and raised her eyebrows. "Tell you what, though, she's got her favorites. And I'm not talking about the females either."

Lee felt an unfamiliar sensation in his stomach. "Who is he?" His voice held an edge that he hoped Troylyn did not notice.

"Well, I'm not a person to spread gossip, but—"

Denny Kincaid strolled in. The tall, lanky man wore an affable smile. At twenty-one, he was the youngest employee at the clinic. He worked as an assistant to the part-time pharmacist dispensing medication.

"Hey. What y'all doin' still here? It's time to close up," Denny said.

Troylyn cut a significant glance at Lee before speaking. "You and Miss Andrea still here."

"There's always something I've gotta do. She stays on me about keeping stuff in order." Denny's pleased smile showed he didn't mind at all.

"Oh yeah, it must be rough working late with Miss Andrea." Troylyn cleared her throat and gathered up a set of notebooks. "See y'all tomorrow."

She gave Lee another meaningful look before walking out of the reception room. Lee got the message. He swiveled in his chair so that he was facing Denny. Denny was nine years younger than Andrea, eleven years younger than Lee. Denny went to a stack of files left on the end of the counter and sorted through them. He mumbled words to a rap song as he worked. Lee frowned. Why would she be attracted to this guy? He was barely out of training pants. His stomach roiled with displeasure at the thought of them as a couple.

"Hey, Miss Andrea, I found that statistical report for ya," Denny called out as he walked down the hall.

"Fantastic, bring it to me," Andrea answered.

Lee drummed his fingers on the desk as he listened to their voices mingling together. When Andrea laughed, Lee's frowned deepened. Maybe they were in on some game at the clinic together. It wouldn't be the first time an otherwise levelheaded woman did something stupid because of a man.

Lee fingers drummed harder and faster on the surface of the desk. Okay, self-examination time. He was letting himself get distracted from his job when it came to Andrea Noble. But that buttoned-down, I-mean-business *fine* woman got under his skin. She . . . intrigued him. Yet he knew better than to let himself be fooled by a pretty package. Not to mention, the lady did not seem blown away by his charm. Lee did not think of himself as conceited, but he'd never had a problem attracting the ladies. Andrea Noble appeared to be totally underwhelmed. *Smart lady, so forget about it, Matthews.*

When he heard the last employee call out a weary "See ya tomorrow," he realized that now was his chance. Lee waited a few more minutes just to be sure, then quietly made his way down the hall to the file room. Four rows of gray metal shelves held patient records. A large copier sat in one corner and a long table in another. He glanced in to see if anyone was there. Finding it empty, he moved on to the small room that served as the clinic pharmacy. Lee tried the door. It was locked as he'd expected. The office the pharmacist used on the days he came was next to it. This door was not locked. It took him only a few minutes to find two drug logbooks from the past three months and a hefty bound set of computer printouts.

After closing the blinds and turning on the desk lamp, Lee spent the next half hour studying the records. The logs were handwritten, with a list of drugs dispensed, with quantities and dates. The pharmacist initialed each entry, with Andrea or Katy signing at the bottom each month. The computer sheets were a record of drugs ordered and received. He would need to find time at least once a week to really dig deep.

Lee glanced up to find it was almost six o'clock. Evening shadows lengthened as the last light of a Louisiana summer day faded. He stretched, then turned off the lamp. As he stepped into the hall, he heard a rustle and the sound of soft music. Only the fluorescent lights of the hallway were on. Light spilled through the open door of Andrea's office. Lee walked to it and looked in. Andrea sat in one of three chairs arranged in a semicircle around a small table near the window. A blues song came from the clock radio on her bookcase. She'd taken off her comfortable shoes and propped her feet up on another chair. Her skirt hitched up one thigh and she rubbed it absentmindedly as she read. He gazed at the way a thick lock of her hair kept falling across her forehead. She pushed it back three times.

Andrea shifted a bit and raised one leg, bending it at the knee, foot at rest on the chair. She looked so different now that she was at ease. The softness of her came through. Gone was the crisp, efficient, in-charge career woman. In her place was a beautiful, relaxed temptress. Her shapely legs were an expanse of smooth caramel. She stretched, her back arching, the buttons on her blouse straining against the ripe fullness of her breasts. Lee breathed in sharply and felt a heaviness in his groin. He took a hasty step back away from the tantalizing sight. Lust pounded through his body. It took all his self-control to fight off the arousal that made his jeans too tight. Several minutes passed before he could collect himself. He rubbed a hand over his face and entered the room.

"Excuse me," Lee said, stopping short.

Andrea jumped up and dropped the folder she held in the process. "Good God!" she yelled.

"It's okay, it's okay." Lee held up both palms to reassure her.

"You scared the crap out of me! What are you still doing here?" Andrea put a hand over her heart.

"I was working late, like you. I looked around and everyone was gone. Or so I thought."

Lee walked farther into the office. The fear in her pretty eyes faded and was replaced with growing suspicion.

"Working late on what? You don't have any dead-lines." Andrea bent down and picked up the report.

"I only meant to work for fifteen more minutes. An hour had passed before I realized it."

"Oh." Andrea seemed uneasy about being alone with him.

Lee pressed his lips together tightly. "I don't bite."

Why had he said that? He looked at her and knew the answer. She stood still in her stocking feet. The top three buttons of her blouse were undone. He could see the outlines of a lacy bra beneath the white poplin. She was an enchanting blend of bewilderment and sensuality. The desire to taste her bit into him with the ferocity of a pit bull. Then Andrea's expression hardened as she smoothed and buttoned her blouse.

"I was just leaving. You should, too." She put on her shoes and crossed to her desk as she spoke.

"I'll walk out with you. It's not a good idea for you to be here alone." Lee leaned against the doorframe while she straightened her desk.

"It's still light outside and the exterior doors are locked." Andrea used her fingers to brush her thick hair. She glanced at Lee and stopped.

"Yeah, but then you've gotta walk behind the building to your car. Only one part of the parking lot is visible from the street."

"I don't take stupid chances. There's a security patrol and I never stay later than six." She gathered up her purse and a stack of files. "But thanks for your concern." Her voice dripped icicles.

Lee's eyes narrowed. The woman was being argumentative for the sake of it. Andrea Noble was stubborn, frigid, and high-handed. The warm, sultry vixen he thought he'd seen moments ago did not exist. To hell with her.

"Forget I said anything," Lee tossed back.

He spun around and strode down the hall. Andrea came right behind him. Part of him wanted to jump in his Acura Integra and peel off. Yet despite the anger stretching his last nerve, Lee waited at the back door while she set the alarm.

It was hot even at this time of day. Late afternoon sunshine beat down on the cement surface. Lee was boiling for a very different reason.

"Good-bye, Miss Noble."

"Good-bye," Andrea said, her tone composed. "I'll see you in the morning."

Lee ground his teeth. The woman was mocking him, and he deserved it. He had no business letting her get under his skin this way.

"Get a grip, man," he muttered to himself as he drove down the highway. He switched the radio on and turned to a hip-hop station. Turning up the volume, Lee tried to drown out thoughts of full, luscious lips and soft, brown thighs.

Five

It was four-thirty and Lee noticed that Andrea's car was not parked in the staff spaces. She was at another meeting at Public Health headquarters in New Orleans. For the past few days, Lee had worked in the afternoons so Andrea and Katy could use the computers. With three of their programs now operating, they needed to access archived records.

Lee sat down at the computer and turned it on. Up until now his work had been pretty routine. He'd spent most of his time scanning records from years back when the clinic had been virtually a one-room shack. Now he was getting to the current records, which would tell him more about the clinic operation and any attempts to hide shady activity. First he needed to start out with a good basic idea of how the clinic was supposed to run. To do that he had to pour through state and federal guidelines. This simple job was turning into a tangle of complications. He'd wanted to be in and out fast. That was the way he handled most cases. Still, it was possible. He just had to put in extra hours, work late. It was probably only a matter of tracking down poor record keeping, bad organization, and maybe some petty pilfering of supplies. So far he'd not come up with more.

Lee pulled up a report on funding. The budget was a maze of money coming from the state, the parish, and the federal governments. No way could the money be misused. Too many eyes were watching and dozens of forms had to be completed to track every penny. Then he noticed something. A section on professional contracts listed names he'd not come across before, with substantial checks being issued quarterly. He printed out the page so his partner, Vince, could run a background check. During a quick run through the rest of the document, nothing caught his eye, so he moved on. Only a small part of the pharmacy records had been entered.

Lee stared at a stack of invoices from pharmaceutical companies and drug administration records. If anyone was fiddling with the drug supply, it was Denny. Lee did not trust that wide smile as much as Andrea did, he thought sourly. Denny was sure of himself. Or did Lee dislike the young man simply because he could make Andrea smile? The thought of this possibility poked at him in the most bothersome way.

"I'm back, Katy. I see you've been holding this place together," Andrea called out down the hall.

Damn it, he'd hoped she wouldn't be here. Her presence was a distraction. Lee didn't want to think too deeply about why. Immediately his mind conjured images of softly swaying hips and caramel brown legs, smooth thighs moving in a sweet harmony of motion. *Focus, damn it!*

After thirty minutes, Lee got a sense of minor discrepancies that he definitely wanted to research. These small blips might not be noticed by a less careful or suspicious examination.

"Hi, Shandra." Andrea walked down the hall, talking to a young mother. "How is little Kendrick doing today? He's getting so big. Come here, sweet boy," Andrea said right outside the door.

Lee could imagine her working wonders to soothe an irritable toddler. He'd watched her with patients young and old. Her caring and dedication to making a difference in their lives seemed quite genuine. There was no doubt that the cool, distant nurse was not the only side of her. Her eyes lit up with true compassion for those most in need. It would be a shame to make the clinic look bad. Andrea had put a lot of work into the place; at least that was his preliminary impression so far.

"Get back on track," Lee muttered to himself in a firm voice.

He set up a special pass code that would allow him to access data only available to Andrea. Then he configured a connection to the mainframe that linked the clinic system to state records. There was a possibility that deliberate wrongdoing might extend beyond the clinic. Or at least Lee would get more information to help in his investigation. It was a painstaking process and required all of his concentration. Lee became lost in the minute detail of learning how to enter the right codes. He would have to set up a temporary password for himself. Except that it would not be temporary. Then he could enter the system at will. As his fingers moved, his mind ran through the ways he would invent reasons to work late. He thought of several means, such as proposing that reports be submitted electronically. They also needed a tape backup system in case the computers crashed.

Lee was so engrossed, an hour passed as if by some magic twist of time. He decided to take a break from staring at the computer monitor. Lee flexed his hands and arms. Then he heard two voices, one deep and the other instantly recognizable.

"Cut it out," Andrea snapped. "This is a clinic, not a singles bar!"

"Aw, c'mon. I'm just trying to make up with ya for the other day," the man said in a wheedling tone.

Andrea frowned at the grinning man when she recognized him. He'd been one of the thugs who had accosted her the first day she visited the clinic. She wondered how he'd gotten in. Without thinking, she'd walked right into the last examination room and pulled the door shut behind her. Her heart thumped. The rest of the staff were up front.

"You must have better things to do with your time," Andrea said, trying to sound as though she were calm.

"Looka here, give me a physical," Bo said. "You s'posed to be takin' care of people, ain't ya?"

"If you leave now, we won't have any trouble," Andrea said.

"Ain't gotta be no trouble. I wanna be friendly with you."

Andrea took a deep breath. "I know we started off on the wrong foot, but—"

"We had our first fuss and now we gonna make up? I like that!" Bo let out a deep chuckle.

"Okay, you've had your fun for the day. Now, we've

got people waiting. Please leave," Andrea said. She still did not raise her voice.

"We haven't finished talking, babe." Bo took a step closer to her. "We got interrupted last time."

"What is your problem? I don't have time for games." Andrea faced him without a hint of fear this time.

"I've got an appointment," Bo said. He pointed to her clipboard. "Darrel Bowman. Check it out."

She glanced down at the list. Sure enough, his name was there. "We'll reschedule you to see the doctor." Andrea turned to walk away and Bo grabbed her arm.

"Okay, I was rude the last time. I really wanted to, you know, apologize. Show you I'm not all bad."

"I'm so touched," Andrea said in clipped tone. "Now, let go of me."

He released his grip. "I mean it. You helped my grandmama out when she had that bad cough last week."

"What's her name?" Andrea was still quite suspicious.

"Miz Lucy Whitefield. She's my mama's mama," Bo said.

"Miss Lucy is your grandmother?" Andrea exclaimed.

"Lives out on Frenchtown Lane," Bo added.

Andrea remembered the feisty old woman and her daughter. Miss Lucy admitted freely to having lived a wild life in her younger days. She was seventy years old, and only health problems had slowed her down. Stella was her fifty-year-old daughter, and still drinking heavily. Andrea had been able to tell by looking at her skin and eyes. They had talked about their children and grandchildren being in trouble all the time. Here stood six feet of living proof.

Bo nodded. "That other bi—I mean that other nurse in charge of the clinic before you didn't even try." Bo held out his hand.

"Thanks. But I'm doing my job."

"Maybe you'll let me treat you to dinner." Bo's eyes glittered now with something other than gratitude.

"Don't mess up a good thing. We were just on the way to getting along."

"Which is exactly what I'm talkin' 'bout," Bo said. He grabbed her hand and massaged her palm in smooth circles with his thumb. "We could get along even better."

Andrea jerked her hand back. "You're obviously in excellent health, so leave."

"Nah, I wanna stay with you."

Before Andrea could react, he'd backed her against the wall. He pressed his lean body into hers, forcing her to feel the hardness of his arousal.

"Come on, I can satisfy you in ways you wouldn't believe," Bo said in a low, husky voice.

"Get away from me," Andrea gasped. She brought her hands up against his chest when Bo leaned in to kiss her.

"Give me a chance and you won't be sorry," he panted.

"What the hell?" she heard Jamal growl.

In two giant steps he crossed to Bo and slapped a large hand on the man's shoulder. He dug his fingers into a soft, fleshy spot between Bo's neck and collarbone. Bo's leering grin melted into a grimace of pain, and suddenly he let go of Andrea.

"I don't think this is part of the exam, is it?" Jamal tightened his grip.

"N-no," the man grunted and gasped in response. "I was just . . . we . . ."

Jamal grimaced in fury. "I know what you were doing. This is a medical clinic, not a strip club. No groping, no suggestive comments. Got it?"

Bo gasped and wheezed. "You gonna break my bone, man. Let go."

"You wanted medical attention, didn't you?" Jamal's voice was calm, cold. "How many times we gotta go through this? *Leave the lady alone.*"

"Awright, awright," the man pleaded, closing his eyes against the pain. "Lemme go and I'll leave!"

Andrea could not take her eyes away from Jamal. There was control in every inch of his muscular frame. She was sure he could really harm the man if he wanted to. But somehow she did not think he would, now that Bo was obviously subdued. With one hand he'd almost brought the huge man to his knees. Still his voice remained level.

Jamal loosened his grip gradually, and Bo let out a long, slow breath of relief. Jamal took his hand away but stood back with a wide-legged stance, ready for action.

"You want to say something to Miss Noble?" Jamal nodded to Andrea.

"Sorry," the man mumbled as he rubbed his shoulder.

"Sorry what?" Jamal stepped close to him and Bo winced.

"Sorry, ma'am."

"And?" Jamal prompted.

"It won't happen again."

"Get out and don't come back," Jamal said. The man glanced at the door as though scared to move. "Go on."

Bo hustled out, but not without throwing a hostile glance at Jamal. "Yeah, right."

Andrea watched as Jamal strode out into the hall to make sure Bo was gone. He was lithe and powerful at the same time. She blinked hard. Jamal Turner was not her type, she argued. He was too charming, too sure of himself, and had serial lover written all over him. She had him down pat, right? No way would she ever fall for the muscle-flexing, beat-on-his chest type of man Jamal was, with his slick talk and sexy walk. Yet her pulse raced. He walked back into the room.

Andrea breathed hard, but not from fear. "Thanks," she said softly.

"No problem. You okay?" Jamal's sharp gaze swept her from head to toe.

"Fine. He didn't really do anything. You didn't give him a chance. How did you know . . . I mean, you got here so fast." Andrea brushed her hair back from her face.

"I was in the computer room and heard your voice. You didn't sound too happy, so I decided to check it out." Jamal walked up to her with worry in his brown eyes. "Are you sure you're okay? You looked rattled."

"No, no. I'm just fine, like I said. Really." Andrea moved away from him as she tried to compose herself.

"If you say so." Still he eyed her as though he wasn't convinced.

"What?" Andrea blushed at the protective force that radiated from him.

"Nothing. I just . . . Nothing." Jamal looked away.

"You must have taken karate courses or something, the way you handled Bo." Andrea glanced at his muscular arms as she spoke.

"Yeah, that and I grew up in a rough neighborhood.

In South Central you gotta know how to take care of yourself." Jamal shrugged.

"I see. Sounds like a scary place." Andrea stared at his lips; the way they moved when he formed words wove a spell that captured her.

"It could be. Just like here, there's good people and bad people that live there. Course, it's not as scenic as Bayou Blue." Jamal smiled.

"Right," Andrea murmured. She stared into his eyes.

Jamal's expression softened; his breathing became audible in the silence that stretched for several seconds. "I mean this place is more beautiful than I'd imagined it to be."

"It is. A lot of trees and plants stay green even in winter. Then there are the bayous and swamps." Andrea chewed her bottom lip gently.

"I'm glad I made this move, Andrea," he said, his voice a soft rumble.

The sound of it, deep with hidden promise, sent a shiver all the way to her toes. "Lucky for me you did come to town. You've saved me twice now."

"I guess that means me working at the clinic is a good thing?" Jamal's dimple deepened along with his smile.

He exuded a potent combination of sexiness and boyish charm at that moment. She wanted to run her fingers through his dark hair and feel the texture of those ebony curls.

"Well . . . I guess it does." Andrea smiled back.

A door slammed and voices approached. Andrea blinked hard and glanced away from him sharply. It seemed to her that the air between them crackled with electricity. Jamal cleared his throat.

"I'll, uh, check around and make sure he's gone," he said.

"Good idea," Andrea replied, her throat tight from the effort not to show how he was affecting her.

"Then we can walk out together." Jamal wore an expression of gentle concern. "That is, if you don't mind."

"No. I was leaving after the last appointment to go to a meeting."

He nodded and walked away. She stared at him for several seconds. Andrea was almost panting at the way his back pockets moved with each stride. It took all her willpower to tear her gaze away from him. Jamal Turner was dangerous indeed. She could well imagine the long line of smitten females he attracted just by curving that full mouth up at the corners. Well, she would not be one of them. After giving Katy several quick instructions, she headed out. Jamal stood at the door waiting for her.

"Keep this up and people will think you're my bodyguard," Andrea quipped.

"You might need one around here." Jamal walked beside her. "And even though you weren't thrilled the board hired me without consulting you, you could use the help."

"I—"

"It's okay." He held up a large palm. "A little muscle isn't a bad idea with the rough characters hanging around."

"Ahem, yes." Andrea could not help but glance at his chest and arms again. "I think we can learn to work together."

"So do I." Jamal waited until she unlocked her car door, then opened it for her. "See you tomorrow."

"Good-bye." Andrea got in and allowed him to shut the door firmly.

He stood outside until she drove out of the parking lot. Andrea glanced back to see him still standing there. When he waved, she waved back. The image of strength and caring stayed with her for the rest of the day.

Andrea looked around her mother's living room. Charlene lived in an upscale town house in New Orleans right off St. Charles Avenue. Vibrant emerald green, deep purple, and royal blue were represented throughout. The fine wool Oriental rug complemented the upholstered furniture. Drapes of deep taupe and green were pulled back from the windows. The room was just like Charlene, bright but not garish. Charming and elegant.

Andrea frowned. Yet it lacked something. This was not a home Andrea would come to at the end of a hard day and feel comfortable enough to leave her shoes in the middle of the floor. Her frown turned into a smile. It was just like Charlene to have the perfect showcase. A far cry from the homey "take off your panty hose and let it all hang out" feel of Gran's house. Gran used to joke that Charlene used to line up her toy teacups just so. Charlene would faint if she were to find a ceramic knickknack on her fancy mantel.

Still, Charlene was making an effort to be maternal. Her invitation for Andrea to "work me into your busy schedule" had held just the right amount of guilt to make her point. Andrea could not be irritated since Charlene wanted to spend more time with her. Today was part of her campaign for them to mend their relationship, which was strained at best. Andrea made a silent promise to put forth more of an effort. Perhaps next time she would invite Charlene out. What could they do together? They had such different interests and tastes. Andrea was turning over this riddle when Charlene entered the room carrying a tray bearing coffee and the doughnuts she knew Andrea loved so.

"Here we go. Hot beignets from Café Du Monde."

Her reddish brown hair was cut short and feathered to frame her heart-shaped face. She was dressed in a taupe short-sleeved silk blouse tucked into white jeans. Silver dangle earrings sparkled as she moved. Charlene reveled in looking even younger than her forty-six years. She was delighted when people expressed amazement that she had a daughter Andrea's age. Indeed, they were frequently mistaken for sisters, a mistake Charlene did not always correct. Andrea gazed at her. Their features were alike. Andrea had always felt she was a copy of her mother, but did not quite capture the spark of the original.

"I told you not to go to any trouble." Andrea sat down at the dining room table.

She knew her mother was far from domestic. Yet Charlene had prepared fresh fruits, juice, and coffee. She'd been determined to make this mother-daughter breakfast special.

"Don't worry, honey. I didn't cut up the fruit." Charlene giggled. "But even I can make good coffee. What kind of Louisiana girl would I be if I couldn't?"

"I hope it's not as strong as Gran makes it. That first cup she gave me almost made my eyes pop. Guess I've been drinking weak Yankee coffee too long." Andrea laughed. "Gran is something else."

"You mean stubborn." Charlene sat down across from her and flipped open a cotton napkin that matched the place mats. "She's got no business drinking coffee."

"She's cut back on the number of cups she drinks. Only one a day. And her blood pressure is just fine." Andrea dug into her bowl of fruit.

"All the same, herbal tea would be better." Charlene sniffed. "But at least she listens to *somebody*."

"Don't start. You two are always digging at each other." Andrea shook her head as if she were chastising two bickering children. "Am I going to have to referee again?"

"Actually I'm in her good graces since I helped you get that job and come home. She usually ignores anything I suggest." Charlene waved her fruit fork in the air.

Andrea stiffened. "Yes, and exactly what did you do to get me the job?"

"Ahem, I know some people in state government. We all belong to the Krewe of Ashanti. When I heard about the clinic—"

"How did you hear about it?" Andrea asked. "You don't visit Bayou Blue very often."

"Are you trying to say I don't keep in touch with Mama? I call her at least once a month."

"She told you about the clinic?"

"She might have mentioned it. I don't recall." Charlene shrugged and sipped from a china coffee cup.

"You talked to that man." Andrea couldn't bring herself to say his name. "Why can't you just tell me the truth for once?"

"Now, wait a minute, young lady. I may only be sixteen years older than you, but I'm still your mother." She put her cup down with a sharp clink.

Any other time, Andrea might have been amused. Not today. A dull, thudding headache started at the base of her skull. It was a familiar attempt to deflect Andrea from a subject Charlene did not want to pursue.

"This move back home was good for us all. Yes, I missed my child. Is that a crime?" Her mother added just the right plaintive note.

"Oh, Charlene, please!" Andrea shook her head.

"Don't call me Charlene," she snapped back. "I'm your mother."

"Only when it suits you," Andrea retorted. Pain flashed across Charlene's face. Andrea immediately regretted her words.

"I see." Charlene got up and went to the window. "I suppose you think Mama really raised you, that I neglected you."

"I'm sorry. I didn't mean it the way it came out. Really."

Andrea searched for a way to back away from this emotional cliff. They'd never openly discussed John Mandeville. As though by mutual agreement, one of them would quickly end any argument that threatened to open that deep wound.

"Maybe I'm not the ideal mother." Charlene's voice was sad and subdued. She turned sharply to face her. "But I do care about you."

Andrea went to Charlene and hugged her. "Of course. I know." She tried to smile. "Guess I'm the latest generation of smart-mouthed Ricard women."

Charlene pulled back and held both of Andrea's shoulders. "I only wanted the best for you, Drea," she said, ignoring Andrea's attempt to lighten the moment. "You have to believe me."

"I do." Andrea smiled. "And I'm glad you're my mommy. Even if I do have to put up with people thinking you're younger than me."

"Oh, stop," Charlene said with a pleased smile. "But you're right about me choosing when to be your mother. I've darted in and out of your life like a bumble bee."

"Now, Char—Mother, I said I was sorry."

"It's time I follow your grandmother's advice to grow up." Charlene assumed a matronly expression.

Andrea looked worried. "And what does that mean?"

"Just that I plan to be here for you. I don't want you to end up on one of those horrible talk shows telling the world how awful a mother I am." Charlene's copper eyes widened.

"Oh, really." Andrea laughed with relief. Her dramatic, lovely mother was back, thank the Lord. "Could you see me baring my soul on national television?"

Charlene giggled. "I guess not." Then her expression grew intent as she swept Andrea from head to toe with an appraising gaze. "In fact, you're *too* restrained. Too serious."

"Not that again," Andrea said with a sigh. She went back to the table and sat down, with Charlene following close behind.

"Your hair is lovely, but my hairdresser Eric could give you a sexy new cut." Charlene lifted a lock of Andrea's hair as though already planning what she'd tell him to do.

"I don't want sexy hair, thank you." Then a vision of that chocolate dream Jamal flashed in her head. "You think he could, you know, fluff it up a bit?"

"Absolutely!" Charlene clapped her hands together in anticipation. "You'd love it."

"Nothing too drastic," Andrea put in quickly with a

frown. She had to put reins on Charlene or who knew what she'd end up looking like.

"Leave it to me." Charlene stood back with one hand under her chin. "And these clothes . . ."

Andrea tugged at her blouse self-consciously. "What's the matter with my clothes? They look fine."

"Pu-leeze. Where do you shop? Frumps R Us?" Charlene frowned at the skirt and blouse set Andrea had worn.

"There is nothing wrong with my clothes," Andrea said, sticking out her chin. "I don't like short skirts."

"Well, there is one thing Mama and I agree on. You need a good man to set your soul on fire." Charlene sat down across from her and winked.

Andrea started, her jaw almost hitting the tabletop. "Gran talks entirely too much. I've got too much work to do to think about him."

"He's a nice enough young man. Why shouldn't you think about him?" Charlene picked up the ceramic coffeepot on a heated base and refreshed both their cups.

"Nice my foot. Jamal Turner may have sucked Gran in, but not me," Andrea said with force.

"Ahem, well, Jamal thinks a lot of you, from what I understand." Charlene dabbed her lips with a napkin and looked at Andrea expectantly.

"Ha! He turns on the charm for any female that's still warm and has a pulse."

Andrea had spent days building up this player image of him. She needed it as a protective shield against his charm. Or was it to protect her from herself? She shook her head, chasing away that thought.

"So this Jamal really turns you on! My oh my." Charlene wore a delighted grin. "Where did you meet him? What does he do?"

"Wait a minute. Didn't Gran tell you?"

Charlene shook her head slowly. "No, my dear," she said, her grin widening.

"Then who told you about Jamal?" Andrea blinked at her in bewilderment.

"You just did." Charlene was the perfect picture of a sleek cat who'd caught her prey.

"I can't believe it!" Andrea groaned in despair. "You set me up!"

"Don't blame yourself. I'm a master." Charlene laughed. "Now, tell all. You know you want to."

"There is nothing to tell." Andrea took her hands from her face and sat up straight. "After Ellis, I'm immune to phony sweet talk."

"I see. That's why you're working so hard to convince yourself he's no good. Because you're *not* attracted to him." Charlene gave her a pointed look.

"That's ridiculous!" Andrea stammered. "The last thing I need is another heartbreak on legs. No way. My whole focus is on serving the patients who need me."

Charlene let out a stream of silvery laughter. "Oh, Andrea. You sound so cute."

"My work is not cute," Andrea grumbled. She squirmed in her seat.

"Don't pout." Charlene reached across the table and patted her hand again. "Relax and be happy."

"I am happy with my *career*." Andrea gazed out the window at the blue skies. "Right now that's enough."

The image of dark eyes and broad shoulders flashed into her mind. Andrea could only imagine what being enclosed in those thick, strong arms would do to her resolve to resist him. He made her feel safe and daring at the same time. Jamal had an assurance about him. He was smart, funny, and sexy as hell. She shivered but wasn't sure if it was from fear of herself or desire.

Charlene studied her. "But work isn't enough now that you've met *him*. Maybe I will visit Bayou Blue."

Andrea snapped back to the here and now. "I've got enough problems with Gran playing Cupid."

"Now, listen, don't accept anything less than the royal treatment," Charlene told her. "After that horrible divorce, you've earned it."

"Mother, I'm not going to date anyone. And this man . . . there's something about him."

"Obviously. He sounds fine as wine with the charm to match. What's not to like?" Charlene laughed.

"No, I mean something strange. He seems out of place." Andrea's brow furrowed as she tried to make sense of her gut feeling.

"In Bayou Blue? That's a big plus in my book," Charlene quipped. "Most of the single men in that town have raggedy pickup trucks, few teeth, and even less money."

Andrea laughed out loud and lost the elusive thread she'd been trying to follow. "You're so bad."

"You know I'm right." Charlene waved a hand in the air.

"You're a treat. I know I should have said it before now, but I missed you." Andrea took her mother's hand.

Charlene's expression softened. "I missed you too, baby. And I really do try my best to help you."

"And I appreciate it." Andrea smiled back at her.

"I think we should celebrate with a shopping trip." Charlene pursed her lips for a moment. "Esplanade Mall is having a huge sale."

"I'm not going to buy a bunch of new clothes." Andrea shook her head.

"You want a seductive new you," Charlene said with a wiggle of her eyebrows.

"No, I don't. But it is time to get my hair done." Andrea stuck out her chin in defiance.

"Whatever the reason, let's go to it!" Charlene dashed into her bedroom and came back with her purse.

Despite her attempts, resisting Charlene proved futile. She teased and charmed Andrea into laughter the entire time. Their first stop in the mall was Charlene's favorite exclusive hair salon. Charlene's hairdresser, Eric, seated Andrea in his chair, and he and Charlene stood at various angles staring at her.

"What do you think, Eric? I say a dramatic feathered bang over one eye, just below the eyebrow." Charlene circled around to face Andrea.

"Hmm, I'm getting a vision." Eric was a tall man the color of café au lait. He sported a small goatee and wore a black coat with the words CHOICES FOR HAIR in electric blue painted on the chest pocket.

"Nothing too, you know, out there." Andrea shifted nervously under their scrutiny.

"Maybe some blonde highlights," Charlene murmured.

"No way!" Andrea cried.

Eric stepped close to her and brushed her hair lightly with one hand. "In fact, the reddish highlights in your hair now are kinda golden in tone. See, what I'd do is—"

"No hair color and don't cut too much either." Andrea jumped out of the chair. "Come to think of it, I don't really need a new hairdo at all."

"Oh, no, you don't." Charlene pushed her back into the chair.

"Calm down, babe. Nobody's gonna do anything you

really don't want." Eric rushed to soothe her anxiety. "How 'bout I get you a Barq's cream soda?"

"Here, sweetie, here's a magazine. You pick out the style you want." Charlene gave her a copy of *Black Hair Magazine*. She shot a sideways glance at Eric, who nodded.

"Absolutely." He went out and came back with a paper cup full of soda.

"Just so we all understand." Andrea squinted at them both in warning. Then she pointed to a picture. "This one."

"That's not very different from what—" Charlene started.

"This or nothing." Andrea pressed her lips together in a stubborn expression.

Charlene gave a gasp of frustration. Then she shrugged and looked at Eric, who shrugged helplessly in response.

"The customer is always right," he said without much conviction.

Two hours later, Andrea gazed in awe at her image. She had to admit that Eric was good at what he did. Her hair was still long in the back, but loose curls were layered around her face.

Charlene sniffed. "It looks cute. But a touch of blonde would make it simply stunning."

She sashayed off before Andrea could respond. Andrea and Eric shared a laugh. She paid him and headed off to a clothing boutique at Charlene's insistence.

"Just a few things," Andrea insisted.

Andrea ended up with three blouses, a new dress, and shoes to match.

"Perfect," Charlene said. She held up a short red skirt.

"You're kidding," Andrea said with a laugh.

"Wear that to a meeting and you'll get whatever you want." Charlene gave a sharp nod and hung it over her arm. "It's perfect."

"I'm not the type to show a little leg to influence people, Charlene." Andrea shook her head once again. Something she seemed to be doing a lot of on this excursion.

"You make it sound like a bad thing." Charlene smiled and waved a hand.

Andrea's smile faded. "I've made it this far without resorting to that sort of thing. My degree and—"

"Yes, yes. You're well qualified. But let's face it, looks count. And men still run things for the most part." Charlene led her to a counter. She took out her credit card and handed to the saleswoman.

"Now you need the right accessories." Charlene turned to Andrea and her arched brows came together. "What's wrong?"

"Nothing."

"You're lying. Well?" Charlene put her head to one side. "It's the clothes."

Andrea swallowed the lump of anger that had risen in her throat. "I'm not you, Charlene." She bit off the urge to add she did not want to be anything like her, that she'd spent years trying not to be Charlene.

"Well . . ." Charlene's voice trailed off. "I thought you'd love it. We do look so much alike, and I look simply stunning in that shade of red. But we can return the skirt."

She spoke rapidly, her eyes clouded with dread. Andrea knew they'd come close to the edge again. Charlene seemed to sense it, too. Her expression pleaded with Andrea not to say more. Andrea's heart pounded as they stared at each other.

"Of course we won't take it back. Not after you spent so much energy talking me into it." Andrea put on a smile.

Charlene looked relieved. "I saw a pair of earrings that would be perfect for you."

Andrea felt tension drain from her shoulders. Once more they'd avoided confronting what truly separated them. Charlene provided more lighthearted banter, and Andrea went along with it. She did not want to face those particular demons. They'd achieved a kind of stasis in this way. Charlene went on about necklaces or something. Andrea nodded and smiled in all the right places as she pushed away family shadows from the past.

Six

Lee arrived at the clinic and walked through the waiting room. "Good morning." Several of the women patients gave him flirtatious smiles.

He went to the computer room to store his canvas bag, then followed the smell of fresh-brewed coffee. Business was booming that morning. Andrea had arranged for a pediatrician to come twice a month for well-baby care. Lee went down a second hall away from the examining rooms to avoid harried moms and screaming kids. This led to the kitchen. It was a good-sized room with a big Formica-topped table and padded chairs. The staff found refuge there for coffee breaks and during lunch. Katy was there filling her Minnie Mouse mug.

"Hello, sunshine," Lee said.

"Don't start with me," Katy muttered. "It's only ten and I feel like I've been here a week."

"Rough, huh?" Lee found a black mug that had become his in the three weeks he'd been coming.

"Listen to that." Katy jerked a thumb over her shoulder toward the racket. "All morning. My God!"

"It was your idea to have certain days for kiddie shots," Lee said.

"Somebody should have given me a good shake, too. Never again. Before the school rush, we're going to spread those appointments out." As though she needed further convincing, a piercing screech sounded.

"That one had the windows vibrating," Lee quipped.

"You think that's bad, try dealing with their mommies. Argumentative and picky, picky, picky." Katy frowned as though tasting something sour. "I'd like to give *them* a nice sharp needle in the butt."

"So you're hiding out back here. Who's helping Dr. Hill?" Lee leaned against the counter and sipped the strong coffee.

Katy laughed and sat down at the small table. "Student nurses. They need the experience."

"You're something else." Lee shook his head.

Katy raised an eyebrow at him. "So are you, from what they tell me. I hear you're a regular one-man SWAT team."

"Very funny," Lee said. He was embarrassed at the look she gave him.

"Lisa and Troylyn are telling the world you're a doggoned hero." Katy grinned at him.

Lee sat down across from her. "Your boss wasn't quite so impressed." He wondered why that bothered him.

"I don't know about that." Katy consoled him with a pat on the shoulder.

"Well, I do. She doesn't bend easily, does she?"

"Andrea can be a hard case. But she really appreciates all you've done."

"Has she said something?" Lee forgot to be irritated. He was curious and hopeful that Andrea felt something positive about him. Anything would do at this point.

"Sure. She's always talking about how much the computer system you set up has helped the clinic."

"Oh." Lee felt a stab of disappointment and guilt in his belly. Most of his overtime was spent gathering evidence that might sink the place.

"Like that tickler system for immunizations . . ." Katy went on about one of her and Andrea's pet projects.

Her voice faded into the background as Lee considered his role in Andrea's world. Would he damage her life's work beyond repair? Yet he had little choice.

There was no real reason the clinic should suffer permanent damage. The more he thought about it, he realized he could be doing Andrea and the clinic a big favor by helping to root out these problems. He could help protect her from being blamed and save the clinic she so cherished. The prospect of being Andrea's hero caused a pleasant sensation to spread up his spine.

"Hel-loo." Katy waved a hand in front of his face. "You haven't been listening."

"Sorry, I was thinking of ways to impress the boss." Lee grinned by way of apology.

"Think improve the clinic. That's the way to this lady's heart." Katy drank the last drop of coffee from her mug and stood.

"I'll keep that in mind," Lee said with a smile.

"Sugar, before you know it, you two will be best friends if you work at it."

Lee pictured Andrea's smile. Her sensual lips curling

up gently at the corners, tempting him to taste, nibble, suck . . . "Yeah. I'll get on that."

"Boy, I can tell you like the idea of pleasing that woman." Katy rinsed out her mug and dried it with a paper towel.

"I was thinking of computer systems that might help," Lee said, casually leaning back in his seat. He sipped his coffee.

Katy turned to him with a smirk. "Yeah, uh-uh. I really believe that one."

"This is strictly business," he grumbled.

He brought the mug to his mouth to cover his growing chagrin. Here he was, a PI who had fooled some of the most dangerous criminals, yet let him have one simple conversation about Andrea Noble and his face was an open book!

"Okay." Katy struggled not to smirk at him. "A new software program, wow-wee."

"Good morning. What new program?" Andrea strolled in. She rubbed the back of her neck wearily with one hand.

"Hi," Lee said. He noticed how tired she looked. "Long day already, huh?"

"I've got this pain in my neck bending over stupid paperwork. The department has a triplicate form for everything." Andrea grimaced.

"Poor kid. What about some ibuprofen?" Katy clucked sympathetically.

Lee crossed the room without thinking. "Here, let me see." He moved behind her and kneaded the tight neck muscles with adept fingers.

Andrea tensed and her eyes widened. "N-no, I'll be—"

"Don't fight it or you'll just ache more," Lee said softly. Gradually her shoulders eased down.

Andrea closed her eyes and relaxed completely. "Thanks. I'll be okay in a minute, though." Still she did not move away from him.

"Better than any pill I've got in the drug cabinet," Katy said. She grinned and waved her fingers as she slipped out the door.

"That feels wonderful. Are you living a double life as a masseur?"

Lee savored the feel of velvety brown skin. Her hair was pinned up in a French roll, but a few wisps trailed down the back of her neck. He leaned forward and caught a scent of flowers. Andrea seemed to unwind and flow with the rhythm of his fingers. She sighed again and tilted her head forward as though inviting him to touch her more. Lee massaged her upper arms and stepped so close his chest touched her back. He inhaled deeply again.

"I actually studied therapeutic massage back in L.A.," Lee said in a strained voice. He was finding it harder and harder to breathe normally.

"Is that gardenia?" he murmured.

"Yes. You like it?"

Andrea exhaled, then arched her back slightly. Her hips brushed his groin. Lee felt himself harden and knew he'd have a raging erection in a few seconds. A voice told him to let go, but his body was having a hell of a time obeying.

"Yeah," he said in a husky voice. "Smells delicious." His hands moved to her waist and he pulled her to him.

The temperature in the room seemed to shoot up by fifty degrees. Lee felt hot all over. His hands moved to her waist, then started lower. Andrea sighed and swayed in his arms. He buried his nose in her hair, savoring the feathery texture, breathing in the womanly scent of her.

"What are you doing?" she whispered huskily, no trace of anger in her tone.

"Helping you relax," he whispered back. His erection throbbed, straining to be set free.

Andrea lowered her head. Lee lifted her hair and brushed his lips against the exposed patch of silky light brown skin on her neck.

The sound of loud voices approaching seemed to wake them both from the dream. Andrea went rigid, then whirled around and backed off.

"Thanks," she stammered as she avoided looking at him. "I feel okay now."

Lee was not ready to let go of the moment. "Are you sure? I could . . ."

Andrea swallowed hard. "I'm positive."

Lee took several deep breaths to collect himself. He should have been grateful she wasn't looking at him. His legs were wobbly as he went to the table and sat down. The pulsing hunger in his crotch eased, but only slowly. *Think of something neutral like football or cold waterfalls!* Lee shifted to ease the discomfort.

Andrea cleared her throat. "So you were in college." She seemed eager to introduce a safe subject.

"Excuse me?" Lee's mind was still foggy.

"You said you studied massage therapy." Andrea put distance between them by going to the counter opposite him. She got a cup and poured coffee into it.

"Yeah, but that was after college."

"What's your degree in?" Andrea glanced at him with interest.

"I only went a few semesters. Too much partying and too little studying." Lee grinned at her.

"Why doesn't that surprise me?" Andrea smiled back at him.

"I'm a grown-up now. Mr. Responsibility, that's me."

Andrea considered him thoughtfully. "I see."

Lee got a sudden chill, a flash that he was in danger, but not the kind he'd been used to as a cop. It was time to put more than physical distance between them. He shied away from troubling emotions like caring too much, emotions he'd suppressed for a long time. Andrea could be up to her neck in whatever was going down. Experience had taught him long ago not to trust appearances. Now here he was shaking like a fifteen-year-old kid in heat. His mind had turned to mush and veered totally off his goal, which was to get answers.

Having recovered from the attack of lust, Lee rose from his chair. "Better get to work. I've got a real tough boss," he said jauntily, back in his role as a flirtatious lightweight.

"She's not as bad as they say," Andrea said jokingly.

Lee paused in the doorway and looked at her. "Nah, not half as bad as she'd like folks to think," he said in a quiet voice.

They stood staring at each other for a few moments before Andrea blinked hard and put her cup down.

"But you're right about one thing, it's time to get busy. See you later." She placed the cup in the sink and walked past him.

Gardenia fragrance floated to him as she went by. Lee felt rooted to the spot. "Right, later," was all he could manage.

He would have to think about a lot of football and cold water to get through this case.

* * *

Andrea gazed around the open field of green grass dotted with tents and booths. The small park was near the center of town. She smiled at people who passed but kept a watchful eye on everything happening. The first big public event staged by the clinic seemed to be going well. Billed as the First Annual Bayou Blue Health Fair Extravaganza, it was set up on a prairie near the center of town. The site was used for carnivals and other outdoor events.

The health fair included fun activities for adults and kids. Face painting, a space walk, and helium balloons were as much a hit with parents as with their children. Red-striped tents covered most of the booths and exhibits. The crowd was not as big as they'd hoped, but Andrea knew it would take time for the clinic to inspire confidence. Her vision was for people from other small communities around Bayou Blue to eventually use the clinic also. Andrea wanted to reach the poor, underserved people in the southeastern third of Lafourche Parish. For now she was more than satisfied with the first health fair.

Gran ambled over to her with two of her lifelong pals, Miss Sandra and Miss Noreen. "This ain't half bad." She nodded to Andrea in approval.

"Thanks," Andrea said dryly.

"No, I thought you'd have some of them lectures on all kinds of diseases that would scare folks into an early grave. You know what I'm talking about." Gran glanced at her pals, who nodded in agreement.

"Lordy, yes," Miss Noreen piped up. "Went to hear a talk on heart disease and almost had a heart attack!"

"You're so right. By the time that lady doctor got

through talking about us old black women droppin' dead, all I wanted to do was cry." Miss Sandra rolled her eyes.

"And don't let 'em start talking about cancer, girl!" Gran shook her head. "Some of them doctors look like the grim reaper himself." This brought a burst of laughter from her buddies.

"Tell you what, this is ten times better. Got me all kinds of ink pens and key rings." Miss Noreen held up a bag of freebies given out by exhibitors.

"Noreen, your house already looks like a swap meet. What you gonna do with all that junk?" Gran said bluntly.

"My grandchildren gotta have pens for school, and people just love these key chains. I give 'em away." Miss Noreen was not at all deterred. "In fact, I ain't through makin' my rounds. Come on before all those little notepads are gone." She walked away with a slow but steady gait.

"Oh yeah, I want some of those, too," Miss Sandra said, following her. "Let's go, Mavis."

"All right, you pack rats. I'll catch up in a minute," Gran said with a laugh. She carried a bulging plastic bag with a home health company logo on it.

"You seem to be doing your own share of packing," Andrea said, eyebrows raised.

"I'm getting health information." Gran pulled a pamphlet out of the bag. "See, this one's on tasty low-fat recipes."

"Oh yes, I do see." Andrea peered down into the bag. "And I also see six ink pens, three pencils, a key chain—"

"Oh, hush." Gran snatched the bag behind her back.

She looked at Andrea, then laughed out loud. "Okay, you got me this time."

Andrea laughed with her and put an arm around her grandmother's waist. They walked in the direction Miss Sandra and Miss Noreen had taken. "If hard cases like you three take home health information, then we've done our job today."

Andrea knew that many poor and elderly people put off seeking medical assistance until their symptoms were severe.

"Don't mind me, sugar. You've done a beautiful job. Your way of bringing this information down home is what we need," Gran said.

"I'm glad to hear you say that." Andrea sighed. "It was a lot of work, but worth every minute." They both looked around.

Gran nodded to where Denny stood with Jamal. Both men helped kids into a giant inflated space walk. "How's Denny making out?"

Andrea followed her gaze. "Better than I expected. He's still a bit undisciplined, but not as bad as some I had to let go."

"His grandmama told me she appreciates you giving him a chance. Helen has been through so much with that boy. Maybe he's finally coming around." Gran watched Denny, her brows drawn together.

"What do you mean?" Andrea looked at Gran.

"You know that's her youngest son's child. His mama is on drugs and Helen's son is in a gang out in Los Angeles. The welfare folks took him away from them and Helen got him when he was twelve. Wild as could be." Gran shook her head slowly.

"He's been in trouble?" Andrea was not surprised.

Denny had the bravado of a young man wanting to prove his masculinity in all the wrong ways.

"Small scrapes, yeah. Skipping school, fighting in class, and shoplifting little stuff like candy bars." Gran sighed. "Helen stuck by him, though."

"He does seem to be trying. Lately he's been more cooperative."

Andrea did not add it had taken at least three heart-to-heart talks with the young man. Denny had a habit of arriving late, leaving early, and doing as little as possible in between. At first he'd shown lots of attitude, while making snide comments under his breath. But over the last three weeks he seemed to be coming around. There was something in him, Andrea thought, some kernel of goodness that made her think he was not a lost cause. There were times when he showed initiative. Then he'd come in another day with that cocky "I'm bad" attitude again. Still, she knew his family and the problems they'd faced. Andrea was determined not to give up on Denny too quickly.

"Well, keep a firm hand. Don't do him any favors just 'cause Helen's in my prayer circle at St. Isidore." Gran pressed her lips together. "Poor thing worked hard all her days and her children broke her heart."

Andrea grinned and pinched Gran's cheek. "Message received and understood, for the third time."

Gran beamed at her. "I'm so proud of you, baby." Then she shifted her attention. This time she pointed to Jamal. "That's another employee you should be happy to have."

Jamal helped a crowd of noisy children into the space walk. Squeals of delight came from the inflated fun room filled with soft plastic balls. Children bounced around inside the bright blue and red contraption. He seemed to take genuine joy in helping the little kids. He was equally proficient in handling them. Andrea watched his powerful arms reach out to cradle an anxious little girl hesitant to join the others. She watched him charm her until she was giggling. So he could be tender and caring.

This thought brought back the memory of his hands on her shoulders, strong and soothing. Andrea blushed at another memory, the hunger to feel his strong and gentle fingers caressing the bare skin beneath her blouse. Her nipples had stayed erect for almost an hour. It had taken twice as long as usual for her to fall asleep that night. She'd kept imagining his lean, muscled frame stretched beside her in bed while he massaged her entire body. Andrea had tossed and turned until two in the morning.

But Andrea also noted the knot of simpering mothers who surrounded him. He grinned and traded banter with them like an old pro. Andrea pressed her lips together. She knew his kind. He was a real smooth operator. The kind of man quite capable of making a woman feel as though she were the only one. Like her ex-husband, Ellis. Lies had rolled off his tongue like melted butter, and Andrea had let love blind her. Ellis had used sweet words and romance as a kind of rose-colored veil to hide the truth. Yet Andrea had gone along with it. Now here she was letting Jamal get to her in the same way. He bent his head down close to a pretty woman dressed in tight denim shorts. The woman laughed at some remark he'd made. There he stood, ready to finesse his way through the female population of Lafourche Parish. Well, he could count out at least one.

"He's okay," she said, and looked away.

"Okay nothing, the man is hot. Look at all those

women. We best get over there and save him." Gran hooked her arm through Andrea's and tugged.

Andrea did not budge. "The way he's grinning, I don't think he needs to be rescued," she retorted.

"He's gotta be friendly. Come on so he can see this cute new outfit you got on up close." Gran straightened the collar of Andrea's red and tan cotton knit shirt.

Andrea did not look at her clothes. She gently guided Gran's hand away. "Stop that. And I'm not going to join his groupies."

"For crying out loud, c'mon," Gran said, and yanked hard on her arm. She succeeded in moving Andrea a few steps, despite her resistance. "You've been to every other booth twice. Quit avoiding the man."

"I'm not avoiding him," Andrea insisted.

"I've been watching you for the last two hours. You went to every display table and made a big circle around him."

"It's got nothing to do with him," Andrea insisted. "My focus has been on the exhibits that are directly health related."

"And you've done your job. Time for fun." Gran pulled her forward again.

Andrea pulled in the other direction. "Katy might need help with her booth on immunizations."

Andrea's body tingled at the thought of being so close to him again. Her physical reaction to Jamal yards away had been strong. She already knew what being close to him did to her body. Watchful eyes would detect any sign that she was attracted to him, and word that Andrea Noble had the hots for sexy Jamal Turner would be all over Bayou Blue by morning.

"You scared of him or something?"

"Don't be silly." Andrea sniffed. "I work with him

every day. He does his job fairly well and that's what counts."

"You're trying a little too hard not to notice him." Gran squinted at her. "And if you ask me, he *does* scare you."

"Ridiculous," Andrea said with force. Still, she could not look Gran in the eyes.

"Then come on." Gran issued her challenge with a twinkle in her eyes. "Being close to rippling muscles and a gorgeous smile shouldn't be a problem."

"Fine." Andrea tossed out the word in what she hoped was a careless tone. "Let's go."

They both strode across the dark green grass. Andrea kept her head up and did not look away from where Jamal stood. She was quite aware that Gran kept darting sideways glances at her. The closer they got to him, the more obvious it became that the space walk was not the main attraction for the mothers. A pretty young thing rubbed her hand along Jamal's arm. Andrea forced a smile despite the unreasonable and strong urge to peel the hussy off him. Denny stood several feet away. He watched the children while talking with another young man. He waved at them and they waved back.

"Hi there!" Jamal called as they approached. "You ladies want to have a go? The crowd is thinning out." He nodded to the space walk where now only two kids jumped around inside.

"Not out here, it isn't," Andrea said. She kept smiling. "No indeed."

"Excuse me while I talk to the boss," Jamal said to the young woman. "Gotta make sure she's happy."

"Bye-bye, Jamal," the woman trilled.

She gave a perfunctory nod to Andrea and Gran before drifting off, hips swaying. She glanced back to make sure Jamal watched. Three women lingered, pretending an interest in the space walk while keeping an eye on Jamal. Andrea rolled her eyes. Gran poked her side with an elbow, a sign for her to behave.

"You're doing a wonderful job, son. Right, Andrea?" Gran said in a bright voice.

"Thanks, ma'am. I'm doing my part for the health of Lafourche Parish."

"Making this health fair fun is an important job, baby. These children might even wanna come to the doctor next time. Right, Andrea?" Gran's prompt this time was firmer as she poked Andrea's side again.

"Of course. The staff and I took that into consideration when we were planning." Andrea wore a staid expression. Maybe she could be near him without having her senses go haywire.

"Yes, we did," Jamal said in a formal tone.

Gran glanced from Jamal to Andrea and back again. She pursed her lips for a moment before she spoke. "Oops, I just remembered something. I'll see y'all later." She walked away at a brisk pace.

Andrea blinked with surprise. Gran was fast putting distance between them. "Where are you going?" she called out.

"I see Father Viator. I need to tell him something about the church bake sale," Gran yelled back without breaking her stride.

Andrea did not see the parish priest, and this was the first she'd heard of a bake sale. She frowned at the back of Gran's flowered blouse as it disappeared into the crowd.

"What a busy lady," Jamal said.

"Yes, she's always up to something," Andrea mumbled to herself.

"I didn't hear you," Jamal said.

"Nothing." Andrea recovered. She began the start of a smooth exit. "Good job keeping the kids happy over here."

"It's not hard. They love this thing." Jamal jerked a thumb at the inflated attraction. "You must be happy about the way the fair has turned out. Good crowd."

"Yes, I'm already thinking about what we'll do next year." Andrea's brows came together. "I'll start lining up sponsors next week. You know, ride on the success of this one while it's still fresh in their minds."

"Great idea." Jamal cleared his throat. "I thought of a few things myself."

Andrea made herself look at him. She gazed up into his eyes, hoping to lessen the impact the sight of his body had on her. It didn't work. There was no way she could take in full lips or dark eyes set against creamy milk chocolate skin and not feel her pulse rate inch steadily up and up. Andrea swallowed hard. The man was pure poison. Jamal looked at her as though he wanted to speak but was searching for words. He seemed to lean forward, inviting Andrea to come closer. Then, without warning, he took a step back from her. His expression became tense, almost angry.

"Excuse me," he said curtly. "I better make sure the space walk is still anchored."

Andrea was embarrassed. Here she stood mooning over him. She behaved no different from the women she'd only moments before held in such contempt. Even worse, he knew it and was making a fast escape.

"I, uh, better go check on . . . other things," Andrea

stuttered. She wanted to kick herself for being so transparent and clumsy.

Jamal walked off quickly. "Sure thing. I've got this under control."

Andrea frowned as he walked away. She was more irritated at her own behavior than at him. She had showed herself as just one more fawning female, and Jamal was not interested, period. Still it rankled that he'd been so quick to escape from her while he'd courted the attention of other women. She turned sharply and marched in the opposite direction.

"You're an idiot, Andrea," she whispered harshly. "He's doing you a favor, so be grateful." Her words did not ease the sting of rejection, or loosen the knot of disappointment in her chest.

Seven

The small sandwich shop was crowded as usual. Lee told himself he was only here for lunch. Yet he scanned the customers looking for one face in particular. Andrea and Katy ate here almost every day. It was close to the clinic, fast, and had great hamburgers.

Lee lingered over making a decision on what he wanted. He would not go back to the clinic just yet. He would relax and enjoy his lunch hour.

Two dueling voices sounded in his head. One called him wise. The less time he spent near Andrea, the better. What he needed was breathing room so he could stop thinking about her as anything except another assignment. Things were adding up, and the total did not look good for her or the clinic. Lee saw discrepancies that pointed to serious problems. Andrea could be involved. Hell, she had to be. She reviewed the inventory records, signed purchase orders, and co-signed with the doctor on all narcotic drugs that had to be tracked. Lee compared records on drugs dispensed and suspected that some of the patients did not exist. He shared receptionist duties with another clerk. Lee's one hasty search revealed names on the dispensary ledger of people who never came in for appointments. Getting away from the clinic allowed him to think objectively. If it looks too good to be true, it is. Lee had been through enough in his life to not just know, but feel, the truth of that saying.

The other voice nudged alive the part of him that wanted to believe, to not be cynical and to trust appearances. It whispered that Andrea was not faking it when it came to her patients. Lee thought about the times he'd seen her easing the fears of an elderly patient or taking extra time with a teen mom. If she was acting, she could win awards, but everything inside him told him that she did care about people. Her smile seemed to inspire confidence in the most nervous patients and defuse angry, resistant ones. It was the same smile that sent shock waves through his body when she directed it at him. Pleasing her made him feel extraordinary and proud. Which was a big problem.

Lee sighed and drank from his cup of cola. He knew very well from his days as a cop in Los Angeles that the prettiest package could be the most deadly. Nothing and no one could be taken on face value, and life was cheap. His younger brother's death at fifteen in a barrage of automatic gunfire had proven it. Nothing he'd done as a brother or cop had helped save Chris. Indifference in the department when it came to minority youth had long rankled. Chris's death had sealed his decision. Lee resigned the day after his funeral. Five years as a private investigator had served to confirm what he already knew. He saw the worst in people, rich, poor, and in between. Which reminded him of another old saying, that looks can be deceiving. His cynicism about life and human nature had been formed by life and reality, he mused.

He just needed to keep his priorities straight, he told himself firmly. If drugs were being taken, he'd have to involve the cops. Lee decided to wrap this thing up quick, report to the cops, and get the hell out of Dodge fast. And Andrea? He gritted his teeth at the thought of her being involved. Despite his hard, cynical outlook, Lee couldn't see it. Or maybe he just didn't want to see it. A *real* big problem.

"Hi, Denise. Our order ready? I think it's in Katy's name," he heard a familiar voice say. He turned to see Andrea standing at the end of the long counter under the PICK UP sign.

She did not see him at the other end of the dining room, seated in a booth. He watched her brush back a tendril of hair from her face. Her thick brown locks were pulled back into a French braid. As she smiled at other customers, his heart turned over. It was a struggle to be such a hardnose. He could not think of her as a criminal, not when she smiled like that. Her face glowed. The smooth brown skin invited him to caress it. She wore lipstick the color of wine—he swallowed hard, wanting desperately to taste her lips. Lee drew in a deep breath and let it out. The physical attraction hit him with force again, reminding him why he needed to avoid her. Lately he'd begun to think of her kindness and her sense of humor. Andrea was not all starched uniforms and stern lectures. Lee frowned at a disturbing truth: he looked forward to hearing her voice. The clinic seemed drab when she wasn't there.

Andrea turned her back to him and he studied the delicate lines of her neck. He remembered massaging her there until he was virtually stupefied with lust. Every nerve ending in his body fired up whenever she was nearby. He'd made a fool of himself once and that was enough. Better to fade into the woodwork and let her leave without seeing him.

Andrea faced the man standing in line behind her and laughed at something he said. The tall, dark man was obviously flirting with her. Lee scowled. Who was this guy anyway? Thoughts of slipping out quietly vanished. Lee slid out of the booth and moved closer, keeping them in view as he listened to their exchange.

"You haven't changed a bit, Brian. Still cracking jokes." Andrea gave his arm a playful punch.

"Well, I can't say the same for you. You've changed, girl. You're ten times prettier." Brian gave her an admiring full-body examination and let out a whistle.

"Still trying to sweet-talk me." Andrea smiled with pleasure.

Lee was at the counter before he knew it. "Hello there," he said, his tone filled with forced cheer.

Andrea faced him. "Oh, hi," she said hesitantly.

"Everybody seems to find this place for lunch, huh?" Lee looked at the man, then at Andrea.

"This is Brian Scott. One of my old classmates." Andrea looped her arm through Brian's. "Brian, Jamal Turner. Jamal's originally from Los Angeles."

"Hey, stop saying *old*! Nice to meet you." Brian stuck out his hand.

Lee grasped his hand and gave it a perfunctory shake before letting go. "Hi. Old pals, huh?"

"Man, this lady has been breakin' my heart since the third grade." Brian pulled a long face.

"Oh, quit. Brian is the most talented guy in town. He acts, sings, and plays a mean blues guitar," Andrea said.

"You're making me blush." Brian grinned at her. "And this one wasn't too shabby singing those songs either."

"Really?" Lee was interested to find out more about Andrea, but not this way. Not from a still-interested ex-boyfriend.

"We used to put on variety shows," Andrea said to Lee.

"Those were the days. Me on guitar and you singing along. We've gotta get together, Drea." Brian pulled her closer to him.

"I know. It's just I've been so tied up with work and all. Maybe this week," Andrea said, anticipation in her eyes.

"We have to set up the case management system," Lee broke in. He tried to keep his voice light, but the effort made his jaws ache.

"I'd forgotten about that." Andrea looked disappointed.

"We might even have to work on it weekends." Lee moved a few inches to stand close to Andrea. "Nights, too."

"I know how that is. I been working overtime myself. So, you just moved here from L.A.?" Brian looked at Lee.

"Yes." Lee crossed his arms over his chest and offered no more chatty details.

"Oh." Brian seemed to process the unspoken message in his posture. "Interesting place. But too big for me."

"Yeah, it can be overwhelming to small-town people." Lee stared back at him.

"I travel quite a bit actually. Guess I just prefer living

where you don't have to fight traffic to buy milk."
Brian's voice held an edge.

Denise placed five white paper bags on the counter.
"Here's your order, Andrea. That's sixteen dollars
even."

Andrea glanced from Lee to Brian. "If I don't get
back with this food, I'm going to be in big trouble. I'll
see you around, Brian."

"Right. I've gotta get moving myself." Brian nodded
to Lee. "See ya."

"Yeah," Lee said in a short tone.

"Baby girl, you just let me know. I'll have a crawfish
boil organized in no time flat. The whole gang will be
there and we'll dance just like we used to." Brian gave
her a quick peck on the forehead. He glanced at Lee,
then left.

Andrea paid for the food and got change back.
" 'Bye, Jamal." She reached for the food.

"I'll carry those." Lee paid for his lunch, picked up
the bags, and cupped her elbow.

"They don't weigh very much," Andrea said.

"Come on. You've got hungry employees waiting."
Lee went to the door and pushed it open.

Andrea paused for a second, then followed him.
"What was all that about us needing to work late? You
told me things were going along just fine." She brushed
back her hair again as they walked down the sidewalk.

Lee felt warm watching the movement of her fingers
against the cotton-soft curls. "Yes, but . . . you need to
tell me what data fields you want set up. Remember, I'm
going to customize the database to your specifications."

"I've already given you the list." Andrea shot a sideways glance at him.

"Uh, not for all the new programs. And we'll need to

review and evaluate the system even after you start using it." Lee felt a rush at a new thought. "It could take another month, maybe two."

They came to an intersection and waited for the traffic light to turn. Andrea looked at him. "Just show me the basics and I'll take it from there. I've used computers since college."

"Why take time from the patients? I know how much you enjoy that part of the job." Lee smiled at her.

"I wouldn't want to put a cramp in your social life. Thanks anyway." Andrea started across the street when cars stopped for the red light.

Lee matched her stride. "But I don't mind. It's worth it. To help the clinic, I mean."

Andrea stopped a few yards short of the clinic. "It's really not necessary. I'm not a tech dummy."

"I didn't say you were. You're great. At your job, I mean." He stumbled over his words like a kid.

"Thanks a lot," Andrea said, her tone dry.

Lee felt as though he'd wandered haplessly into alien territory. He stood close to her, his body ignoring the small voice of caution in his head. That voice had saved him too many times to count. And right now it was telling him to back off.

"Yeah, on second thought, it might not take that much after all," Lee said curtly. "Better relieve Terri so she can get lunch." He started to turn away but stopped when she touched his arm.

Andrea's expression had softened. "I didn't mean to sound snippy. It's just we need to be careful about overtime pay. The board is breathing down my neck about expenses."

Lee's antennae went up. "The clinic is having money problems?"

"The accounting records are scrambled. I'm working with an auditor from the state fiscal office now. I think it was just poor record keeping really." Andrea sighed.

"That's what I keep hearing."

"We have to meet layers of bureaucratic rules about medical care standards and the budget."

"I guess you could go months without knowing which end is up with the money or other stuff." Lee glanced at the clinic.

"Oh yes," Andrea said with a nod. "And I'm just beginning."

"Easy to get it all tangled up," Lee said. *Easy to cover your tracks,* he added to himself.

"Very easy. But I've got good staff like Katy and Denny. Thank goodness we're in this together." Andrea started walking again.

Lee walked beside her. "You've got a big job on your hands, eh?"

Her full lips lifted in a ghost of a smile. "Well, we finally agree on something."

"Yeah." Lee smiled back.

"From now on I promise not to be so touchy," Andrea said. "And, Jamal." She stopped at the clinic entrance.

Lee's body temperature shot up when she looked at him. Her mouth was full and moist, her expression open. "Yeah?" he managed to choke out.

"I value you, too. We're a team." Andrea's lips curved up gently. "Don't think I haven't noticed all the time you've spent getting our systems up and running."

Lee felt tiny, needlelike jabs of guilt in his chest. "Just doing my job."

"You're going above and beyond your job. Thanks."

Andrea tilted her head to one side and a wisp of hair trailed down her right cheek.

"I'm trying to do my part," he murmured, unable to take his eyes off the sweep of dark waves brushed back from her face.

Lee wanted catch the dark lock and twirl it around his fingers, to feel its texture. He wondered if she sensed the crackle of attraction between them. The sound of traffic receded. Andrea seemed to move closer to him. Her gaze traveled from his face down his body and back again. When her lips parted, he held his breath. Then the clinic door opened and a mother came out, admonishing her little boy.

"Hush. I'm not buying you candy," the woman said, and pulled the wailing child behind her. "S'cuse me, y'all."

"Sure," Andrea said as she made a wide path for them.

Andrea cleared her throat as she glanced away from him. They both watched the mother and child walk off, still wrapped in a battle of wills.

"I'll bet Katy and the student nurses are really yelling for their burgers by now. I'd better get inside before they come looking for me." Andrea opened the door before he could and walked in.

"Then you'll need these." Lee shook the bags he still held. He grinned at her.

"Oh, right. Thanks." Andrea blushed prettily. She grabbed the bags and hurried inside.

Lee went to the reception desk so Terri could take a break. He barely listened as she gave him a brief rundown on what needed to be done. He checked in several patients who had appointments. Yet he was just going through the motions. His mind was on Andrea. She'd been very frank about the state of the budget records. Why would she tell him if she was up to something? Maybe it all went back to the previous directors.

His cynical side spoke right up. Most of the staff whispered gossip about what was wrong at the clinic. To deny any problems would look even more suspicious. There was no doubt she'd inspired loyalty from the staff. She could just as well be building up her own shell of protection. Andrea made it a point to let everyone know she was in charge and hands on. Lee pushed aside sympathetic leanings. Get the goods, then get paid. If she wasn't involved, fine. Lee would move on, whatever happened.

Andrea tapped her ink pen on her desk rapidly. She considered the reports in front of her. The budget was enough to make even the most experienced bureaucrat dizzy. The clinic received funding from a complex set of federal and state sources. With each came an equally complex set of strings attached. Still, she'd managed to figure it out; at least she'd thought so until today. The patient statistics and money spent did not add up. They kept dancing around like jumping beans. *Now what?* Andrea chewed on the end of her pen. For the third time she called Denny into her office.

"Yes, ma'am." Denny came in and stood before her desk.

"How many of these patient charts have you found?" Andrea tapped her copy of the list of names she'd printed out for him.

He bent forward and peered down to where she

pointed. "Let's see, out of twenty-five, about seven so far. It's been wild all day. I'll get back on it now."

"I don't get it. Close to seventy thousand dollars was spent on follow-up treatment and home visits, according to Thelma Cresson's reports," Andrea murmured to herself.

"Miss Cresson had her own way of doing things, that's for sure," Denny said with a frown. "Uh, I wasn't gonna say anything, but . . ."

Andrea glanced up at him. "What?"

"I don't wanna get caught up in nothing." Denny rubbed his chin, eyes wide. "But like, I don't want nobody getting in trouble for something they didn't do."

"I don't have a clue what you're talking about." Andrea rocked back in her chair.

"They're gone and we get all the blame." Denny fidgeted with his hands.

"She told you what to do and you had to follow orders. I understand. So tell me what happened." Andrea waited as he seemed to silently debate whether to talk.

"If I lose this job, won't be easy to get another one. My grandmother needs me to help." Denny looked at her with desperation in his dark eyes.

"I know that, Denny." Andrea stood and walked to him. "And I know how hard you've tried over the last few weeks."

"Miss Cresson has a lot of big-time connections. She's still pissed, pardon my language. But she said anybody that helps you will go down, too." Denny blinked hard. "I ain't been no angel, Miss Noble."

Andrea sat down in one of two chairs in front of her desk. "Let's talk." She patted the forest green vinyl seat cushion and Denny sat down next to her.

"Guess you heard I gave my grandmother lots of trouble staying out late, drinking, and running with the wrong crowd. I swear I was never arrested, for nothing serious, that is." Denny spoke in a rush as though saying it quickly would convince her.

"Yes, I've heard."

"My mama kinda dumped me on my dad, and he . . . got his own problems." Denny hung his head and clutched both knees with his hands. "Bottom line is, I raised myself."

Andrea felt a flood of compassion for him. She'd known the anguish of feeling abandoned by her own mother. Charlene had escaped the boredom of Bayou Blue and left Andrea for party trips to New Orleans all the time when she was younger. Gran had been wonderful and loving in her comforting maternal way. Yet inside, Andrea suffered. For years Andrea had believed that it was her fault, that she'd been a bad girl. Looking at Denny now, she could see herself fifteen years ago. Like him, Andrea had hidden the hurt under a facade. Hers had been the workaholic overachiever in high school and college. Denny had obviously adopted the bad boy pose.

"You've had it hard. But tell me the truth and I'll do everything in my power to help you," she said.

Denny looked at her searchingly. "You really mean that, huh?" he said quietly.

"You've got a good heart. I can see it in the way you treat people. No matter how bad you think it is, lying will make it worse." Andrea waited once more.

Denny looked away. "Miss Cresson did private nursing on the side. She referred patients to herself and billed the clinic for it."

Andrea frowned. "But I'd have seen her name on pay

invoices. No way is an employee allowed to get paid for services they should provide here."

"Health Services, Inc., is owned by her friend. Miz Ruth had a contract with them. They billed Medicaid through the clinic."

"I can't say I'm surprised." Andrea shook her head. "So what's that got to do with you?"

Denny's gaze slid sideways again. "I helped her do paperwork. She paid me extra. She said it wasn't illegal."

"But you knew better," Andrea added.

Denny nodded. "We was always juggling."

"Show me what you did, okay?" Andrea stood.

Denny's brows pulled together in a worried expression. "But—"

"I'm not asking you to help gather evidence against yourself," Andrea broke in. "You were following instructions, right?"

"For sure." Denny's face muscles relaxed a bit.

"Then show me these doctored records." Andrea jerked a thumb toward the file room.

"Yes, ma'am."

"And, Denny?" Andrea put a hand on his shoulder to stop him. "Your grandmother has reason to be proud of you these days."

Denny stared at his shoes. "Nah, I still got a ways to go. Anyway, I got an idea where most of the files were put up." He darted off ahead of her.

For the better part of the morning they sifted through a stack of paper that made Andrea want to scream. Getting a clear picture of the situation was not quite as easy as she'd hoped. The invoices listed Health Services, Inc., not Thelma Cresson. Andrea read through the files and boiled with outrage. The woman was crafty. Andrea would have to consult with the auditor, but her gut feeling was that they should make the best of it and start from scratch. The clinic would only suffer from more bad publicity, especially since it would not be easy to prove anything. Besides, Andrea wanted to start fresh and give the staff successes. Morale had been low when she'd taken over. No need to pull it down again when the guilty would escape punishment anyway. With iron determination and Denny's enthusiastic assistance, they managed to put the records in order for the auditor. Andrea marveled at their achievement. She gave Denny permission to take extra time for his lunch break as a reward.

Andrea gulped down a turkey sandwich at her desk while reading regulations for a new program. The confusing requirements threw another curve at her. After the morning she'd spent, Andrea once again felt an urge to scream. The phone rang and she snatched up the receiver in exasperation. She'd never get through at this rate.

"Yes," she said through clenched teeth.

"I know, boss lady," Terri began in her best diplomat's voice. "But, uh, John Mandeville is here to see you. Says he won't take up much of your time." She said the last sentence in almost a whisper.

"He's standing in front of you?"

"You got it."

"Give me five minutes, then bring him back."

"Sure will."

The first thing Andrea did was clear anything from her desk that might attract his attention. No need to give him a reason to get in clinic business. Terri knocked on her door just as she finished.

"Here you go, Mr. Mandeville."

"Thank you, dear," John said.

Andrea waited until the door closed behind Terri, then spoke. "So we finally meet."

"Thanks for letting me barge in. I know how busy you are." He did not seem to mind her scouring look. "I've wanted to talk to you for a long time."

"I see." But Andrea did not see at all.

"I know this is awkward. The circumstances, I mean." He still stood near the door. "I've heard nothing but good things about what you've done here." John waved a hand around to indicate the clinic.

"It's been a team effort," Andrea said.

"Leadership makes the difference. It's obvious your staff respects you."

"Thank you. Please, have a seat."

Andrea studied him, trying to determine if the man lived up to the myth. How many years had it been since she'd last seen him? At least twenty, she mused. Charlene had taken her on a trip to New Orleans and they'd met John at the Audubon Zoo. Of course, she hadn't known he was her father then. Ten years old, Andrea had quickly warmed to the handsome man who'd bought her a stuffed tiger and all the cotton candy she could eat.

He was certainly handsome in a rugged way. John Mandeville had aged well. She searched his face for any resemblance, any shared features. Except for a faint likeness around the nose and chin, she had Charlene's features. His eyes were black and so was his hair, with just a touch of gray at his temples. Realizing she was staring, Andrea cleared her throat.

"So what can I do for you?" she said.

"I was going to ask you that." John tapped the arm of the chair with his fingertips. "Anything you need here in the way of equipment, just ask."

"We have everything we need."

"Health care is sky-high these days. Is your budget okay? I have some influence."

"The budget is fine. We've been able to expand a bit."

He nodded. "You've got classes on nutrition and a clinic for babies. Impressive start."

"Thank you again." Andrea wondered what he really wanted. It was difficult to believe he'd shown up just to heap praises on her. She was working up the nerve to ask outright when he spoke again.

"Your mother is bragging about you. Charlie is proud as can be, and so am I," John said with a wide smile.

Andrea stiffened. "Charlie?"

He laughed. "Oh, I had a habit of calling your mother that as a nickname. She didn't like it too much, though, still doesn't."

"Is that right?" Andrea said with an edge to her voice.

The tone of her question was not lost on him. "We're on good terms."

"Hmm."

"Andrea, I really hope we can get to know each other."

"Why?" Andrea tossed the blunt question at him.

"Because . . ." He seemed to struggle for words for a few moments. "I care about you. I always have, no matter what you might have heard."

Andrea continued to stare at him. Irritation competed with curiosity. Curiosity won. "What exactly did you have in mind?"

John lifted a shoulder. "I don't know. We could meet for lunch and talk."

"Get to know each other over lunch," Andrea echoed.

"I'm not saying I can be a father figure to you after all these years. All I want is to know you better."

Andrea's chest tightened with emotion. "I *had* a wonderful father."

"Look, I didn't come here to upset you." John leaned forward. "I was just hoping that somehow we could—"

"Sure. I could get to know Grandma Isabelle and my half sisters and brothers. Let's have a great big family reunion."

"You're angry. I'd better go." He stood.

"What about dinner? Say tomorrow night?" Andrea gave a sharp laugh. "I'm sure your wife would be thrilled."

"I didn't mean it like that."

Andrea stared at him with a stony expression. "I was sure you didn't, Mr. Mandeville. I won't sneak around to see you the way my mother did." She bit off the words as though they tasted bad in her mouth.

"Of course not."

"I'm not Charlene. And frankly, I know as much about you as I care to." Andrea stood also.

"Of course, this is sensitive for my family." John sighed. "But you've got it wrong. Charlene and I were two wild, reckless kids who fell for each other."

"I didn't hear the word 'love.' " Andrea glared at him. "Or did I miss something?"

"Yes, we loved each other. Sometimes being in love isn't enough. I never disrespected Charlene. Never," he said.

Andrea stared into her biological father's eyes. She felt nothing, no pull, no connection. It was a measure of the man's arrogance that he could even face her after thirty years of neglect. And that line about being in love with her mother was just that, a line.

"I don't believe you. Why should I?" Andrea said in a cold voice. "You took the easy way out."

"You don't know the whole story," he insisted. "At least let me tell you my side."

"Actions speak louder than words," Andrea snapped. "Or I should say *in*action."

John took a step toward her. "It's not that simple. We were both scared kids and—" He broke off and shook his head. "I'm really sorry, Andrea, but I'm not a monster."

"What do you want from me?"

"A chance. I know I should have done some things differently."

"So I'm a loose end you want to tie up to soothe your conscience," Andrea said, acid lacing her voice.

"Maybe," John answered promptly. "Maybe it's because the older I get, the more I regret what I did to you and Charlie. But I really want to do whatever I can to help you. That's no lie."

Andrea hesitated. He was her unfinished business as well. "Let me think about it for a while," she said, finally.

"Here." He handed her a business card. "Just tell my secretary your name and she'll put you through."

"I can't promise I'll call." Andrea took the pale blue card with embossed gold lettering.

"I understand." John gazed at her for several moments. "I can only imagine what you've heard about me over the years. Of course, some of it's true." He wore a boyish grin.

"Well, I . . ." Andrea paused. He'd know she was lying if she tried to say it wasn't all bad. It had been.

John's expression changed to one of earnestness. "But I never, *never* did anything deliberately to hurt you. In my own way I tried to protect you and Charlene. Will you keep that in mind?" He held out his hand.

"Yes," Andrea said softly. She put her hand in his large one. He held it firmly for a few seconds before letting it go.

"Thank you. Good-bye." With a nod and a smile, he walked out.

So much for wondering what Charlene saw in him. John Mandeville was indeed an irresistible force. Andrea stared at the card without really seeing it. She wondered if it was finally time to talk to her mother about him, and if they were ready after so many years.

Eight

✳

Lee's partner, Vince Jefferson, strolled into his office holding a can of cola. He took a swig from it and plopped down on one of the chairs facing Lee's desk. Lee had the Friday afternoon off from the clinic. He'd taken the opportunity to catch up on two other investigations he and Vince were close to wrapping up.

L & V Investigations was headquartered in a modest four-story building in Harahan, a small bedroom town outside New Orleans. The cozy reception area leading to their suite held a desk with a phone and word processor for their part-time secretary. Down a hall were two offices, one for Lee and one for Vince. Another room the size of a large closet held a photocopier and desktop computer. A combination fax machine, scanner, and printer was on a table in the corner.

They specialized in background checks and loss prevention, a fancy phrase that meant they helped businesses keep employees from stealing them blind. But they were willing to take on the occasional odd job, like the clinic investigation. Especially since Lee's check of John Mandeville had revealed deep pockets. The ability to get paid played a large part in their decision to take a case.

"So how's the big undercover thing going? Lots of nice cash flow will come from it."

"Getting deeper than I wanted it to," Lee said. *In more ways than one,* he thought, remembering Andrea's smile.

"Like what?" Vince's attention was split between Lee and a report he scanned.

"From what I can tell, there's been some theft of funds. Food vouchers are missing, equipment's been 'misplaced,' that kind of thing." Lee frowned.

Vince dropped the sheet of paper he was reading and shrugged. "About what we expected. Same old same old. What business doesn't have employees with sticky fingers?"

"Yeah, but this is a medical clinic with a *pharmacy,*" Lee said.

"Oh-oh, drugs disappearing? Bad stuff, man." Vince shook his head.

"I don't know for sure," Lee added quickly. "The records are such a mess it's hard to tell."

"That could be deliberate. How high up does this go? Boss in on it?"

Vince posed the question as he would for any case. Usually Lee's response would have been routine and automatic. Yet in this instance, the question caused his stomach to churn. He cared about the answer—too much, in fact.

"I don't think it involves the new director," Lee said.

"But you don't know for sure. From what you've told me, I bet it does." Vince waved a hand.

Lee looked at him sharply. "What makes you say that?"

"It's a small clinic and he—"

"The director's a woman. Andrea Noble." *And what a woman,* he mused.

"Whatever. She's gotta see all these reports herself, inventories and such. Am I right?" Vince pointed a forefinger at him.

"Probably. I'm not sure yet," Lee said hesitantly.

"Course she does." Vince propped an ankle on his knee. "Plus, it's a small town and everybody knows everybody else's business. She's in on it."

"She doesn't seem like the type," Lee mumbled.

Andrea worked long hours and was turning the quality of patient care around in Bayou Blue. In fact, the clinic was quickly gaining a reputation throughout Lafourche Parish because of her. It wasn't just the medical care, it was the time she took to really listen to patients. She made them feel respected and valued. All of this did not fit Vince's view of the situation. Why would she destroy the very thing she labored to save?

Lee shook his head. "I just don't think so, Vince. I've gotten to know the lady."

"Crooks come in all shapes, sizes, and colors."

"She's straight up on everything I've seen so far," Lee said.

"Exactly what have you found out?" Vince asked.

"Not much more than what I've told you. The place was in chaos from sloppy management, still is for that matter. Andrea's working like crazy to clean it up."

"Is she, now?" Vince's eyebrows went up.

"Yeah," Lee said distractedly. "She puts in twelve-hour days. She's got the local politicians watching her every move."

Lee wore a slight frown as he gazed at the view from his window. It wasn't scenic like the countryside surrounding Bayou Blue. The neighborhood contained an assortment of fast-food restaurants, corner stores, and a shop that sold liquor and discount cigarettes. Burglaries were common, and armed robbery almost accepted as a given. There was very little in the way of grass, just concrete and a few sickly shrubs. The drab surroundings matched the views Lee and Vince held. Both had been cops and had seen the nastiest side of life imaginable. What little good they stumbled over seemed almost an accident. Maybe he was too cynical. His ex-wife had told him that often enough. Still Lee could not fit Andrea into such a dim picture of the world. In spite of his sour outlook on human nature, something about her made the world brighter. Lately he'd begun to believe that one person could make a difference.

"Anyone working there could have taken advantage of those screwed-up records," Lee said.

Vince's eyes narrowed. "Is she pretty?"

Lee looked at the folder on his desk. "Yeah, you could say that."

"So maybe her sweet face has you convinced she's innocent." Vince's thick black eyebrows went up.

"I'm looking at the evidence, period." Lee threw an irritated glance at Vince before looking away again.

"Uh-huh." Vince's terse response said it all. "Brother, it's time to shut it down and get out."

"I don't know." Lee's gut resisted the idea of leaving Bayou Blue and Andrea behind so quickly.

"It's a criminal matter. Give Mandeville a full report and tell the local police about the missing drugs."

"I've got to know more before I can give a thorough report. Like I said, those records are really screwed up bad." Lee avoided Vince's gaze.

Vince pointed a thick forefinger at him again. "I smell trouble. Don't let a nice body and pretty face suck you in."

Lee grunted. "Not a chance. And don't give me that look," he snapped. "But you're right about the sheriff."

"I'm getting a bad feeling about this case." Vince squinted at him. "Let's get our money. Let Mandeville and the sheriff deal with the rest of the garbage."

"Yes, Mother," Lee teased.

"Good. Now tell me what you think about this thing with the Latham Company."

Vince went on to describe his investigation into suspected corporate espionage in a New Orleans advertising agency. Lee listened, but his thoughts were on Andrea. Vince was wrong about her. Lee's suspicions had eroded with each day as he worked beside the lovely nurse. In truth, he now wanted to prove Andrea's innocence. For the sake of the clinic, and the people of Lafourche Parish, he told himself in a firm voice.

Lee was afraid the state department of health would decide the problems at Bayou Blue Clinic called for drastic measures. Poor record keeping was one thing, but missing drugs something else altogether. Patients would have to travel fifty or sixty miles to another clinic. Those without transportation would not get care at all. Lee grimaced at the thought of how children would suffer as a result. He would do whatever he could to save the clinic. Vince's gruff voice broke through his thoughts.

"That's what I've got so far. What do you think?"

Lee blinked at him. "Sounds good."

"Yeah, so I'll be through with them today. You

should be finished in Bayou Blue soon, right?" Vince squinted at him.

"Right, right," Lee said.

"Man, your mind is on her." Vince stood. "Listen to your big brother, leave her alone. You've already had enough grief to last you a lifetime."

Lee tensed at the memory of his bitter divorce and custody battle. He'd lost too much over the years, his mother to drugs and alcohol, his brother, Chris, to the streets. And now he realized that Denny reminded him of his brother way too much. Vince was right, Lee had begun to think of ways to save Denny from himself. Maybe he could do a better job than what he'd done with his baby brother. Losses, he'd had his fill of them. Which was why he guarded his heart. Lee vowed to avoid Andrea. No more good-byes, no more getting his heart kicked like a damn football. And if he jailed another filthy gang that specialized in ruining young lives, all the better.

"My mind is on getting a check out of this dude Fred Jones. He's been dodging us for days. Now leave so I can get some work done." He picked up the phone and punched a number.

"Yeah, right. Like I believe it," Vince retorted, and left.

Lee sighed when he was gone and tried to focus on something other than Andrea Noble.

Andrea walked into the clinic and couldn't help but smile. Kids were everywhere, climbing over the furniture and bouncing around like cute jumping beans. Exactly as she'd planned, she thought happily. This waiting room had been added on especially for children.

The walls were painted with baby animals, flowers, and clouds in bright, cheery colors. In one corner a four-year-old little girl happily hugged a stuffed giraffe and babbled to it. A burst of giggling to Andrea's right caused her to turn around. Jamal had a group of six children captivated with magic tricks. His tall, muscular body made him look like a mighty giant compared to them. His thick arms bulged as he waved them. The playful gentleness he exuded was in sharp contrast to the raw physical power implied by his stature and build. A gentle giant, Andrea thought. Jamal Turner was not just a pretty face. He really seemed to care about people.

"Now, where did that mysterious magic coin go?" Jamal reached behind a little boy's ear and then showed them a big gold Mardi Gras doubloon. "Mickey, you've been hiding it all along!"

"Oooh," came a chorus of childish voices.

"Make the stuffed rabbit appear again, Mr. Jamal," a boy called out, followed by the clamor of shouts.

"Yeah, we wanna see that one again!"

"Where's bunny?" A five-year-old girl clapped her hands.

"Hey, I've done that one three times already," Jamal said with a weary laugh. He rubbed his forehead. "I better see what's taking Miss Katy so long."

"Stay with us!"

"We wanna play some more!"

He was hemmed in on all sides. "Now, come on. I've got to get some work done."

Andrea smiled. The strong man who had rescued her twice now needed to be rescued, and from a mob of children, no less. He spotted her and tried to escape.

"Miss Andrea is here to take over," he said. His voice and eyes pleaded with her.

"You've got things under control. See ya." She waved her fingers at him and started to back out, but stopped when he yelled.

"No, wait!" Jamal quickly handed out toys from a box, then made an end run around the children and cut off her exit. "I'm just helping out. Lisa and the other student nurses are running late."

"If they don't come, you might have to stay in here," Andrea said with a wicked grin.

"Please tell me you're joking!" He glanced around him in distress.

Andrea laughed at the expression of alarm on his face. She couldn't torture the poor man. "They just got here. I was coming to tell you they're helping Katy set up now."

"Whew! You almost gave me a heart attack, woman."

"You had them eating out of your hand." Andrea nodded at the children.

"I'm winging it, to tell you the truth." He rubbed his hands together and followed her gaze. "I'm used to trying to amuse one kid, mine. And he has to give me help most days."

"You're married?" Andrea felt a stab of dismay. Something in her voice must have betrayed her.

"Divorced," he said softly.

His eyes seemed to hold a message, but Andrea was afraid to read it. "Oh," she said, and glanced away. To her relief, Lisa bounded in.

"I'm sorry, y'all. We got held up at school. I'll take over," Lisa said in a breathless voice.

"Am I glad to see you," he said with vigor as he gazed at the young woman.

Lisa blushed. "Really?" She smoothed down the front of her bright pink scrub shirt.

"They might look cute, but they'll eat you alive when they get bored. You got here just in time." He laughed and gave her a big-brother pat on the shoulder.

"But you're so wonderful with children, all of the patients actually," Lisa purred. She looked at him with adoration written all over her pert face.

Andrea groaned inwardly with irritation, at herself as much as Lisa. The young woman only mirrored what she must have looked like only seconds before, a foolish woman simpering over a man. An image of her mother flashed through her mind. Charlene was a master at the art of flirting. Andrea had made it a point not to behave like her. Not that Jamal didn't turn on his special brand of charm at the drop of a hat. He loved the attention he generated from women of all ages. Well, she would not join the Jamal Turner fan club.

"I'd better get back to work." Andrea turned to leave.

"Me, too," he said quickly. He said good-bye to Lisa and followed her down the hall. "Hey, thanks for staying with me."

"No problem." Andrea did not risk looking at him again. "We're a team."

"Yeah. Listen . . ." His voice trailed off.

Curiosity made her glance at him briefly. "Yes?"

"I . . . I really like working here. A lot more than I expected to," he said, eyes averted to some point past her shoulder.

Andrea was captivated in spite of her attempt to be cool and professional. This brawny man who could make thugs cower seemed to have a shy side, too. There was no macho seductiveness flavoring his words now. He seemed genuine. Still she held back. Getting caught up in some guy was not what she wanted or needed, a little voice reminded her. Andrea looked away.

"Like I said, we're a team. I'm lucky to have good people working here. It makes work pleasant," she said with forced cheer, and continued toward her office.

"Very pleasant," Jamal said with emphasis.

Her heart thumped faster at his tone. "Yes, well . . ."

Andrea got to the door to her office and turned to find him standing only inches away. She gasped at the heat generated by being so close to him. The broad expanse of his muscular chest filled her vision until all else seemed to fade. The whole world tilted in his direction. His body called to her, enticing her to stroke it with the tips of her fingers. Andrea looked up into his eyes and breathed in the scent of his aftershave. Her gaze traveled down his face, back to his chest. It rose and fell in a hypnotizing slow motion.

"You're the reason, you know," Jamal said softly.

"I am?" Andrea's head swam when she looked into his eyes.

"Yeah. You're the reason this place has a whole new feel to it." Jamal gazed at her hair. He tucked a stray tendril back in place.

"Thanks," she replied, thrilled more by the intimate gesture than of the compliment.

The sound of Katy's voice broke the spell. Andrea stepped back and leaned against the doorframe.

"Thanks, Mrs. Williams. We'll see you in two months. We're ready for the next one, Troy," Katy said from an examining room down the hall.

"Right this way, ma'am," Troylyn replied.

Andrea tugged at her blouse, feeling as though she'd been caught necking in the hallway. Indeed, her mind and body had taken a sharp turn into an erotic zone she'd thought was dormant. Obviously Jamal Turner had awakened it. She would have to find a way to work with him and not be affected. Talk about a challenge, she mused. Months of celibacy had made her vulnerable, Andrea told herself. It was nothing deeper. She wouldn't let it be anything more. Andrea stood straight as Katy, Troylyn, and the patient walked by. She even risked looking into those eyes again. What she saw stunned her. Desire lit his dark eyes. Then in a split second a curtain dropped and he was back to normal. Had she imagined it?

"As I was saying, I'm really pleased with our progress. Everyone is working hard," she said in her prim nurse voice again. She went into her office.

He exhaled slowly and walked in with her. "Yeah. Even Denny. I don't know what kinda scare you put in him, but the kid is working like a dog."

"Denny's a good person deep down. He just needs a firm hand," Andrea said.

Jamal nodded. "I notice you've given him more responsibility."

"He's earned it. Katy, the pharmacist, and even a couple of the doctors have told me how much he's changed."

"Is that right? Listen, I could help him out, too." Jamal looked at her with his head cocked to one side. "He's putting in a lot of hours."

"That's nice of you, but that would double your workload." Andrea went to her desk.

"I don't mind. It's not like I'm giving up an active social life," he joked.

Andrea glanced at him sideways and cleared her throat. "I find that hard to believe. You've got women fluttering around you like bees to honey," she said, hoping her tone sounded casual.

"There's no one special, at the moment," he replied.

The last phrase sent a now familiar tingle down her spine. Andrea had to do something to stop it from taking over again.

"Yes, well, a positive male role model would be good," Andrea said.

"Like you said, he's not a bad kid." Jamal grinned. "I'll start on those records he's buried under."

He smiled at her, dimple and all. It was as though he deliberately let go one last sensuous salvo before leaving. Andrea shook herself to recover. She dove into a voluminous single-spaced bureaucratic report to block out thoughts of his strong hands touching her in all the right places.

The husky man the color of burnt cork stared at Denny through hooded eyes. "What you gonna do?"

They stood in a cluttered, dirty apartment in Bayou Blue's only subsidized housing complex. There were four cinder-block duplexes, painted drab mint green. Three other men watched with implacable expressions. They were one third of what passed for the local gang in Bayou Blue. Yet they had ambitions to go further and do bigger things. Ty'Rance, their leader, had decided Denny could help them. They had grown up together in Bayou Blue, both running the same dusty streets and getting into trouble. Now Ty'Rance was convinced Denny could use his L.A. contacts to help him.

"Look, Ty, that new lady they put in charge, uh, she keeps an eye on everything. I dunno 'bout all this." Denny licked his lips nervously.

"When you took my money you knew, punk. We had an understanding." Ty walked close to him, cutting off any chance Denny might have to escape. "You knew payback time was comin'."

"Yeah, I'm sayin' . . ." Denny's mouth worked for a second until he registered the threat that hung heavy in the air. "The clinic doesn't keep heavy drugs," he finished lamely.

"Don't lie to me. My cousin Shonda already told us they got local anesthetics, sometimes even stuff like Soma." He referred to the highly addictive muscle relaxant.

Denny rubbed his mouth with a shaky hand. "What I meant was, they don't keep much of that stuff around. And the pharmacist keeps a list."

" 'And the pharmacist keeps a list,' " Bo mimicked. "Man, this dude takin' us for fools."

"Look, you ain't backin' out, so get that outta your head." Ty'Rance thumped Denny's chest with a thick forefinger.

"I didn't say I wasn't gonna help y'all." Denny raised both arms as though to protect himself from a blow.

"First, you pay back the three thousand you owe me. Either I get cash or I take it outta your ass." Ty thumped Denny harder to make his point.

"Right, right," Denny agreed eagerly. When the big man walked away, he rubbed his chest.

"Now, tell me again about the setup." Ty went to a lumpy old couch and sat down hard.

"Three days a week I work with the pharmacist. I can get in the drug room without it looking suspicious then," Denny said.

"Okay, but you can get a key other days if you tell one of the nurses you need somethin', right?" Ty asked the question as though he already knew the answer. His icy gaze did not waver.

Denny rubbed his jaw with a nervous jerky movement. "Sometimes the pharmacist makes up prescriptions on the spot if the doctors leave orders."

"So you can pretty much come up with a reason to get in anytime you want," Ty'Rance said as he leaned forward. "You can fix up the books so they don't know nothin' is missin'."

"But I can't—"

"Then make up some invoices and order more drugs," Ty'Rance cut in.

"Forge her name?" Denny's eyes were round as saucers.

"No, say 'Sign here, I'm gettin' extra goodies to sell on the street,' " another gang member barked. "What a chump!"

"What you think you gonna do?" Ty glared at him impatiently. "You can get the blank forms an' you know what to do, right?"

"Yeah," Denny said reluctantly.

"I'll tell you what to order. There are some drugs we can cook and make into powerful stuff."

"Yeah, designer drugs," Bo piped up. "Damn, Ty. We can clean up!"

"Right. We can corner the market around for miles. Even make some sales in New Orleans. Yeah, I like that." Ty'Rance wore a smile as he looked around at the others.

"We got to be real careful now." Denny wore a thoughtful and more relaxed expression. "Listen, after my debt gets paid, how 'bout I earn some money, too?"

Ty'Rance tilted his head back and stared at the ceil-

ing for a few minutes. The others waited in silence. He
lowered his head and looked at Denny again. "You set
this up right and we'll see."

"Okay!" Denny blurted out. His anxiety seemed replaced now with enthusiasm.

Ty held up a palm. "I said we'll see. First you gotta
produce."

"Yeah, sure."

"Now you talkin' sense, boy. I was beginnin' to think
you was all into that nine-to-five crap." Ty lit up a cigarette and sucked on it.

"I'm gonna make enough to set up a nice savings ac-
count for Granny, then I'm heading back to L.A. I've
got it all planned," Denny said with a lopsided grin.

Ty eased down into the cushions. "Uh-huh. One
thing at a time."

Two days after his last heated encounter with Andrea,
Lee sat in front of the computer monitor without seeing
it. He'd put off digging deeply for too long. Why? The
answer blinked in his head like the black cursor on
the computer screen: Andrea. Lee did not want to find
the link proving she was involved. But he would need to
do a report soon for Mandeville and the advisory board.
There was no way around it.

With a sigh, he scrolled through the now computer-
ized drug inventory. There was a tracking chart for the
purchase of medications and their use, which linked to a
spreadsheet. The pharmacist entered quantities dispensed, which in turn subtracted from totals. It took
only a few keystrokes to know the amount of drugs that
should be in the cabinet. Lee gazed at the figures for

thirty minutes. He noticed a gradual increase in orders. Yet according to his count, the number of patients had remained the same. He wrote down long chemical names of drugs so he could look them up. Later he would check purchases against dispensary records. Before Lee could react, the door to the record room swung open. Denny came in and looked at the monitor over his shoulder.

"What you doing?" Denny asked.

Lee switched to a different screen. "Checking these programs I installed. I'm taking a break from entering data. Man, these records are jacked up." He pointed to a stack of folders.

Denny gathered the folders into his arms. "I'll take care of these."

Lee stretched and leaned back in the chair. "Okay. Just show me the invoices."

"What invoices?" Denny looked at him with a frown.

"Purchase invoices, purchase orders? If I'm going to help keep track, I've got to see it all."

"I'm taking care of that, too. Just, uh, help me file some papers in the patient records. I mostly got this stuff wrapped up." Denny dropped a folder, then three more when he bent down to pick the first one up.

"Lots of things are disappearing around here. We can cover each other if we both make sure all the paper is right." Lee cocked his head to one side. "You're not worried about anything, are you?"

"Don't come in here accusing me of anything," Denny said, his voice strained.

Lee dropped his voice. "Lots of drugs being ordered. Wonder why."

"It's a clinic, man! I don't have time for this."

Lee held up both hands, palms out. "Whatever you got goin' on is your business."

"*My* business is right," Denny snapped. "I work here and that's all you need to know. There is nothing going on. Nothing."

"Cool. But Miss Noble asked me to put the records in the computer. I'll know what ought to be here, equipment and medical supplies included."

"So do it and quit bothering me!" Denny blustered. "Man, I'm going back out front."

"I can help," Lee said quietly as he leaned forward.

Denny glanced at him sharply, then looked away. "I don't know what you're talking about."

"Okay. But if you get jammed up, let me know."

Denny stood up straight, his expression guileless. "I'm working with Miss Andrea to clean house, Jamal. If you know anything about missing clinic property, then you better tell me."

Lee had to admire the kid's audacity. Denny seemed quite confident of himself. It meant one of two things. Either Denny really was innocent of any wrongdoing or he had what he thought was a foolproof system for covering his tracks. His cocky expression made Lee suspect the latter. Also he and Andrea had been working closely together. Could it mean Andrea was in on it and would back him up?

"A person could make some good money. If somebody wanted to, I mean." Lee shrugged.

"Which is why a lotta folks got fired, right?" Denny shot back.

"Yeah," Lee answered. They gazed at each other in silence for several seconds. "Guess they were stupid."

"You got that right. See ya." Denny walked out with a long, cocky bounce to his steps.

Lee felt frustrated and depressed. His instincts told him to keep trying. But it bothered him more than he cared to admit that Andrea might be involved. Lee turned back to the computer. He had put considerable time into learning the art of forensic records examination, the new term for sniffing out a rat. He would keep at it no matter where the trail of crumbs led him.

Nine

The Plumbers Union Hall was decorated with a combination of artificial greenery and real flowers. Andrea looked around the large meeting room that had been transformed into a grand ballroom for the fund-raiser. Local businesspeople and Bayou Blue society were just as decorative in their finest. Andrea wore a plastic smile. These kinds of functions were now part of her duties as director, and she wasn't thrilled about it. Yet the clinic was also supported by local funds, and Bayou Blue was by no means a wealthy town. Such events would allow her to implement programs tailored to meet the needs of Lafourche Parish residents. To that end, Andrea would just have to grin and bear it. Thinking of all the people who would benefit helped her get through it.

The Zydeco Rockers played a series of lively tunes that coaxed more and more couples onto the floor, but Andrea's focus was not on partying. This was a business affair for her. She circulated through the crowd, making contacts and answering questions about her health initiatives. A plump redheaded woman in a bright orange chiffon dress appeared beside her.

"Miss Noble, I'm Hester Chappelle of the Bayou Rouge Chappelles." Hester flashed a wide grin at her and waited for a response.

Andrea did not miss her cue. "Of course, everyone knows the famous Chappelle family," she said with a nod. "Who doesn't love Fireball Creole pepper sauce?"

"Ours was first!" Hester declared, then giggled. "Every member of my family has to say that or be disinherited." She referred to the decades-old rivalry with another famous Louisiana family who had a world-renowned hot sauce.

"Are you enjoying yourself?" Andrea accepted the offer of a cup of punch from a passing waiter. Another round of chitchat would leave her throat dry again.

"So-so. The subcommittee did a fair job." Hester glanced around the crowd. "I suggested we have a biker theme, but . . ." She lifted a shoulder.

"That would have been interesting." Andrea suppressed a shudder at the idea.

"The Summer Sensation thing is okay, I guess."

"Well, we do have a wonderful turnout," Andrea said. There were well over one hundred people in attendance.

Hester glanced around the room. "Hmm. I especially wanted to meet you."

"Really?"

"I admire all those fabulous programs you have. Community service is a particular interest of mine." Hester beamed. "I helped to set up rose gardens for the homeless in over fifteen cities."

Andrea gazed at her speechless for a few seconds. "Now, that is something."

"I know it sounds strange, but bringing beauty into their lives is just as important as food. And they can sleep on grassy patches, too." Hester spoke with pride.

"Guess they know to avoid the thorns," Andrea murmured. Then froze at the expression on Hester's face.

Hester blinked rapidly in confusion, then her face cleared and she burst into laughter. "You're a delight, Miss Noble. I'm going to tell my brother to write a nice big check for the clinic." She patted Andrea's shoulder and left still giggling.

Andrea sighed with relief as she watched the woman drift away to join other wealthy friends. Hester seemed to be repeating the story to them. Andrea smiled and waved when Hester pointed to her.

Just then Katy emerged from the crowd, a plate of hors d'oeuvres in hand. She wore a pink pantsuit and her dark hair was pinned up.

"See, boss? I don't know why you were worrying. You're doing a great job of schmoozing," she said.

"Nice word for brownnosing," Andrea quipped. "And I've come close to stepping in it three times since I got here."

"Relax, your work speaks for itself. You've got heavy hitters in your corner." Katy cleared her throat and nodded to her left.

Andrea glanced at John Mandeville and his wife, Victoria, standing with another couple. He looked over at her and raised his wineglass in greeting. Victoria Mandeville followed his gaze. Her thin mouth clamped shut. Andrea turned away from them.

"Katy, tell me the truth. Is there gossip about John Mandeville controlling the clinic?"

"No way, folks are too scared of him," Katy answered bluntly.

"So you know," Andrea said.

"Yeah, well . . ."

"Oh God! Just what I need!" Andrea rubbed her forehead.

"Trust me, no one is going to risk the infamous Mandeville wrath," Katy whispered. "Come on, boss. Relax."

"Sure, relax," Andrea said, and resisted the urge to look at the Mandevilles again.

"Ooh, I love this song. I'm going to find my date and boogie," Katy said with a wide grin. She tugged at Andrea's arm. "I said forget it, Andrea. Okay?"

"Okay." Andrea forced her mouth to curve up into a smile.

She watched Katy leave with a sigh. At least Mandeville was staying well away from her. Andrea decided to put even more space between them and moved through the crowd. Gran grabbed her arm.

"Everybody's having a good time," she said, her voice raised so she could be heard over the music. "Why aren't you dancing?"

"This is business for me, Gran. You know that. I'm being watched and judged." Andrea tilted her head to indicate the people around them.

"Pooh," Gran said with a dismissive wave of her hand. "They're already impressed if they've got any sense. Have some fun."

"From the way you were kicking up your heels with Mr. Walter, I'd say you're having enough fun for both of us." Andrea grinned at her.

"We're just friends."

"Oh, yeah. Tell me another one," Andrea teased.

Gran blushed. "Hush your mouth."

"I think he's cute. And a real nice guy."

"Isn't he, though?" Gran smiled, then squinted at Andrea. "What are you doing for male company?"

"Don't start."

Andrea put an arm around her and they strolled toward the tall doors that opened onto the terrace. A warm wind blew in the scent of the bayou and gardenias planted around the courtyard. The floor was made of a dark green stone tile. Antique-style lampposts provided a soft lighting. Six wrought-iron round tables with matching chairs sat in a circle around an area left clear for dancing.

"Baby, you're lonely," Gran said.

"For the one hundredth time, I'm not lonely," Andrea said in a patient tone as though talking to a child.

"Yes, you are."

"I don't have time to be lonely. Besides, I'm surrounded by people ten hours a day."

"I'm talking about romance, girl, and you know it."

"Let's not have this argument again." Andrea kissed Gran's cheek as they went outside.

Gran held up a finger. "I don't argue, I discuss. And I think—"

"Yes, I know what you think," Andrea broke in. She led her to an empty table. "Sit down and listen. I know you want me to be happy."

"Exactly, and you need—"

"I need time. Please, Gran. I've got so much on my mind these days." Andrea rested against the chairback and let out a deep breath.

Gran smiled affectionately. "You're right, cher. Sit and take in some fresh air. Enjoy yourself."

"Are you kidding? I'm working just as hard tonight

as I do at the clinic. Don't let the hors d'oeuvres and music fool you. I'm being sized up." Andrea glanced at the people scattered around the terrace.

"Oh, stop. They're too busy eating and dancing."

"They're not that busy. Especially not the board members. It's so important to build our credibility. I'd better circulate some more." Andrea started to rise, but stopped when Gran shook her head.

"You've been on your feet for an hour or more. You sit here and let me get you some more punch and food." Gran stood.

"There's no need to make a special trip. I'll be back inside in a little while," Andrea protested.

"I was going to get more food for myself anyway." Gran moved off at a brisk pace. "Just stay right there."

Andrea opened her mouth to call her back, but realized it was no use. Gran was through the doors and fading into the crowd already. Andrea laughed to herself. Still, she enjoyed this brief respite from smiling and talking. Being out under the deep blue sky with silver stars twinkling overhead was peaceful. The band was evidently taking a break. Andrea glanced at her wristwatch. It was near eleven o'clock. The party was set to wind down at midnight. She'd been here since seven. Gran was right, her feet were starting to complain. Andrea slipped off her black pumps, flexed her toes, and gave a soft sigh of relief. Another breeze brushed her face and she closed her eyes and breathed in the fragrant smell of home, wet grass, and bayou.

"Miss Mavis sent me out on a mission."

Andrea's eyes flew open. Jamal stood in front of her holding a small, round tray with two plates of food and two glasses of punch. He looked stunning in a black suit cut stylishly with narrow lapels, a crisp white shirt, and a black, green, and white silk necktie. The suit jacket was tailored to fit his broad chest. A tiny shock of electricity started at the base of her spine and spread through her hips. Andrea just gazed at him for a moment. His cologne floated on the breeze and snaked itself around her until she shivered. Obsession for Men, Andrea thought hazily. Appropriately named, given the effect he was having on her. Then Andrea realized she must be gawking at him. She'd successfully avoided him most of the evening as he circulated among the guests.

"What?" she managed to blurt out.

Jamal held up the tray. "She said you needed to be revived after working so hard. So here I am."

Andrea's mind took an erotic turn at the speed of light. She could think of all kinds of ways this gorgeous man could refresh her. He put the tray on the table with a graceful movement.

"Yes, here you are," she murmured. Andrea looked away from him. She hoped it would clear her mind. "Thank you."

"You're welcome. May I sit down? That was a long walk." He gazed down at her with a soft smile.

"I'm sorry," Andrea stammered out. "Of course, please."

He folded his long frame into the wrought-iron chair. "You should be pleased with the turnout."

Andrea struggled not to stare at him again. He stood out from every other man present. His every gesture seemed to capture her.

"We have a lot of support from the community," she said.

"I noticed you doing the network thing." Jamal took a bite out of a small ham sandwich.

"The entire board is here." Andrea gazed through to

the ballroom. "The mayor, aldermen, all of them are keeping a close eye on us."

"Yeah, this is a business function in disguise." He nodded.

"Exactly. Of course, good food and music make it easier to open up discussions." Andrea laughed. "Something we understand very well in south Louisiana."

"Tell me about it. Since I moved here I've had to really exercise more. Too many fried-shrimp po' boys," he said, and patted his flat stomach.

Andrea studied his build. From where she sat, he was doing a great job of keeping in shape. "Men can eat whatever they want without worrying the way we do. It's all these fat cells."

"I wish," he said with a grunt. "You should be with me at the gym. It's rough lifting those weights and doing chin-ups."

"You could handle anything with those muscles," Andrea blurted out before she realized it. "I mean . . ." She stuck a cookie in her mouth to cover her confusion.

"Thanks." Jamal swept a glance over her from head to feet. "You must work out, too. You look positively . . . fit."

Andrea squirmed under his examination and tugged at the hem of her ivory sleeveless party dress. "I try to run at least three times a week. Honestly, I haven't kept up. Too many long hours at the clinic."

"Best thing to fight off tension," he said.

"That's something I get plenty of these days." Andrea wanted to steer the conversation back onto safe ground. "Every day I uncover some new horror that curls my hair."

Jamal leaned forward. "Yeah, things have been pretty bad. The records are like a puzzle somebody threw in the air. You have to wonder how those people got any-thing done," he said, referring to former clinic staff members.

"Tell me about it!" Andrea said with a groan. She lowered her voice. "Patient records are still screwed up. But we've made headway a little."

"What about the pharmacy?" Jamal took a sip of punch, then put down his glass. "I heard Bill Larissey is about ready to quit."

Andrea scowled at the mention of the part-time phar-macist. The man constantly criticized Andrea's attempts to organize the clinic.

"He's a pain in the . . . well, you know. Everyone works with me except him," she said.

"The inventory and dispensary are a mess."

"No kidding. Why should it be different from the rest of the place?" Andrea retorted.

"I guess you're sorry you took this job." Jamal used his forefinger to trace an invisible line on the tabletop.

Andrea let out a long, slow breath. "It's worse than I was told, and that's the truth. But all in all, I'm glad to be home. And for the first time in years I feel like I can really make a difference, one that I can see."

Jamal gazed at her with a thoughtful expression. "You didn't feel that way in Chicago?"

"Some days I did. But most of the time I just felt overwhelmed." Andrea smiled. "Could be I was never cut out for big-city life. What about you? Aren't you bored down here after Los Angeles?"

"Not really. I was ready for a change after my di-vorce," he said with a shrug.

Andrea detected a note of sadness in his voice. "Yeah, I know what you mean. Chicago definitely lost its appeal for me. Funny, but I started thinking about home more after I got the final divorce papers."

"Yeah," he said quietly.

She looked at him. "But you were home. Why leave?"

"For one thing, my ex-wife moved to Houston. I'm closer to my son now," Jamal said.

"How old is he?" Andrea was intrigued at the image of him as a father.

"Jake is six going on thirty-five," he quipped.

"And you left the rest of your family in L.A.?"

He paused before answering. "My childhood in L.A. wasn't exactly sweetness and light."

He'd left his home to escape. Andrea knew a lot about trying to outrun pain. The signs were there beneath that layer of strong, cool dude. His face cleared like a cloudy sky giving way to sunshine. He turned his bright smile on her.

"Anyway, here we are right where we want to be," he said.

"Please," Andrea said with a groan. "I'd much rather be seeing patients."

"But you know being in charge means you can do more good for more people," he said, and gazed at her with his head tilted to one side.

"Yes, I'm tired of complaining about what 'they' should do. I'm going to do it," Andrea said.

"You want a career, not just a job. Do what you want for once, right?"

Suddenly Andrea felt a click deep inside. He understood her. His tone, his expression, and even the way his eyes reflected the soft lighting cast a spell and made her believe he could see into her heart. It wasn't logical.

They hardly knew each other outside the clinic. As she gazed back at him she caught a glimpse of something in his eyes and thought she understood him, too. He was searching, like her.

"Right," she murmured, unable to look away from his dark eyes.

When the band started to play, he looked over his shoulder, then back at her. "Let's dance," he said, and held out his hand as though the matter were already settled.

Andrea was out of her chair and in his arms before she realized what was happening. The music seemed to wrap itself around them until she imagined they were all alone in the world. The tune was a rhythmic blues love ballad. The lead singer's rich tenor added a poignant note that made the air vibrate. Andrea tensed when Jamal gently placed his open palm against the small of her back. Her hand rested inside his larger one. Without fanfare, Jamal pulled her closer until their bodies touched lightly. Andrea fought to slow her breathing when he rested his chin against her forehead. Her nipples hardened and sexual craving washed through her body. Andrea bit her lip to hold back the soft moan that threatened to tumbled across her lips. She became pliant under his touch as he led her in a Creole two-step.

"How am I doing?" he said close to her ear.

"Just fine," Andrea whispered, and snuggled closer.

"I took lessons from a friend."

"Hmm?" Andrea inhaled the scent of cologne on his skin, a salty mix that was intoxicating.

"Dancing. My pal's girlfriend showed me how," Jamal said.

"Yes, dancing," she mumbled.

Andrea was thinking of a different kind of dance. For

the first time in years she felt totally free. There was only this moment, music, and the sensation of being in his arms. She wanted to cup his face in both hands and press her lips to his. As though her desire conjured up the reality, she was gazing into his eyes. His mouth came closer.

"Andrea . . ." His voice was husky and low.

"Yes?" Andrea whispered.

"You look beautiful tonight." Jamal said. "Simply beautiful."

Andrea took a deep, shaky breath. "Th—" His lips grazed hers teasingly, cutting off her reply.

Jamal pulled her closer, his forehead resting against hers. For a long, delicious moment Andrea felt suspended in time. They seemed to float on a cloud, moving in harmony to the music. He started a fire that raged out of control deep inside her. Andrea gazed into his deep brown eyes and trembled in his arms, wanting more of him. Then the music stopped and the other dancers applauded.

Jamal held her a moment longer, then took a deep breath. He stepped back and let go of her hand. "I think we'd better go in."

Andrea swayed, still off balance and reluctant to let go of the moment. "I suppose."

"Some rich guy might want to drop a stack of cash for the clinic." He tugged at his tie and smiled at her.

The magic was gone and the composed charmer had returned. Even his smile seemed closed to her. *How dare he turn it on and off like a light switch*, she fumed silently. And she'd been so willing to surrender. Now he stood there gloating. Andrea's eyes narrowed as she glowered at him.

"Like you said, this isn't a simple party," she

snapped. "In fact, few things are what they appear on the surface. Excuse me." Andrea spun around and marched off.

"I'll go with you. You might need more refreshments." Jamal used the advantage of his long stride to catch up to her.

"No, I won't," she said without looking at him.

"Did I do something wrong? I thought we had a nice dance." Jamal smiled and nodded at several people.

"Yes, we did. Just a dance," Andrea said, looking at him sideways.

Jamal studied her for a few seconds. "Sure. A dance."

"It's over," Andrea said. She started to walk away when his hand on her arm stopped her.

"I think we should talk." Gently but firmly he led her to a corner away from a knot of other people. He seemed flustered and at a loss about how to proceed.

Andrea was not sympathetic. "Well, make it short. As you reminded me, I've got business to take care of."

"We work together," he began.

"This is not news to me. Of course, it was a surprise since I didn't hire you."

"I guess what I'm trying to say is—"

"Hold it," Andrea broke in with an angry frown. "Don't flatter yourself. Number one, I'm too busy for your player games."

"It's not like that."

"Number two," Andrea pressed on, ignoring his comment, "I'm not interested in dating, and if I were, you wouldn't be my first choice."

His dark brows drew together in irritation. "I only meant—"

"Number three, I don't date men I work with. So

calm down, you're safe from me," Andrea finished, her voice like a razor blade.

His expression softened as he gazed at her. "I wasn't trying to be a smooth operator, okay? We both felt it. And it could make things . . . complicated."

He didn't have to say what "it" was; Andrea knew full well. Yet she would not give him the satisfaction of acknowledging the powerful attraction she felt.

"I agree." Andrea lifted her chin and gazed back at him coolly.

"Good." He looked away. "See you later."

"Yes, at the clinic." Andrea wanted it plain that she did not want to see him again tonight.

"Right," he muttered, and walked off without looking back.

"Yeah, right," she shot back, determined to have the last word.

Andrea congratulated herself on being a blue-ribbon idiot. Her hard-won common sense had turned to mush. She watched him go. At least she'd told him off. Her moment of triumph was tempered by the memory of being in his arms. Andrea shook her head as though to clear heated fantasies from her mind. When she glanced up again, she gasped.

"Lord, can things get any worse?" She groaned.

Charlene's grand entrance on the arm of the handsome George Leduc told her the answer was obviously yes. Leduc was a well-known sculptor in New Orleans, and equally well known as a womanizing prima donna. John Mandeville and his wife were across the ballroom. Andrea watched the scene unfold with dread. The crowd was smaller now as people were leaving in groups. Charlene's musical laughter floated across the room.

Suddenly John spotted Charlene and his smile froze. Victoria followed his gaze, then spoke close to his ear. At first it seemed John did not hear her. Victoria spoke to him again, this time with an angry expression. Then they turned and headed for the nearest exit. John could not resist glancing back just once at Charlene. So did Victoria, but with a look of pure hatred. Andrea gasped when Charlene smiled sweetly and waved to them.

"Hi, darling," Charlene gushed as she approached Andrea. "Let me introduce you. Oh, but you met him several years ago, didn't you?" She hugged George's arm and beamed at him.

"Yes, I certainly remember your lovely daughter." George wore a smarmy expression.

"Hello," Andrea said dryly. "You've missed most of the party, Charlene."

"Sorry, baby. We got a late start. But I'm so proud of you." Charlene made a kissing motion toward her without touching her lips to Andrea's cheek. "My Andrea is the director of the local clinic. She's saving lives every day."

"How marvelous." George looked at Andrea as though something very different was on his mind.

"George, how wonderful to see you. How is your work going?" a woman called out.

"Excuse me. Must make nice to possible rich patrons." George stroked the thin mustache he wore and sauntered off.

Andrea rolled her eyes. "Good God, Charlene. Where do you get them?"

"What?" Charlene flipped the long white silk scarf she wore over one shoulder.

"That," Andrea said, nodding at George. He simpered

and flattered a rotund woman in a shocking pink chiffon dress.

Charlene eyed her date for a moment before replying. "George isn't so bad. And he is so absolutely fine."

"He knows it better than anyone else, too," Andrea said with a scornful expression.

"Don't let that arrogant pose fool you. He spoils me like crazy." Charlene wore a catlike smile of satisfaction.

"Your taste in men hasn't improved," Andrea muttered.

"What, sweetie?"

Charlene's attention had drifted to John and Victoria. They stood at the door, trapped by another socialite from a prominent family who kept talking. Victoria's expression was stretched so tight her skin seemed about to crack as she nodded at the woman. John darted furtive glances at Charlene. The minor drama was not missed by a number of people present, including Gran. Charlene flashed a dazzling smile at him. John looked at George and then back at her. He turned away sharply and guided Victoria out with one hand on her elbow. The socialite's startled expression told Andrea that he'd cut through her chatter, interrupting her in midsentence. Andrea groaned under her breath.

"You had to make a scene, didn't you?"

"I didn't do anything." Charlene wore an innocent expression.

Andrea shook her head slowly. At that moment she caught sight of Jamal across the room. His gaze shifted between Andrea, Charlene, and where the Mandevilles had stood seconds before. Andrea tensed with anger toward him again. She'd come close to making a big mistake tonight. Charlene's antics brought the age-old fear that she was indeed like her mother, always choosing the wrong man. Andrea tried to learn from Charlene's mistakes. Yet she had not seen through her former husband. And here she was caught up in the beguiling charms of another man, one whose motive seemed clear. Andrea glanced away when Jamal looked at her and smiled.

"I think that puts an end to this evening for me," she said. "I suppose you'll be leaving soon." Andrea knew Charlene's main purpose had been achieved, to taunt John and Victoria.

"I came to support you, but George is giving me the silent signal that he wants to leave. Bye-bye, my brilliant baby girl." She rattled out the words so fast they sounded like one long sentence.

Charlene hugged her and blew another kiss before she breezed off. Soon she and George were leaving. All eyes followed the handsome couple who'd caused such a stir. Andrea avoided Jamal. She collected Gran and managed to leave without feeling too conspicuous. Gran was silent for the first five minutes of the drive home.

"The party was really nice," Gran said, stealing a sideways glance at Andrea.

"Most of it anyway." Andrea kept her eyes on the road ahead.

"Charlene's got too much nerve." Gran huffed. "I'm gonna tell her just what I think."

"Don't waste your time, Gran. When has she listened to you or anyone before?" Andrea spoke with bitterness.

"Well, she shouldn't have spoiled your night. Downright selfish is what she is. And you were having such a good time with Jamal," Gran blurted out, then pressed her lips together.

"And by the way, no more matchmaking stunts, especially not with him of all people," Andrea said angrily. "He's exactly the kind of man Charlene would choose."

"But he's not—"

"No more," Andrea cut her off. "Understand?"

"You don't have to bite my head off," she grumbled. "Just trying to help you come out of your shell."

"Like Charlene?" Andrea said, sarcasm dripping like acid from the words.

"Okay, okay."

They rode in silence all the way home. Though she was angry with Charlene, she also was grateful. She'd needed a dose of reality. Andrea felt she'd had a close call with Jamal tonight. She promised herself it would not happen again.

Ten

Denny sat at the desk in the clinic pharmacy, filling out a stack of forms in triplicate. Lee watched him for several seconds, backed up a few steps down the hall, and whistled as he approached. He came to the open doorway in time to see Denny stuff the forms in a desk and lock the drawer.

"Hey, man. What's up?" Lee said in a happy-go-lucky tone.

"Nothing. I thought everybody had left." Denny stood and crossed to a shelf of labels and other items. "I'm here getting everything set up for tomorrow. Bill will be here, you know."

"Yeah, I know. Pretty nice outfit you got there." Lee leaned against a cabinet and crossed his arms. "Worth a nice chunk of change."

"I guess."

"I knew this guy back in L.A., did a great business on

the side selling medical equipment." Lee picked up a box of cotton swabs, examined them, and put them down again.

"Oh yeah?" Denny spoke without looking at him. He set up the electric typewriter used to print labels for medicine packages.

"Yeah. Made good money, too. Real good money." Lee leaned forward to speak right over Denny's shoulder. "Bet you know what I mean."

"I don't," Denny said quickly. Too quickly.

"Look, I didn't just get off the bus from Stupidville," Lee tossed back at him. "I got eyes."

"You've got nothing but some wrong-ass idea," Denny said angrily.

"Uh-huh." Lee sidled up to him with a swagger and lowered his voice. "I've made a few contacts around town. And you hangin' with Ty'Rance Wilson is my imagination?"

Denny grew still for a second, then continued arranging supplies on the counter. "What do you know about Ty?" he said, his tone cautious.

"Enough to put two and two together. I'm good with math."

Lee let his words sink in. His old undercover-cop instincts took over. This opportunity was too good to pass up. He'd set up a deal and then let the local police take over. When Denny said nothing, he went on.

"I wouldn't mind meeting the dude myself. I've just been looking for the right hookup."

"A college boy like you?" Denny looked at him from the corner of his eye. He was still on guard.

"Like I told you, I have contacts in L.A. We made big money, too. I can help you out, man." Lee adopted the bragging gangsta tone he'd heard so often as a cop.

"Maybe you're full of big talk and nothing else." Denny now turned to face him. There was a spark of interest in his black eyes and a cunning expression on his boyish reddish brown face.

"Nah, I can deliver what I'm talking about." Lee gazed back at him with a serious expression.

"I don't know." Denny rubbed his face with one hand.

"Set it up and I'll do the rest."

"Ty don't play. He's into some heavy stuff," Denny said.

"Humph, heavy as it can get out here in the sticks."

"You got into it with Bo. He's one of Ty's boys." Denny stabbed a forefinger in the space between them. "He won't like you too much."

"Bo is a chump. Ty won't get too far if that's the kinda help he's using," Lee said with a grunt of derision.

"Yeah, well . . ." Denny rubbed his face again and thought some more. "They don't know you."

Lee decided not to push him for now. "Okay, man. But we can still do business. Then once we show him a profit, he'll probably be a lot more friendly."

"Whatcha mean?" Denny took his hand down and relaxed somewhat.

"You and me can work inside the clinic. He won't know the difference, right? Long as you give him what he wants." Lee wore a sly smile.

"Right, right." Denny nodded and stared at the wall, deep in thought.

Lee eyed the young man. Denny was more than cautious, he looked scared. Lee played a hunch. "How much you owe him, man?"

Denny looked at him sharply. "Who says I owe him anything?"

There was no mistaking it, there was fear in his eyes. "You shakin' bad to get your hands on money. I figure you either owe somebody dangerous or you're on drugs." Lee cocked his head to one side. "Maybe both."

Denny licked his lips and shook his head. "Look, man, I don't know you."

"Yeah, you do. I'm the brother that's gonna get you outta that hole you're in."

"Uh-huh. And what's in it for you?"

"Same as what's in it for you, cash. Only I know how we can make some profit without sharing it with Ty." Lee winked at him.

"I'll think about it," Denny said after a while. "I'm not saying anything else."

"You're too paranoid, dude." Lee slapped his back and grinned.

Andrea walked past the door and paused. "Hi. You guys are here late again?"

Denny smiled at her. "Yes, ma'am. But I'm on my way out now. 'Bye." He slid past Lee without looking at him again.

" 'Bye, Denny. Thanks again for taking care of those invoices," Andrea called after him. She glanced at Lee again. "I'm headed for home myself in a few minutes. I'll lock up." She seemed to be anxious for him to leave.

Lee crossed his arms. He could not afford to slip again. This attraction had worked its way beneath his skin, and he was not happy about it. Only two nights ago he'd lost his senses. His whole body had responded to Andrea under some stars and a crescent moon. Now he tensed in anticipation of another onslaught.

Andrea wore a light gray tailored pantsuit, the jacket open at the collar. Sterling silver hoop earrings gleamed against her brown skin. No amount of effort she made to dress in a conservative, businesslike manner could disguise the lush curves of her breasts and hips. How would it feel to run his hands over her skin, to follow the curve of her body with the tips of his fingers? Was her bare flesh beneath the fabric as smooth as that exposed at her throat? Lee's libido stirred to life and he hastened to cut it off at the pass.

Whether it was her fragrance, the way her lips glistened like ripe dark fruit, or moonlight madness, the reason didn't matter. Lee was not one of those brothers with brains in his crotch. Somehow she'd almost gotten through to that place in his heart he closely guarded. The last thing he needed was to lose his head over a woman, especially this one. She could be just one more cute crook.

"Hey!" Andrea said, waving her hands at him. "Did you hear me?"

"Sorry, I was thinking about something I've gotta do later," Lee stammered.

"I'm sure your social life is busy, so I'll hurry up." Andrea brushed back her hair and walked to her office.

"I—" Lee almost blurted out a denial but caught himself. Luckily she seemed not to have heard him anyway. "I'll wait at the back door," he called out.

"Okay," she answered from a distance.

What was his problem? The simplest thing was to let her think he was a player, act as though he indeed had a lover. Maybe that would help. In fact, he should contact one of the women he saw occasionally. Being with Katina was pleasant enough. An evening with a woman who made no demands might just do the trick to help him fight off this madness. Yet the thought of being with any other woman left him feeling flat as week-old cola. This was really crazy! Lee had never felt this lost, even when he'd courted his ex-wife, Kristen. There could be something to this Louisiana voodoo after all, he mused, shaking his head.

"What's wrong?"

Lee started at her melodious voice near his shoulder and spun around. "What?"

"You seemed to be thinking about something deep," she said. Andrea gazed up at him, her head cocked to one side.

He looked into the clearest, most beautiful pecan brown eyes he'd ever seen. "Not really," he murmured.

Andrea turned and set the alarm. "If you say so. Let's go." Her tone was crisp and distant.

He followed her down the short hall and through the door. He waited as she locked the door. Head up, Andrea marched ahead of him to her car, with the heels of her pumps tapping military style. Nothing in her manner indicated she even remembered their close encounter the other night. Lee felt a mixture of relief and annoyance. He'd never had trouble attracting beautiful women, even as a teenager. It was not egotism, just a fact. Not every relationship had worked out the way he'd wanted, though. Lee had grown tired of the love games by his mid-twenties. It would be great if movies and romance novels were right, that love could last. But he knew better. Uncomplicated companionship was the best option. Passionate longing only led to misery. The passion Andrea inspired should be enough to warn him she would only let him down. Lee had had enough of letdowns to last him a lifetime. His heart hardened against the seductive woman who could smile and turn his body to jelly. Good, he was glad she could turn to ice water at will.

Andrea reached her car. The headlights flashed when

she turned off the alarm. "I'll see you tomorrow. Denny tells me you may be through with the records *A* to *G* soon. Sounds great."

"Yeah, great," Lee echoed. He squinted in the late afternoon sunshine and assumed a casual pose. "See ya, boss lady."

"Good-bye. Don't party too late." Andrea opened the driver's-side door and gazed at him.

There seemed to be a question in her voice. Did she want to know if he was seeing someone? Here was his chance. If she was interested, that could mean . . . nothing, it meant absolutely nothing. Damn! He felt like a mixed-up teenager. This was a case and she wasn't in the clear by a long shot.

"No problem, I'm used to it," he said in a jaunty voice.

He whirled around and strode to his Integra without looking back. Lee could not trust himself to be alone with her for any length of time, at least not for now. As he drove away he talked himself down from the dizzying effect she'd had on him.

Lee entered John Mandeville's office suite. The pretty secretary was gone for the day since it was after six in the evening. He'd arranged for this first report to take place when they could meet with the most privacy. The office building was practically empty on a Friday night. Lee walked across the thick ocean blue carpet. He stopped at the sound of an incensed female voice. The door was open, but the speaker was on the other side of the spacious office. The thin woman in an expensive mauve dress stood with her back to Lee. Mandeville rumbled an expletive.

"I don't believe a word you say. You knew Charlene Noble would be there!"

Lee recognized the woman. Victoria Mandeville glared at her husband. She folded her arms to her chest, causing the gold bracelets on her wrists to jingle. They seemed to be at a standoff.

"Give it a rest, Vicky." John walked to the bar.

"I won't put up with being publicly humiliated," Victoria spat at him.

Lee moved to the side to make sure neither would see him. Andrea's mother had some connection to Mandeville?

"Don't be so melodramatic. That was over years ago." In contrast, John seemed quite calm.

"I saw the way you looked at her. You weren't exactly hiding it!" Victoria shouted.

"Get a grip, woman," John barked. His voice came closer and then the door shut firmly. His response was inaudible. Their voices were now muffled through the thick oak door.

Lee was left to ponder the brief part of their exchange he'd heard. So Andrea's mother and Mandeville had been, or still were, lovers. He was not at all surprised that John had not told him the whole story. Private detectives were used to having their own clients lie to them. Here was another reason to get out of this case fast. He walked out into the hallway, not a moment too soon. The door leading to John's office swung open a second after he was gone.

"Now I know why you were so interested in that clinic. There's a limit to what I'll tolerate, John," Victoria said.

"I'm interested because it benefits the community," John said in a mild tone.

"Your community spirit is about as plentiful as honest politicians. You're making money, lots of it, or you wouldn't give a damn about the Bayou Blue Clinic."

"The previous director wouldn't see reason."

"You mean he was someone else's puppet and not yours," Victoria shot back. "You don't care about what happens at that place. You're always involved in a racket of some kind. Papa says—"

"Your high-class family have their own brand of racket, darlin'." John laughed.

"We never wallowed in filth," Victoria snarled at him acidly.

"You mean he never lowered himself to get his hands dirty, he paid others to do it," John lobbed back at her. "Don't forget how well I know Papa Trosclair's business."

"Then you know how powerful he is. Stay away from Charlene Noble."

When the outer door opened, Lee hurried in the opposite direction toward the elevators. He strolled back toward Mandeville's suite as though he'd only just arrived.

"Evening, ma'am," Lee said as he nodded at Victoria.

The angry woman merely shot a brief glance at him as she walked by. Lee took the opportunity to examine her up close. Victoria was attractive but not pretty like Charlene Noble. Expensive clothes and makeup, and the benefit of what Lee guessed was a high-priced hairstylist, helped. He strolled on, mentally tossing around this new information. He entered the office suite for the second time. John Mandeville turned as Lee walked in.

"Hi, Mr. Mandeville. Sorry I'm late," Lee said.

"Actually you're right on time," John said. He glanced past Lee to the door with a sour expression.

"If you say so." Lee shrugged. He followed John into the office. He sat down in one of the soft leather chairs facing the huge desk.

"Been a long day, Lee." Mandeville sighed like a man carrying the weight of the world.

"Guess ordering people around is tiring."

John smiled at him. "Let's have a damn drink." As he worked, he continued to talk. "Actually, being the boss is exhausting. But luckily I've got sharp people working for me."

"Uh-huh." Lee did not sympathize with the problems of a rich businessman. He took out a small pad and reviewed his notes.

John came and sat down in the chair next to him. He handed Lee a cut-glass tumbler of amber liquid. "Best cognac I've ever tasted."

"Thanks." Lee put the glass on a round table between them without drinking from it. "Here's what I've got so far. I think at least one employee has been stealing from the clinic. I'm pretty sure he plans to steal drugs next. Probably already has, but with those records, I can't tell."

"And the director?" John sipped from his glass.

"The guy could have been involved, but at this point I can't tell." Lee flipped the pad closed.

"I was referring to Ms. Noble," John said. He looked at Lee hard. "You must have some opinion by now."

"Nothing definite. I mean, she signs invoices and has been slow to delegate. So . . ." Lee had to force the words out. "She might know what's going on."

"I see." A muscle in Mandeville's jaw tightened.

"Bottom line—the place needs a major overhaul and the cops should be brought in."

"No, we can't do that. I want you to handle it." John

delivered his decision in a determined voice. He looked every bit the CEO.

Lee raised his eyebrows. "This isn't a simple matter of employee theft. I suspect this kid has gang connections."

"But you don't know for certain, right?" John said.

"State auditors and the police can use what I've put together so far."

"Listen," John said, and leaned back in his chair. "You know how important that clinic is to poor folks around here. I don't want to call in the bloodhounds unless we're absolutely sure."

"Which might cut into your profits?" Lee said in a flat voice. "And just what is your connection to Andrea Noble?"

"I participated in the hiring process, gave the search committee my input," John answered smoothly.

"That's all?" Lee gazed at him, head tilted to one side.

"This is a small town. I know the family." John lifted a shoulder.

"So you know or knew Charlene Noble *very well*," Lee said.

John's mild expression hardened. "You're being paid to investigate that clinic, not my private life."

"I could do a better job if you told me everything."

"I've told you everything you need to know." John's dark eyes glittered with ire.

"I don't think so," Lee said in a level tone.

"I hired you to get to the bottom of management problems, not to follow up on gossip," John snapped.

"This isn't just to satisfy my curiosity," Lee shot back coldly. The man's arrogance grated on him. "We're talking drug theft and possibly involving the feds."

His mention of the federal authorities had the desired effect. The color drained from Mandeville's face. He went to the bar and poured more cognac into his glass even though it was not completely empty.

"That's preposterous." John spoke over his shoulder. "You're really stretching to make this thing bigger than it is."

"If they steal drugs and cross state lines to sell them, it could well be a federal case." Lee, didn't think so, but he wanted to rattle Mandeville.

John turned around with a composed look. "You don't even know if there is theft of drugs, much less a gang connection."

He had to admire the man's ability to bounce back. "True. But from my experience, the signs are there."

"Fine. We'll deal with it *if* that's the case." John drew himself to his full height and looked down at Lee.

"No, I'll notify the local police and let them decide." He stared back at John. Several seconds ticked by in tense silence.

John nodded. "I can live with that. Harley Boudreaux is a fishing partner and a real reasonable guy."

"I'll let you know what the sheriff says."

"Better yet, I'll set up the meeting," John said in a take-charge voice. "I'll give you a call by tomorrow morning."

Lee didn't like it, but he decided not to argue the point. "Okay. Tomorrow," he insisted.

"No problem." John smiled now, the genial southern gentleman again. "Now relax and finish your drink."

Lee did not feel like drinking with this upper-class version of a used-car salesman. "No, thanks, I've got to get going." He walked out.

As he drove to New Orleans, he tried to reconcile his gut reaction to Andrea with his cop's instinct. Years of scraping up humanity's garbage told him not to be deceived. Mandeville's reaction when asked about Charlene and Andrea told him there was a missing piece, a big one. A sick feeling formed in the pit of Lee's stomach. He did not want any more reasons to suspect Andrea's motives, but they kept popping up like poison mushrooms.

It was a sunny Saturday morning. Andrea got up at six o'clock to get an early start. Moving day had finally come. She was all packed and ready to move into her apartment. The small complex of one- and two-bedroom flats was only a mile from the clinic downtown. Gran stood with both hands on her wide hips as she surveyed the suitcases and boxes.

"Still don't see why you can't stay here," Gran said with a stern face.

"We've been through this," Andrea warned with a squint.

"All right, all right. It just seems the last couple of months flew by too fast." Gran pinched Andrea's cheek gently. "I got used to my little pecan candy baby being home again."

"You'll see me at mealtimes more than you want to."

"You come by every day if you want, cher." Gran winked at her. "I've tasted your cooking."

"Hey! It's not that bad," Andrea protested.

"Needs work, child." Gran's dark eyebrows went up. "Gotta improve so your husband and six babies won't starve," she teased.

"You've been out in the sun too long. Six kids? No way."

"The right man will change your mind, I bet." Gran chuckled, thoroughly enjoying Andrea's reaction.

"I love you dearly, but you're dreaming." Andrea laughed at the notion.

"We'll see."

Andrea shook her head. "It's amazing how you manage to work marriage into every conversation."

"Okay, I give up. You're bound and determined to be single." Gran smiled.

Andrea was suspicious of this early surrender, but said nothing. "Good. Now back to the real world, carting all my junk out of here. I can't believe how much of it there is."

"Yeah, a strong man is on his way to help," Gran called over her shoulder as she left the room.

"Uncle Curtis is coming?" Andrea closed and sealed another box.

"Nope." Gran's voice came down the hallway from Andrea's old bedroom.

"Cousin Leonard? No, he's working offshore for the next three weeks." Andrea tripped over one of three large shopping bags. "Damn!"

"Watch your mouth," Gran said as she entered the living room again.

"Nothing wrong with your hearing." Andrea wrapped the last of her black figurine collection in plastic bubble material. "So who is my hero?"

The doorbell rang and Gran darted out to the foyer. "I'll get it."

"Okay," Andrea said in a distracted tone. She rummaged through a large box.

Gran bounced in and spread her arms with a flourish. "Surprise!" she chirped. "He was so sweet to offer when I told him we needed a pair of big male arms."

Andrea froze for a split second, then turned around slowly. "Hi," she stammered.

"Hi," Jamal said, his voice rich and deep.

Eleven

Andrea was speechless. She glanced from him to Gran, then back at him. Jamal gazed at her with a twinkle in his brown eyes. He was dressed in a plain white cotton T-shirt and faded blue jeans. The soft T-shirt molded to the muscles of his chest. Andrea was lost for a moment as she enjoyed the view. Her gaze traveled down lower. Faded denim, not tight but fitting well, covered his narrow hips and muscular thighs. Her sex-o-meter was spiking off the scale. Andrea could feel the moisture forming between her legs. Damn! All he had to do was walk into a room in simple clothes and she quivered. A thrill went through her when she realized Jamal was staring at her as well. He pressed his lips together and took a deep breath.

"Uh, I'm here to help you move. Miss Mavis said y'all couldn't get anyone else. All your cousins had to work." Jamal wiped his top lip and looked away. "Ahem, what do you want me to move first?"

"You . . . I mean . . . What?" Andrea felt giddy.

"What do you want me to move first?" Jamal asked, still avoiding her gaze.

Andrea collected her senses. "Right, right. Those boxes can go. But I don't think they'll fit in your trunk."

"No problem. I borrowed a friend's truck." Jamal easily lifted a large box of books.

Gran peeked out from behind him, a wide grin on her face. "My, my, such a strong young man."

"If you can just get the front door," he said.

"Andrea, open the door for Jamal." Gran left the room. "I've got to check on something."

"Don't go far because I want to talk to you," Andrea said in a measured voice.

"Sure, cher." Gran blinked at her with a mild expression, then bustled off humming.

They were left alone and Andrea felt awkward again. She smiled at him nervously. "Well, here we go," she said without moving.

"Uh, this box is starting to feel heavy." Jamal nodded toward the door to prompt her.

"Of course." Andrea groaned inwardly. She was destined to make a fool of herself in front of this man.

She scurried past him to the front door. Jamal walked by, leaving behind a refreshing scent of soap and mint aftershave lotion. Andrea swallowed hard. Somehow she had to get out of this frame of mind.

"I put some old blankets down in the bed," Jamal called over his shoulder.

Andrea gasped at the vivid image she had of them naked on a downy blanket in the back of his friend's truck. She fanned her face with one hand. Her red cotton shirt stuck to her chest with perspiration.

"Good thinking," she managed to stutter.

"Yeah, well, I've gotten good at moving. One divorce and then a move across the country." His full lips went up into a dimpled smile.

"Me, too," she murmured. Andrea inhaled fresh air to clear her head. "I'll get some of the smaller stuff."

She rushed off, hoping busywork would act as an antidote to him. An hour later they had the largest and heaviest items loaded in the truck.

Gran came outside. "There are just a few odds and ends left. I'll bring them in my little car, later on."

"I thought we'd pack my car and follow Jamal. That way he could go on home." Andrea glared daggers at her.

"I've gotta stop for groceries and get my medicine. Wait, Rowena needed to come with me." Gran looked at Jamal. "My friend Rowena can't drive right now 'cause of her cataract surgery."

Jamal's lips twitched as he appeared to try to fight off laughter. "Yes, ma'am."

"So it might take me a while, two, maybe three hours." Gran raised her eyebrows at him.

"Yes, ma'am. I got ya." Jamal wore a mock serious expression. "I'll take care of her for you."

"I can't believe this." Andrea glanced at Jamal from the corner of her eye.

"What?" Gran's big, dark eyes widened with innocence.

"Come on, Andrea. What about furniture?" Jamal gently guided her to the open passenger door.

"It was delivered yesterday afternoon," she said, still looking at Gran. "But—"

"Go on, cher. I'll be along at some time or other." Gran waved gaily and went in the house.

When the door shut firmly, Andrea ground her teeth in frustration. Jamal seemed not to notice. He went around the front of the forest green Dodge Ram and got behind the wheel.

"All set," he said, and beckoned to her from inside the cab.

"I'm taking my car," Andrea burst out. She could not sit so close to him for even a few miles. No amount of air conditioning would keep her cool. "I've got to get it there anyway."

Was it her imagination, or was there disappointment in his eyes? Yet he smiled immediately. "Sure thing. I'll meet you there."

"But how do you know where it is?"

"Your grandmother gave me directions," he said with a grin.

Andrea groaned and shoved the truck door shut. Mavis Ricard had some kind of nerve. Andrea fumed and rehearsed the tongue lashing she'd give Gran before the day was through. She drove behind the shiny truck down Highway 1 toward town. Their eyes met as he stared into the rearview mirror. He smiled and gave her a thumbs-up sign. Her irritation subsided as the warm wind rushed through her open car window. Still she chafed at Gran's insistence on interfering in her love life. Jamal must have cast some kind of spell over that woman. He certainly seemed to have a knack for it, she mused, thinking of the way women lit up when he was around. Jamal was handsome, sexy, and seemed to be a caring man. She'd seen him be tender and funny with patients. Andrea also admired the way he'd become as much a mentor to Denny as a co-worker. The younger man looked more and more to Jamal for guidance. Then there was the sexual chemistry between them whenever Jamal got close to her. Just thinking about the way they'd touched that night at the fund-raiser made Andrea's heart pound. Andrea had been unable to think straight when he put his muscular arms around her. The sensation of resting against his rock-hard chest had left her weak with desire.

All in all, Jamal Turner seemed to be Mr. Right. So why fight it? She tried to think of the logical reasons she had vowed to stay clear of a relationship. Those reasons were pretty good. She needed time and space after the knockout punches from Ellis. One of the social workers in the Chicago clinic where she'd worked had advised her to take time to regroup. She needed to feel good about herself again.

The truth was, Andrea did not trust her judgment in choosing men. Ellis had seemed to be a stable kind of guy. A college professor who taught business, he talked endlessly about management styles and corporate culture. He dressed conservatively and talked about family values. Yet he'd turned out to be a dog in geek's clothing. Like mother, like daughter? No way! She was not going to repeat Charlene's pattern of hooking up with chumps.

Andrea gazed ahead at the rearview mirror and saw his lovely brown eyes again. She took a deep breath. As for Jamal Turner, he was not even in disguise. He smiled and women stumbled over each other to be near him. He was funny and a smart aleck. Women loved being near him, and he knew it. He was good-looking, a smooth talker. There was nothing conservative about Jamal. The clothes he wore weren't flashy, but didn't hide his fabulous body. There was nothing restrained about the animal way he walked, like a graceful panther, or the way he spoke his mind. Jamal Turner was definitely not the kind of man Andrea thought she wanted or needed. In short, he was the kind of man Charlene was drawn to. An excellent reason to run screaming in the opposite direction.

He smiled at her in the rearview mirror again and she automatically smiled back. On the other hand . . . why not accept that what you see is what you get? *He's a nice guy, go with it!* Andrea sighed. She'd left Chicago convinced that she had the question of men and relationships settled.

"Gran, this is all your fault," Andrea grumbled out loud. She turned up the car radio. Maybe loud music would clear her confused thoughts.

It was another hot day, typical for late June in south Louisiana. The China blue sky was cloudless. Andrea savored the heat, contrasting it to the bone deep cold she'd endured during those long Chicago winters. The road stretched ahead, with rich green grass on either side. Moss-draped oak trees grew tall and wide, their massive branches curved down to the ground. Egrets flew overhead, their snowy white bodies gleaming in the sunshine. It was hard to be in a grumpy mood on a day like today. They approached town and Jamal turned down the street leading to her new home.

Andrea looked at herself in the car mirror and nodded. "I'm in control. I'll thank him and send him on his way."

Following him into the lot, Andrea parked in the space next to the truck.

Jamal got out of the truck and stood with both hands on his hips, looking around. "Nice place."

Andrea joined him. "Yeah, I really like the way it's designed."

The exterior's wood walls were stained a dark reddish brown that blended with the surroundings. Palms and compact shrubs had been planted along the sidewalks. A cozy courtyard featured a fountain in the middle of a pond. The complex was deliberately small, only sixteen flats. Each building had two floors.

"It's nice and quiet. My apartment is over here." She got the keys out of her purse and led the way to her ground-floor flat.

"Hmm, you think this is a good idea?" Jamal walked around the corner of the building. "A second-floor apartment would be better for a woman living alone. But at least these windows look secure."

"Sure they are. I checked it out," Andrea said. "And the landlord has a security system installed, see?" She pointed to the control pad.

"Good idea," he said, but continued to look around.

"Not that I'll need all the protection. But thanks for worrying about me, Dad."

He grinned. "I get the point. Just wanted to make sure you were secure."

"Thank you, sir." Andrea made a playful curtsy. "You've saved me twice so far. Guess I'm lucky to have a knight in shining armor."

"Yeah, guess so," Jamal said softly.

They gazed at each other for a few moments. He took a step toward her and Andrea panicked. She unlocked the front door. Without looking back, she went inside the apartment.

"Okay, let's start the fun stuff. I'll turn on the air conditioner," she said, and hurried ahead of him.

"It is pretty hot in here."

Andrea turned around to find him only inches away. "Yeah, I'll put it on high to cool things off."

His lips parted slowly. "I like a hot climate," he said.

"I do, too. But not this hot. Let's lower the temperature so I can think straight," Andrea murmured.

Jamal lifted a hand as though to brush her hair, then held back. He blinked like a man waking from a trance and took a couple of steps back. "I'll, uh, start unloading."

"Yeah, right, unload."

She watched him walk away with a mixture of excitement and relief. There was no mistaking it, she'd seen desire in his eyes. Andrea found a tissue in her purse and dabbed at the sweat on her forehead. The next two hours or so would be a test, but she was determined to pass it.

It did not take long before the living room of her apartment was filled with boxes and bags. Andrea once again marveled at how much she'd accumulated. They unpacked the kitchen items first, then tackled the living room. In no time they'd set up her compact disc player and arranged most of the books on a corner bookcase.

"Nice furniture. I like the colors," Jamal said as he continued to unpack a box of CDs and cassette tapes.

"Thanks." Andrea once again admired the sofa set. The fabric had an abstract pattern of cool blue, mauve, and green that matched the green carpet. "I find it soothing."

"Yeah. You've got a really nice place here."

"Once I get all this junk organized." Andrea pushed back a tendril of hair from her eyes. "It could take months with the hours I put in at the clinic."

"I'll help," Jamal said promptly.

Andrea cleared her throat. "I'm sure you've got enough to do in your time off."

"Not really. I know how it is to live out of boxes. I've done it twice." Jamal spoke matter-of-factly.

"So you live somewhere in Bayou Blue?"

Jamal did not answer immediately. "No, in Harahan."

"You drive a long way. Why not work closer to home?" Andrea kept her tone conversational. Still, she was fascinated to finally find out more about him.

"Because I found a job in Bayou Blue. This is beautiful." Jamal had unwrapped a small wooden sculpture of a woman and child. It was carved from mahogany.

"I found it in a small shop on the island of Sint Maarten." Andrea walked over to where he stood. "That started my collection."

"I love going to the Caribbean. Brazil is another favorite." He carefully placed the piece on the shelf of another bookcase. Then he unwrapped other figurines and arranged them artfully.

"You're a world traveler, huh? Lucky you." Andrea watched him take care with the position of each piece. "And an artist at heart, it seems."

Jamal smiled at her over his shoulder before turning his attention back to his task. "I've got my own modest collection of Haitian and African art. There you go." He put the last piece on the third of four shelves.

"Perfect." Andrea smiled at him.

"So when were you on Sint Maarten? Maybe we bumped into each other."

"On my honeymoon almost ten years ago. My husband met his future mistress that week," Andrea said. She frowned and pushed the memory away.

"Oh," Jamal mumbled. "Well, at least you got some good art out of it, right?" He wore a cautious smile.

Andrea looked at him for a few seconds in stunned silence, then burst out laughing. "I never thought of it that way. You're so silly. How did you know I wouldn't punch you?"

"I counted on your great sense of humor. Plus I can move pretty fast." He laughed with her.

"Uh-huh. Now let's see how fast we can both move. I can't stand all this clutter."

They traded jokes for the next two hours as they worked. Andrea gave him directions on moving the furniture once most of the boxes were empty. They hung up pictures, put her bed up, and threw away mounds of newspaper used to cushion her belongings. By one o'clock they were both tired and hungry. Andrea collapsed on the sofa with a groan.

"My back aches, my feet hurt, and I'm sweating like a construction worker." Her head fell back on the cushion and she closed her eyes.

Jamal sat next to her. "Well, at least you're a cute sweaty construction worker." He sniffed the air. "And not too stinky."

"Hey!" Andrea smacked the top of his head with a small throw cushion. "You're supposed to tell me I'm completely wrong. You flunk the southern gentleman test."

"C'mon, give me some credit. I did say you were cute and sweaty." Jamal ducked a second swing at his head.

"I forgot that sense of humor could be used for evil purposes."

"I give up." Jamal raised both hands. "The truth is, you're not cute."

"You're asking for it." Andrea raised the cushion again.

He closed one large hand around her wrist. "You're

beautiful." His gaze swept over her. "All the time, in every way."

Pleasure surged through her body at his touch. Instantly she forgot about keeping distance between them. In fact, she wanted him closer. As though pulled by a powerful magnetic force, he leaned toward her. Andrea dropped the cushion and met him halfway. He gave her one light kiss, then another, then another. Andrea closed her eyes as his tongue traced a fiery trail along her bottom lip before tasting the inside of her mouth. His gentle probing continued until they both moaned softly. Andrea felt a shiver begin at the base of her spine and fan out until every part of her body seemed to vibrate.

Jamal's hands slid from her back to her hips. Andrea savored the heat from his body beneath the cotton T-shirt. She gasped when he kissed her neck. His lips brushed down the open neckline of her short-sleeved shirt. She wanted him to touch her everywhere. Andrea undid the top four buttons and tilted her head back. He eagerly nuzzled the soft mounds of exposed flesh above the pink lace bra. The only sound she heard was their heavy breathing. Andrea buried her fingers in curls of dark hair as he continued to kiss her breasts.

Jamal found the front hooks and opened the bra. Andrea gasped as he nudged the fabric aside with one hand. Jamal circled one nipple with his tongue delicately before taking it in his mouth. The sensation of his teasing caress made her ache for more. It was a sweet mixture of pleasure and pain, a sexual hunger that gripped her with a vengeance. From a distance Andrea heard a voice that seemed not her own but had to be.

"Here, please," she whispered, and offered her other breast to him.

"Yes, baby."

He opened the last buttons of her shirt. Andrea watched in ecstatic fascination as his head bent down toward her erect nipples.

The phone rang. Neither moved as it jangled five times.

Jamal gripped her tighter. He nibbled one nipple gently with his full lips, then moved to the other. "Ignore it," he said hoarsely.

"Yes," Andrea breathed. She had no intention of answering the phone.

The phone stopped, but then the door chimes played a musical tune. Andrea's head began to clear ever so slowly. "Wait, I . . ." Her effort to swim out of the haze of desire was blunted by his insistent tongue on her nipple again, this time faster.

"No, they'll go away." To make the point how much he wanted her, Jamal put his hand between her legs.

Andrea bit back a loud moan. "It could be Gran."

The door chimes rang again and a female voice called out, "Miss Noble, Shirley Sharp, the manager. I wanted to give you the checklist."

Jamal continued to nip at her flesh hungrily. "She'll get tired and leave."

Andrea pushed Jamal's face away from her body with great reluctance. "Just a minute," she yelled back.

"It's obvious she knows I'm in here," she whispered.

"Damn!" Jamal muttered, and took a deep, shaky breath as he sat back. "I've gotta throw cold water on my face . . . and a few other places." He stumbled to the half bath a few feet down the hall.

Andrea hastily fastened her bra and buttoned her blouse. She checked herself in the mirror, combed her hair with her fingers, then went to the front door.

Ms. Sharp was buxom, well past thirty-five with hair

dyed a deep copper that matched her brown skin. And she was apparently very curious about her new tenant.

"Hi," the woman said as she peered past Andrea into the apartment. "Uh, I didn't mean to inconvenience you and your friend. I guess you had to climb over boxes and all."

"No problem," Andrea said in a bright voice. "Come right in. We were in the back bedroom—putting things in the extra closet," she added quickly when the woman's auburn eyebrows shot up.

"Right." She wore a knowing smile. "Anyway, I forgot to give you this list. Mark anything that needs repair. That way we can catch problems early."

"Thanks, Ms. Sharp." Andrea almost snatched the paper from her hands. "I'm sure everything is just fine."

"Yes," Ms. Sharp said without moving. She glanced around. "You've really done a lot in a short time."

"Hard work and determination, I guess." Andrea smiled at her and cleared her throat. "But we've still got quite a lot to do."

"Of course, having your furniture delivered the other day helped." Ms. Sharp lingered as her gaze darted to the hallway. It was obvious she wanted to see more.

"It certainly did." Andrea rolled the two page checklist into a tube and tapped it against her thigh. "Is there anything else? We really want to finish and get some lunch."

"No. Just be sure and get that to me within the next five working days." Ms. Sharp seemed reluctant to leave.

Andrea almost cried out with joy when the phone rang again. "Well, if you'll excuse me."

"Certainly, of course. I . . . Oh my," Ms. Sharp blinked when Jamal strolled down the hall. She stared at his chest.

He nodded to her. "Hi. I'll get it." He went down the short hallway to the kitchen and picked up the cordless phone on the counter.

"I'll be sure and bring the checklist no later than Tuesday." Andrea fought the urge to push the woman out.

"Good." Ms. Sharp patted her hair and batted her eyelashes. "Let me know if there's anything I can do to help."

"We're doing fine, thank you," Andrea said crisply, annoyed at the way she ogled Jamal.

"I'll bet," she said with a sigh that reeked of envy. "Well, good-bye."

" 'Bye." Andrea ushered the woman out and shut the door behind her with a firm thump. "Some nerve," she muttered under her breath.

"What was that?" Jamal came out holding the cordless phone.

"Nothing." Andrea tugged at her blouse.

"It's your grandmother," he said. He held it out to her without walking closer.

Andrea took the phone. "Hi. On your way?"

Andrea fervently hoped so. Gran would add a much-needed buffer zone. True to her devious matchmaking intentions, Gran made an excuse. She gaily twittered that she was sure Andrea didn't need help. But help was the one thing Andrea needed most. Being alone with Jamal proved one thing: she could not trust herself to think rationally.

"But you've got more of my things and . . . A club meeting you forgot about, huh? Yes, I'll see you tomorrow." Andrea punched the off button. Awkward silence stretched on for what seemed forever.

"Listen, about what just happened between us," Jamal started, then stopped.

Andrea shifted her weight from one foot to the other. "It's obviously a bad idea. I mean, we work together. I'm the boss."

"It was my fault. I kinda got out of hand when you smiled at me. You've got the prettiest eyes I've ever seen and—"

"Don't go there again." Andrea stepped back. She took a deep breath and let it out.

"Of course. I mean, it would just complicate things at the clinic. No way would it ever work." Despite his words, Jamal looked at her with a question in his dark eyes.

Her breasts tingled with the tactile memory of his caress. He'd known just the way she wanted and needed to be touched. She forced herself to look away.

"Exactly. It could affect staff morale," Andrea replied.

He walked close to her but kept both hands at his sides. "Maybe not."

"You know better. The last thing we need is a hot romance interfering with our working relationship. Not to mention, the board would question my judgment, and they'd be right." Andrea rubbed her eyes. "I must have lost my mind."

"Then we've got an even bigger problem. This thing between us isn't going away, Andrea," he said softly. "It just keeps getting stronger. What do you suggest?"

"I don't know."

"If you want me to resign, I will," Jamal said solemnly.

"No!" Andrea said forcefully, then cleared her throat.

"I mean, we're mature and experienced enough to handle it."

"Sure," he said without conviction. "So we'll work together like nothing happened?"

Andrea lifted her chin. "Okay, there's a kind of basic physical attraction. But we both know giving in would be a disaster, so I say we try to stay out of each other's way for a while."

Jamal nodded slowly. "How long do you think it will take? A few days? A week? A month?"

"I don't know," Andrea blurted out in exasperation. "We'll take it one day at a time."

"Okay." Jamal was silent for a few moments.

Andrea did not look at him. She was afraid that her fragile resolve would disintegrate if she did. Still, she could almost cut the tension and ambivalence in the air between them. Both of them were holding back.

"Maybe it would be easier if we talked it out," Jamal said.

"Well . . ." Andrea shook her head.

"In a neutral place. I think trying to ignore it will only make things worse. Let's get it out in the open."

"Maybe discussing the objective reasons we should only be colleagues will help." Andrea risked a glance at him.

"Let's go somewhere, have lunch and talk."

Andrea thought about his suggestion for several seconds. "No, I think you'd better leave."

"Yeah, maybe you're right at that." He took a deep breath, slapped his palms against his thighs, then turned to leave. "See ya round."

"Right."

She watched him walk away. It was sixty seconds of internal debate. The urge to shout for him to come back warred with her practical self. She could not afford to jeopardize her credibility by plunging into a torrid affair with a handsome employee. Not to mention the danger to her sense of emotional security. Fear of another painful betrayal loomed larger than any concern about the opinions of others. If any man was a heartbreak on two legs, it was the alluring, sensuous Jamal Turner. She had to get over this insane lapse in judgment. Andrea stared out the window for another two hours. She didn't get any more unpacking done that day. It would take days for the tingle to fade, if it ever did.

Twelve

Charlene bounced into her living room carrying a tray with glasses of diet cola. "Here we are, darlin'. I'm so glad you called. I just knew we'd have fun once you got home." She beamed at Andrea.

"I thought we should talk."

"Wonderful. You know, I think as adults we can discuss things so much easier." Charlene took the slice of lime from the edge of her glass and dropped it into the soft drink. She sipped from it and sighed.

"I'm so glad you feel that way," Andrea said.

She tapped a foot on the carpet and prepared to broach the subject of Charlene's act at the fund-raiser. It had obviously been aimed at John Mandeville. For days Andrea had debated bringing it up at all. Yet if she was to live in Bayou Blue within a stone's throw of her controversial and flamboyant parents, some kind of understanding was essential. Charlene could not stage such stunts using Andrea as a pawn.

"I understand you and that fine young man are really hot for each other," Charlene said with a sly smile.

Andrea stared at her in surprise, then blushed. "If she's going to spread gossip, Gran should at least get it right. We're co-workers on good terms."

"Very good terms, according to Mama. She—"

"Has been sticking her little nose in my private life and I won't have it," Andrea broke in. "Jamal is nice, but not for me. I'm through with it."

"I don't know why you keep fooling yourself. I could see it in both your eyes that night of the fund-raising party. Hot!" Charlene made a hissing sound and laughed at Andrea's scowl.

"Speaking of that night, just what were you trying to prove?" Andrea folded her arms across her chest.

"Prove? I merely came to support my daughter's efforts on behalf of a worthy cause." Charlene showed no sign of guilt. She sipped from her glass again.

"You went there to prance in front of John Mandeville and his wife. Admit it."

"I could care less what that crumbucket and his crummette think. Believe me." Charlene wore a smug half smile.

"Charlene—"

"I've told you a million times, call me Mother. And what is this tone? You sound like Mama, for goodness' sakes." Charlene brushed back her hair with one hand.

"You knew he'd be there," Andrea pressed on, pointing a forefinger at her.

Charlene lifted a shoulder. "I didn't think about it really."

"Mother," Andrea said through clenched teeth.

"All right, so maybe I did have reason to think he would be there." When Andrea's lips pursed with disapproval, Charlene pouted. "It's a free country, for crying out loud!"

"Listen to me, this isn't a game. The clinic is too important to a lot of people. You could even say it's a lifeline. We can prevent serious illness, even premature deaths, with the care we give. I—"

"Fine, fine. No lectures. Sheesh, you're more like your grandmother every day." Charlene put her glass down.

Andrea sighed with frustration. "And you act more childish the older you get."

"Now, just a minute, young woman, I've had enough of your condescension." Charlene glared at her.

"Charlene—" Andrea bit off the rest of her sentence when Charlene's mouth flew open. "Mother, you never thought that maybe your dramatic scenes might affect my ability to work and live in Bayou Blue?"

"These people know better. John wouldn't allow it, baby." Charlene patted her knee. "Don't you worry."

"You've overlooked something. Victoria Mandeville has influence of her own."

"Pooh! Vicky may be a poor dresser and a little plain, but she's not stupid. She won't cross John, not on this." Charlene smiled with confidence.

Andrea tried to figure her mother out, something she'd been trying to do since childhood.

"You seem very sure of that."

"I am. The board is behind you one hundred percent. Of course, you're doing a fantastic job," Charlene said. "We told them so. It's better to let them take credit for finding a wonderful director."

The word "we" rang in her ears as loud as a bell. Still Andrea kept control. "Thanks. And thank John for me."

"He was happy to do it after I . . ." Charlene's voice faded. Her eyes widened with alarm. "Let me explain."

Andrea stood up. "Oh, you better believe I want to hear an explanation."

"There's that tone again."

"You lied to me from day one. What was your story? Oh yeah, some pal of yours in Health Services told you about the job. I should have known better."

"Andrea, calm down!" Charlene stood and tried to get her attention.

"I don't need or want his help. Why can't you understand that? He wasn't there for me."

"What does it matter? He owed you that much and more! I never lied about wanting you home, wanting to get closer to you." Charlene raised her voice to be heard.

Andrea continued to pace and talk. "I don't want anything from him. Louis Noble was more man than he'll ever be. He was my father in every true sense of the word."

"You listen to me, Andrea. I did it for you."

Andrea whirled around and faced Charlene. "For me? I'm supposed to be happy you crawled to that man again for me?"

Charlene's eyes narrowed. "I've never crawled to him or any man," she snapped.

"John Mandeville never once lifted a finger to help you or openly claim me. We're his dirty little secret. The way he snuck around with you shows what he thought about us."

"You stop it this instant." Charlene shook a finger in her face.

"And you let him do it! You were so happy to bag a

rich man, you didn't care about your self-respect or me!" Andrea shouted. "In fact, I'll bet you used getting me a job as an excuse to see him."

Charlene flinched as if she'd been slapped. Her eyes glistened with tears. "How dare you talk to me this way," she said in a wavering voice. "I've made a lot of mistakes in my life, but you could at least give me some credit. I made a choice to be with John, that's true. But if you think I ever let him debase me, then you don't know me very well."

"You two met in the shadows, ducking and hiding so his white society pals wouldn't be offended." Andrea did not back down.

"We kept our affair secret, yes. It was reality back then, Andrea. We were just kids trying to figure out what we felt and what to do about it. Interracial dating wasn't just frowned on. It could get someone hurt, even killed."

Andrea shivered at the grave tone of Charlene's voice. Her mother's expression was just as solemn, her face pinched. Andrea had never seen her so stricken.

"Did something happen?" Andrea asked quietly.

"Daddy wanted to confront John. It took two of his brothers and all three of your uncles to hold him down when he found out." Charlene sank onto the sofa. "Mama begged them to stay all night to make sure he wouldn't do something crazy. I would never have been able to live with it if he'd been hurt."

"My Lord," Andrea murmured.

"I was young and in love, or at least what I thought was love." Charlene massaged her forehead. "Even after I married Louis, it took me years to realize how stupid I'd been."

Andrea thought of the whispers about Louis and how

his marriage to Charlene had changed his life for the worse. Always the talk ended abruptly when they realized Andrea was nearby. Charlene seemed in the mood to talk openly about Louis and their marriage for the first time. Questions crowded her head, but dread froze her tongue. It was still a subject too painful to broach. Andrea recoiled from probing such a tender wound. Not yet, she told herself. She wasn't ready.

"I didn't mean to be so bitter." Andrea tried to hold back the tears, but they escaped anyway.

Charlene hugged Andrea. "I know I haven't been the best mother, but I do love you."

"And I love you, too, Mommy." Andrea closed her eyes and breathed in the scent of her mother's expensive perfume. "I'm sorry for those awful things I said."

"Shh, don't even think about it again."

Charlene crooned soothingly and cradled Andrea in her embrace. They held on to each other for comfort. Once more they'd successfully backed away from the past.

Charlene went to her bedroom and came back seconds later with a decorative box of facial tissues. They smiled at each other self-consciously and dabbed at their eyes.

"I'm glad we talked about this. I really am," Charlene said between delicate sniffles. "You know, I think we've made a breakthrough. And we didn't have to go on one of those trashy talk shows to do it!"

"Oh, Charlene, you're too much!" Andrea smiled in spite of herself. Her mother could always charm her way out of anything too somber.

"So you're not mad at me." It was a statement of certainty. Charlene was her old self again. "I knew you'd understand."

"Hold on, I didn't say what you did was right," Andrea protested.

"Oh, will you just admit the ends justified the means!" Charlene waved a hand dramatically.

"Charlene," Andrea said with eyebrows raised.

"You're back in the bosom of your loving family, you love your job, and those poor patients are getting the best care they've had in years."

"It's more than the way John Mandeville behaved thirty years ago. He's trouble. Everything he's involved in seems to be shady." Andrea crossed her arms again. "Now I wonder just how much of the gossip about the clinic is true."

"We both know about gossip. We've been the subject of it before." Charlene made a rude noise. "Don't pay attention to it."

"It's more than gossip. The records are a mess and I can't find some valuable equipment." Andrea grimaced. "I'm going to take another look at those files. I was blaming it all on incompetence. Now . . ."

"Of course that's all it was," Charlene piped up. "Listen to me, John is a ruthless businessman and he may break a few rules."

"A few rules? What about that insurance scandal ten years ago?" Andrea stared at Charlene.

"He was never directly linked to anything illegal."

"At least no one could prove it. He's slippery," Andrea said.

Charlene ignored the dig and pressed on. "Andrea, John is far from perfect, but I've known him for a long time. He'll only go so far."

"Which is pretty far. John Mandeville could get away with murder in this state even if they found him standing over a dead body holding a gun," Andrea retorted.

"Don't exaggerate," Charlene said with a wave of her hand. "Besides, John wouldn't waste his time on petty theft."

"Oh, I get it. Because he wears thousand-dollar suits and steals millions, this would be beneath him?" Andrea frowned at her reasoning.

"I never said he was a thief, so don't put words in my mouth." Charlene shook a finger at Andrea's nose. "Shame on you, believing nasty talk about your—"

"*Don't* call him my father," Andrea cut her off. "You know how I feel about that."

"Okay, okay." Charlene sighed. "Anyway, the point is, he's not as bad as you think."

Andrea pressed her lips together. Charlene had tried for the past fifteen years to convince her not to despise John Mandeville. It didn't work. In her own strange twist of logic, Charlene had thought Andrea would turn to him as a father figure after Louis died. At first Charlene had been terrified when Andrea finally found out the truth when she was fifteen. Then she'd openly talked about John. The result was that Andrea's loyalty to Louis, her true father, had deepened and her anger toward Charlene had increased. In her mind Charlene had never appreciated Louis. Charlene's voice broke through her thoughts.

"Well?"

Andrea blinked back to the present. Strange how the feelings from her childhood were still so vivid and strong. "Well what?"

"Are you going to see John?" Charlene leaned forward with a serious expression.

"You two cooked up some scheme. This is too much. You're having an affair with him!" Andrea fell back against the sofa cushions.

"There is nothing between us except that we both want the best for you. I swear it, Drea." Charlene put a hand on Andrea's arm. "He really would like to make up for all those lost years."

Andrea shook her head. "We're not exactly the Brady Bunch. I can't blend into his family."

"Well, of course not. But you can have an adult relationship with him. So it'll be . . . different as far as father-and-daughter relationships go."

"Different is right!" Andrea retorted. "Charlene, what am I going to do with you?"

"Call me Mother." Charlene patted her hand and sat back.

"Oh my God," Andrea said with a groan, and covered her face with her hands.

"You don't have to decide this minute. Think about it." Charlene popped up and went to the kitchen with the tray and glasses. She returned moments later.

Andrea looked at her. "You must know this whole situation is bizarre. The only reason I considered living in Bayou Blue is because he lives miles outside of town."

Charlene sat next to her and smiled with catlike satisfaction. "I figured you'd think of that."

"Wonderful. And here I thought *I'd* made the decision to come home," Andrea said.

"You did, baby. I just helped you to it, that's all," Charlene replied.

"Well, you did make one good point. I can't see John Mandeville caring about petty theft. But I don't see why he cares about a health clinic that serves poor people." Andrea held up a hand when Charlene started to speak. "Please, don't tell me he's just saintly."

"Frankly, he likes being in control the way his daddy

and granddaddy were all those years. Mandevilles have been running things in Lafourche Parish for over eighty years."

"Thank you for that honest explanation." Andrea gazed at her in surprise.

"As I said, you're not a little girl anymore. I want our relationship to be special." Charlene's expression sincere. "And John wants to get to know you, too. He's mellowed in the last few years. Maybe it's because he's not close to any of his children."

"I'll have to think about it some more." *A whole lot more,* Andrea added silently.

"Fine, subject closed." Charlene tilted her head to one side. "Now back to you and that magnificent man. You're so lucky to have him working right next to you all day long."

Andrea glanced away from Charlene. " 'Working' is the right word, nothing else."

"So you keep saying. I can't understand why you're fighting it. If it were me, I'd—" Charlene stopped when Andrea squinted at her.

"There are a half dozen reasons why Jamal is Mr. Wrong."

"I'll bet you can't remember one when he smiles at you, my dear," Charlene said shrewdly.

"Which makes him even more dangerous," Andrea tossed back.

"And it makes you even more scared. You want to reason your way through everything. But the heart doesn't care about reason, logic, or if two plus two equals four."

"I don't want to make another mistake," Andrea said quietly.

Charlene put an arm around Andrea and pulled her close. "There are no guarantees. It'll be an even bigger mistake to pass up what may be the love of your life."

"That's a stretch," Andrea said quickly. "I hardly know him."

Charlene sighed. "I wish there was a man that looked at me with that kind of passion in his eyes."

"Oh, come on," Andrea said. Still she shivered at the memory of how they'd touched.

"Now who's not being honest?" Charlene murmured. She kissed Andrea's cheek lightly, then got up.

"It's almost twelve. Let's grab lunch, maybe a couple of shrimp salads, and talk some more."

Andrea and Charlene spent the rest of the day together. They did indeed talk, but of nothing too deep or serious. Sitting at a patio table at Copeland's on St. Charles, they spent a pleasant Sunday afternoon. As she drove home to Bayou Blue, Andrea pondered the two new men in her life and Charlene's advice on both.

It was another manic Monday. Andrea was grateful for the madness, though. It meant she had not seen Jamal. Andrea was not sure if she could face him without remembering the heat of their embrace. She spent the morning either in her office or Katy's, handling administrative chores. After three hours of paperwork and phone calls, Andrea was able to take a deep breath and a break. Katy brought her a mug of steaming coffee.

"Here you go, boss lady. I figured you needed this after that conversation with the district manager," Katy said.

"Bless you." Andrea accepted the cup and sipped from it. "Wonderful!" She rocked back in her chair.

"I could tell from your expression it wasn't pleasant." Katy leaned against Andrea's desk.

"Not the best way to start the week, no." Andrea started to say more, then stopped. She got up and closed her office door. "Some of the missing equipment is state property. How could two computers, six chairs, a desk, and an X-ray device be misplaced?"

"This office is too small for that, and we both know it." Katy grunted and leaned back in her chair.

"That was Karen Normand's point on the phone. And of course, she brought up the missing coupons." Andrea shook her head slowly. "I told her all we can do is our best to find out what happened, then move on. But . . ." She put the coffee mug down.

"Yeah, we've still got problems." Katy tapped a finger on the side of her ceramic mug. "So what are we gonna do?"

Andrea rocked and thought while Katy sat with a pensive frown on her face. Minutes ticked by as they sipped coffee and pondered solutions to their problems. After a time, Andrea let out a loud sigh.

"Katy, I'm going to document everything that's missing and follow the trail as far as I can." Andrea looked at her. "That includes questioning former staff again."

Katy's eyes widened. "Whoa, does that include Thelma? She and those slimy relatives of hers won't be happy."

"I'm not going to be intimidated. I'll haul her rear end before the board of aldermen if I have to. This involves parish money."

"Uh, you've been away a long time. Let me explain the facts of life around here. Three of her cousins are big-time contributors to election campaigns for at least two police jurors and three town aldermen." Katy pursed her lips.

"I know. So let *them* sweep it under the rug. At least we'll have done everything we could," Andrea said.

"And made some enemies in the process, boss lady."

"They're already pissed with me. Ask me if I care," Andrea said.

Katy grinned crookedly. "You got a point, darlin'. Besides that, they're not dumb enough to mess with Mr. John Mandeville."

Andrea tensed. "What have you heard? What are people saying about him and the clinic?"

"Just that he's the power behind the scenes. But what else is new. He—" Katy broke off and stared at her. "What's wrong? You look like you just ate something bad."

"Nothing. Forget it. Go on with what you were saying."

"You know how he likes to keep his finger in every pie." Katy went on a diatribe about interference from local politicians.

Andrea relaxed a bit as Katy's voice faded into the background. Thank God there was no talk about her and John Mandeville. But then most young folks wouldn't know and their elders would be too scared to talk about it openly. No one would risk Mandeville's legendary wrath. He held too many jobs in his hands. Still she did not care for herself as much she did about the effect on the clinic. What was that old saying about sins of the father? In this case it was mother and father.

"But forget those clowns. We'll focus on what counts, the patients," Katy said.

"Yeah. I'm not really worried about it. I just don't want it to cloud the real issue, which is our impact on health problems." Andrea gazed out her window at passing cars on the downtown street.

"I know." Katy sighed and sipped the last of her coffee. "Have Denny and Jamal made any progress on sorting through those records?"

"I haven't talked to them yet."

"Remember that you're supposed to meet with them. The sooner we have answers for Ms. Normand, the better." Katy stood.

Andrea's stomach fluttered at the thought of being close to Jamal so soon. At least they would not be alone. "I'll meet with them later on today."

"I think things out front have slowed down. Want me to get them for you?" Katy opened the door. "Might as well deal with it now. I know that woman. She's like a dog with a bone."

"Sure," Andrea said after a pause. The last thing she needed was to let Katy or anyone else detect tension between her and Jamal. That would start a whole new set of rumors spinning.

She smoothed the front of her tan cotton shirt. It was neatly tucked into a navy blue skirt. Andrea inhaled and exhaled five times in preparation for his appearance. As seconds ticked by she drummed her fingers on the desk blotter. Realizing it, she laced them together to keep them still. Jamal knocked on the half-opened door and walked in.

"Hi," he said.

Andrea cleared her throat. "Hi."

He entered cautiously, unsure of his reception. "Katy said you wanted to meet with me."

"Yes, and Denny. I want to know how much progress y'all have made with the records." Andrea kept her gaze on a point just above his shoulder. "Is he coming?"

"Denny drove his grandmother to a cardiology appointment. He won't be back until after lunch sometime." He shut the door behind him.

Andrea blinked at the closed door. "Oh."

She bit her lower lip, then looked up at him. He couldn't give her a break, could he? Here he stood, fine as ever in khaki chinos and a sage green knit cotton shirt. The short-sleeved shirt emphasized the rippling muscles in his arms whenever he moved. The familiar craving to touch him hit her full force.

"We could put this off until you can meet with both of us. If you'd be more comfortable, that is."

"No," Andrea said sharply. She lifted her chin. "Why wouldn't I be comfortable with you?"

"I guess I shouldn't assume this is as hard for you as it is for me," he said in a quiet voice.

Andrea picked up an ink pen and fidgeted with it. "How is that?" The flutter of anxiety in her stomach was replaced with anticipation.

"I know we agreed on all the reasons we shouldn't get involved."

"Very good reasons," Andrea said.

"Sure, and I still agree," he rushed to add. Then he sighed. "But keeping the other day out of my mind isn't so easy."

"We knew it wouldn't be." Andrea risked a brief glance at him. Looking into those eyes was too much and she turned her gaze away quickly. "But we did agree that getting involved was a horrible idea."

"We never said 'horrible,' " he replied. "I mean . . ."

"No, I didn't intend for it to come out that way," Andrea put in. "Just that it's not a very good idea. Right?"

Jamal didn't answer right away, but when he did, his response lacked conviction. "Yeah."

Andrea swallowed hard. She squared her shoulders and lifted her chin. "Right. We'll get over it." She forced herself to smile and hoped that it looked more genuine than it felt. "On to business then. I hope you have good news about the records."

Jamal nodded as though silently agreeing to follow her lead. "About the records, let's see." He sat down in the chair across from her. "There's still a lot of missing pieces."

"I said *good* news." Andrea's brows drew together.

"Sorry, but you know what condition the last crew left them in." Jamal lifted a shoulder. "I'm surprised we were able to put together as much as we have. But we still can't exactly track all medications or even find all the invoices we need."

"Darn it!" Andrea slapped an open palm on the desk.

Jamal stared at her. "I thought you weren't that concerned about it."

"The previous director submitted a final report. I was to tie up a few loose ends and then start fresh. At least that's what I was told at first." Andrea grimaced. "But now I'm being held accountable for finding out what happened before I got here."

"They can't really blame you, can they? I mean, it didn't happen on your watch." Jamal leaned forward, elbows propped on his knees.

"Yeah, well, I haven't made friends with some of the decisions I've made recently. Especially about personnel."

"You mean that nurse who was the clinic manager and Shonda. Got ya." Jamal rubbed his chin. "They've both got friends in high places. At lot of Shonda's relatives run errands for some of the local politicians."

"How do you know all this? You've only been in

Lafourche Parish a few months." Andrea raised an eyebrow.

"Almost a year really."

"There are people who've lived in Bayou Blue for twenty years and they're still considered outsiders." Andrea's eyes narrowed. "And the natives don't talk about certain things to outsiders."

"I've made some good friends in the last few months. Especially working here." His brown eyes twinkled. "Folks appreciate it when you help them out."

"And it loosens their tongues, eh?" Andrea laughed.

"Let's just say they like to chat." Jamal tilted his head to one side.

"I may not have said so, but you do a great job around here. And not just with computers and filing. I've seen the way you pitch in and talk to the patients." Andrea smiled at him. When he smiled back the world seemed brighter.

"Thanks. That means a lot to me," he said.

"And I really appreciate the way you've gotten through to Denny."

"He was messing up pretty bad, huh?" Jamal wore a serious expression.

"Between us, I was afraid I'd have to fire him." Andrea shrugged at his raised eyebrows. "He handled a lot of things for Thelma and the rest of those bums. It looked as though he knew more than he was telling."

"But you don't feel that way now?" He gazed at her intently.

"Honestly, the jury is still out. But he's gone a long way toward proving himself. You can take a lot of credit for helping his attitude. He seems to follow your lead," Andrea said.

Jamal shifted in his seat uncomfortably. "Don't give me too much credit."

"I know you spend some of your free time with him."

He looked up at her sharply. "You do?"

"Sure. And I think it's great. He's a smart young man. With the right guidance he could really make something of his life." Andrea's businesslike reserve was slipping fast. She couldn't help it. Jamal was a caring, giving man despite the devilish persona he adopted at will.

"Don't be too sure I'm the right role model." He seemed uneasy with the compliments.

"I wish I could take your picture right now." Andrea grinned. "You look so humble and bashful. I expect you to say 'Aw shucks' any minute."

Jamal shook his head. "No, just being honest. I was a wild kid myself once, and I can't say I'm completely reformed. So don't fit me with a halo just yet."

"Okay, so I'll hold off on the halo. But I still say you're a good guy." Andrea felt a warmth now that went past physical desire. She had a growing respect for him as a man.

"Thanks." Jamal stood up quickly as though eager to escape. "Look, I think I can help you out on those records. Give me a few more days, maybe a week."

"Do what you can. And don't put in too many long hours," she said softly. "You look tired."

Jamal turned to leave, but hesitated. He faced Andrea again. "I haven't been sleeping all that well for the last few days."

"Tell me about it," she murmured. "Too much on my mind, I suppose."

"Yeah, that's probably it." He gazed at her for several

seconds, then started out again. "I'll let you know something as soon as I can."

"Thanks," Andrea called after him. "Then we can get back together."

Andrea stared at the spot where he'd sat for a long time after he was gone.

Thirteen

Lee arrived at the Lafourche Parish sheriff's substation in the small town of Cut Off at 5:50 that evening. He made it a practice to be ten minutes early for appointments he was uneasy about. It gave him a chance to look around. He didn't like the idea that Sheriff Boudreaux was Mandeville's pal.

The building was red brick and small. Three deputies passed him in the space of two minutes, each wearing sober expressions as though intent on fighting crime. Lee looked around for a few minutes. He read the bulletin board and observed the activity around him. At 5:59 he gave his name to a female deputy at the front desk and sat down on a wooden bench to wait. Mandeville strode in seconds later. He grinned at the attractive woman with shocking red hair and freckles that stood out against her fair skin.

"Hey, Tish. How's life treating the cutest law officer in Louisiana?"

"Can't complain, Mr. Mandeville. Well, I could, but who wants to hear?" She grinned. "Go on back."

"All right, darlin'." John turned to Lee and shook hands with him. "Hello, Matthews. Let's go on down to Harley's office."

Mandeville walked on unchallenged. Several deputies spoke to him by name. Lee looked around as he followed him. They went through a large room with desks. Two burly white deputies watched Lee with hooded expressions. Mandeville led them down a short hall at the end of which was a door with a frosted-glass window. Mandeville went in without knocking. The room was small with a gray metal desk in the center. The only items on it were a phone and one file folder. Sheriff Boudreaux stood up when they entered. He was thin and developing a slight paunch. Lee guessed his age at somewhere around fifty. His brown hair was streaked with gray and starting to thin at the top.

"How y'all doin'?" he said in a thick Cajun accent. "I haven't seen you in a while, T-John. And when you do show up, you bring bad news." His bushy brows drew down.

"Hey, Harley. You look good." John slapped his palm into Boudreaux's hand and shook it firmly. "Think of it this way, we're going to help you keep this parish safe."

"Uh-huh." Sheriff Boudreaux grunted and turned his attention to Lee; his frown deepened. "With a private detective?"

"Harley, Lee Matthews is one of the sharpest private detectives around." John pointed to Lee with an affable expression.

"Yeah," Boudreaux said. He shook Lee's hand and

dropped into the chair behind his desk. "So, John, tell me. Why are you a citizen crime fighter all of a sudden?"

John and Lee sat down in two faded pea green vinyl chairs. "I've been working with Bayou Blue to help them get that clinic on its feet."

"Got your hand in everything as usual." Boudreaux's mouth lifted at one end.

"I'm interested in improving the community, yes." John smiled at him. "Unfortunately the clinic hasn't lived up to my expectations."

"What you mean is two or three folks over at the clinic screwed the place up."

"Yes, but it goes deeper than that. Some of the equipment is missing. That's bad enough. But Lee thinks we've got a more serious problem brewing." John nodded to Lee.

"Actually I think a serious problem is about to get a whole lot worse," Lee said.

"How's that?" Boudreaux rocked his chair back and forth. He looked at John instead of Lee.

"I'm pretty sure drugs have been stolen from the small clinic pharmacy," Lee answered in a firm voice.

Boudreaux's easygoing expression disappeared when he looked at Lee. "You got proof?"

"I've been working at the clinic for almost two months. The records are in shambles. We can't be sure all the drugs were given to patients," Lee said.

Boudreaux shrugged. "Don't mean somebody's been stealin' 'em. Could be you just had some sloppy record keepers."

"That's only part of it. One of the employees is involved with a local gang. I think he's been stealing for them."

"We figure they're selling the stuff on the street. A lot of drugs could move through the clinic," John said in a grave tone.

Lee wanted to laugh but kept a straight face. "Yeah, right. Anyway, I told this kid that I want in on the deal. Denny might tell me more any day now."

"But he hasn't said anything yet?" Boudreaux asked.

Lee shook his head. "No. He's more than likely checking it out with Ty'Rance Wilson. He's—"

"I know who he is," Boudreaux broke in. "He's scum, has been since he was a kid."

"Yeah, I get the impression he's a bad guy, real mean," Lee said.

"Humph, I know of more than a few boys carryin' scars he gave 'em," Boudreaux said with a sour grimace. "I'd like nothin' better than to personally escort him to Angola."

Lee nodded. The Louisiana State Penitentiary in Angola, Louisiana, was one of the toughest prisons in the South. It housed some of the meanest convicted felons in the state. Most were carrying sentences of twenty years or more. The percentage of those doing life was high as well.

It was obvious Boudreaux did not like private detectives. That, and the sheriff's personal interest in taking down Ty'Rance, gave Lee hope he could soon pull out of the whole sticky mess. Like most cops, Boudreaux wanted to handle crime in his territory without outsiders butting in.

"What I can do is put together all the facts, throw in a couple of theories, and let you take it from there," Lee said.

"Of course, Lee's built up a relationship with this Denny Kincaid," John put in.

"I've gotten about as much as they need. I'm sure a deputy can be placed inside the clinic and learn more." Lee's eyes narrowed as he looked at Mandeville.

"But that will be starting over. Denny won't confide in somebody new right away, if at all." John turned to Boudreaux, but said no more.

The sheriff glanced from Lee to John. "I think I see where this is headed. Forget it. You know damn well we don't use no civilians to do undercover work."

"Bull! You use informants all the time," John retorted.

"Yeah, but they ain't private eyes," Boudreaux said with a sneer. "The last thing I need is for this fella to get shot up. Him or his next of kin will be suin' the taxpayers for a million bucks."

"Lee knows what he's doing," John said with confidence.

"It don't take nothin' but a week of half-assed trainin' to get a private investigator's license in this state," Boudreaux retorted.

"I was on the Los Angeles police force for five years and an L.A. County sheriff for a year before that," Lee said in a clipped voice.

But Lee was not offended. He'd felt the same when he was a cop. In fact, he welcomed the sheriff's attitude. He would just as soon extricate himself from this case and move on. There was one big downside, but he dodged that train of thought.

Boudreaux looked at Lee with less scorn. "Okay, so you're not the run-of-the-mill idiot gettin' mixed up in po-lice business. I still don't like it."

"Which is understandable. And you're not exactly starting over. You know where to look and what to look for," Lee said.

"On the other hand, T-John here has a point." Boudreaux sat forward and put both elbows on the desk-top. "The Kincaid kid trusts you. We can find out more a lot faster with you in there. Get them boys in jail faster, too."

Lee pressed his lips together. "Maybe."

Lee also understood the advantage of finishing what he'd started with Denny, but he sure as hell wasn't going to say it. Sheriff Boudreaux was silent for several minutes as he pondered his options. Without warning, he picked up the receiver of the phone and punched in three numbers.

"Ted, come in here a minute," he said, then hung up. "Ted Tullier is the chief deputy that covers this end of the parish. He's a smart guy. I want his opinion."

They waited for only a short time before a tall black deputy with a military-style haircut came in. His uni-form, dark khaki shirt and dark brown pants, were spot-less. Ted nodded to the two men before speaking to his boss. Lee concealed his surprise that Boudreaux would put a black man in charge of anything.

"Yeah, Sheriff. What's up?" Ted leaned against the closed door.

Boudreaux summarized the situation in a crisp and concise manner that surprised Lee. His down-home, folksy manner was gone. Lee revised his opinion of Boudreaux. This was no stereotypical old-time southern sheriff.

"Mr. Matthews here is on the inside right now. Ques-tion is this, do we want him to stay or do we take over?" Boudreaux rocked back in his chair and fished a cigar from a desk drawer. He chewed on it without lighting up.

Ted studied Lee for several minutes. His expression gave nothing away. "You went undercover before?"

"Yeah, as an L.A. cop," Lee replied.

"O-kay." Ted's gaze flicked to Sheriff Boudreaux. "You know how I feel about Ty'Rance and his crew. I've been hearing he wants to take his gang to another level."

"Yeah," Boudreaux rumbled around the cigar in his mouth. "Ain't satisfied being small-time scum."

"I'll bet it was him or one of his boys that shot up Lucky Dufour's house the other night." Ted looked at Lee. "I figure it was payback. Lucky is trying to move in on him."

"Drive-bys? Bad sign." Lee knew all too well that rural wanna-be gangsters had begun to pattern themselves on big-city crooks.

Ted nodded. "Ty is trying to organize a bunch of petty thieves and punks. He wants more profit and power."

"Sounds like you've been keeping a close watch on him," Lee said.

"For the last five years at least." Ted turned to the sheriff. "He's closer than we've ever gotten." He nodded in Lee's direction.

"Them boys ain't just a problem for Bayou Blue either," Boudreaux said.

Lee watched the two men, both silent and deep in thought. He recognized the familiar bond between two policemen who worked closely together. Their communication was a form of verbal shorthand. Each understood the other's train of thought so well, long discussions were unnecessary.

"Sheryl," Ted mumbled, more to himself than anyone else.

"Who?" Lee asked.

"Sheryl Fosse, one of the deputies that patrols Bayou Blue and towns in that district. She can be your backup in case things go bad." Boudreaux's eyes narrowed. "Don't tell me you got a problem with female law officers."

"None at all, just asking." Lee grinned.

"Good, 'cause Sheryl will clean your clock if you catch an attitude." Boudreaux grinned back at him.

"I'd do it, but Ty'Rance knows I'm on his tail." Ted grimaced. "But they're used to seeing her patrol the area. He'd get suspicious if I start showing up more."

"Makes sense," Lee said.

Lee listened carefully as the two men discussed shifting around patrols to free Sheryl even more. He was impressed with their use of up-to-date policing techniques. Using new computer programs, they concentrated patrols on problems areas. Boudreaux and Ted exchanged a terse plan.

"So where do we go from here?" Mandeville glanced from Ted to the sheriff.

Boudreaux stood and crossed to him. "You know as much as you need to, John. Don't worry. We gonna get this thing wrapped up and save that clinic for you."

"One thing, Harley, let's make sure Miss Noble isn't pulled into anything dangerous," John said with a pointed look at the sheriff.

Sheriff Boudreaux nodded. "I understand, T-John," he said quietly.

Lee glanced from the sheriff to John. What was that about? Mandeville's protectiveness seemed almost personal. Then Lee thought of Andrea's mother. Maybe John had promised Charlene that he'd take care of her daughter no matter what.

Mandeville stood and smoothed down the front of his expensive sport shirt. "Good. I'll leave it in your capable hands. I've got my hands full with the board about this."

"One way or the other, we'll get it straight." Boudreaux slapped him on the back. "We'll talk with Matthews here a little longer. You don't need to know the dirty details."

Mandeville looked at him. "In other words, get out, eh?" He chuckled. "All right, I'll leave it to the professionals." He waved at them all and walked out of the office.

Lee waited until the door had banged shut. "What was that about the board?"

"John is in a political tug-of-war about the clinic, among other things." Boudreaux waved a hand as though to dismiss the subject.

"Sorta like Ty'Rance and Lucky, two dogs fighting over the same bone," Lee observed. He glanced at Ted, who cleared his throat.

Sheriff Boudreaux's dark eyes flashed irritation for a second, then he forced a smile. "John is a leading citizen. We try to keep leading citizens happy."

"I see," Lee said with a raised eyebrow. He knew very well that the sheriff's job was as much politics as law enforcement.

"Keeping down crime is our number one priority," Sheriff Boudreaux said in a clipped military tone. He clamped his jaws shut.

"I know that," Lee said without a hint of sarcasm. Police chiefs all over the world had to juggle doing the right thing and pleasing power brokers.

Boudreaux let out a long breath. "John ain't a bad fella, just used to getting what he wants, when he wants it. Know what I mean?"

"I know," Lee said.

"So let's talk about how this thing is gonna play out." Boudreaux went back behind the desk and sat down again.

Lee paid close attention to the men as they gave him more complete information on Ty'Rance's background and the gang. Although Ted did most of the talking, the sheriff filled in a few blanks as well. They finished an hour later, and Lee drove back to his office in Harahan, but his mind was still in Bayou Blue.

Denny did not impress him as capable of holding his own with Ty'Rance. The young man wanted to make fast money and prove his manhood. Still, Lee did not sense he was ruthless and unfeeling the way the men who surrounded Ty'Rance were. At least Denny had not reached that point yet, but a lifetime of disappointments and hard knocks certainly gave him the potential. Denny's feelings of discontentment and resentment simmered just beneath the surface. He was on the edge and Ty'Rance was ready to give him a push. Lee thought of Andrea.

She was grateful to him for taking time with Denny and he was setting a steel trap that would close on the kid. Guilt gnawed at him.

He could almost smell the alluring scent of her perfume, a light floral fragrance that she wore to work every day. Andrea seemed to think of Denny as a younger brother she was determined to save. Of course, it could all be an act. Lee gripped the steering wheel. He wondered once more if he was allowing himself to be lulled by her beauty.

Before meeting Andrea Noble, Lee would have sworn that was impossible. Growing up on the meanest streets in South Central had left him with a tough outer shell. His childhood had been cut short as a result. The one thing Lee had learned was to be wary. His practice was to keep everyone at a safe distance—less chance of getting stabbed in the back. Yet being with Andrea day in and day out was messing with his head. Suddenly he felt his life was an emotional desert. It was so good to joke with her about experiences they'd shared or listen to her talk about her dreams for the clinic. Lee yearned to be able to talk with her about his goals, too. But he couldn't, not without lying to her. He couldn't even tell her who he really was.

"This damn case." Lee pounded the steering wheel in frustration.

In the past few years, Lee had longed to meet a woman like Andrea. Someone he could let in. And now he couldn't even be sure she was for real. Once more he forced himself to admit the possibility that she could be involved in a crime. Lee's stomach tightened. If she wasn't, Andrea wouldn't forgive his role in bringing Denny down along with the gang. He'd have to get over this infatuation. No way could it lead to anything lasting. Lee knew all about good-byes. This would be just one more for him. But he still had his son. Lee vowed to take off the coming weekend and drive to Houston. The thought of seeing Jake's eyes light up and hearing him shout, "Hi, Dad!" soothed his ragged nerves. At least for now.

Andrea sank onto the sofa at Gran's house. The pattern of yellow daisies and green leaves on the fabric soothed her. It had been weeks since she'd been able to take a deep breath and relax like this. The scent of baked chicken, hot rolls, and lemon furniture polish was like a hearty "Welcome home!" Although she did not regret getting her own place, her apartment seemed sterile. Long hours at the clinic prevented her from adding the lived-in domestic touches to it. There were at least five boxes she still had not unpacked.

"I knew it. You work too much. Now you're about to collapse." Gran squinted at her. "This is the first time I've seen you in almost a month."

"Two weeks," Andrea muttered.

"Still too long. And you're losing weight." Gran leaned forward in the overstuffed chair that matched the sofa. "These clothes are hanging off you, girl."

"They are not," Andrea said. She looked down at the dusty pink skirt and white blouse. "Anyway, I could stand to lose a few pounds."

"Nonsense. Men like a woman with meat on her hips." Gran slapped one of her hips to illustrate her point.

"Then I shouldn't have any trouble with dates," Andrea quipped. "And I'll pass on those creamy mashed potatoes dripping with gravy, thank you very much."

"What foolishness! You been hanging around them northern women too long."

"Gran, you're a southern snob," Andrea teased. "Anyway, I'll have a helping of your delicious okra and tomatoes and a salad."

Gran wrinkled her nose. "Suit yourself. Supper will be ready in a little bit." She squinted at Andrea again.

"Now what?" Andrea tucked one leg under her.

"Speaking of dates, have you and Jamal been out yet?"

"Will you let me take care of my own love life?"

"What love life? I'll never get to argue with Charlene about your wedding at this rate," Gran retorted with a grunt.

"I refuse, absolutely refuse, to have this discussion, so drop it," Andrea said in a crisp tone. She glared at her grandmother.

Gran drew her shoulders up and clasped her hands in her lap. "Fine. Snap at me for being concerned about your happiness."

"That's enough, Gran dear," Andrea said through clenched teeth.

"You're so grouchy because I'm talking sense. You'll be sorry you passed up that prize of a man, missy," Gran went on.

"I'm still bruised from the last 'prize' I had." Andrea grimaced at the thought of her ex-husband. "Or would you prefer I heal quickly, like my mother? She moves to a new man at the speed of light."

"You've got a different temperament from Charlene, always had." Gran grew thoughtful for a few seconds. "But she's not as bad as all that."

"Please! You always said Charlene is too flighty, ready to jump from one thrill to the next." Andrea squirmed down against the cushions to get more comfortable.

"I know, but I wasn't always right about Charlene," Gran murmured, more to herself than to Andrea.

Andrea looked at her sharply. Gran's expression was somber. She seemed to be looking inward. "That's a switch. I remember some of the shouting matches you two had."

"I know, and I'm not saying she didn't make mistakes," Gran said.

"More than just mistakes, Gran. Charlene went after what she wanted no matter who got hurt."

Gran looked at her, her dark eyes filled with sympathy. "I know you blame her for making Louis unhappy.

But, sugar, there's two people in a marriage. Louis played a part in some of what went wrong."

"Sure, he didn't lie down and let her walk on him. She wanted money and fine clothes. Daddy was a working man who didn't have cash to throw around." Andrea had a bitter taste in her mouth. "I don't blame him for losing his patience and his temper."

"Don't judge your mama so harshly, cher. Louis had problems even before they were married." Gran picked at a loose thread on her flowered shirt.

Andrea frowned slightly. "I never heard anything like that. What kind of problems?"

Gran was quiet for a moment as she continued to fiddle with her skirt. "He was always kinda unusual even as a boy. But Lord, Louis was crazy about Charlene! He followed her around like a puppy from the time they were ten years old. Never stopped either. Girls were wild for him, too. He had thick black hair, long eyelashes, and hazel eyes. But he didn't notice any girl but Charlene. Like to killed him when his folks moved to Houston when he turned thirteen."

Andrea remembered the tall, gentle man with the soothing voice. "Daddy was sweet and sensitive. Too sweet for Charlene."

"Yeah, 'sensitive' is one way to put it. You know he came back to live with his aunt two years later just to be near Charlene. Course, she was boy-crazy by then." Gran shook her head.

"Daddy never stopped loving her, even when she hurt him," Andrea said in a quiet, strained voice. "I remember how he enjoyed talking about the first time he saw her. His face would glow."

Gran shook her head. "It was almost too much. I

mean the way he loved her so hard," Gran said in an odd tone.

Andrea gazed at her. "He was devoted and loving. Not what I'd call faults in a man."

"Charlene used to say she felt like she couldn't breathe sometimes. I would tell her she oughta appreciate the boy more. Funny how time changes things. Years later I saw her side. It was too late by then." Gran rubbed her hands together. "Maybe things would have turned out different if I'd understood."

Andrea looked at her. "I don't understand what you mean."

"Charlene and I argued over every little thing. She tried to tell me about Louis, even dropped hints about John Mandeville. Course, she didn't come out and say who he was," Gran added quickly when Andrea's eyes went wide. "I'd talk up Louis. I must have told her a hundred times to be thankful such a kind boy loved her so much."

Andrea felt a stirring of unease but did not know why. Maybe it was the tense expression Gran wore as she talked about Louis. "And you were right."

Gran gazed at her. "Louis made Charlene his whole life, and not in a good way. Not for either of them. Charlene can't be tied down. Even as a baby she liked to run free. I never was happy letting her be who she was. I tried to keep her locked up when she was a child. But she'd sneak out and go down the road or climb trees. I tried to change her. So all we did was fuss and fight. Didn't make a bit of sense." Gran stared into the past.

"Charlene grew up and made her own choices. You're not to blame for the way she treated Daddy," Andrea insisted.

"I'm not saying I am." Gran looked at Andrea. "What I am saying is you need to understand your mama better. I'm trying to explain why she's like she is."

Andrea's grimace softened. "Honestly, I don't think she's intentionally malicious. Charlene doesn't consider consequences. She sees what she wants and goes after it."

"That may be true, cher. But like I said, there's always more than one side to a story." Gran pressed her lips together.

Andrea felt a chill as though a winter breeze had swept into the room. Gran's words sounded ominous. "Are you trying to tell me something?"

Gran was silent for almost a full minute. She sighed. "I'm just saying it's not fair to hold a grudge against your own mama. You were just a baby. You don't know everything that went on between your mama and papa, no one does."

Andrea stared at Gran. "There *is* something you're not telling me."

"Have you ever asked her about what happened between her and Louis or John Mandeville?"

"Neither of us would know where to begin. I'm not sure it would change anything."

Gran leaned toward Andrea. "Charlene is scared of losing you forever. It's up to you, baby. Talk to her."

Andrea was surprised at Gran's attitude. She'd always been so critical of her middle child. It intrigued Andrea. Yet it frightened her, too.

"I'll think about it, Gran," Andrea said.

Lee studied the drug logs and pretended not to notice Denny had entered the records room. Denny stepped behind a tall metal cabinet. He watched Lee for a moment, then backed out and came down the hall again, this time making noise so as to be heard. Lee shoved the log back in a drawer.

"What's up?" Denny said.

"Nothing," Lee replied with a grin. "Just working hard."

"Got some people that wanna meet you." Denny leaned against the desk and stuck his hands in his pants pockets. "I told 'em about your contacts."

Lee remained calm despite the adrenaline rushing through his veins. "Sure. What time?"

"Not tonight. Friday. I'll let you know what time later," Denny said tersely. He nodded with a grave expression.

"Sounds good." Lee held out his hand. Denny slapped his palm against his and grasped it tight before he let go.

"See ya." Denny strolled off.

Before Lee could process this latest development, Andrea appeared in the doorway. He smiled. Her thick hair was tousled. Lee could imagine her tugging at it while working. The woman was sexy no matter how she tried to hide it.

"Hey," she said, "didn't I instruct you not to work long hours?"

"I don't always follow orders. My teachers used to say I had a problem with authority." Lee stacked four computer disks in a small storage container.

"Evidently." Andrea walked further into the room. She glanced around, picked up a few files, and gave them a cursory inspection. "Denny tells me you've got over half the patient histories stored in the database."

"Yep. I'm up to *M*. It should be downhill from here.

There sure are a lot of Landrys and Leblancs," Lee joked.

"Don't celebrate yet. We're big on Marchands, Oubres, Thibodeauxs, and Trahans." Andrea smiled at the mock look of horror on his face.

"Damn! I wish you hadn't told me that," Lee said, and put a hand to his forehead.

"Wait, I forgot about the Ricards and the Roussell clan."

"You're gonna give me nightmares." Lee smiled back at her.

Andrea had a devilish twinkle in her brown eyes. "Oh, and then there's—"

Lee put a finger on her lips. "Stop. I'll be up all night muttering letters of the alphabet."

Her lips were warm and supple to the touch. They stared into each other's eyes. Lee remembered the feel of her silky skin. Opening her blouse had been like unwrapping a lovely package. His breath caught when he realized she was staring at his mouth. She felt the same way.

Andrea took his hand down slowly and held it. "Sorry," she said softly. "Didn't mean to disturb your sleep."

"Too late, you've already done it," Lee whispered, his voice hoarse.

Lee closed his fingers around her hand. He did not want to let go. Everything else suddenly faded into the background. The investigation, Denny, and the clinic were minor details he would deal with later.

"So what do we do now?" he said.

Andrea blinked as though the question confused her. "We had this talk a couple of weeks ago." She made only a token effort to pull her hand away.

For Lee, the most important thing in his world at that moment was to hold on to her. "We didn't really settle the question, and I can't stop thinking about you."

"All the same complications apply," Andrea murmured.

"Then I guess we better talk again," Lee said quietly. "Dinner?"

Andrea blinked as though trying to wake up. "I don't know."

He needed to be with her. "Please."

She hesitated for only a moment, then nodded. "Okay, I'll get my purse."

"I'll wait here."

Lee watched her back up a few steps, then turn and leave. When he was alone, unease crept through him. Every minute he was near her, the tangle grew more knotted.

She came back, her hair now brushed into place. His gaze traveled down the curve of her chin, traced the graceful sweep of her neck and the round outline of her breasts beneath her blouse. He thought of holding Andrea again so close he could feel her heartbeat. The prospect made any possible complications seem irrelevant.

"I'm ready," Andrea said.

"Me, too," Lee replied. He followed her out.

Fourteen

"I knew it was a good idea to let you decide," Lee said. He looked around.

"This place has excellent food and a nice view." Andrea nodded at the floor-to-ceiling windows ahead. "Bayou Lafourche is gorgeous when the sun sets."

They stood in the lobby of Savoie's Seafood House, waiting for a table. The restaurant was crowded even though it was still early. All around was the clink of silverware and the murmur of dinner conversations. A smiling waiter approached and they were taken to a table near a window.

The waiter placed the menus on the white tablecloth. "How is this? You could wait for a terrace table if you prefer."

"This is fine with me," Andrea said when Lee looked at her.

Lee held Andrea's chair, gazing at the mass of dark

hair that framed her lovely face. He resisted the temptation to bury his face in it. Instead he sat down next to her.

"The food is legendary, even for south Louisiana," Andrea said. She turned and seemed startled to find his face inches from hers.

"I'm not all that hungry. But I'll take your recommendation about what to order." Lee savored being so close to her.

"I'll have the broiled shrimp. They've got great softshell crab," Andrea said as she looked at him.

"Sounds good. I'll have that as well." Lee was not thinking of food.

"And their trout is the best for miles around."

"Sounds even better," Lee replied.

Andrea tilted her head to one side. "You're not even looking at the menu."

Lee picked it up, read quickly, and put it back down. "Trout it is."

Andrea laughed as the waiter came over again. He took their orders and darted off. "You don't linger over decisions, I see."

"Not when I find what I want," Lee said promptly.

Andrea looked away. "Are we talking about dinner?"

"Not entirely, no."

An awkward silence fell between them. Lee could not call back the words now. He'd taken a wild leap into unknown territory. His attraction to Andrea was extraordinary. Still, his old instinct urged him to be cautious. He pushed down his hunger and sat back from her.

"This is the worst timing in the universe," Andrea blurted out. "You know what I mean?"

"You better believe it." Lee heaved a deep sigh. He thought of the circumstances surrounding their relationship.

"But we're here anyway." Andrea toyed with the edge of her linen napkin.

"Yeah." Lee stared down at the tabletop as though looking for answers.

"So," Andrea said.

"So," Lee echoed.

The waiter appeared with two salad plates heaped with romaine lettuce. "Here you are. Enjoy." He flashed a professional smile before leaving.

"You were saying?" Andrea glanced at Lee.

Lee cleared his throat. "No, you go on."

"I . . ." Andrea pursed her lips. "Darn, this is hard! Typical, you know? Just when you think you've got your life in some kind of order, pow!"

"No kidding. I was finally sure I knew at least some of the answers after my divorce. No more letting emotions rule my head."

"Me, too." Andrea smiled softly. "I believe it's called deluding yourself."

"But I never expected to find someone like you here. Hell, I didn't expect to find you at all." Lee had had no idea such a woman existed, a woman who could set him on fire with a glance.

Andrea lifted a shoulder. "Neither one of us was looking."

"But we found each other anyway. Bad timing and all." Lee looked at her again and let the world slip away.

"We could fight the feeling and avoid each other at work." Andrea looked at him for a response.

"I've been trying that for weeks," Lee said quietly. "Hasn't worked so far." He took her hand in his. "I can't just be a friend, Andrea."

"I know." She stared at their entwined hands.

They sat silent for a long time, content to touch. The

warmth from her skin seeped into his body and his heart. Andrea was the woman he wanted, and he wondered if it was fair to her under the circumstances. He knew deep down it was selfish. Yet he'd waited all his life to feel this complete.

The evening summer sky was bright orange mixed with blue. Sunshine slanted across the tables, throwing shadows across the dining room. The scenery added a perfect setting for this moment.

Lee reluctantly let go of Andrea's hands when the waiter came over with their entrees. The man glanced at their untouched salads.

"Was the salad to your liking?" he asked.

"Yeah. Just leave them here," Lee said.

"Sure thing," the waiter said. He rearranged the table and put the larger dinner plates in front of them. "Enjoy," he repeated, and left.

"I've got an idea," Lee said. "Let's just be discreet for a while. I mean, no need to rush."

Andrea raised her eyebrows. "I always thought you were bold. The kind of guy who did as he pleased and to heck with what people thought."

"I can be sensible once in a while," Lee tossed back. "I can keep a secret."

"Hmm, then I've got a lot to learn about the real Jamal Turner." Andrea smiled at him.

Lee's stomach churned. "Right." He looked away quickly.

"Did I say something wrong?" Andrea put a hand on his arm.

He forced a smile that he hoped looked more genuine than it felt. "No, of course not."

"Then tell me what you're thinking."

"It just hit me that you're the most beautiful woman

in the world and you want to be with me. I don't deserve it," Lee said. He did not have to pretend. The emotion behind his words was very real.

Andrea brushed her fingers along his jawline. "Don't be silly. You're a sweet man beneath that cocky attitude," she said softly.

"I hope you remember that later when the demon comes out," he teased. Yet he caught her hand and held it tightly.

"The demon?" she said, cocking an eyebrow. "Is that what they call it these days?"

Being with her and talking this way tore down his defenses. He wanted her to love him so hard, all would be forgiven. Was there such a thing? Lee had long ago concluded that love everlasting was a fantasy for fools. Only chumps fell in love so hard they couldn't think straight. For his part, he'd always been in the driver's seat when it came to women. Until now, that was. Here he sat going against his survival instincts, all because of a pair of big brown eyes and full lips attached to a no-nonsense nurse of all things. Yet he could not stop if he wanted to, and he did not want to stop. Not when she looked at him that way. He'd just have to damn well find a way to deal with all the complications.

"I think I can handle it," Andrea said with a half smile. "Now let's eat this great food before it gets cold. Then I'm going to take you for a ride to my favorite spot."

"Where is it?" Lee let go of her hand and picked up his fork.

"About a fifteen-minute drive from Gran's house. We can leave my car at my apartment and take yours." Andrea tasted a small slice of roasted potato served with the shrimp.

"Sounds good."

The next hour and a half felt right. They seemed to both be relieved to get past the stage of fighting their mutual attraction. Now they could relax. Beneath the surface, they had more in common than either had thought. Lee made his first delightful discovery about her. Andrea had a quirky sense of humor beneath that starched exterior. For two hours they swapped jokes and talked about other shared interests. Andrea's laughter came from deep in her throat and sent chills up his spine. He loved the sound of it. The waiter came and removed their empty plates.

"Let's see, we've covered food, favorite colors, and vacation spots," Lee said as he held up three fingers. "What's left?"

"I hope you love the blues, 'cause I'm a blues fanatic," Andrea said.

"You know, I listen to it every once in a while since I moved south. R and B and hip-hop are more my thing." Lee put his arm around her chair.

"I can take you to the best nightclubs in the state and make you a convert like that." Andrea snapped her fingers.

"I'll bet you can," Lee said with a laugh. "Name the time and place. I love New Orleans."

"I'm talking about right here in Lafourche Parish, cher. And Baton Rouge has blues artists that are international stars."

Andrea went on with a spirited lecture on the blues clubs and festivals of south Louisiana. Lee listened to most of it, but mostly enjoyed seeing the sparkle in her eyes. Andrea stopped in midsentence and looked at him.

"I'm chattering on like a squirrel on speed. Sorry." She blushed.

"Don't be. I'm enjoying every minute," Lee said. "And learning a lot, too."

"You're being tactful. But I did warn you I'm a fanatic. Now it's your turn." Andrea leaned toward him and lowered her voice. "Tell me your deep, dark secrets."

He laughed. "I'm a pretty shallow dude. Something you pointed out to me once."

Andrea's mouth flew open. "No I didn't!" she protested.

"Well, you sorta implied it a couple of times. All muscle, no brains or sensitivity. That's what you thought, admit it." Lee stared at her hard.

"I . . ." Andrea squirmed under his scrutiny.

"Andrea, tell the truth," he prodded, enjoying putting her on the spot.

"All right, I did," she admitted. "But you thought I was a stuck-up, rigid nitpicker." Andrea pointed a finger at his nose.

"I never thought you were stuck-up," Lee said with a grin.

"Funny, very funny," Andrea said, and gave his arm a playful swat.

"So we both made terrible first impressions." Lee gazed at her hair and face. "Now we know better, or at least we're starting to."

"Yes," Andrea murmured.

"A pretty good start at that."

Lee leaned close until their lips met. Awareness of where they were brought him up short. Andrea sat back and took a deep breath.

"We should go before it's dark. You won't be able to see what I want to show you."

"Let's hit it then," Lee said.

In short order, they paid the bill and drove to her apartment. Andrea parked in her reserved space and joined Lee in his car. She gave him directions as they drove through the countryside. They rode with the windows down, zydeco music blasting from the radio. Andrea tried to teach him to sing along in Creole. They were weak with laughter after only one song. Andrea broke off from the lesson and pointed down a gravel road.

"Turn here," she said.

Lee looked around. On both sides of the road stretched tall grass, palms, and swamp oak. Dusk combined with the thick foliage made the woods seem darker. Grayish green Spanish moss hung down from tree branches like long beards. Crickets chirped and birds called to each other from high overhead. The scene was almost mystical.

"This is what I love about Louisiana. You can escape to a subtropical paradise by driving a few miles and taking one turn down an old dirt road."

"Yeah, I missed it more than I realized," Andrea said. "Not that I've had much time to enjoy it. The clinic—"

"Don't even mention the you-know-what," Lee broke in. "This is your time to relax. I'm going to see to it that you do."

"Is that so?" Andrea smiled at him.

"Believe it. No talk about work, records, or patients."

"Yes, sir," Andrea said, and saluted. "Just keep following the road. We're almost there."

Lee followed another curve in the twisted road and came to a clearing. He blinked in amazement. There was a gravel parking lot full of cars to their left. Straight ahead was a sprawling old house set on the banks of Bayou Blue. Lights and music spilled from the windows. Lee turned off the engine.

"This is fantastic!" Lee stared wide-eyed. "What is this place?"

"Poppa's House of Funky Blues. Poppa's for short." Andrea laughed. "You should see your face right now. You look like you just stumbled on some magician's castle."

"Poppa must be a magician to have this kind of place in the middle of nowhere." Lee grinned.

"No magician, just an old south Louisiana bluesman who got tired of life on the road. This property has been in his family for four generations. His great-grandfather built the house."

"Wow," was all Lee could say.

"He was my dad's best friend. Come on." Andrea tapped his arm.

They got out of the car and walked to the low-slung porch leading inside. There was a white banner with blue letters hanging over the front door. It said DON'T COME IN IF YOU AIN'T READY TO PARTY! Andrea nodded to it.

"Well, can you past the test?" She stared at him.

"Oh, yeah," Lee said smoothly.

They stepped inside what must have once been the living and dining rooms. Tables were arranged on either side of the door, with a small dance floor in the middle. An archway indicated that a wall had been taken down. Straight ahead was a raised semicircular platform. A four man band played a bouncy blues song that had the audience snapping their fingers, nodding, and tapping their feet. A tall black woman with shocking red hair met them. She balanced a tray of beer bottles on one hand.

"Hi, I'm Bébé. Y'all sit anywhere. I'll be back in a minute." She sashayed off on long, graceful legs.

Andrea walked to a table near the window. A breeze blew in, making the white gauze curtains flutter. Ceiling fans helped keep the interior of the club comfortable. The band ended the tune to applause.

"What do you think so far?" Andrea said once they were seated.

"I'm wondering how you could stay away from this place," Lee said. He propped both elbows on the rough surface of the round table.

"There was a lot of work at the . . ." She paused when he held up a finger. "At the you-know-what," Andrea finished.

Bébé appeared right on cue with a basket of mixed nuts and pretzels. She put it on the table. "What can I get y'all?"

"Two Abita beers," Andrea said promptly. She turned to Lee. "You'll love it. It's a Louisiana brew made from spring water in the famous Abita Springs."

"Got ya." Bébé was off again.

"Man, and I thought I knew Louisiana." Lee smiled at her.

"No way. New Orleans is more like a neo-European city. You gotta get the whole flavor of the Bayou State, cher," Andrea teased.

As if to confirm her statement, the band started to play again. This time the song was slow and poignant. The lights in the nightclub muted. A miniature glass oil lamp was on the table between them. Andrea's brown eyes glowed from its tiny reflected flame.

"I'm looking forward to future field trips," Lee said softly.

Her mouth curved up deliciously. "Discreet field trips?"

He leaned forward and kissed her lips. "Absolutely. Now let's forget about the world. Dance with me."

Lee led her by the hand onto the dance floor. There were other couples dancing, but he didn't pay attention to them. He held Andrea in his arms and let the rest of the world go away. There was only the music, the way her body perfectly fit against him, and the sweet smell of her perfume. She put both arms around him with her hands holding his shoulders. Her head rested against his chest. Her hips swayed in time to the music, matching his rhythm as well.

Lee felt himself harden slowly, desire pumping through him. He'd never been so aroused by a simple dance before. Andrea snuggled closer, molding her pelvis against him. Lee choked back a moan and gripped her tighter. Andrea raised her face to him and he kissed her lips, this time hard. He tried to satisfy a lifetime of hunger with the sweetness she provided. Yet a thousand years of kissing her would never be enough. Lee knew what he'd only suspected and feared the first time they touched. He would love her even if it broke his heart.

"Ahem!"

A deep, gruff male voice startled them both and broke the spell. Andrea looked over Lee's shoulder and smiled. Lee scowled and turned toward the source of a most unwelcome interruption.

"What?" Lee growled.

"The song is over, that's what. Y'all the only ones still on the floor," the husky man said. His bushy eyebrows went up to his receding hairline as he glanced at Andrea. "Hey, baby girl."

"Poppa Ben!" Andrea let out an embarrassed laugh. "You look wonderful."

"For an old man, you mean. Let me get a look at you." Poppa Ben took a step back and put his fists on his hips. "Pretty, just like your mama. And who is this?" He nodded to Lee.

"Jamal Turner, meet Ben 'Poppa Blues' Lavergne." Andrea went to Poppa and kissed his cheek.

Lee smiled and shook hands with him. The older man's grip was strong. "How ya doin'?"

"Doin' real good for a relic." Poppa tightened his grip to prove his point. He stared at Lee steadily.

"Yep, I can tell," Lee said. He extracted his hand and flexed it.

"Cut it out, Poppa. I'm not eighteen anymore," Andrea said, and pinched his arm. She turned to Lee. "Poppa used to intimidate my dates."

"I'm just sayin' hello is all." Poppa wore an innocent expression.

"Sure you were," Andrea quipped.

"Nice to meet you, sir. Anybody that looked after Andrea is all right with me." Lee grinned at him.

"There you go. I got a feelin' we gonna be buddies." Joe clapped a huge hand on Lee's shoulder that made him rock back on his heels.

Lee blinked from the impact. "I'm really glad to hear it."

"Let's sit down. Hey, Bébé, bring us some beer," Poppa shouted.

"On it's way," she called back.

Poppa led them back to their table and they all sat down. They laughed and talked for a time. He was a jovial teddy bear of a man. Yet he skillfully questioned Lee about his job, education, and family history, all with a pleasant smile. Lee mused that Poppa Ben would be an asset to any private detective agency.

"How's Charlene? Haven't seen her in over three months." Poppa sipped from a mug of beer.

"I can't believe Mama's been here at all!" Andrea said with a look of surprise. "She's always saying how dull it is in Bayou Blue."

"Been comin' to my place off and on for the last couple of years at least. Guess she's gettin' homesick in her old age," Poppa said with a chuckle.

"I wouldn't advise you to mention old age to Charlene," Andrea warned.

Poppa laughed heartily. "Oo-wee, she'd take my head off! Look, I better get back to work. You two have a good time. Not that you won't." He winked at them and laughed again when Andrea blushed.

"Poppa Ben," she muttered, and pursed her lips.

"I remember being young and crazy in love." Poppa clapped his hands together. "I'm gonna have the guys play a special dance tune just for you. Take care of our baby girl, son. Don't make me come lookin' for you." Poppa wore a mock scowl to punctuate his pretend threat.

"No, sir. I don't want that!" Lee held up both hands.

" 'Bye, sweet," Poppa said.

He planted a kiss on Andrea's cheek, shook hands with Lee, and ambled off. He went to where the band leader sat drinking at the bar and said something to him. The man gave a thumbs-up sign to Andrea and Lee.

"Poppa is too much," Andrea said with a smile of warm affection.

"He seems like a good man." Lee waved to him, then turned to Andrea.

"He is. Poppa Ben and Daddy were closer than a lot of brothers. They were so much alike." Andrea gazed across the room at him.

Lee recognized the pang of loss in her expression. "You were still a kid when your dad died, huh?"

Andrea nodded. "Almost ten. He was killed in a car accident."

"That's rough. At least you've got good memories, though." Lee drank from his glass.

She looked at him. "And you don't?"

He shook his head. "Nope," he said in a clipped tone.

"That bad, huh?"

"He was no-good dirt," Lee said, his voice flat.

"And your mother?"

"I used to blame her for a lot of what happened, but she did her best. She went through a lot for us." Lee stared down at the table.

"Yeah, I guess there comes a time when you have to stop blaming your parents." Andrea leaned forward until her arms rested on the tabletop.

"I guess you're right," Lee said. He reached out and she placed her hand in his.

Without saying more, they'd reached an understanding. Later they would talk about the past. For now, no more needed to be said.

At that moment a long, sensuous note came from the guitar of the bandleader. The sound seemed to reach out and wrap itself around them. Lee and Andrea got up at the same time. They came together without saying a word. Once again Lee burned at every point where their bodies touched. Andrea rested her lovely face against his chest and held him. Lee wanted to protect her from all harm. He rubbed her back as he pressed his lips to her forehead. In seconds desire flooded him with such force he felt dazed. Andrea looked up, her brown eyes gleaming.

"I'd like to leave now," Andrea whispered.

They stopped moving to the music. "Are you sure?" Lee whispered. He brushed his lips against the smooth skin of her cheek.

"Yes."

Poppa came over and they said good-bye. They drove back to her apartment. The night closed around them, making the inside of his car intimate and cozy. Jazz played softly on the radio. The closer they came to her apartment, the more Lee's heart raced.

He followed her inside without hesitation. He made no protest when she turned on the compact disc player or dimmed the lights. Lee did not hold back when she came into his arms with a sigh. His blood pounded wildly through his veins when she guided his hand to her breast and kissed him. His fingers caressed her until the nipple pebbled through the fabric of her blouse. He moaned deep in his throat as he hardened beneath the gentle stroke of her fingers.

Andrea used her other hand to unbutton her blouse. Lee's hands moved on their own, pushing sleeves down her arms until she was free of the garment. He traced a line with his lips down her neck and to the soft mounds of flesh above black lace.

She pulled his shirt from his pants and ran her fingernails along his spine. Lee gasped at the sensation and buried his face between her breasts. They undressed each other slowly, savoring each moment. Lee unhooked her bra, then pulled back to admire her full brown breasts, the nipples peaks of milk chocolate. He leaned forward and licked them hungrily. Through a luscious haze, he felt her hands rubbing his thighs. Andrea grasped the bands of his briefs and pulled them down. Impatient to be near her, Lee broke off caressing her to yank them off. He stood still and looked at her. She wore only the black lace panties that matched her bra. Her skin was like luminescent burnished gold in the shadow of one small lamp. She walked toward him and caressed the head of his erect penis. Lee groaned and pulled her to him. He buried his face in fleecy curls of thick brown hair that smelled of jasmine.

"Are you very sure?" Lee said hoarsely.

It was the only note of caution he could muster. He'd reached the limit of his self-control. Still, he gently rubbed one of her nipples with his thumb to be sure of her answer. She did not disappoint him.

"Yes, yes, yes," Andrea sighed between peppering delicate kisses across his chest.

She used both hands to drive him senseless, alternately squeezing and stroking him. Lee picked her up and Andrea wrapped her legs around his waist. They kissed and caressed as he carried her to the bedroom. Andrea let go long enough for him to sit on the bed. She pushed him on his back and straddled him. He relished the way she took control.

"Nice bedspread," Lee mumbled between kisses. "Get rid of it."

"No time," Andrea said, rocking her hips against him until he was senseless.

Lee nipped her flesh gently as she moved against him. "You feel so good," he gasped.

Andrea kissed his shoulders while combing her fingers through his hair. Lee groaned when her fingers closed around him. Her tongue traced a fiery trail down his chest and back up again to his neck. She stood and took off her panties with slow deliberation, staring into his eyes as she pushed them down her hips and thighs.

Then she disappeared into her bathroom and came back with a square foil packet. He nodded when she held it up. Andrea tore it open and surprised him. She knelt in front of him and expertly fitted the condom over his penis, her fingers gently caressing him.

"Now, please!" Lee said hoarsely, reaching for her.

She mounted him and eased his penis inside her. Lee cried out as she began a rocking motion that made him forget everything else. Every nerve ending felt raw and belonged to her. Control was the last thing he needed or wanted. He gave himself over to her completely.

Andrea seemed to know exactly how to move. Every few minutes she shifted her hips just right, sending him to new heights of ecstasy. He uttered guttural shouts in a voice he did not recognize as his own. Lee reached out and squeezed both breasts in his hands, rubbing the nipples with his thumbs until she cried out, too.

"Faster, baby," Lee moaned. He strained forward in a frantic effort to feel more of her.

Andrea lifted up and down faster, harder, until both dripped with sweat. They crashed together, crying out each other's names. Lee saw and felt a white-hot flash. His world dissolved into only one explosive moment when he strove to make the feeling last. His orgasm seized him and he lost all reason. He lifted them both up with one powerful thrust. Andrea screamed, shuddered once, then tightened around his penis. Then Lee's body went limp; the only sensation was Andrea's weight on top of him. He heard her panting as if from a distance.

After a few seconds she sat back and carefully lifted her body. She rolled to lie beside him in one smooth motion.

"No," he gasped.

Lee pulled her back to stretch full length on him, her head resting on his chest. He did not want to lose the delicious heat radiating from her skin. It was heat they'd ignited together. Spent and satiated, he felt the world come back. Music drifted to them from the speakers in the living room.

"I've never felt this good before," Lee whispered in a shaky voice. Somehow he could not find words to explain how deeply she reached inside him.

"I know. I feel it, too." Andrea nuzzled his skin with her lips and lifted her face to him. She wore a dreamy smile. "And I don't care what people say."

"Are you sure?" Lee combed her tangled hair with his fingers.

She settled her cheek against his chest again. Relaxed and content, Andrea sighed. "I'm sure, Jamal."

Lee flinched at the sound of only one of many lies he'd told her. What had he done?

Fifteen

The next day, Lee was back at work and trying to concentrate on the real reason he'd come to Bayou Blue.

Denny came into the records room. "It's on for Friday night," he said, and slapped Lee on the back. "Awright?"

Lee nodded to him. "Sure. What time you want me there?"

"Eleven is when the party starts." Denny grinned. He shuffled his feet in a hip-hop dance. "We gonna get paid some real money, man."

"Keep it down," Lee said. He got up from his seat and looked down the hall.

"Ain't nobody around, man. Relax. They all got patients or something." Denny chuckled and continued to dance.

"I wasn't asking to go to a party, Denny. What's up with that?" Lee frowned at him.

"We always get together. Like, you know, combining business with pleasure." Denny bobbed his head. "Gonna have some fine women in the house, too."

Lee's eyes narrowed. He wondered if Denny was luring him into a setup. "I'm into business, all right? I get plenty of pleasure elsewhere."

"It's not like that," Denny said. He stopped clowning around when Lee's expression did not change. "Okay, look, don't get all tense."

"I don't want no crap, Denny." Lee pointed a finger at him.

"I'm telling you it ain't no big deal. Ty is into serious business. Trust me."

"Uh-huh," Lee said with a grunt.

"The party goes on up front and we get down to business in the back." Denny waved a hand. "That's all."

"What did you say about me?" Lee doubted Denny would give him the whole truth, but asked anyway.

"I said there's this dude from South Central got some contacts. I mentioned the Crips and a little something about making big money." Denny grinned again. "That got their attention."

The Crips had a solid base in Shreveport, Louisiana, a city in the far north of the state. Gang leaders with family ties in the area visited to escape violent retaliation from rivals. Shreveport was a sleepy small town compared to Los Angeles. Unfortunately the young men had kept themselves busy by organizing a Louisiana branch of the Crips. The Bloods, another ruthless L.A. gang, had taken root not long after.

"Just so they understand I'm serious." Lee sat down again, but didn't return Denny's smile. "If y'all want to make real money, you have to put business first."

"Trust me, these dudes are lookin' to get paid like us." Denny nodded with vigor.

"Yeah? Then I don't advise them to wait around too much longer. The Latino Kings are moving in fast, and they're getting strong in New Orleans." Lee crossed his arms.

"Damn! I heard a bunch of those chumps got deported." Denny sat down on a small stool across from him.

"Don't think that's gonna stop them. Blink once and those guys will own this state." Lee propped his elbows on his knees. "I'm telling you what I know."

"Yeah, they're vicious. Hey, what say we hang tonight? Help you get in with my boys," Denny said with a grin.

"Sure," Lee said.

"We can go to Sonny's Pizza Place. The women go there, too, man. Got some fine bi—" Denny broke off when Andrea appeared suddenly. He coughed loudly to cover the profanity he'd used.

"Hi." She glanced briefly at him, then longer at Lee.

"Hi, Miss Andrea. How are you doin' today?" Denny put on his good-boy expression.

"Great, as a matter of fact." Andrea smiled at Lee.

Denny looked from Andrea to Lee. "I've got some work to do up front. See you later." He winked at Lee and left.

"Hi," Andrea said again, and sat down on a chair next to him.

"Hi." Lee smiled. "I think Denny picked up on the vibrations."

"You think?" Andrea glanced over her shoulder, then turned back to him. "We're not that obvious, are we?"

"No, I guess not."

Another lie. He was not at all sure of what he could handle anymore. But there was no turning back.

Andrea breathed in and out. "About last weekend."

"Yes?"

"It was fabulous. Let's do it all over again, beginning with Friday." Andrea leaned forward slightly.

"Uh, I can't."

Andrea's smile faltered. "Oh . . . I understand."

"No, it's not like that," Lee said, brushing his fingers across her cheek. "I promised Denny we could hang out more. In fact, we're having pizza tonight."

Her smile brightened again. "That's great. I'm glad you and Denny are getting close."

"Yeah, well . . ." Lee's face felt stretched tight with the effort to force his mouth to smile back.

She touched the tip of her forefinger to his chin briefly, then sat back. "You're good for him. We can get together another time."

Lee looked into her eyes and saw traces of the passion they'd shared. "What about tonight?" he blurted out without thinking.

"Oh?" She gazed at him, head tilted to one side.

"It might be kinda late. But I'd really like to be with you," he said. That was no lie.

"Call me," Andrea said.

His heart warmed at the happiness in her eyes. "For sure," Lee said.

She smiled at him and left the room. A few minutes later Denny strolled back into the file room. He leered at Lee and nodded in the direction of Andrea's office.

"No hard feelings." Denny leaned against a desk.

"What are you talking about?" Lee turned his back to him.

"I was going after that. She's fine, even if she's older

than me. But you got there first. Guess I moved too slow."

"Stop dreaming, youngster. Slow or fast, you weren't going anywhere," Lee said over his shoulder.

"Cocky. I see your game. Smooth move, man." Denny chuckled.

"Smooth how?" Lee swiveled the chair around and faced him again, arms crossed.

"Get in with the boss lady and make our way even easier." Denny wore an expression of admiration as he nodded. "Yeah, I can see we're gonna do big things."

Lee ground his teeth to hold back his temper. He was as angry with himself as he was with Denny. Not only was he lying to Andrea, but he'd made her the object of lewd speculation.

"Ms. Noble is a fine lady. She cares about you," Lee said in a controlled voice.

"Too bad she cares about you more." Denny grinned.

"Look—"

"Hey, hey, don't go off about it, man." Denny held up a palm. "I'm just saying it's good for business."

"Right," Lee muttered, and swallowed the anger he felt. He could not get out of character now or Denny would get suspicious. "So Friday is definitely on?"

"No doubt about it," Denny said promptly. He winked at Lee and went down the hall whistling.

Lee rubbed a hand over his face and sighed.

Andrea hummed a tune as she worked late in her office. The long day didn't bother her because Jamal was at the end of it. Everything seemed to be going her way. Her days at the clinic were fulfilling. Both of her new programs were drawing rave reviews from the people she'd most wanted to please, the patients. The clinic's advisory board was happy with her latest progress report. The state health department seemed ready to forgive and forget. Andrea's assurance that there was no serious breach, merely a lack of a paper trail, had helped, of course. Bureaucrats loved documentation. But they liked they way her programs satisfied federal officials even more.

Best of all, she got to see Jamal every day. The days were sweet, but the nights were fantastic. She sighed and stared out the window at the lovely view.

Buildings on both sides of the street cast long shadows in the late afternoon sunshine. Most had been built over fifty years ago and had antique charm. The oldest building, a hotel built in the late nineteenth century, had been renovated along with a dozen other structures. A local landscaper had helped city officials plant trees and flowering plants along the streets. Downtown Bayou Blue was coming alive again.

So was she, Andrea mused. It was just a year ago she'd alternated between feeling numb and being angry. The memory of strong hands kneading her breasts and hot kisses rushed back. That she could be fulfilled both professionally and with a man was a wonderful discovery.

"Ahem, I was going to say don't work too hard, but . . ." Katy stood in the door. She wore a teasing grin.

Andrea blinked her way back from the sweet reverie. "I'm just taking a break."

"I hear ya." She came and dropped into a chair. "You know the old saying, 'Careful what you wish for'? Well, we're living proof. I'm beat, boss lady."

"Speaking of busy, it's time for me to review invoices

and the drug record again. Look at what I found." She handed Katy a trade journal.

"Effective inventory controls in clinic settings," Katy read. "So?"

"I've written up a new procedure, a lot of it based on that article. Sally helped, too."

Katy stood. "On that cheerful note, I'm going home. What about you?"

Andrea brushed back her hair and smiled. "For once, I'm going to leave on time."

"Good for you." Katy stood and walked to the door. "Trust me, the work will be here when you get here in the morning. Staying late won't change a thing. Good night."

"Have a nice evening," Andrea called after her.

She stayed in her office a while longer to straighten her desk and files. The voices of staff faded as they left for the day. Andrea followed soon after. She walked out the door and saw Denny getting into Jamal's car. They waved to her as they drove out of the parking lot.

"Have fun," she called out to them.

Andrea considered the two men. They were so much alike. Jamal still had traces of a reckless young man. Maybe that was why he understood Denny and why Denny listened to him. But beneath that brash grin and confident animal stride was a kind heart. Andrea smiled. Jamal was a real man. Later tonight she would hold him close again and tell him so.

At home, the hours dragged by. She tried to keep herself occupied by reviewing the reports she'd brought home. Yet her gaze kept drifting to the clock.

"Come, on, girlfriend. He said it would be late. Now you're mumbling to yourself. Not good."

Andrea stretched to relieve the tension in her shoulders. She put her feet up on the sofa and settled back to read. The first report was a blistering assessment of the clinic, completed two years ago. Andrea intended to contrast their progress with the problems cited. To do that, she would attack the most troubling issue. The improvements in tracking drug inventory would be the first portion of her annual report. She put the audit aside and went over the printout she'd gotten from the clinic database.

"Hmm, I must have made a mistake somewhere," she said.

According to what she'd written, at least ten invoices were missing. Each invoice had a six-digit number. Andrea had decided to keep them in sequence as part of the new inventory procedures. Yet the numbers skipped around. Still, she was not too concerned since the amount indicated on the printout roughly matched her review of the drug stock. More than likely, Denny and Jamal were behind on entering data. Andrea tossed the papers aside and tapped a foot nervously. Maybe there was something interesting on television. She sat pressing buttons on the remote. Channels flew by.

The doorbell was a welcome sound. Checking through the peephole first, Andrea opened the front door. Jamal was an even more welcome sight. He wore a white shirt with a dark green stripe down one side and jeans that hugged his lower body.

"I'm later than I thought I would be. If—"

"You're right on time." She took him by the hand and pulled him inside.

He pointed to the piles of folders. "Do you ever stop thinking about the clinic?"

Andrea looked at the papers, then quickly gathered them up. In seconds they were stashed away in the extra bedroom she used as a home office. She strode back to the living room with a smile.

"I'm not thinking about it now," she said. "Let's have a drink. White wine okay?"

"Yeah, sure." Jamal sat down on the sofa.

Andrea went to the kitchen and poured them both a glass from a bottle taken from the refrigerator. "So did you bond with Denny over hamburgers?" she said as she walked to the sofa.

Jamal smiled as he accepted the glass from her. "It was pizza, and I guess you could say we did."

"Good. I'm glad you came over." Andrea sat next to him and drew her knees up onto the sofa cushion.

"If you're tired, I'll understand. It was a long day at the clinic. I was running from the minute I stepped in the door. So were you."

"But we're standing still now." Andrea lifted her glass to him in a toast. "To the weekend."

"You know it," he replied, and raised his wineglass.

Andrea watched him as she sipped wine. Jamal drank deeply as though thirsty. "You look tired."

"Like I said, a long day." He did not look at her.

"Well, now you can relax." Andrea turned off the television and turned on the stereo radio, using another remote. "How's this for setting the mood?"

"Nice," he said without looking at her.

"Tell me more about yourself."

Jamal shifted positions and glanced at her. "Not much more to tell. I'm from Los Angeles. I moved here about a year ago after my divorce. That's about it."

"And you have a son," Andrea said.

"Yeah," Jamal said with a wide smile. "One good thing that came out of a bad marriage."

"What's he like?"

"Smart and smart mouthed." He laughed. "Seriously, he's a good kid. Doing great in school now. He had a rough time after the divorce."

"Children do take it hard."

"I should have been there more for him." Jamal's expression became solemn. "My ex-wife reminds me of that every time I visit."

"It's great that you moved to be near him."

"Guilt. I've got a lot of that," Jamal mumbled.

"And a lot of love for your child," Andrea added. "You're a good father and a good man, Jamal."

"Ahem, thanks." He tapped a tightly clenched fist on the arm of the sofa and didn't look at her.

"You mentioned that relatives lived nearby," Andrea said.

"A couple of aunts in New Orleans, and cousins in Baton Rouge."

"Do you visit them often?"

"Holidays mostly." Jamal drank the last of his wine and stood. "Think I'll have more wine."

Andrea stood. She put her hand over his as she reached for the glass. "Let me get it."

"No, I can . . ." His voice trailed off when he gazed into her eyes.

She stroked the back of his hand with her fingertips and moved close to him. "Why don't we both have some more," she whispered, and covered his lips with her own.

She teased his lips wider with her tongue until he gave in completely. He tasted sweeter than ever as Andrea kissed him greedily. Yet he seemed to be holding back. Andrea ached to touch him and to feel his touch.

She pulled away long enough to put both wineglasses on the sofa table. When she turned to him again, she was disappointed to see him checking his cell phone.

"I've been paged. I'll just return this call." He turned away as he punched the keypad.

"Sure. I'll get those refills," she said.

Andrea went to the kitchen and poured more wine for them both. She was sitting on the sofa when he came back. Jamal gazed down at her with a tight expression.

"Listen, I gotta go," he said.

"Go?" Andrea blinked at him.

"I just wanted to come over for a few minutes and—" He raked long fingers through his dark hair.

"What is this about, Jamal?" Andrea stared at him in confusion. "Did we have a fight and I missed it?"

"No, no, it's not you. It just that things are moving kinda fast." He seemed to struggle for words.

"Give me a clue, Jamal, because I'm lost." Andrea's heart pounded at the sudden turn his mood had taken.

He gazed at her. "I guess what I mean is . . ."

"Wait a minute, do you think I'm getting too serious because I asked about your family?" Andrea said. She frowned at him. "Take it easy. I'm not desperate."

"I didn't mean—"

"I enjoy being with you, but I'm not trying to push you someplace you don't want to go." Andrea's temper rose toward the boiling point.

"Sure." He rubbed his jaw and took a deep breath.

Andrea's anger dissolved at the look of acute distress on his face. This big, strong man was afraid of getting hurt again, something she understood very well. She moved close to him, but didn't touch him.

"My marriage went bad and the divorce was worse. I felt the same way you did," Andrea said.

"So, we should take it easy this time around." Jamal looked at her. His eyes said he wanted to hold her, but he did not move closer.

"I don't want to own you and I don't want to be owned, okay?" she said quietly.

"Okay. Look, I'm sorry for taking you through drama. I don't know what the hell is wrong with me." Jamal looked genuinely puzzled with himself. He took a deep breath and let it out.

"Leave if it'll make you feel better. But I can promise you one thing. I'll make you feel a lot better if you stay."

Andrea watched his expression. She understood his fear. She felt it herself. What would she do if he decided to run?

I'm stronger now. At least that was what she wanted to believe. Still, she clenched her teeth so hard her jaw ached.

Jamal came to her with one long step and took her in his arms. His kiss was gentle, searching, as though he needed to be reassured. Andrea gave him what he wanted. Her response was to mold herself against him until their bodies were a perfect fit. They went to her bedroom without speaking. Once there, Jamal let her undress him. She massaged his shoulders and back until his muscular body relaxed beneath her fingers. Andrea stripped down to only the fuchsia bra and panties she wore.

"I'm going to keep my promise," she whispered close to his ear.

She lit all three wicks of a long, vanilla-scented candle that sat on her dresser. When she returned to the bed, Jamal took control. He pulled her panties down over her hips and thighs, kissing the soft flesh until she moaned for more. Reaching up, he unhooked her bra. Andrea took it off and sank down onto the bed. The sensation of his long, hard body stretched atop hers made her moan in pleasure. With a brief pause to put on a condom, he mounted her and slowly, maddeningly eased his penis inside. Andrea felt an aching need that was both pleasure and pain as she lifted her hips to take in every inch. She gasped each time he thrust.

Then his gentle probing gave way to a frenzied pace. Andrea matched the rhythm of his hips with her own. They clawed at each other, their bodies slapping together as they sought to tame a primal hunger. Faster and faster they went until the queen-sized bed shook with the force of their thrusts. An orgasm started deep inside her until it spread in waves, a force that pulled her into bliss. Andrea panted his name low, then screamed once. She wrapped her legs around him and rolled her hips frantically, taking every drop of pleasure he had to give. Jamal let out a deep, guttural groan as he stiffened inside her. He came and pushed Andrea over the edge into another orgasm. Their movements slowed, then stopped. They lay still in each other's arms.

"Are you going to stay?" Andrea whispered.

Jamal braided his fingers through her hair. "Yes."

Lee gazed at Andrea and smiled. They were on the bayou behind Gran's house. She was teaching him to fish Louisiana style with a cane fishing pole. Andrea wore a frown of concentration as she watched the small red and white float bounce on the gentle waves of water. A wire basket of flopping perch and sacalait floated in shallow water between them.

"They're not biting now. Guess it's gotten too hot. The best fishing is early in the morning," she said quietly, as though afraid to scare away what few fish were left.

"Maybe they saw you hooking their pals and took off," he said in a stage whisper.

She squinted at him. "Such a comedian."

"We've been at this for two hours and haven't caught anymore fish. I'm hungry." Lee rubbed his stomach.

"You haven't really tried," she shot back.

Lee stuck the end of his fishing pole into the soft mudbank and walked over to her. "I've been distracted. Do you have any idea how good you look from behind in faded blue jeans?" he whispered as he put both arms around her waist.

"Why can't you just admit I'm a better fisherman?" Andrea whispered back.

"No, you fight dirty." Lee pressed against her. "You put on this tight T-shirt to throw me off my game."

"I did not!" she said hotly. "I— Wait, I've got another one."

Lee stepped away from her. Andrea reeled in another perch as Lee cheered her on. Her face glowed. Sunlight brought out red highlights in her dark hair. He smiled as he watched her. She seemed perfectly at ease despite years of big-city life.

"Looks like Gran will have enough for a fish fry," Lee said with a grin.

"To feed my huge family? We'd have to do a lot better than this. So pick up that fishing pole." Andrea took the fish off the hook and dropped him into the wire basket.

"I say it's time for a trip to the fish market," Lee teased.

Andrea glanced at the fish, then at him. "I say you're right. This is hard work!"

"Then let's quit for the day and relax."

"Amen!" Andrea said with a smile.

They packed up their catch and hiked back to the house. Gran made a big fuss over the fish, taking them from Andrea and shooing them back out the door after they'd washed their hands. They walked back to the bayou hand in hand, Lee carrying a wicker basket of goodies Gran put together for an impromptu picnic. Andrea had a large cotton blanket for them to sit on while they ate.

"Let me show you another special place," Andrea said.

She led him down a footpath overgrown with thick grass. Wild ferns and honeysuckle bushes grew on both sides of it. They were sheltered from the pounding Louisiana sun by a thick canopy of trees overhead. Lee felt as though he were in a magical forest being led to temptation by a beautiful nymph in blue jeans. He followed happily.

"Just how far do you plan to take me, woman?" Lee pretended to be out of breath.

Andrea turned around suddenly and pulled him into her arms. "How far do you want to go?"

Lee kissed her full lips. "You know the answer to that," he murmured.

She slipped out of his embrace and tugged him by the hand. "Then come on."

They went a few feet farther before entering a clearing. An expanse of dark green grass stretched to the edge of another section of Bayou Blue. The water made a gentle lapping sound against the bank. Swamp oak and ash trees surrounded by thick shrubs farther back provided patches of shade. A warm breeze blew, rustling the leaves of bushes and trees.

"Here we are," she said. "One of my favorite playgrounds when I was a kid."

"You were lucky. All I had was a few clumps of yellow weeds and concrete," Lee said.

Andrea spread the blanket on the grass near a large oak tree. She sat down and patted the spot beside her. "Well, now you're here with me."

Lee dropped the insulated basket on the blanket and sat down next to her. "A big improvement."

"It really was bad where you grew up, huh?" Andrea rested her chin on his shoulder.

Lee paused before answering. He tried not to think about his childhood too much. His mother had turned to alcohol and drugs to escape. His younger brother, Chris, had turned to a gang for security.

"Yeah, pretty rough. High crime rate, high unemployment, lots of despair, everything you see in those gang movies."

He could have added that his mother and brother had suffered a real tragic ending. Instead he pressed his lips together. The less he said, the better.

"And it still bothers you." Andrea massaged his arm to comfort him.

"I'll carry that life with me forever. But at least my son doesn't have to live it," Lee said with conviction. "He's going to have better opportunities and a safe environment."

"Children need stability." Andrea wore a pensive expression.

"Yeah, my ex and I finally grew up and put Jake first. No more sniping at each other in front of him, no more custody drama."

"That's great. Being caught in the middle is awful," she murmured.

"What about you? Growing up in Bayou Blue must have been just about perfect. Small town, big, loving family around you." Lee thought of how different their lives had been.

"Not perfect, not at all," Andrea said. "My mother and I have a kind of truce these days. But we've had our share of battles. My daddy . . . Their marriage wasn't exactly a good one."

"I'm sorry, baby. I guess the big city doesn't have a monopoly on misery."

"No way." Andrea looked up at him. "I think it's wonderful the way you put Jake first. Boys need positive male figures."

Lee suspected she was thinking of Denny. Guilt pricked at him like a fine, sharp needle. He rubbed his cheek against her dark hair and made a silent vow to help the young man as much as he could.

"Hey, we're way too serious for this picnic," he said in a playful tone.

She smiled at him. "You're right. No more heavy social commentary."

"So what do we talk about?" Lee said, brushing a dark, curly tendril of her hair away from her face.

Andrea gazed up at him. "We don't have to talk about anything." Her full mouth curved up in a seductive smile.

"I like the way you think, lady," he whispered, and kissed her hard.

Andrea lay down, pulling him on top of her. "You taste so good," she mumbled, her lips pressed against his. She guided his fingers underneath her T-shirt.

Lee caressed her breast through the lace bra until her nipple hardened. "What if someone—" She smothered his words with an urgent kiss.

"Nobody will find us," she whispered. "Now, hush and give me what I want." She pulled her T-shirt off in one graceful move.

His breath caught at the sight of the white lace bra against her café au lait skin. Without taking her eyes off him, she undressed completely.

"Are you sure some fisherman won't stumble on us?" Lee took off his clothes quickly despite his words. He was on fire to have her. He removed a condom from his pocket and put it on.

Andrea shook her head slowly. "Private property. Besides, no one can see us from the bayou through the thick brush."

She went to him and their bodies melded together like two pieces of a puzzle. A breeze across the water did nothing to cool their heat.

"I'll never be able to look at an oak tree the same way," he murmured. He gasped when she rubbed against his erection.

"The way nature intended it to be," she whispered with a soft laugh.

Lee held out as long as he could. Andrea drove him deeper into a lustful frenzy by licking his lips as she rocked against him. She nibbled on his shoulders, moving her hips faster, then slower. With an explosive moan, Lee lifted her.

"Now," he rasped.

As Andrea lowered herself slowly, he moaned at the shock of hot velvet closing around him. He clutched at her and thrust hard. They made love hard and fast, with no slow buildup this time. When Andrea came, her muscles tightened around his penis. She whispered his name over and over. The sensation sent him into a frenzy. His orgasm exploded, leaving him shaking in her arms.

"I've never felt it like this before," he said, his voice husky with emotion.

"Loving you is beautiful," she murmured, and kissed his neck.

They stretched out on the blanket spoon fashion, with her back tucked against his chest. They lay quietly for several minutes, both pondering the wonder of what they'd shared.

"I wish I could freeze this moment and stay right here with you forever," Lee said softly.

"No worries, nothing but carefree days of fishing and making love." Andrea squirmed in his arms. "Only one problem."

"What?" He nibbled her earlobe.

"We probably wouldn't fish that often." She laughed.

"Now, *that's* a problem I'd like to have," Lee said, laughing with her.

"Don't worry, baby. I'll get the clinic straightened out and we'll have more time together." Andrea sighed happily.

Lee's laughter died at the mention of the clinic. There was no escaping reality, not even in such a magical moment. He had come to Bayou Blue for a serious purpose. A purpose that would end this little bit of heaven much too soon.

"That's what we need, more time," Lee said quietly, and held her tighter.

Sixteen

Three days later his partner sat across from him in his apartment just outside New Orleans. Lee's mind twisted with indecision. He'd given in when he shouldn't have. Now he had to find a way out. He should have avoided Andrea and concentrated on the case. Why couldn't he have walked away? No mystery there. He'd looked into her eyes and leaving was not an option. Every detail of their lovemaking came back to him vividly, hot memories that burned him even now. The way she wrapped her legs around him left him weak. He wanted to taste her sweetness all the time. Not a minute of the day passed when he didn't think of Andrea.

"Well?" Vince's deep voice broke through his musing.

Lee shook off the haze he was in and looked back at him. Vince sat on the patio chair across from him, wearing a frown of disapproval.

"She's not in on it," Lee said defensively.

"Uh-huh. And that's your totally objective opinion," Vince tossed back. "Yeah, right." He took a long sip from a can of beer.

Lee sprang from his chair and paced. "I shouldn't have told you about us," he muttered in irritation.

"You told me after I put two and two together, my brother," Vince said. "I figured something was up. Two months on one simple case. In and out, that was the plan, remember?"

"Sheriff Boudreaux wanted me to stay in," Lee growled. "It wasn't just Andrea."

"C'mon, you're talking to me. You've tied up more complicated cases in less time."

"This is different." Lee stared across the small patch of ground that was his urban backyard.

"Damn! Don't tell me, you're in love," Vince said with a sour note in his voice. He drew a huge hand over his face.

The word "love" sent a chill up Lee's spine. He didn't want to talk about his feelings for Andrea, not even with his closest friend. Besides, he could not face the thought of what would happen in the future. All good things came to an end. What he'd shared with Andrea went way above good, to beautiful. In the light of day Lee realized the pain would be that much more intense. At this point the best thing he could do was wrap up the case without hurting either of them too much. That meant he would protect Andrea from the whole ugly mess. He spun around to face Vince.

"Look, I can finish this in three weeks."

"I say two." Vince held up three thick fingers and ticked them off as he spoke. "You've met with the small town scum wanna-bes. You know what the kid's been up to. Give Sheriff Whatsit the info and let him take it from there."

"I don't know if I can." Lee rubbed his chin.

"No, you don't know if you *want* to," Vince replied.

"Two weeks starting when?"

"Monday." Vince nodded when Lee glanced at him sharply. "Yep, I mean tomorrow."

"That's it. I just disappear." It sounded so cold and final when Lee said it out loud. But that was what he wanted, right?

"I'm not totally heartless. I can see you care about this lady. Two weeks is stretching it, but you can break it off gently." Vince shrugged.

"Yeah." Lee walked back to him and sat down heavily.

Vince lifted the can to take another swig, but paused with it halfway to his mouth. "You *are* going to stop seeing her?"

Lee shook his head slowly. "She's not like the rest, Vince. I know this sounds like a stupid line from some stupid love song, but Andrea is special."

Vince sighed and put the can down on the table. He drummed his fingers on the tabletop for several seconds. "I wasn't gonna say anything, but—"

"I know what you're going to say. Don't let a sexy body make me lose my head. Letting women tied to a case get to you is the first fatal mistake for cops and private investigators." Lee rattled off the admonition Vince had given numerous times over the years.

"That's not it. I got kinda worried about this so-called simple case getting too dangerous. I did some checking up on the principles." Vince paused, his jaw clenched tight.

"You don't need to go behind me like I'm some rookie," Lee said with a scowl.

"I know that," Vince snapped. "Stop being so damn touchy. We've watched each other's backs since day one."

Lee raked his fingers through his hair. Vince was right, of course. More than once they'd delved deeper on each other's cases when they had a lead that would help. "Sorry, man."

"Forget it," Vince said, and waved a hand in the air. "But you ain't gonna like this."

Vince wore a deep frown as he leaned forward. A cold chill, this time fear, went through Lee despite the thick Louisiana heat.

"What?" Lee said, his throat constricted.

"I finished the background on Mandeville and Andrea Noble. He's no dummy. I had to really dig deep," Vince said.

"And he's up to his neck in shady dealings. I suspected as much." Lee shrugged.

"Mandeville's interest in the clinic is more than just as a concerned citizen. He's majority owner of a medical supply business that sells to the state, including the Bayou Blue Health Clinic."

"I'm not surprised. So he wants to make sure he keeps a fat contract." Lee began to relax, but Vince's expression stopped him. "There's more?"

"He's ripping them off," Vince said. "The usual stuff, billing more than they should."

"Some of his political enemies are trying to get him?" Lee remembered the snatch of conversations he'd overheard at Mandeville's office.

"That little clinic could bring him down. All they have to do is find one loose thread to follow and the whole scheme could unravel."

"With his money, he'll survive." Lee lifted a shoulder. "And I never thought his motives were pure anyway."

"He can't afford another scandal *and a criminal investigation*. Some of his empire hasn't bounced back yet. He was heavily invested in Asian markets. Top notch lawyers charge a lot of money."

"So he hired me to investigate." Lee nodded. It only confirmed his low opinion of the man.

"Good way for him to keep one step ahead," Vince said.

"No wonder he was so eager to have me follow up on the gang connection. He wants time to clean up his mess and get attention away from the contracts." Lee rocked back in his chair. "I knew he wasn't just interested in helping the poor."

"Not hardly," Vince retorted.

"What goes around comes around. Mandeville will get his sooner or later. Besides, Andrea won't let him rip off that clinic. She's too dedicated to the patients," Lee said.

Vince let out a puff of air. "Lee, she's his daughter."

"What the hell are you talking about?" Lee's eyes narrowed. He let the chair fall forward.

"Andrea Noble is John Mandeville's wrong-side-of-the-blanket daughter. I'm sorry, man." Vince fell back in the chair. He seemed drained from the act of delivering bad news.

"Are you sure?" Lee clenched his hands into fists.

"It's not on her birth certificate, but I tracked down Louis Noble's sister in Lake Carlos. Course nobody talks openly."

"There's no way to confirm thirty-year-old gossip," Lee snapped. He glared at his partner.

Vince's expression was sympathetic despite Lee's anger. "Louis Noble married her mother and adopted Andrea, thinking she was his. When he found out the truth, he started drinking heavily and doing cocaine. He went on a binge and crashed his car. The sister is still bitter about it."

"That doesn't mean it's true," Lee protested. He got up and paced. "Maybe they never liked Andrea's mom. Maybe—"

"Charlene Noble and Mandeville quietly settled her claim for child support when Andrea was born. Mandeville's rich daddy wrote a check for seventy thousand dollars." Vince drew an envelope out of his shirt pocket.

Lee took the photocopy of the court record and read it. His fury grew with each sentence. Charlene had agreed not to press any further claims in exchange for the money.

"Damn it, I should have known." He held the papers so tight, they crumpled at the edges.

"I didn't find any evidence Andrea's hooked up with Mandeville to pad prices. But—" Vince broke off as though unwilling to make the final accusation.

"She might even have an interest in some of Mandeville's businesses." Lee's mind raced ahead at the possibilities. "Hell! I'll bet she's known all along that I'm a private investigator."

He laughed bitterly, a sour taste in his mouth. Andrea had succeeded at beating Lee at his own game. Those whispered words of passion were an act. Most of his life he'd run from women who wanted more than he could or would give. This time it was the other way around. He'd fallen in love with a woman who didn't care for him at all. Vince's voice finally pierced the rage that fogged his brain.

"Lee, listen to me. I'm not sure she knows about you. Mandeville is a crafty snake. It could be in his interest to keep her in the dark," Vince said loudly to get his attention.

Lee paced and thought hard. "But why wouldn't he tell her?"

"To protect her or himself. And another thing, Andrea and her mom might have their own agenda. This thing is like the twisted plot of some southern gothic novel." Vince threw up both hands. "Just give the sheriff what he wants and forget about the Addams Family."

Lee's expression hardened along with his heart, or at least he tried to harden his heart against her. But one thing he did know. He would kick her to the curb for sure. He'd learned long ago to cut his losses with beautiful women who lied.

"Yeah. I'll bag more than one crook before I'm through." Lee's jaw hurt when he clenched his teeth.

Vince stared at him intently. "Meaning?"

"I'm going to help put those gangstas in jail and expose Mandeville's scam," he said.

"And what if Andrea is involved?" Vince pressed.

Lee rubbed a hand over his face. He closed his eyes and thought of holding her in his arms naked beneath a bright blue sky. She'd definitely gotten through his cynical armor. He had to get over it. Fast.

"Whatever happens, happens. The board hired me to find out exactly what's going on, and that's what I plan to do. I'll get the job done," he said, his voice strained.

Andrea laced her fingers together and rested her hands on the top of her desk. She studied Denny's sullen expression. This was not at all the reaction she'd expected, and certainly not the one she would tolerate. The informal meeting had started off on a cordial note. After twenty minutes of her trying to get a straight answer about discrepancies she'd found in the inventory, Denny had become irritable. Now both stared at the printed reports like two chess players planning their next move.

"Well?" Andrea said to break the silent standoff.

"I don't appreciate it. Okay, so maybe I did get in a little trouble when I was young. That's no reason to act like you want to search my house or something." Denny gestured with both hands to dramatize his outrage.

"I didn't accuse you. I've said that a half dozen times in the last five minutes." Andrea spoke in a level tone even though her temper was steadily rising. "But you know one of my priorities is to improve accountability with inventory. Especially when it comes to drugs."

"Like I haven't been giving up my nights and weekends to get the place straight!" Denny blurted out. "This is the thanks I get."

"I know how hard you worked." Andrea ground her back teeth.

"I can't help it if the place got run into the ground. I wasn't in charge. Awright?"

"This is about the inventory and invoices for the past three months. Forget the last director and what happened then." Andrea picked up the printed record from the database. "Over fifteen numbered invoices have disappeared. And this bill seems to indicate two very expensive digital drug scales and a microscope were ordered." She waved the discarded carbon of the clinic credit card.

"I don't know," Denny mumbled. "You can't even read all the numbers. How you know when that stuff was ordered?"

Andrea could not argue with him. She could only read the brand names and a few numbers. Most of it had been torn off. The slip of paper had fallen out from between two rolling file cabinets.

Andrea nodded. "True. But what's with this attitude, Denny?"

"I can't do my work with everybody looking over my shoulder, giving me orders. Man, it's working my nerves."

"I'm not asking any more from you than I expect from all the staff, including myself. We can't afford many mistakes. All eyes are on us."

"Yeah, yeah, yeah," Denny mumbled under his breath. He stared at the floor.

"Excuse me. Maybe I can help." Jamal stood in the door, but did not come in. He glanced from Andrea to Denny.

Andrea looked up and smiled. "No, but thanks any—"

Denny jumped from the chair. "Man, she riding me about some stupid reports. Tell her, Jamal. We've put those records back together."

"He's right. We keep finding missing forms. But we did the best we could." Jamal nodded.

"Yeah, even Dr. B says they're in the best shape he's ever seen 'em." Denny referred to the pharmacist.

Andrea placed both hands on her desk, palm down. "Fine. Then I need to know which sets of invoices have been ordered since my first day here."

"There's no way to know that," Denny said promptly. "The box with sixty packs was opened. They were all jumbled up."

"Yeah, you're right," Jamal added.

"Who opened the box?" Andrea said tightly. This was beginning to seem like a game of dodge.

"The previous director—" Jamal began.

"Shonda did it—" Denny said.

They broke off at the same time. Denny cast a side-long glance at Jamal. Jamal did not look at him but shrugged.

"Like we said, no way to tell. I mean, we both think somebody else did it," Jamal said calmly. "You'd probably get a different answer from each staff person."

Andrea turned to Denny. "I want you to put all the invoices in order. Make a list of any missing numbers and give it to me by the end of the day."

Denny seemed on the verge of another angry outburst as he stared hard at Andrea for a few seconds. "Okay," was all he said. He walked out with one last furtive glance at Jamal.

"I thought a war was about to break out in here," Jamal said. He wore a jaunty grin as he closed the door.

"It started off peaceful enough. Then all of a sudden I've got this attitude coming at me." Andrea relaxed against the back of her chair. "I don't know what got into him."

"He's under a lot of pressure. Take it easy on him." Jamal sat down across from her.

"I've been doing that since I walked through the door," Andrea replied. "But I can't go back to the old way this place was run."

"What's the big deal? A few missing invoices and a few extra drug cartons. I'll bet we can make it all come out right." Jamal waved a hand.

Andrea wondered at his casual response to her concerns. "We've got to go beyond doing better. Bayou Blue Clinic has to be damn near perfect. We've talked about that."

"Yeah, but hell, it's like the contracts. Nothing is going to be perfect. You oughta know."

There was something beneath Jamal's smile, and it wasn't humor. Andrea studied him for several seconds. "I don't get it. What do contracts have to do with the drug inventories?"

"I'm just saying it's all the same thing. We do what we can to keep the right people happy."

"Yes, and part of that is doing things the right way." Andrea studied his expression. She sensed some change in him.

He shrugged and stood up. "Whatever. I'll help Denny as much as I can."

"Want to have dinner later?" Andrea asked. "I make a mean spaghetti and meatballs. It's about the only thing I can cook."

"I've got plans with a couple of buddies."

"Why don't we make it Friday then?" Andrea said.

"Yeah, I'll call you." He left and shut the door behind him.

Andrea frowned. There seemed to be a flippant, almost sarcastic tone underlying Jamal's words. Strange that he happened to come in during her meeting with Denny. She looked down at the printed reports again and thought of Jamal's comments. A meeting that was supposed to be open and shut had left her with two mysteries on her hands. What was going on?

The scene should have been idyllic. The sunset on the Mississippi River in downtown New Orleans was lovely. Andrea and Jamal strolled along the Riverwalk. Dinner had been nice, but Jamal was back to being the charmer, all bright and shiny on the surface. Andrea tried all evening to pierce through the act to find the sensitive man underneath. Jamal seemed to dance away with the agility of a boxer ducking punches. His emotional defenses were up and she didn't know why. She was frustrated and struggling not to show it. This wasn't the man she'd gotten to know.

"Let's sit here for a while," Andrea said. She took his hand and led him to a bench.

"Sure." He held her hand lightly, but let go when they sat down.

"I'm glad the week is over." Andrea sighed. She put an arm on the bench seat behind his back. "But this is a perfect way to end it. I haven't seen much of you all week."

"That place has been crazy." Jamal gazed at passersby.

"Let's not talk about the you-know-what," Andrea said in a stage whisper.

"I don't blame you with the way things are going." Jamal glanced at her, then went back to people-watching.

"You mean with Denny and the invoices?" Andrea sighed. "Yeah. I still haven't figured out what's up with him."

"Maybe he's right. It's not like a few missing pieces of paper are the worst thing that's happened."

"I know the staff must get tired of hearing it, but we can't afford mistakes." Andrea frowned at him. "You think I'm too demanding?"

Jamal turned to her with a half smile. "Nah, just judge him by the same standard you set. You know, the contracts."

Andrea was confused by the sudden turn away from Denny to herself. He'd made a reference to the contracts the other day after the confrontation with Denny.

"You keep bringing that up. Is there something bothering you about the contracts?" she said.

"Oh, c'mon. Allgood Healthcare, Inc., has a fat contract. Most of that equipment is overpriced," Jamal said.

"You're right, but it's what the market pays. Medicare and Medicaid allow suppliers to charge them higher prices. It makes no sense, but it's legal."

"Yeah, I guess that makes it okay," Jamal said, his voice laced with cynicism.

Andrea took her arm from around him and sat up straight. "No, but it means I have to set priorities. So a few small companies pad their profits. The state and federal folks need to fix the problem."

"Right, let somebody else worry that shoddy equipment costs everybody big bucks. That's the way it goes." Jamal looked at her.

"I haven't heard complaints about shoddy equipment," Andrea said.

"Have you asked? Or are you too busy 'networking' with the big dogs?" Jamal looked away.

"What do you mean by that?"

"Nothing. Just forget it," he said.

Andrea was through being patient. "Oh, no. You've dropped a few nasty little comments that need to be explained, and fast."

"Look, it's your business. You've got people you want to take care of," he said with a tight smile. "I know how it is."

"I have no idea what or who you're talking about, Jamal. And I'm tired of playing guessing games. If you've got something to say, say it," Andrea said with a glare.

"Like you don't know John Mandeville owns a big part of Allgood Healthcare."

"Felice Allgood owns that company. It's registered with the state as a female-owned firm and gets extra help getting contracts."

"Felice Allgood fronts for her husband, Norman, one of Mandeville's pals. The happy couple was at that fancy party a few weeks ago." He rattled off the facts in a dry voice.

"You talk like they're my friends, too. I don't know them personally," Andrea broke in.

"Poor Norm. He thinks he got a good deal. He doesn't realize that Mandeville slept with his wife." Jamal gave a harsh laugh.

Andrea had a sick feeling in her stomach at his revelations about John. Her mind raced with the implications until all else was blocked out. She'd wondered about John's sudden devotion to his civic duty. For all she knew of him, John only wrote checks and let his wife deliver them at society charity functions. Andrea definitely intended to find out more. Suddenly she looked at Jamal through narrowed eyes.

"What was that crack about me wanting to take care of certain people?" she said tightly.

"Hey, Mandeville is an important man in a *lot* of ways. That's why he gets the goods. Right?" Jamal wore a sly grin.

Andrea was startled by his expression. His eyes glittered with scorn. In an instant it vanished and he laughed lightly. Jamal turned his head. When he glanced back at her, his expression was all charm again. Could he really believe that she'd agree to such a slimy scheme?

Once again her parents had succeeded in messing up

her life. Andrea felt sure Charlene knew about Mandeville's real motives. They were two of a kind in a lot of ways. Even though she had no part in it, Andrea felt guilty.

"Sins of the father," she whispered low.

"What?"

Andrea shook her head. "Nothing. I didn't know about John Mandeville's connection to the Allgood contract."

"Politics rules down here. And powerful people get their way, especially rich ones." Jamal shrugged again. "That's the first thing I learned when I moved to Louisiana."

"I've monitored compliance with each contractor, including Allgood. I didn't find anything irregular," Andrea said. "Just being politically connected doesn't make them crooks."

"Uh-huh." His expression was still cynical.

Andrea glared at him. "Not everyone in Louisiana is a scumbag crook."

Jamal held up both palms. "Hey, it's cool with me. My only point was, Denny might be doing business as usual."

"Then he'll be doing business according to regulations and state law. *That's business as usual now*." Andrea was offended by his attitude.

"Sure."

"Are you saying I'm in on some kind of under-the-table activity?" Andrea's voice rose with anger.

"Maybe it's hard to fight the system." Jamal looked away. "Or fight against certain people. Like I said, Mandeville is one of the richest and most powerful men in the state."

Jamal thought she'd been influenced by Mandeville's

position. Andrea hated the resignation in his tone. She cared deeply what Jamal thought of her, and it hurt that he assumed she'd compromise herself in any way. What else could he think, given the facts?

Yet this was not the time or place to tell him about Mandeville and her mother. She simply was not ready. Especially since her mind still reeled from this new information. First she would find out more from the best source possible. If John Mandeville wanted to have a relationship with her, it would have to be built on honesty. This would be a perfect chance to see if rumors she'd heard about him were true.

"You're right."

Jamal gazed at her with an impassive expression. "I am?"

"Status and money make a difference in this country, not just in Louisiana. I can't change some things. But I would never, *never* let a patient suffer because of politics. Do you think I would? Well?" she said angrily when he didn't answer immediately.

Jamal twisted a stray tendril of her hair around one finger. "I wouldn't want to believe it," he whispered.

"Then don't. I thought you knew me better." Andrea brushed his hand away.

He sighed deeply and his expression softened. "I'm sorry. Come on now, forgive me. I should know better. Please, baby."

Andrea slowly put her arms around his neck and touched her forehead to his. "There will always be gossip floating around Bayou Blue. Not much else to do in town."

She closed her eyes and took a deep breath. The aroma of soap and shaving cream on his skin was delightful. He stroked her cheek with one forefinger. Their noses touched first, then their lips.

"To hell with it," Jamel said fiercely. "I don't care about contracts or anything else. Not when I'm holding you."

He enfolded her in a strong embrace and kissed her deeply. Jamal seemed determined to drive out the world. It worked. Andrea stroked the hard muscles of his back, wishing she could rip the shirt off and feel his bare skin against hers. She gasped for air when he pulled away.

"Are we ready to go home?" he said close to her ear.

Andrea pressed her cheek against his smoothly shaven cheek. "Yes indeed."

Hours later she was alone in her apartment with sweet memories. She could still feel his arms holding her as they'd made love. Andrea sat on the side of the bed, brushing her hair and humming. She watched the small television without really paying attention to it. An old black-and-white movie was on. A hard-boiled detective was grilling a suspect.

"So how do you know all this? You got too much info for an innocent guy. Talk or I'll toss you out of here," the actor growled.

Andrea sat up straight. She hadn't thought about it until now, but how did Jamal know so much about All-good Healthcare, Inc.? He knew more than she did about the clinic contract. That had never been part of his job. He knew details about the company's owners and more. And he knew way too much about John Mandeville. Andrea tugged at the belt of her terry cloth robe as she considered it all. She went over the scene with Denny in her mind. That was where it had started. But what did it all mean? A knot of anxiety formed in her chest. There was no use pretending. Jamal had behaved strangely for the last few days. The old voice of suspicion came back, and his relationship with Denny took on a more ominous aspect. If Denny was doing something wrong, it was likely Jamal would know. Andrea remembered how he'd stepped in to defend Denny. She shook her head. He was only being overprotective.

The issue of Denny's sloppy work was minor. Mandeville was the bigger problem. He was more involved in the clinic than he or her mother had let on. She would meet with John Mandeville. Then she would have a long talk with Jamal. There must be no secrets between them, no matter how well intentioned. They would both have to face unpleasant facts.

Seventeen

"I don't like it one damn bit!" Sheriff Boudreaux shook his head vigorously. "No sir, not one bit."

"That guy is no Sunday school student, Matthews." Chief Deputy Tullier said with a skeptical expression.

Lee paced the small square of sickly green tile in the chief's office. For the last forty-five minutes he'd tried to convince them Denny was just a kid caught up in a bad situation. For a while he'd thought they would agree. Now they had shoved him right back where he'd started. Guilt had eaten away at him for weeks. Andrea's lovely brown eyes haunted him. There was admiration in them whenever she talked about his special relationship with Denny. For all his swagger, Denny was scared of Ty'Rance. Denny needed to be rescued from himself as much as from Ty'Rance. Part of the young man wanted the easy money. Yet Denny also knew he was in way over his head. Lee thought about Chris and his mother. He hadn't been able to save them from the kind of evil Ty'Rance and his gang spread around, but he could damn sure try to save Denny.

Chief Deputy Tullier's eyes narrowed. "Did you tell Denny already without talking to us?"

"Of course not," Lee said. "I want to be able to tell him he can cut a deal."

Sheriff Boudreaux grunted. "The DA is up for reelection. He's always yappin' about how he's tough on crime."

"Uh-huh. We gotta get a lecture on what the taxpayers expect every time we go to him." Tullier's lip curled with derision. "He's running scared."

"His pitiful conviction rate is why," Boudreaux said.

Lee chafed at the injection of local politics. "Look, he can pull in bigger fish than Denny. That's the selling point. Tell him how great he'll look at the press conference."

"He'll love that. I can just see him standing in his office rehearsing his speech. He's got a big mirror in there," Tullier said with a grin.

"Yep, stares in that thing every time he walks past it." Sheriff Boudreaux chuckled. "Wants to make sure he's pretty for the cameras."

"Ty'Rance is working hard to set up a major drug ring, guys. He's one mean dude," Lee said.

"Yep, we know." Sheriff Boudreaux's smile vanished.

The three men grew silent. Lee thought back to Ty'Rance and those cold fish eyes. There was not a hint of compassion or human feeling in them. Lee had met men like him before. They could laugh about inflicting pain. Killing rivals was considered part of life.

"Like I said, your pal could get a lot of nice press if he prosecutes that dirtbag," Lee said finally.

"Not to mention if he gets a conviction," Sheriff Boudreaux said.

"But he'll need solid evidence to put Ty'Rance away a long time." Lee perched on the edge of the sheriff's metal desk. "Denny can help us get it."

"A lot of folks would be happy if we put Ty'Rance in prison." Tullier shot a glance at his boss. "The DA needs their votes and he knows it."

Sheriff Boudreaux rocked in his chair and chewed on his cigar awhile longer. "Say we go along with it. We bring Denny in and put the fear of God into him."

"Yeah. Tell him the ugly facts of life if he doesn't cooperate," Tullier added.

"Denny won't be a hard sell if we do it right," Lee said. He looked at Tullier and then at the sheriff.

"How do you know he won't say, 'Blow it out your ass!'?" Sheriff Boudreaux's thick eyebrows bunched together into a line. "We've got nothing on him. Denny hasn't come out and admitted anything except that he owes this guy."

"Yeah. He hasn't said he pilfered drugs from the clinic. Or that he's stolen for Ty'Rance," Tullier said.

Lee had to admit they made a good point. Whatever his faults, Denny was smart. He'd consider his options with lightning speed. Young men like Denny had a cunning sense of survival.

"True. He could run back to California and pay his debt from a safe distance," Lee said. "That way he could get off the hook and not have to inform."

"And we wouldn't have a damn thing on Ty'Rance." Sheriff Boudreaux grimaced. "We'd be the last ones to know he's got his gang fully organized."

"Yeah, right about the time we start cleaning up dead bodies from drive-bys," Tullier said with a deep frown.

"Unless . . ." Lee said thoughtfully.

Sheriff Boudreaux stopped rocking the chair and sat forward. "I'd be tickled pink to hear any good ideas. Especially if it means Ty'Rance will spend a lo-ong time in prison."

Lee took a deep breath. What he would suggest was a risk and would seem cruel to most. But he'd gotten to know Denny quite well. His hostility toward any kind of authority and the police in particular might lead him to bolt. He might even tell Ty'Rance. It would likely be an anonymous call given his fear of the man. But Denny's fear was the key.

"It's done all the time," Lee said with shrug. "We tell Denny that we'll let Ty'Rance think he talked anyway."

"A dangerous bluff." Tullier shook his head slowly. "Denny could get scared and run to Ty'Rance to convince him it's a lie."

"He'd end up floating in the swamp," Sheriff Boudreaux said bluntly.

"Denny's not that stupid. He knows Ty'Rance would kill him in a second." Lee felt sure that he was right. Still, there was also a chance *they* were right. Lee counted on his instinct about Denny and human nature.

"You know him, huh?" Tullier rubbed his chin.

Lee sat down in a faded green vinyl chair. "Look, I know it seems cold. But Denny won't last long running with Ty'Rance. He's not vicious enough."

"So you want to save him from himself." Sheriff Boudreaux looked at Lee with a half smile. "Now you're a social worker instead of a private detective."

"I'm sick of watching young black men self-destruct, yeah. Call it whatever you want," Lee said with heat. He did not add that guilt weighed in heavily, too. Guilt that stretched back to his own brother.

"You're not the only one," the sheriff replied, his smile gone.

"Amen," Tullier added in a sober tone.

"Then let's do this thing," Lee said, and stood. "I'll bring him in. I can think of a story."

The sheriff glanced at Tullier. The chief deputy nodded. "No, I've got a better idea."

They spent the next hour planning where they would meet and how to proceed. After much wrangling, Sheriff Boudreaux decided to ask a plainclothes state police trooper to handle it. An unmarked car would stop Denny on his way home from work. The trooper would take him to a state police substation where they would be waiting.

"When?" Tullier asked.

"Soon as possible. This week?" Lee glanced at the sheriff.

"I'll see what I can do," Sheriff Boudreaux said.

"Call me at this pager number when it's set up." Lee handed him one of his business cards.

"Got it." The sheriff gave a sharp nod.

Lee said his good-byes and left. The drive to Harahan was long, but not because of the miles. He was sure his reasoning was sound. In more than one instance Lee had correctly predicted Denny's behavior. Andrea was right that they'd become quite close. Anger boiled up again.

His instincts had failed him where she was concerned. Every time he looked into those big brown eyes that mirrored caring and sincerity, his suspicion evaporated. It was hard for him to be coldly objective when he was near her all day every day. She was so warm and . . . No, he had to fall back on his training as a cop and his experience with the nasty side of human nature. He had to put aside emotion so he could see the entire situation clearly.

She probably owed her daddy a great deal, starting with a nice paycheck and cushy job. Then Lee shook his head at that conclusion. It didn't add up. He'd seen Andrea do things for patients she didn't have to. But what was it she'd said? Something about working around the politics. Maybe she'd compromised her ideals and made a deal with the devil. Maybe she thought it was the only way. Lee had faced hard choices in his life. It wasn't fair of him to make assumptions. He understood what she was up against. He hoped she would understand him in turn. Yet he also knew that with those kinds of deals, the devil usually won.

Lee turned his car around and headed back toward Bayou Blue. He picked up the slim cell phone and punched the number pads. "Mr. Mandeville please. Lee Matthews." Several seconds passed before Mandeville picked up. "Hello. We need to meet today. One hour is fine."

Andrea wasn't in the mood to work late today. She drove to a small home-furnishings store to get a few things for her apartment.

"Charlene always says shopping is the best medicine," Andrea said out loud. "Let's see if she's right."

Her mind was on Jamal Turner. The man pulled more surprises from his sleeve than a magician. Once again she wondered at the change in his demeanor lately. He had something on his mind, some problem that he would not share. Andrea suspected that it involved her. If not for the passion in his eyes when he looked at her, she might think he was about to leave. The thought of living without him filled her with dread. He constantly seemed to pull away, then come back to her, as if he were trying to work up the nerve to break things off completely. Andrea tried to imagine never making love to him again. She certainly could live without him. Yet she knew that it would take a long time for the aching hunger for him to go away.

A billboard caught her eye as she sat at a traffic light. It read GULFCO—WORKING FOR A BETTER FUTURE IN LAFOURCHE PARISH. The Mandeville family's corporate empire. It's main office was *here*. She tapped her fingers on the wheel and drove on when the light turned green.

In the store, Andrea browsed through a selection of framed prints and decorations, but her mind was elsewhere.

"Do you have a phone book?" she asked the salesclerk.

"Sure. What are you looking for?" The short blonde wore a smile that said she wanted to help.

"Gulfco." Andrea walked to the glass display case that doubled as a checkout station.

The clerk put the book on the counter. "I can give you directions if you want. Houma is so small you'd have to try real hard to get lost."

"Yes, thank you."

Andrea wrote on a notepad in her day planner as the woman talked. Minutes later Andrea drove toward Gulfco. She told herself it was just to get a look at the place. For some reason, she wanted to see where Mandeville did business. The clerk had been right. In ten minutes she was in front of the six-story gray brick building. Andrea parked in one of the two parking lots.

"Now what?" she asked herself.

Andrea knew the answer immediately. She would go inside. It was unlikely that John Mandeville would appear in the lobby. He probably had a private entrance like the typical corporate CEO. Still, she was nervous as she got out of the car. She took her time walking toward the entrance, ready to duck if she even thought she saw him. When she got to the double glass doors, Andrea took a deep breath and opened the door. The lobby was quiet, with one security guard on duty. It was decorated in soft blue, gray, and beige, with tall plants in huge pots arranged around it. There was a snack shop with several small tables and chairs. Andrea stared at the building directory. Gulfco occupied most of the offices. There were two law firms, an insurance company, and a doctor's office in other suites.

"Need some help, ma'am?" the tall, husky guard called out.

"No, thank you," Andrea said. "I found what I was looking for."

The man smiled and nodded. He continued to scan the parking lot. The smell of hot bread made her stomach rumble. She'd only had a small salad of wilted lettuce for lunch. Andrea followed the aroma to the counter.

An older black woman in a white apron appeared from behind a rack of potato chips. "Whatcha need, boo?"

"Just looking." Andrea stared at the list of menu selections on a wall behind the counter.

"Take your time, bay," the woman said in a Creole accent. "Tell you what, got some real good fried shrimp po'boys."

"Sounds tasty." Andrea's mouth watered at the prospect. "But I try not to eat too much fattening stuff."

The woman gave Andrea a head-to-toe glance. "Pooh on that, bay. You got a good figure. One little po'boy ain't gone hurt."

Andrea pursed her lips. "Let me think about it some more."

"I'll be here," the woman called out with good humor. She smiled as though confident of another po'boy sale soon.

Andrea started to walk away from temptation when she stopped short. "What the—"

She watched Jamal enter the lobby. He smiled at the guard as though they knew each other.

"Hey, there. On your way to see the big man, huh?" the guard said.

Jamal strolled over to where he stood. "Yep. How've you been, Bert?"

"Real good for an old man."

"C'mon. You're still young and full of spark," Jamal said.

"Humph, being a cop for twenty years ages a man."

Andrea's mind raced. She stood inside the snack shop close enough to catch odd snatches of their conversation. The two men continued to exchange small talk, most of which she couldn't hear. Jamal was here to see the "big man." John Mandeville was a big man around here. But that made no sense. She could not imagine why Jamal would go to see him.

"I got here early, but I better get going," Jamal joked.

"Yeah, don't want to keep John the Great waiting," Bert laughed. "See ya later."

"See ya later, man. Take it easy."

Andrea peeked around the corner of wall that hid her from view. She jumped back when Jamal walked past. Her heart beat triple time. Any second she expected him to turn and confront her.

"You all right, bay?" the counter woman asked with a frown.

Andrea was afraid Jamal would hear her if she spoke. She nodded and plastered a smile on her face. The woman shrugged and went back to sweeping the floor. Andrea risked looking out again in time to see him disappear into the elevator. She waited a few seconds, then went to the guard. He stood behind a high desk and made notations in a journal.

"Excuse me," she said.

The guard looked at her and smiled. "Yes, ma'am."

"I have an interview with someone in Gulfco. She said that I should go to their executive suite. Is that Mr. Mandeville's office?"

"Sure is, on the sixth floor. In fact, they own the building. Just lease the other office space."

"Oh, I see." Andrea stared at the directory again.

"Well, good luck. I'm sure you'll do fine." Bert grinned at her, then went back to his task.

"Thanks."

Andrea walked to the elevator. She pressed the button and waited, her mind blank. A group of chattering people got off and she boarded the elevator. The ride up seemed to take forever, but when the elevator stopped, she was afraid. She stood still, unsure if she had the nerve to get off.

"This is it, ma'am. You did punch the button for the sixth floor," a man said. He tapped a leather portfolio against one leg, obviously impatient to go home.

Andrea blinked out of her daze. "Sorry."

She stepped out. The walls were of oak panel, stained to make it look dark and rich. Thick ocean blue carpet cushioned her steps. She went past a series of doors. Smartly dressed men and women moved at a brisk pace. There was a large reception area with two sofas upholstered in dark blue and gold fabric. In the center a petite brunette sat at a desk. She was on the phone, so Andrea waited until she hung up.

"May I help you?"

"I'm looking for Mr. Mandeville," Andrea blurted out.

"He's expecting you?"

"Yes." Andrea pressed her lips together. Another lie in less than fifteen minutes. She froze, afraid the woman would check with someone.

"Go right down that hall, take a right, and his secretary will help you."

"Thanks," Andrea stammered.

She walked in the direction the woman had pointed. It was a short distance, yet in seconds Andrea talked herself into leaving at least three times. Suddenly she turned the corner and saw Jamal. His back was to her as he talked to the secretary. Andrea stood rooted to the floor. *Now what?* The decision was taken out of her hands when the secretary looked at her.

"Yes, ma'am?"

In the same instant Mandeville swung open one of the wide double doors. "Come on in, Lee." His mouth fell open. "Andrea?"

Jamal spun around, eyes wide with dismay and shock. "Damn!"

She stared at Jamal, then looked at her father. "What is going on here?"

"So, you say he's cool." Ty'Rance gathered a handful of peanuts from a can. "You know the guy well enough to stick up for him?"

Denny licked his dry lips before answering. He glanced around at the three men. Ty'Rance had called a meeting at the apartment he sometimes shared with one of his girlfriends. They all stared at him with dull eyes. Bo leaned against the wall in Ty'Rance's shabby living room. Another sat in an old ladder-back wooden chair. The third stood behind the leather recliner where Ty'Rance sat. The bass from the music in the next room made the walls vibrate.

"Tell her to turn that crap off or I'll throw her and the damn CD player out," Ty'Rance barked.

The man standing behind him turned and stomped out without speaking. Seconds later the music stopped. He came back and took his position again.

"Sure, Ty. I wouldn't have brought him to you if I didn't trust him," Denny said.

"Yeah, but you're dumb as dirt." Bo sneered at him. "How you know he ain't a cop?"

"Look, I been talking to the guy for months. He's South Central all the way." Denny made a chopping motion with his left hand. "I know my people."

"Humph!" was the husky man's only reply. He shifted position, but continued to lean against the wall.

"Now, now. Don't insult my little partner." Ty'Rance threw a few nuts in his mouth. He chewed slowly as he gazed at Denny.

"Guy looked okay to me when we met that time. Don't seem like no cop," the second man in the wooden chair said.

"That don't mean nothin'. You ain't no smarter than him," Bo retorted.

"Oh yeah?" The man started to get up from the chair. He froze at a look from Ty'Rance.

"Sit down, fool." Ty'Rance scowled at Bo. "And, you, shut up."

Denny rubbed his hands together. His eyes darted

around at the hard faces, all frowning except the man standing behind Ty'Rance. He smiled grimly at the scene, but said nothing.

"Uh, if y'all wanna forget the whole thing, it's okay with me. I mean . . ." Denny's voice faded to a croak when Ty'Rance turned to him.

"It ain't okay with me, though." Ty'Rance stood and walked to him. "This is what we gone do. You get the goods and I'll tell you where to take them. Anything go down, it's on you." He poked Denny's chest with a thick forefinger.

"Wha-at you mean?" Denny blinked rapidly at him.

"You know damn well what I mean. If the cops show up, you better not talk." Ty'Rance's voice was matter-of-fact.

Denny nodded without speaking. Sweat rolled down the side of his face. Ty'Rance turned his back on him and talked to the other three men. Denny sank down on the sofa and listened. He twisted his hands together nervously. The men nodded while Ty'Rance did most of the talking.

"What you doin' way over there, li'l partner?" Ty'Rance barked over his shoulder. "Come over here."

"Yeah, sure," Denny stammered. He wiped his forehead with one hand and joined them.

Ty'Rance draped his beefy arm around Denny's neck. "I think we gonna do all right. What you think?"

Denny's lips pulled back in a strained smile. "Right, right. We'll make lots of money." He winced when Ty'Rance's huge arm closed tighter around his neck.

"I'm counting on it," Ty'Rance said.

Eighteen

Andrea stared at him. "LeRoyce Matthews."

"Lee," he replied.

"What?"

"I'm called Lee. A nickname, sort of." He felt unnerved by the cold look in her eyes.

"Who are you really?" Andrea asked the question softly.

He knew what she wanted to know about him went beyond a simple identifier. Andrea's question sought to delve deeper to the real man beneath the name. Lee inhaled and let out air slowly. Right now, in front of Mandeville, he could only offer facts.

"I'm a private investigator out of New Orleans. L & V Investigations, Inc. Mr. Mandeville hired me on behalf of the board of directors." Lee spoke quietly, in the same voice he'd use to break bad news to the families of crime victims.

"To investigate me?" Andrea stood, her body stiff.

"No, of course not," Mandeville broke in. "We suspected serious wrongdoing, maybe even criminal activity connected to the clinic. We made the decision to hire an investigator before you were hired."

"You planted a private investigator in my clinic without telling me. I'd say you didn't trust me either." Andrea spoke to Mandeville but still looked at Lee.

"At the time I didn't know what was going on," Lee said fervently. "I didn't know you. Now I do. You really care about that clinic."

"Thank you so much," Andrea said, acid dripping from each word.

"Andrea, sit down and let's discuss this rationally." Mandeville moved to her and put a hand under her elbow.

"Don't worry. I won't turn into a hysterical female." Andrea jerked her arm from him and sat down. She glared at Mandeville.

Lee looked at the two of them. He didn't see any resemblance. Andrea looked like her beautiful mother. Both women had clear, silky skin. Both moved with grace. Yet the determined set of Andrea's jaw did remind him of Mandeville. Or maybe it was all in his mind now that he knew she was Mandeville's daughter. Lee blinked when she looked at him sharply.

"Well?" she said, and pressed her lips together.

It was obvious she wanted Lee to answer. "Since I have office skills, we thought my being an employee at the clinic would be better. I needed to see things from the inside, get the trust of employees."

"So you could turn them in," Andrea snapped.

"Yes, if they were hurting the clinic and patients," Lee replied.

He took a shot at what he knew was important to her. It was an obvious ploy to appease her. Cheap tactic? Maybe. But he could not stand to see the contempt in her eyes. The strategy did not work.

"As if you care about a rural clinic out in Podunk." Andrea's eyes narrowed. "You're good, Mr. Matthews. I have to say you're very good."

"I started to care a great deal. I got to know some of the patients. Then it became more than a case of employee theft," he said, his brows drawn together. Lee hoped she could hear the truth in his voice.

Andrea laughed dryly. "Oh, please, Mr. Matthews. It's getting really deep in here."

Lee flinched at the way she called him "Mr. Matthews." "I mean it, Andrea. Every word."

"So many words in the last few weeks. Now I'm supposed to pick through the lies. Which words were true?" she asked, her face a stiff mask of anger.

"I know you're upset," Lee said.

" 'Upset' doesn't begin to describe how I feel." Andrea's eyes were bright with tears.

For a moment a slight tremor of her bottom lip betrayed her. She looked away from him at some distant point through the window of Mandeville's office as she gathered her strength. When she gazed at him again she seemed to have gained control once more. Mandeville glanced from her to Lee and back again, his expression curious. Lee could tell Mandeville picked up on the subtext of their exchange.

"Let's talk this out. Andrea, we all want the same thing: to save the clinic. That was the whole point of hiring Lee. We all know that you're committed to those poor folks. The board knows that you've done one helluva job, baby." Mandeville sat in the chair next to her and patted her arm.

Andrea's head snapped around. "Don't patronize me! I can guess whose idea it was to hire a private investigator."

Mandeville cleared his throat. "Well . . . I did think we could find out what was going on much faster this way. Maybe you don't realize how close the state was to shutting the place down," he added defensively. "The inspector general wrote a scathing report to the secretary of health and hospitals."

"Of course I know. I read it my first week on the job."

"I went to a meeting with those folks two weeks before we hired you. The item on their agenda was closing the Bayou Blue Clinic."

"As I said, I know very well just how bad things were. I've been through the files," Andrea said with an edge to her tone.

John remained calm in the face of Andrea's wrath. "Then you know we had to take action."

Lee decided it was wise to remain silent for the time being. Then Andrea turned to him. The passion he'd seen in her eyes was gone. He wondered how to get it back or if he even could. She hadn't heard the worst yet.

Andrea gave a short, scornful laugh. "So you hired a private detective to go undercover in a little rural clinic. Overkill, don't you think?"

"The board agreed that hiring Lee was a good plan. As you know, equipment is missing. Worse, drugs are missing." Mandeville wore a grave expression. "The last thing we need is drug dealers using the clinic."

"Oh, please!" Andrea blurted out. "That's a stretch even for you two."

"There is pilfering, Andrea. Face it." John gazed at her steadily.

She tapped her foot for several seconds. "All right, something is wrong. But it could just as well be poor judgment and lax paperwork."

"Now who's stretching it?" John said in a tolerant tone. "Lee has done an outstanding job of gaining this Denny Kincaid's confidence. He's learned that Denny is a gang member and—"

"What?" Andrea shot out of her chair.

"Calm down," John said.

"Lee, what is he talking about?" She stood with legs apart and hands on hips.

Lee stared back at her. His voice was even when he spoke. "I suspected Denny within the first two weeks I was there. He always seemed to be the last one with equipment before it disappeared. Then I found out he'd volunteered to help the pharmacist. I checked him out. He's been hanging out with a gang."

"You checked him out." Andrea's chest rose and fell faster with each word he uttered. "Go on."

"I got to know him and he introduced me to the gang leader. He has been stealing for them, Andrea." Lee sighed. "I'm sorry. I know you really like the kid."

"Let me see if I understand. You pretended to be his friend so you could help him get arrested. Is that right?" Andrea's brown eyes flashed with fury.

"Just a minute," John broke in before Lee could speak. "Denny was only too willing to steal even more when Lee suggested it. That's how Lee confirmed his suspicion."

Andrea seemed to vibrate with barely controlled rage. She continued to ignore Mandeville. "Only after *he* dangled juicier bait in front of him. You trapped Denny!"

"Don't be silly. He didn't ask the boy to do anything he wasn't already willing to do," Mandeville said.

Lee glanced at him sharply. "Let me handle this."

"Yes, give me one of your slick explanations," Andrea said.

"Denny was headed down a dead-end road. He's in debt to this gang leader, Ty'Rance. Stealing from the clinic is Denny's way of paying him back. I can help him."

"Oh yeah, you're helping him. Right into a jail cell," Andrea shot back.

"He was headed that way without anybody's help," John put in, determined to have a say.

"Keep quiet!" Lee yelled at him in exasperation. "Honey—"

"Don't give me that 'honey, baby' crap!" Andrea shouted. "Just tell me the truth for the first time!"

"I'm trying to. You're not listening with an open mind. As usual, you're making snap judgments," Lee said. His patience was gone.

"Just because I'm not falling for your famous charm?" Andrea snapped.

"If you used your head instead of thinking with your emotions—"

"You've got nerve!" Andrea shouted. "My emotions have nothing to do with it."

"C'mon. You're angry because I found out what you didn't. Denny pretended to be some helpless kid and you fell for it," Lee replied heatedly.

"You're the most arrogant, deceitful, two-faced snake I've ever had the misfortune to meet. And that includes my ex-husband!" Andrea's voice bounced off the paneling of Mandeville's office.

"So now we get to the heart of it. This is about us," Lee tossed back. "And do we have to hear about your ex again?"

"Don't even try it. The bottom line is, you lured Denny into more trouble!" Andrea glared at him, chin out.

"Hey, time out, you two!" Mandeville said loudly.

He walked between them, forcing both to move back. He stood with both feet planted apart like a boxing referee. Andrea panted, but said no more. She turned away and went to the window. Lee took a deep breath to calm down.

"Ty'Rance is cold-blooded. He's a suspect in at least two murders. He'd have Denny killed without batting an eye. I've got a chance to save him," Lee said with fervor.

Andrea turned to face him. "How?"

"If he helps the sheriff catch Ty'Rance, he can cut a deal on the thefts. I can't promise anything because we have to get it from the DA, but he could get probation and no prison time."

Lee watched the frown of concern wrinkle her brow as she considered his words. He wanted badly to caress the lines away, to hold her close and say it would be all right. However, that was an even bigger promise he could not make. Andrea looked at him. More than anything, Lee wanted to see understanding and forgiveness in her eyes. Her eyes narrowed.

"So this gang leader Ty'Rance is dangerous."

"A suspected murderer," John said quickly. "He needs to be taken off the streets."

"Then he hasn't survived by being dumb, which means he's cautious and can sniff out a lie fifty feet away." Andrea stared at Lee coldly. "You'll put Denny in even more danger."

"It's the only way," Lee said.

"The hell it is. Get Denny arrested now for theft. I'll fire him from the clinic. That way Ty'Rance won't blame Denny."

"Andrea . . ." Lee raked his hair with his fingers.

"Ty'Rance can't say Denny deliberately backed out on his debt. Denny won't have to risk his life and—"

"Andrea, no," Lee cut in.

"What do you mean, 'no'? There's no reason to put this young man's life on the line. We've got a chance to keep him out of prison. I'm sure he'll get probation." Andrea seemed desperate to convince him.

"It won't work," Lee said.

"You don't care about him enough to try!" she said.

Lee walked over to her and grabbed both her shoulders. "Listen to me. Denny can't simply walk away. Ty'Rance won't forget or forgive. He might even think Denny messed up on purpose to screw him."

Andrea twisted free of his grasp and backed away. "This is all your doing. Denny's blood will be on your hands."

"Now, now, dear," John clucked in a tone meant to mollify her. "Let's not fight each other. We've got a serious problem on our hands."

Andrea faced him. "You make me sick," she hissed.

"Now, hold on, young lady." John's voice was taut.

"I don't want to hear it." Andrea swept him with a scornful gaze, then whirled to face Lee again. "You wanted to be the big hero who brought down the big, bad gangsters."

"Get real, Andrea." Lee waved a hand at her.

"I've been calling you by some made-up name for

weeks. Lies must be second nature to you." Andrea looked at him with distaste.

"If you hadn't been so busy kissing butt and covering for Daddy, you would have seen the trouble. Hell, it was right under your nose," Lee snarled.

"What did you say?" Andrea's eyes were wide.

He walked closer to her. "I've heard Louisiana politics involves kinfolk deals. Maybe you were hired to protect your father's interests."

"What the hell!" John growled. "That's a lie!"

Andrea swayed as though he'd slapped her. "How did you . . ." Her voice trailed off.

"I'm a slimeball private eye, remember?"

My *real* father was Louis Noble. But yes, John Mandeville is my biological father," Andrea said in a strangled voice. She spoke as though the words were bitter pills in her mouth.

"Andrea, I—" Lee reached out for her, but she drew back.

"He has no 'interest' in the clinic. None." Andrea looked at John. "Tell him."

"I'm only trying to help improve the community. Part of the effort is to upgrade health care," John said promptly.

"He's the silent partner in Allgood Healthcare, Inc. They've made about a million dollars in the last two years, most of it from state contracts. One is with—" Lee broke off when she held up a hand.

Andrea looked at John. "So that's it," was all she said.

"Our discussions had nothing to do with contracts or medical supplies. Nothing I advised the board to do benefited me," John said smoothly.

Andrea glanced at each of them in turn. "You two

have a lot in common." She walked away from them both and sat down heavily.

"The fact is, we've got to deal with this situation. We don't really have a choice," John said.

"No. Ty'Rance told Denny weeks ago what he expected from him. He wants his money. And he'll make Denny pay in some other way if he doesn't get it." Lee watched Andrea. His words had no effect. He sighed and sat on the edge of John's huge desk.

Andrea stared ahead at the wall without looking at Lee or John. "Now what?"

"I have to finish it out," Lee said. "And you've got to show up at the clinic and behave normally, Andrea."

She closed her eyes and rubbed them with the tips of her fingers. "So I'm part of the act now."

"Lee is right, Andrea. We've got to go through with it. Remember we're doing this for the clinic." John nodded.

"Your concern is touching," Andrea retorted.

"It's the best way I can protect Denny," Lee put in. "Think about it, Andrea. Put aside what you think of me."

She looked at him briefly, then turned her head away. Lee could see that Andrea was indeed considering his argument. A few moments of tense silence passed before she spoke.

"I don't have much choice. You've gotten the sheriff and state police involved." Andrea stood and walked to the door. She put a hand on the doorknob, but did not turn it. "One more thing. Forget about ever having a relationship with me. That goes for both of you," she said with her back to them.

"Baby, you're overreacting," John replied with force. "Your mother and I—"

"I mean it." She turned around, raking them both with a look of cold contempt.

Lee did not answer. He didn't know what to say. Once again he'd lost something precious. Maybe it had never been real anyway and the fantasy was over. He watched her walk out. Despite his effort to harden his heart, a small piece of him went with her.

"She'll cool off and it'll be all right." John frowned. He did not sound as confident that were true.

Lee stood straight. "You better hope so."

John glanced from the open double doors to Lee. "What does that mean?"

"If it hits the fan, you could get that expensive suit dirty," Lee said.

He strode out of the office without giving John a chance to respond. Lee was sick of the entire business. Yet there was no easy way out for him now. He drove down the highway thinking of Andrea and the hate in her eyes.

Two days later, Lee sat in his office staring out the window when Vince walked in. The big man was dressed casually in chinos and a knit golf shirt. Vince grunted as he eased his solid bulk down into the chair facing Lee's desk.

"Man, people never cease to amaze and disgust me."

"Oh yeah?" Lee said in a distracted tone, still looking out at the dingy scenery below their third-story office.

"You know I'm tracking down backgrounds on Latham's employees, right? Turns out the main suspect is one of his female managers and he's doin' her. Naturally he doesn't tell me this." Vince's eyes narrowed. "Are you listening?"

"Yeah, yeah. You're breaking the Latham case wide open," Lee said irritably as he waved one hand at him.

"What's up with you?" Vince said, a slight frown on his face.

"Not much." Lee's jaw muscle tightened.

Vince said nothing for several seconds as he studied Lee's expression. "How's the Bayou Blue investigation going?"

"It's going," Lee said shortly, and swiveled his chair so that his back was to Vince.

"So you're going to save that kid Denny, huh?" Vince asked, his bass voice calm.

"I'm going to damn well try," he said.

Lee's hand closed around the arm of his chair tightly. He'd seen too many lives destroyed and suffered too many losses in his thirty-two years.

"You look like hell, man. You getting any sleep?"

"We've both been working mad hours on too many cases." Lee swung the chair back around and shuffled papers on his desk. "We need to wrap up some of these that aren't going anywhere."

"Uh-huh." Vince watched him for a moment. "Those circles under your eyes got anything to do with a certain case involving a pretty nurse?"

"Don't start with me, Vince. I've got a lot on my mind." Lee did not meet his partner's gaze, but kept sorting through files.

"Yeah, I'll bet. Okay, she got to you in a big way. What are you gonna do about it?"

"Nothing. It's over," he said gruffly.

Lee grimaced at the sharp ache his own words brought. He'd spent the last two nights trying to numb that pain. Years of shielding his heart had been useless. Andrea had knocked down his wall of steel the first time they kissed. She'd put cracks in it with one smile. It seemed like forever since he'd held her in his arms. He wanted to bury his face against her skin and feel her heartbeat. All that was gone. *Accept it and move on,* he told himself once again.

"If you say so," Vince said with a worried look in his dark eyes. "But—"

"I'm going to get out of there soon. Before I leave, I intend to make sure Denny is safe and the clinic isn't shut down." Lee was determined to leave as little destruction behind as possible.

"Yeah, you can at least do that much for *her.*" Vince wore a wise expression mixed with sympathy. "I know, my brother. I know."

Lee stared down at the reports without seeing them, his face stiff with grief. "I'm going to miss her, Vince. She was the best thing that happened to me in a long, long time," he said quietly.

Vince leaned forward, both elbows on his knees. "If she feels the same way you do, then you can work it out, man."

For several moments Lee considered his friend's words. He wanted to believe he could find a way back into Andrea's heart, but he knew better. The look of hurt, contempt, and disappointment in her eyes that day in Mandeville's office went too deep.

"No, Vince, we won't. Anyway, I've done enough damage," he said, his voice hoarse with regret for what he'd lost. "I'm going to make sure I don't do any more."

Nineteen

Andrea spent a quiet Sunday afternoon with her grandmother. They sat on Gran's front porch. She needed the solace of Gran's domestic haven. It helped dull the anguish of not seeing Lee. Still, it would only come back to swallow her up once she was alone. *Alone*. The word echoed in her mind. Being alone had not seemed a tragedy before a tall, dark, and dangerously alluring man had entered her life. He was everything she did not need, she told herself constantly. Lying was his stock-in-trade, deception his method of operation. TROUBLE should have been tattooed in bold letters on his forehead. And yet . . .

"What's wrong with you, child?" Gran put aside the knitting needles and white shawl she was working on. "You're moping around like your pet fish died."

"Nothing is wrong. I'm just resting."

Gran watched Andrea in silence, rocking slowly.

"Uh-huh," she said deep in her throat, her way of saying "Like I believe that!"

Andrea drew both legs up on the large, cushioned seat of the swing. Gran grunted and picked up the half-finished shawl from the table beside her. Andrea exhaled in relief when Gran seemed to become absorbed in the stitches.

White cane ceiling fans overhead creaked as they stirred the warm summer air. The scent of freshly cut grass floated on the breeze. White egrets and heron circled above. Their long wings were outstretched as they sailed along like airborne ballet dancers. Usually Andrea found pleasure in one of nature's best performances, but not today.

Thoughts of Lee and Denny rattled around in her head. Dread was her constant companion. Denny had made so many mistakes in his young life. Andrea feared that taking up with Ty'Rance would prove to be a fatal one. Of course, Lee had sworn to protect him. He was strong, smart, resourceful, and daring. She'd sensed it the first day they met. Lee would charge in with a take-no-prisoners determination. She prayed that he would not take too great a chance. Considering the whole situation, Andrea worried that she'd been too harsh with him. One more source of apprehension to keep her awake until the wee hours of the morning.

Andrea pressed the heel of her right hand against her forehead. The dull thud of a tension headache plagued her.

"You can't hide anything from me. I know exactly what's going on." Gran's tone was matter-of-fact. "That young man is more than he seems."

Andrea dropped her hand and stared at Gran. "Wha-at?" she stuttered.

"He acts cocky, Mr. 'I'm so cool it just rolls off my back.'" Gran did not pause from making a pattern in the lacy yarn. "Way I see it, he's trying to convince himself he doesn't need tenderness and love. But he does."

"Oh," Andrea said, tension draining from her body.

With her thoughts full of the investigation, Andrea's first thought was that Gran somehow knew everything. It was irrational, of course. But the extraordinary events of the past few days left her open to believe anything was possible.

"It's plain to see, cher."

Andrea stood on unsteady legs and walked over to the small table between them. She poured herself a glass of lemonade from the pitcher. "What is so plain, Gran?"

"You two had a fight. You're both being stubborn, trying to teach each other a lesson." Gran gave a tolerant chuckle. "Young folks."

"Yeah, that's it." Andrea went back to the swing and dropped down onto the cushion again. She pushed it into a lazy sway.

"Okay, might as well tell you now. Then you can get over being mad by the time he gets here." Gran's voice was mild. "I told Jamal to come over."

Andrea squeezed her eyes shut. "Not again! Gran, you're unbelievable."

Gran did not flinch in the face of Andrea's wrath. "Don't try to make this about me. You two were made for each other."

Andrea crossed her arms defensively. "No, we're not. Trust me, he's not the prince you think he is."

"You find out he's married with seven kids?" Gran cut in sharply.

"No, but—"

"On the run from the police? Broke outta prison maybe?"

"Of course not," Andrea replied. "But—"

"He's been tipping with another woman in town?" Gran's dark eyebrows went up to her hairline.

"No—" Andrea tried to retort, but Gran beat her to the punch.

"Then it makes no sense to keep up this silliness. Bet y'all fussed about something that means nothing when you really look at it." Gran clicked the needles together as she stitched with a smile. "Good thing you got me to point it out."

Andrea floundered for some plausible way to explain. "He's not the man I thought he was. We're so different."

"Sure. He jumps into life with both feet. You like to sit down and plan, then stick one toe in to see if it's okay." Gran laughed.

"I'm not that timid," Andrea replied with irritation.

" 'Cautious' is the word I'd use," Gran said.

"And what's wrong with that?"

"Nothing, long as you don't take it too far. But when it comes to love, sometimes you oughta close your eyes and jump."

Andrea grimaced. "I did that once. I landed flat on my face in the dirt. I'll keep my feet on the ground from now on."

"Let go of the past, cher." Gran shook her head. "Jamal isn't Ellis."

"Yes, but who is he?" Andrea murmured low. She imagined him, tall and smiling as though he'd played a joke on the world.

Gran didn't hear her. "Stop making him pay for what some other man did," she said.

Andrea swung her legs to the floor. "I'm leaving. You two have a fine time sipping lemonade." Her sandals slapped angrily against the porch's wooden floor. She went through the side door to the living room.

Gran was undisturbed by her anger. "Sure, baby." She smiled and started another row in the pattern.

"Where are my car keys? I put my purse right here and now it's gone."

"Check in the back bedroom," Gran called out with good humor.

Andrea huffed in frustration. "I haven't been in there, Gran—" She came back to the porch and stood with both hands on her hips. "Okay, you've had your fun."

"What, cher?" Gran affected an innocent expression.

"You've gone one step too far this time, Mavis Louise Ricard."

"Brush your hair a little bit. Here he comes." Gran nodded toward the road.

Andrea followed her gaze in time to see Lee's sporty dark green Integra turn in to the driveway. "I'll deal with you later, missy," she hissed with a scowl.

Lee parked and got out of the car. "Afternoon." He smiled at Gran.

"You gonna thank me one day," Gran mumbled low to Andrea. Then she beamed at Lee. "Hi, baby. I got a glass of lemonade waiting for you."

Lee climbed the porch steps in his long-legged stride. "Thank you, ma'am. Hello, Andrea," he said. His smile was tense when he glanced at her.

"Hello." Andrea clipped off the word.

"I'm going in," Gran announced without ceremony. She was gone before Andrea could say anything.

"Moves pretty fast for a woman her age," Andrea

muttered under her breath. She turned to face Lee. "You should have known better than to come here."

He gazed at her for a few seconds. "I guess you're right."

"What did you expect, a warm welcome? Did you think I'd fall into your arms?" Andrea glared at him in defiance.

"No." Lee took a deep breath and let it out. "Look, maybe the way we started complicates our future."

"You're good at something else, understatement!" Andrea blurted out. She walked away from him to the edge of the porch.

"So it's hopeless," Lee said in a flat voice.

"You're just like my so-called father. But then I'm stupid. I should have figured out he was somehow hooked up with the clinic. Not that my mother would ever tell me the truth!" Andrea spoke with bitterness.

He walked close to her. "You didn't know about his connection to the clinic or the contract?"

"How dare you judge me! I don't have to prove anything to you." Andrea put distance between them again by moving away.

"I'm sorry, Andrea. I know it's inadequate, but it's the truth. I'm so sorry," he said quietly, his voice deep and intense.

The emotion implied in his words tugged at her heart. Andrea fought the urge to look into his eyes. She would yield if she did. Wasn't that how she'd let Ellis make a fool of her? The men in her life were like evil magicians. They were masters of illusion capable of pulling sincere declarations out of thin air. This time she would not cooperate with the sleight of hand. Andrea faced him with her chin up. They studied each other for a time. She sensed he was looking for a vulnerable spot. Well, she wouldn't show him one.

"Okay, so you're sorry. Fine, but nothing changes," she said in an even tone.

Lee nodded once. "All right. Let's go for a walk."

"I said—"

"We need to talk about something else. I can't risk Gran overhearing," Lee whispered. He glanced toward a window.

Andrea followed his gaze and saw the curtain twitch. "Let's go."

They left the porch and walked around the house to the backyard. The summer sun was a bright white light. Heat waves shimmered above the blacktop road that ran in front of the house. Andrea led him to the backyard and toward the oaks trees. Here shade and a breeze that carried the scent of the bayou made being outside more bearable. She led him to one of the benches her grandfather had made. They sat down.

"Things are moving with Denny. Ty'Rance gave us a list of drugs he wants. Pills for pain, muscle relaxants, the works." Lee took a piece of notepaper from his pants pocket and showed it to her.

Andrea read the list. "Some of these are addictive. Most are mild. But they can be mixed with other drugs."

"Exactly. Ty'Rance is putting together his own drug lab. They didn't sell all of the equipment Denny stole from the clinic."

"You need a Drug Enforcement Administration number to order this stuff." Andrea forgot her anger. She looked at Lee.

"He's going to forge your pharmacist's signature.

Bill's been pretty sloppy about leaving his authorization number lying around," Lee said.

Her eyes narrowed. "I can't believe Denny thought up such a scheme on his own. You were a cop."

"Andrea, get serious. These are drug dealers. They know as much about DEA numbers and the chemical properties of certain drugs as any medical professional. Probably more."

"Yeah, yeah, yeah," Andrea said as she waved a hand. She hated to admit that he was right.

"And what Denny didn't know, I'm sure Ty'Rance or some other gang member taught him." Lee leaned against the back of the bench. "They didn't need me to coach them, that's for sure."

"Now what?"

"We bring Denny in and tell him what we know," Lee said.

Andrea's heart rate sped up until it thumped like a drum. The danger of their situation rushed in on her with greater force than before. It seemed only yesterday that she'd found out about Lee, Denny, and the investigation.

"Oh God," she murmured. "It's happening so fast."

"That's the way these investigations go sometimes. You have to be ready in case things speed up. The bad guys set the timetable." Lee sat forward, elbows on both knees.

"You've done this many times before?" Andrea glanced at him in curiosity.

"A few back in L.A. I did backup and went undercover." Lee rubbed his large hands together.

Andrea stared at him for a long time. He seemed to be thinking back to his past. She tried to imagine him as a police officer. "I think of you as having a big problem with authority. It's weird to think you became a cop. Or were you ever the bad boy you told me about?"

"Yeah, that was the truth. I got into a few scrapes. Nothing serious, though. I got to know a couple of black cops in this basketball league. Real good men, ya know?"

"They took an interest in you," Andrea said.

"Sure did." Lee smiled with affection. "They weren't as tough as this old preacher that lived down the street. Reverend Rooney was a character. Between them they helped keep me straight."

"But you left the force. Why?"

Lee's smile vanished. He stood and walked away, looking into the woods. "I thought being a cop meant making the world a better place. After a while, I just got sick of seeing the ugliest side of humanity. Some cops weren't much different from the punks we arrested. Then my little brother got killed." He seemed to bite off the last sentence. "I lost those idealistic dreams."

"So that was the rough time you mentioned," she said softly.

Lee shook his head. "I'm not going to stand by and let Denny die," he said forcefully, his baritone voice a low, dangerous rumble. "I'm going to save him."

Andrea stared at him. He seemed to have grown even taller. The look of resolve stamped on his face left no doubt that he meant it. She began to believe that Ty'Rance had more to worry about than Denny. Yet she still felt a kernel of fear. Andrea stood and walked to him.

"Remember what you told me? Ty'Rance Wilson is smart and vicious. That's a deadly combination." Andrea put her hand on his powerful forearm without thinking. "Be careful, Lee."

He looked down at her hand. Andrea savored the solid feel of him. Heat seemed to flow up her arm and spread through her entire body. He looked into her eyes and she wanted to hold him close. A bone-deep hunger almost took hold. Her nipples hardened and rubbed against the satin fabric of her bra. Andrea wanted him to hold and caress her. She was only inches away before she knew it. Lee's chest rose and fell rapidly.

"Right," he growled, his voice hoarse. This time it was he who moved away. "I managed to convince the sheriff and state police to make the arrests away from the clinic."

Andrea stood with her arms down, hands balled into fists. She couldn't believe she had almost kissed him! Lee rubbed his eyes and sat down again.

"Damn! I'm losing it," he grumbled.

"Am I still a suspect?" Andrea asked.

"No, not anymore." Lee stood. "Look, let's try to put aside personal feelings for the next few days. We can't afford to let it distract us. It could lead to dangerous mistakes."

Andrea wrestled with her fury toward him. He was right again. They had to concentrate on the investigation. Denny's life could depend on it. So did Lee's life.

"Of course." Andrea's tone was short and businesslike. "What do I do?"

"Nothing," he answered quickly. "I want you as far out of this as possible."

"Fine time to consider that after you . . ." Andrea's voice trailed off when he frowned at her. "Sorry. Go on."

"Denny is going to make excuses to work late. He's been practicing Bill's signature and making false entries on patient records," Lee said.

"The invoices are preprinted with the DEA numbers. We keep those locked up."

"Like I said, Bill's been careless. He's left them around where Denny could take several."

"I'm going to fire that moron," Andrea burst out. She paced in front of him.

"Yeah, but wait until this is over," Lee said. "Then you can hang him up by his thumbs if you want."

"Not a bad idea," Andrea retorted. "But I was thinking of another body part."

"You've got quite a temper, Nurse Noble." Lee's mouth twitched as though he was trying not to smile.

"Guess I've got a touch of drama queen from Charlene after all," Andrea said with a shrug.

They gazed at each other for a second, then both looked away. Lee cleared his throat. Andrea closed her eyes for a moment, then opened them again. Her head reeled; she was dizzy from the wild swing between desire and animosity. Lee Matthews introduced more drama into her life than Charlene ever had. He'd shaken up her ordered existence. Andrea could deal with Charlene. She could even handle Mandeville sticking his nose into her clinic, albeit behind the scenes. But she'd spent long hours pondering how to handle Lee. More to the point, she had to handle her fierce appetite for Mr. Wrong.

"I better go," he said.

"Yes," Andrea replied weakly. *Leave before I do something stupid like rip your clothes off!* She took a deep breath to steady herself, then took two more.

"I won't tell you much from now on. Can't risk it. 'Bye." Lee hurried off as though he needed to escape.

"Good-bye."

She watched him stride across the grass until he disappeared around the house. Gran must have returned to the front porch. They spoke briefly. Seconds later his car engine roared to life and she heard the crunch of tires on gravel. He turned onto the paved road and Andrea watched his car head off toward town. She walked slowly toward the house, deep in thought. When she got to the front porch, Gran was in the rocker working on the shawl again.

"There now. No bloodshed and the sky didn't fall," Gran said.

"We didn't kiss and make up either," Andrea said in a dry tone.

"You will." Gran spoke with confidence. "You will," she repeated.

"No more nudges from you, Miss Mavis." Andrea shook a finger at her. She sat on the top step of the porch.

Gran sighed noisily and stopped knitting. "Stubborn since you were a baby."

"You don't know what happened between us, and it's not up for discussion," Andrea said quickly when Gran's mouth flew open. "Trust me, we're better off apart."

"My lips are sealed," Gran said.

"I doubt that," Andrea quipped.

Gran raised one eyebrow at her. "No need to get smart, missy. You've made your point. You're grown and it's not my place to interfere."

"Thank you."

"Maybe I was wrong to get you two together in the first place." The click of needles punctuated Gran's statement.

"You were trying to help. Besides, nobody held a gun to my head and made me go out with him." Andrea gazed off down the road in the direction Lee's car had gone.

"You'd think I learned my lesson with Charlene. Sometimes I think most of what happened was my fault. Your mama does have good intentions at times." Gran heaved a deep sigh.

"That's ridiculous, Gran. Did you know she went to John Mandeville to get me this job?" Andrea made a hissing sound. "I should have figured that one out."

"She was trying to help," Gran said.

"I was dumb enough to actually consider meeting with that creep."

"Charlene wanted you back home. So did I."

Andrea turned around. "You knew? But I thought you despised him."

"What harm did it do? You were tired of Chicago and wanted to come home. He got you a good-paying job." Gran rocked faster.

"John Mandeville has his finger in the pie. He's got fat contracts with the state, including one with the clinic." Andrea frowned as though the man stood in front of her.

"I don't think Charlene knows any of that. How did you find out?" Gran asked.

Andrea started to answer, then caught herself. She'd said too much already. "I was reviewing contracts and asked some questions. The point is, he tried to use me."

"I don't think that was the main reason he hired you, cher." Gran shook her head slowly.

"I never thought of you as naive, Gran," Andrea said. "How much money are we talking about?"

"Several thousand dollars at the clinic alone." Andrea tilted her head to one side. "Why?"

"John Mandeville loves being rich like his daddy and

granddaddy before him. Them folks chase a dollar like hunting dogs after a rabbit," Gran said with an expression of disapproval.

"That's what I'm talking about," Andrea put in.

"John Mandeville is powerful. If push comes to shove, he doesn't need you to help him. Besides, that little money is nothing to him. He's worth millions." Gran stared at Andrea.

"You're trying to tell me he decided to get paternal after almost thirty years? Please!" Andrea waved a hand as though dismissing her point.

"I'm saying he didn't have to listen to Charlene."

"So why did he? Guilt? I find that hard to believe," Andrea replied.

"Life is complicated and people are even more complicated, Andrea."

"Oh, you don't have to tell me." Andrea thought of the men in her life. "I learned about that thirty years ago from Charlene."

"Don't be so hard on her." Gran heaved a sigh. "Maybe if I hadn't been so strict, Charlene wouldn't have been so wild."

"You were trying to help her. In fact, you might have been too easy on her, considering."

"No, cher. I didn't talk to Charlene, I ordered her around when I should have listened."

"Even Charlene admits that she was a handful," Andrea said with a half smile.

It seemed Gran did not hear or see Andrea. She wore a faraway expression. "She was willful, that's true. But I could have been a little less willful myself. I pushed her to marry Louis, and look what happened. Lord, Lord," she said softly.

Andrea turned around to stare at her. Something in

her voice struck a strange chord. "You said that before. What did you mean?"

Gran blinked rapidly and avoided looking at her. "It's best you talk to your mama about it."

"We can't," Andrea said. "At least we've never been able to."

"Then it's time you did," Gran said.

"You've always told me the truth. Now I'm asking you to tell me what you meant." Andrea left the steps and sat in the chair next to Gran.

"Charlene should be the one to tell you." Gran chewed her lower lip. It was obvious she felt torn.

"But she won't. You know how I hate secrets." Andrea gripped the smooth wood of the chair's arm. "I feel like my entire life has been ruled by ugly secrets."

"This doesn't really involve you directly. There are things that go on in a marriage that don't concern anybody, even the children." Gran paused as though considering how or whether to continue.

"Daddy tried to make Charlene happy. I remember him doing all kinds of things to please her." Andrea spoke quietly to coax her.

"That's your childish memory, cher. Guess it looked that way to you." Gran did not look at Andrea. She wore a slight smile. "You were so crazy about Louis."

"He was gentle and loving." Andrea gazed at Gran. "Every little girl's dream daddy, and a devoted husband."

"Mais yeah, on the surface he was that," Gran mumbled.

"Everyone has a few faults."

"Sometimes a man can love too hard. Matter of fact, I don't know if you could call it love. Louis wanted to possess Charlene." Gran shook her head again. "Charlene can't be boxed in by anybody. I learned that when she was a baby."

"I don't see how loving someone with all your heart is a bad thing," Andrea said.

"Loving someone is a joy. But Louis was . . . what's the word?" Gran was silent for a few seconds. "Obsessed. He was obsessed with holding on to Charlene."

"That sounds harsh, Gran." Andrea was stunned by the force of her words.

Gran stared at the ground. "I'm gonna confess something I never told anybody. I kinda thought it was possible Louis wasn't really your daddy. But since him and Charlene had been together and she said so . . ."

"And you wanted them to get married because he was a good man." Andrea finished for her.

"Like you said, he was so in love with Charlene. He'd do anything for her." Gran closed her eyes. "It turned out to be the worst thing for both of them. Charlene couldn't stand the way he clung to her. Louis got to drinking and using drugs."

"What?" Andrea gasped. The world seemed to spin out of control. "That just can't be. I would have known . . ." Her voice died away at the sorrowful expression Gran wore.

"To you he was a sweet, lovable man. But he had another side."

Andrea closed her eyes and tried to steady her breathing. "If this is what Charlene told you—"

"No, cher. I'm telling you what I know for myself," Gran cut her off in a gentle yet firm voice.

Both women sat still and did not speak or look at each other. The only sounds came from around them: the whirring of the ceiling fans and birds calling to each other. The occasional car rushed by on the road. Andrea neither heard nor saw any of it. She was too engrossed in trying to absorb Gran's revelation. Gran spoke first.

"I'm sorry, cher. Your mama is gonna hit the roof when she finds out I told you."

Andrea's face ached from tension. She fought hard not to scream. "Was Daddy drunk the night he died in the car wreck?"

Gran did not answer right away. First she reached out and grasped one of Andrea's hands. "He'd just left a bar. There was a lot of alcohol in his blood, along with cocaine."

"So all these years I've only known half the truth," Andrea whispered.

"Your precious memories were all you had left of him, cher. Your mama didn't want you to lose those, too." Gran squeezed her hand tighter. "Talk to her about it."

Andrea looked at her sharply. "There's more, isn't there?"

"It's been a long time since we faced the pain. Talk to her," was her only reply.

Gran stood as though the effort was almost too much. Her steps seemed stiff as she walked into the house. Andrea could have pressed her for more, but did not. She'd heard more than enough for now. Her view of the past had been turned upside down in seconds.

The afternoon slipped into evening without Andrea noticing. She rocked back and forth slowly. Soon the flash of headlights appeared as cars whizzed by on the road. Gran came out.

"Come on inside, baby. Let's look at some television. You can spend the night here with me." Gran put an arm around her shoulder.

Andrea lifted Gran's hand and kissed it. "Thanks,

Gran. But I better go home. I don't have anything to wear to work."

"Stay home tomorrow. You deserve to rest."

Andrea's thoughts rushed back to the present and Lee. She didn't have the luxury of withdrawing into a shell of self-pity. It wasn't her style anyway.

"No. I'll be fine, cher," Andrea said. She wore a shaky smile as she looked up into Gran's eyes. A tear slipped down her cheek.

Gran pulled her from the chair and into her arms. Andrea buried her face in the cotton fabric of Gran's dress. Gran smelled of lemon and nutmeg. She hummed an old Creole song soothingly as Andrea cried.

Twenty

✻

Lee kept his composure even when he saw Andrea at the clinic. It took every ounce of control not to rush to her side. She looked drained. Her smile was brittle as though it would shatter at the least pressure. Each time staff approached, she rubbed her forehead before answering their questions.

"You okay?" Katy gazed at her with a concerned frown. She placed the back of her hand on Andrea's forehead. "You look weak to me. Something's wrong."

Lee tensed when Denny stopped sorting forms to look around. "Too many long days. I've tried to tell her about that," he put in quickly.

Andrea's gaze darted to Lee, then away. She brushed Katy's hand away. "I'm all right."

"Boss, you got that stressed-to-the limit pallor," Katy insisted. She took Andrea's wrist and checked her pulse.

"Cut that out," Andrea said irritably. She shook free

of Katy's grasp. "Anybody would think I'm at death's door."

"Yeah, and black folks don't turn pale," Denny joked. Still, he stared at Andrea with interest.

"Denny's right. Too many late nights, babe," Lee put in. He walked close to Andrea, wearing a sly grin.

Katy's eyebrows shot up. "Re-ally?" she said. She and Denny exchanged glances.

Denny laughed. Amusement replaced the watchful look in his eyes. "Good move, man." He winked at Lee.

"Can we talk in my office?" Andrea's voice was taut. Her brown eyes were bright with fury as she looked at Lee.

"It's kind of an open secret anyway, Andrea," Katy said. "So don't be too hard on him. Miss LouAnn's niece's daughter lives down the road from Miss Mavis and she saw y'all—"

"Right, right," Andrea cut her off and looked at Lee. "My office." She marched down the hall ahead of him.

"Duck and weave, bro," Denny said to Lee, and laughed again. "Yell if you need to be rescued."

"I can handle her." Lee wore a cocky grin.

"Maybe, maybe not," Katy tossed in.

Lee mused that Katy might well be right. He headed for Andrea's office expecting an explosion. When he walked into the room, Andrea stood in the middle of the floor, shapely legs apart and arms crossed. Her red skirt fell just above the knee. Andrea was crisp and professional in a classic white linen shirt and navy blue blazer. But at that moment she wore the murderous expression of a warrior princess. She looked beautiful even if she did want to strangle him.

"Close the door," she commanded. The door had

barely clicked shut when she spoke again. "Just what the hell do you think you're doing?"

Lee walked around her to stand at the window. He parted two slats in the blinds, then faced her again. "Lower your voice, babe."

"I'm not your babe," she snarled. "And how dare you treat me like your hoochie in front of my staff!"

"I did not," Lee said mildly.

" 'Too many late nights, babe.' " Andrea mimicked him by imitating his deep voice and performing a swaggering walk. "Why didn't you just announce we had nonstop sex all weekend?"

Lee started to laugh, then choked it off. "Ahem, I wish I could have."

"I don't think juvenile humor is called for, Mr. Matthews." Andrea's voice seemed to strain with the effort not to shout.

Lee struggled to get serious again. "You're right. I apologize."

Andrea lifted her head and stared at him. "For what? You've done so much lately. Seems to me you toss out apologies a little too quick and easy."

"I'm sorry I had to lie to you. I'm sorry that Denny is in danger. And I'm sorry if I've done anything to hurt you. The last person I'd ever want to hurt is you, Andrea."

At this distance the sweet smell of her was too faint to satisfy his need. He took a step toward her and she stepped back. A fist seemed to tighten around his heart in that instant.

"No, stay right there. Don't try that oily charm on me this time." Andrea voice shook and she looked uncertain.

"How long are you going to punish me? That's what it is, you know. Being without you is pure hell," he said. His throat felt raw with emotion.

Andrea hugged herself as though for protection. "This isn't the time or place. We've got this investigation going and—"

"It's simple. I love you. Can you love me?"

Lee balled his hands into fists. He'd asked the one question that had frightened him more than any gang. Poverty and the stigma of his birth had left a scar. Lee was not sure he could be loved, not if he let down his mask.

Andrea swayed and caught the edge of the desk for support. "Please, I can't deal with it right now." It was more a plea than a rejection.

Lee crossed to her instantly and took her in his arms. "Don't let it get to you, baby. I'm here," he murmured close to her ear.

Andrea pushed against his embrace, but her resistance lacked force. "Not now, Lee. We'll talk about us, but not now."

"We don't have to talk about us. But don't pretend you don't want me to hold you. I sure as hell need to even if you don't. Do you know what it takes for me to admit that?" he whispered.

"I think I do," she whispered back, and rested her head on his shoulder.

"Then come back to me," he said, his voice soft and urgent. "I need you more than I can say, Andrea."

"I can't think straight, not after everything that's happened. My head is swimming. Sometimes it's all I can do to keep from screaming."

"You need me, too. Let me be there to hold you at the end of the day." Lee held her tighter.

Andrea sighed shakily. "I just don't know . . ." Her voice faded as she lifted her face to his, their lips almost touching.

Sounds of the busy clinic intruded suddenly. Thuds signaled doors opening and closing. Loud voices came from outside the office, then receded. Disappointment washed over him when Andrea pulled away. She tugged her jacket and straightened the collar of her shirt. The fragile magic spell was broken.

"You shouldn't have told our personal business," she said crisply. "Even if it is *unfinished* business at this point."

Lee accepted her need to regain composure. "I wanted to distract Denny."

"And you used my personal life?" Andrea squinted at him.

"Telling him about our affair seemed logical. He thinks I seduced you as part of our plan. That should keep him from being suspicious."

She thought for a time, then nodded once. "So you'll tell him about the investigation soon?"

"Yes. I'm going to tell him you don't know anything. I'll say we didn't know if you were in on it." Lee gazed at her lovingly. "I want to make sure you're safe just in case."

Andrea looked at him with wide eyes. "Just in case what? Has something happened? I thought the sheriff would be close by when you . . . do whatever it is you plan to do."

Lee smiled to reassure her. "We've prepared for all possible contingencies."

"You sound like those FBI types at press conferences. They talk that way when it's really bad." Andrea stared at him with a troubled frown.

"I won't lie to you, things could get tight. Especially after we talk to Denny." He walked to the window and gazed down the street.

Lee recognized the young man in a T-shirt and low-slung blue jeans standing outside the clinic. He was one of Ty'Rance's boys. Smoke from a cigarette curled around his head. The man walked down the block and went into a sandwich shop.

"Lord, I hope Denny doesn't do anything crazy." Andrea rubbed her eyes. "He'll feel trapped and betrayed."

The nervous exhaustion in her tone yanked his attention back inside. Lee turned from the window. "You can't do anything about Denny. The clinic is doing fine. Go home and get some rest, Andrea."

"I have a meeting in Houma at two this afternoon." She rolled her shoulders to ease the tension. "If we finish early, maybe I'll go home."

Lee wanted to massage her tired muscles until she relaxed. He stared at the lips he'd kissed with raging passion and tenderness, both ways equally delicious. He wanted to taste them now so badly it hurt. His short time with Andrea had taught him just how lonely he'd been. Andrea had given him the one thing he'd never had, real love. There was no way he could lie to himself. His life would never be complete without her. That realization kept him awake at night. Maybe he couldn't make her happy. Maybe they were too different. The least he could do was protect her and the work she cherished.

"I'm going to work like hell to make sure this thing ends fast and peacefully," he said softly. He turned and walked to the door.

"I know you will, Lee," Andrea replied.

Lee glanced back at the way she said his name. She did not return his gaze. The spark of hope died quickly.

Andrea had already gone to her desk and started work on some task. He must have imagined the note of tenderness in her voice. Lee walked out and did not look back again. Denny met him halfway down the hall.

"Say, man, I didn't hear any screaming or furniture flyin'. Guess you must be okay." Denny smirked at him.

Lee forced himself back into the role of an egotistical playboy. "More than okay, my brother." He smiled through the pain.

"Damn, you're sharp. You got the lady all hot for you." Denny shook in head in admiration. "I'll bet she—"

Lee grabbed the front of his shirt, jerked him into the storeroom, and kicked the door closed. "Keep your mouth shut," he growled.

"Say, you must be losing your mind! Let go of me!" Denny glared at him. Something in Lee's eyes must have warned him to be still. He blinked rapidly and stopped struggling. "What's the matter with you?" he said in a more subdued way.

"Don't talk about her like that." Lee's voice cut through the air between them. "You hear me?"

"Yeah, yeah. Don't trip, man."

"Just leave her out of this," Lee said. He let go of Denny's shirt.

"All I meant was she wouldn't question us too close. Gettin' all out of place over one little comment," Denny muttered under his breath. He smoothed the wrinkled fabric.

Lee slowed his breathing and counted to ten. "I'll pick you up at about eight tonight. We need to talk before we get with Ty'Rance."

"What for?" Denny's eyebrows came together. "Everything is set."

"You know these guys. You think they're gonna really give us a fair share of the profits?" Lee stared hard at Denny.

"Sure. They need us." Denny wore a cocky expression.

"Use what little brains you've got, Denny," Lee shot back. "Ty'Rance is going to finance even bigger stuff. We need insurance. A way we can start our own operation."

"Uh-uh, no way." Denny's eyes widened with fear. "I'm not about to cross Ty'Rance."

"We won't have to. We can strike a deal with him. Look, I can't go into detail here. Later, okay?" Lee grinned and slapped him on the back. "I'm telling you, we can get rich and Ty'Rance will help us."

Denny still seemed unsure, but the mention of money brought a glitter to his dark eyes. "All right. But pick me up after ten. Uh, I've got some business." His gaze slid sideways.

Lee stared at him. "Oh yeah? Maybe I can help."

"Nah, nothing serious. A little something I gotta wrap up. A sideline before we get to the real business." Denny nodded with a cocky grin.

"Uh-huh." Lee's eyes narrowed with doubt. His instinct for danger kicked in.

Maybe Denny was hatching his own plan. The appearance of a gang member watching the clinic made him feel even more sure something was wrong.

"Look, instead of you picking me up, I'll meet you. Save you gas, man." Denny slapped his shoulder lightly in a friendly gesture that didn't ring true.

"Okay. Meet me at Brown Sugar. They've got a new dancer called Pepper I want to check out. We can mix business with pleasure."

"That'll work!" Denny hooted, their tussle seemingly forgotten. "See you tonight."

Lee nodded and opened the door. He watched Denny stroll off. The young man did not know he was walking right into a carefully woven net. Lee only hoped he could use it to pull Denny to safety. He decided to follow him to make sure.

Andrea drove down the highway toward Bayou Blue. The meeting in Houma had ended a half hour later than she'd expected. She'd been given a long list of new guidelines. It meant her next quarterly report to the state would have to be twice as long.

"And the darn thing is only due in one month," Andrea grumbled to herself.

She would have to figure out a way to capture the new data. Andrea decided to get started immediately. Her first idea was to modify two of the databases Lee had customized. *He had been Jamal then*. Andrea's grip tightened on the steering wheel.

Lush bayou scenery flew by as she guided her Nissan Sentra around the curves of Highway 20. For several hours she'd been somewhat distracted by the tedious talk of bureaucratic red tape. Now thoughts of Lee came rushing back. She glanced at the clock. The minutes were ticking away. Once again her mind whirled with "what ifs," the questions that tied her stomach in knots. The worse part would be waiting and not knowing. Hard work had always been a means of dealing with stress. Andrea headed for the clinic. It was just after four o'clock by the time she parked in the lot. She entered through the staff entrance, using her key. The babble of voices told her appointments were still going full tilt.

She passed by an exam room where Katy sat with an elderly man.

"Mr. Hoffman, why don't you get a hearing aid?" Katy yelled.

"Don't need it. I can hear just fine," he said with a stubborn expression.

Katy puffed in frustration and tried again. Andrea smiled. Mr. Hoffman had been refusing to get a hearing aid for three years.

Terri answered one call after another. One of their consultant physicians, an internist, bustled past. His attention was on the set of X rays in his hand. He called out an order to one of the part-time nurses. Andrea went to her office. She left the door open. At least she could take comfort in the familiar sounds.

"Boss lady." Terri, the receptionist, peeked in the door. "Just wanted to let you know Denny and Jamal took off a half hour ago."

A fist closed around her heart. Some intuition told her that wasn't part of Lee's plan. "What did they say?"

"Not much as far as I can remember." She shrugged. "I tell ya, this place has been crazy. With the phones ringing every second and—"

"It's important, Terri," Andrea said sharply. When Terri blinked at her in surprise, she forced a smile. "I mean they left you guys short. They better have a good reason."

"Katy didn't think it was a problem. They both been working late almost every day. Lisa and Troylyn took turns and helped with the phones."

"I see." Andrea did not hear Terri as she chattered on about the day they'd had.

"Anyway, some kinda stomach bug is going around. Kids and grown-ups have either shown up or called all day. I . . ." Terri eyed her. "Say, are you feeling okay? You look a little sickly yourself."

"I'm okay. So they just left at the same time?"

"Denny got a call from his grandmother. He said she'd forgotten about a doctor's appointment." Terri continued to stare at Andrea. "Are you sure—"

Andrea waved away her question. "Positive. I'm fine. What about Jamal?"

"Something about . . ." Terri frowned with concentration. "Right about then the dietician Miss Henderson called. Before I forget, she wants to have her first nutrition class for nursing mothers next month."

"Great, wonderful. What about Jamal?" Andrea fought to control herself. She wanted to shake the information from Terri's memory.

"Shoot, tell ya the truth, I don't remember what he said. I think he told Katy, though."

"Damn!"

Terri jumped. "I-I'm sorry. It's just there was so much going on."

"No, no, Terri. It's not you. I, uh, just remembered something I need to do. Thanks." Andrea forced another smile. Her mouth felt tight enough to crack at the effort.

"Okay," Terri said, her tone hesitant. She made a hasty retreat.

Andrea's mind raced wildly. The two men had left much too abruptly for her to think it was coincidence. But what could she do? Lee had made it clear she was to keep her distance. Sound advice since she had no experience fighting crime. She stared down at the papers on her desk without reading them. She tried working, but her thoughts kept skittering off. Distraction by any means was impossible now. Sometime later Katy tapped on the doorframe.

"What's goin' on?"

"Tying up loose ends," Andrea replied. She shuffled a few files to make it seem plausible.

"Oh." Katy walked into the office. "Terri says you're pissed off about something."

"No I'm not. It's been a long day. That stupid meeting didn't help." Andrea rubbed the back of her neck.

Katy fell into the chair with a grunt. "Yeah, well, count your blessings you weren't here. All hell broke loose. I even sent a couple of old folks to the emergency room."

"Rough, huh?" Andrea leaned against the back of her chair.

"We handled it. Sugar, boring looks good to me right now." Katy grinned. She tucked a stray tendril of dark hair behind her ear.

"You enjoy working here, don't you?" Andrea said.

"Yep," Katy promptly replied. "A bad day in this clinic is better than a good day at a lot of places I've worked."

Andrea sighed. "I'm glad to hear you say that. I know I can drive you guys hard sometimes."

"You only expect us to do our best," Katy said. "Which is the way it should be."

"I want the staff to feel good about their work."

"We've got great people. Everybody cares about and respects the patients." Katy wore an impish grin. "Course, you did clean out all the deadweight, ya know."

"Please, don't make me relive those first few days." Andrea gave a shudder.

"Like I said, you did a super job finding the right women and men. Like Jamal." Katy raised an eyebrow at her.

Andrea ignored the look Katy gave her. "Speaking of which, why did he leave a little early today?" This time she made sure to keep her tone casual.

"He wanted to go by the bank before it closed. Something he couldn't handle in the drive-through." Katy stood. "Come on, let's take off."

"In a minute. I've just got a few more ends that need tying," Andrea said with a grin.

"Okay. But when Bill and the doctor leave, you leave with them," Katy ordered as she shook a forefinger at Andrea.

"Yes, ma'am." Andrea sat straight and saluted.

Katy chuckled. "Good night, boss lady."

"Good night, and for the gazillionth time, stop calling me that!" Andrea pretended to be frustrated.

Katy only grinned and waved good-bye. Andrea smiled with affection. After a time she got up to stretch her legs. She walked through the clinic and felt pride at what she saw. Bayou Blue Clinic had decent equipment, clean exam rooms, and a neat lobby. Yet the turnaround went deeper than appearances. The health education classes were now a popular feature. Canceled or missed appointments were down by 15 percent. Overall, things were going well. With one exception. Andrea thought about Lee. In her mind the future of the clinic now rested in one strong set of hands.

"But what in the world is going on?" she murmured. "Where are you right now?"

Lee followed Denny's battered late-model Chevy at a safe distance behind a line of traffic. As he'd suspected, Denny was not going to his grandmother's house. Instead he turned right down Hopper Street. Lee glanced

around to get his bearings. Denny parked in front of a
brick house surrounded by a chain-link fence. A BEWARE
OF DOG sign warned visitors off. Yet Denny did not hesi-
tate to open the gate and walk quickly to the front door.
The sound of barking started immediately from the direction of the backyard. Lee parked a block away between two other late-model cars. He had a clear view of
the house across a trash-strewn empty lot next to it.

Finally Denny came back onto the open porch.
Ty'Rance was right behind him. The first part of their
conversation was inaudible. Lee moved quietly through
the underbrush to get closer. Denny seemed to be desperately trying to convince Ty'Rance to do something.

"No, I changed my mind. Just do what I told ya to
do," Ty'Rance said gruffly.

"But she's gonna wonder if I show up like that with
some strange dudes. She could—"

"Play your part and bam! We get what we need and
you get paid."

Denny tried once again. "But Jamal—"

"Screw him. I decided we don't need some smart-ass
from California. I don't trust the punk." Ty'Rance
shoved Denny down the steps. "Wait for my call." He
headed for the front door.

"Look, Ty, I don't think we oughta . . ." Denny's
voice died away when Ty'Rance turned to face him
again, his cold, dark eyes narrowed to slits.

"You tellin' me you not gonna do it?"

"N-no."

"All right then." Ty'Rance raked him with one last
menacing look before he went back inside the house.

Denny sprinted to his car and peeled off. Lee remained hidden for several minutes to make sure both
were gone. Then he went back to his car. He unclipped

the small cell phone from his belt and dialed as he got in the car. He scanned the surroundings, on the alert for members of Ty'Rance's gang.

"We've got a problem. No, we can't put off talking to him. We've got to do it fast."

Lee's heart raced as he explained that Ty'Rance changed plans. From what he'd heard, they would show up at the clinic and rob the place. He hung up the phone and pressed the accelerator. All he could think of was Denny's reference to a woman. It had to be Andrea. Lee would find out exactly what was going on if he had to rip apart every member of that gang.

Twenty-one

✦

Streetlights cast shadows through the car as Lee drove along the narrow streets on the outskirts of Bayou Blue. They'd met at the strip joint, but stayed only a short time. Denny had been distracted and nervous, though he tried to hide it. Lee had suggested they go to the R U Ready, another rough juke joint favored by local criminals.

"Say, man, where you taking me?" Denny rubbed his chin.

"I need to make a stop first. Some guys that can hook us up. You know, like I was saying before." Lee glanced at him sideways before looking ahead again. He steered the car down the dark highway away from the small city's lights.

"Ah, ya know, I think I changed my mind. Just drop me off somewhere. I don't feel like going to the club."

"C'mon, relax and jam awhile. The meeting won't

take long." Lee punched Denny's left arm playfully. "You'll make money enough to pay for lots of special performances." He gave a coarse laugh, but Denny didn't share in the joke.

"Look, man, I don't want to cross Ty'Rance. Besides, he's already asking questions about you."

"Such as?" Lee kept his tone level.

"Just the usual stuff with him," Denny said quickly. "These guys are real suspicious."

"So he's checking me out?"

"I dunno. I guess. Say, stop at Club Hot. I'll catch you later."

"Don't punk out on me, man. This won't take a minute." Lee continued to drive.

"I'm not feeling too good."

"What's wrong with you? Anything happen with Ty'Rance I should know about?"

"No, no. Uh-uh." Denny fell silent and stared out the window.

Lee drove for three more miles before he came to Houma. Denny was so wrapped up in his own thoughts, he didn't pay attention to where they were. They turned down a street and parked in front of a plain brown building.

"Hey, man. This better not be a setup," Denny opened the car door and looked around without getting out.

"Relax."

"I hope these guys know what they're doing." Denny continued to dart nervous glances to his left and right.

"We wouldn't be here if they didn't," Lee said with a dry laugh that scratched his throat. "Come on. Stop looking like a scared chicken or you'll get them all jumpy."

Lee knocked four times and the door opened. Deputy

Tullier stood dressed in a tan T-shirt and blue jeans. He nodded them in without speaking. Lee led Denny down a short hall to the first room on their left. Sheriff Boudreaux and two other men dressed casually sat in a circle around a small table. One of men rose quickly to face Denny.

"Arms up son," he said gruffly.

"What the fu—" Denny blinked rapidly.

"Just do it," Ted barked loudly.

When Denny raised his arms, the man frisked him from his chest down to his ankles. "He's clean," he said to Ted.

"Ty'Rance was right! You're a damn cop!" Denny spun around to leave, but Deputy Tullier's towering frame blocked his exit.

"Take it easy, son," Sheriff Boudreaux said in a calm voice.

Sweat rolled down Denny's face. He looked around frantically in search of a way out. "Forget you, man. I ain't sayin' nothin'!"

Deputy Tullier pushed a chair into the back of Denny's knees. "Sit down," he growled.

"I'm not staying," Denny said. "You can't arrest me 'cause I haven't done anything."

"What about theft?" Sheriff Boudreaux said.

"You can't prove I stole nuthin' from that clinic!" Denny shot back. "I'm not the only one that works there."

"Who said we were talking about the clinic?" Deputy Tullier put in.

"Not real smart," one of the men sitting next to Sheriff Boudreaux said.

Denny looked at Lee. His eyes sparkled with hostility. "I was stupid to trust you. I should have known better. My good pal! You're no different from—" He broke off and swallowed hard.

Lee knew Denny's background. Denny was no doubt thinking of the father who had mistreated his mother and abandoned him. Lee met his gaze without flinching. He had to focus, to numb his emotions. The danger was all too real for Denny. Still, the sting of guilt was sharp.

"I'm trying to save your ass!" Lee snapped. "You think you got a bright future with Ty'Rance and his kind?"

"Only two ways to go with him, prison or the cemetery." Deputy Tullier folded his arms across his chest.

Denny glanced from Lee to Deputy Tullier. "Brothers doing the white man's dirty work," he spat at them.

"Don't give me that bull! Ty'Rance has killed more brothers than any cop around here," Deputy Tullier barked. "Just so he can sell crack to our kids and kill more."

Denny glared at him. "At least he's for real."

"Don't be such an idiot!" Deputy Tullier took a step toward him.

Lee put a hand to the big man's chest. "All right, enough of that. Look, I know you don't want Ty'Rance's foot on your neck. You want a way out. We can help you."

"That good cop, bad cop routine is so old it's on crutches." Denny slumped in his chair with a sullen, defiant expression. "Shove it."

"You little—" Sheriff Boudreaux began, but stopped when Lee raised a hand.

Lee leaned down until his face was a few inches from Denny's. "I'll get to the point. They've got enough to put you in jail. But they're willing to cut a deal."

"If I turn informant, right? Like I said, shove it,"

Denny broke in before he could continue. He wore a stubborn frown.

"This isn't an invitation to a party you can refuse," Lee shot back. "You'll be tossed in jail and Ty'Rance will think you talked."

"I hear the guy is paranoid as hell," one of the other officers said mildly.

"Yep," the other man said.

"Killed two guys by the time he was fifteen. Served juvenile time for one. Never could prove he did the other dude," Deputy Tullier added.

Denny licked dry lips. "Y'all need to work on this act. I'm not buyin' it." His voice wavered in spite of what he said.

"With Ty'Rance as a 'friend,' you don't need us as enemies. I could have let them take you down right along with him, Denny." Lee stared at him.

"I can't believe this shit." Denny closed his eyes.

"Think!" Lee yelled. "They've traced the stolen supplies to you. But they want more than a petty theft conviction. They want Ty'Rance off the streets," Lee said.

"So the little fish get ground up so they can catch the big fish," Denny said bitterly. "Like you care what happens to me."

"I could have gone along and let them get you on drug trafficking. Minimum sentencing for conspiracy applies, life without parole." Lee had to punch through to him with grim facts. "Who's going to take care of your grandmother, Denny?"

Denny covered his face with one hand. "Aw, damn!"

"Either way you were going to be arrested, but our way, you could get probation. Take the chance to be there for her." Lee stood back again.

"I need time to think. Give me a day or two." Denny rubbed his eyes with both fists.

"No, you make a decision before you walk out of here. Either get with the plan or go to jail," Sheriff Boudreaux said.

Denny looked up at Lee. "Did you tell them I stole stuff from the clinic? Is that how they found out?"

Before Lee could answer, Deputy Tullier spoke up. "We suspected you long before that."

"Thanks, but I'm going to be straight with him," Lee said. "You were one of several strong suspects. I helped narrow it down. I don't want to see you in prison for the rest of your life, Denny."

They stared at each other for several minutes. The other men waited without intruding on the silent communication between them. Denny heaved a deep sigh.

"All right. I don't have a choice anyway," he said.

"No, but maybe after this is over you'll have better choices for your life," Lee said.

"Yeah, right." Denny looked away from him.

Lee knew full well how the young man felt. Denny had only bad experiences behind him. That kind of childhood made it hard to expect anything good. Lee had gone down that lonely, bumpy road for too long. Yet for a brief time he had not been alone. He thought of Andrea as the others took over talking to Denny.

"So you've gotten all settled in, I see," Charlene said with a smile. She glanced around Andrea's apartment.

Andrea gazed at her for a second or two. She could read Charlene like a book. "Go on, tell me how the decor could be improved."

"It looks just fine. I love that sofa and chair." Charlene looked distracted even though her smile remained.

"Thank you," Andrea replied, surprised. "What's wrong?"

"Does anything have to be wrong for me to visit you?" Charlene twisted the strap of her leather-trimmed straw summer purse.

"You talked to Gran." Andrea gazed at her. "Now you know I know."

"She had no right to tell you," Charlene blurted out, frowning angrily. "Louis drank a bit, but really you know how Mama can be. Stray an inch from the path of righteousness and . . ." She lifted a shoulder. "You get that from her, being judgmental, I mean."

Andrea ignored the dig. "You should have told me about Daddy years ago, Charlene. Daddy did more than 'drink a bit.' Tell me the truth for once. I can take it."

"It wasn't all that bad," Charlene protested. She sighed. "Louis was under a lot of stress."

"He died because he was driving drunk," Andrea said. The words rang out cold and sharp. Charlene winced. "Isn't that right?"

Charlene covered her face with both hands. When she took them down, her expression was pinched. She seemed to have aged in an instant. "It wasn't all his fault," she said. Her voice was so low Andrea leaned forward.

"Someone got him drunk?" Andrea said.

"Yes." Charlene clasped her hands together in one tight ball.

"Who?" Andrea sat very still and waited for an answer. She could hear the ticking of a crystal clock on the bookshelf across the room. "Charlene?"

"I did." Charlene closed her eyes. "At least, I might as well have. I pushed him to it. He found out about . . ."

"That I wasn't his child," Andrea said. Her mother's response stunned her.

Charlene shook her head. "No, he'd suspected that all along. But it didn't matter. He loved you just the same. In fact, he didn't want to know for sure. I think he convinced himself after a while that you really were his daughter. Louis was like that. So different, even as a little boy."

"I don't understand." Andrea stared at her mother.

"He was so intense. Sometimes he'd get quiet for days at a time. Just wouldn't talk." Charlene pressed her lips together as though in pain.

"What happened between you? You weren't even with him that night."

"No, not in the car. Before that, though." Charlene took a deep breath and let it out. "Louis found out I'd started seeing John again."

"Oh, my God!" Andrea murmured. She gazed at her mother with a grimace that mirrored the abhorrence she felt. "How could you do that to him?"

"Let me finish before you pass judgment, Andrea!" Charlene said, her voice loud and commanding. "My marriage to Louis was a disaster. He needed to control everything about me. My hair, my clothes, everything. He insisted on approving anything I bought. If he thought it wasn't appropriate, he'd make my life miserable until I took it back. Three times I refused. Just got fed up and said no. You know what he did?"

Andrea felt a chill at the look on Charlene's face. "What?"

"I came home one day and he'd ripped two blouses, a

dress and a pantsuit to shreds with a straight razor."
Charlene hugged herself. "He left them in a pile on the
floor right by the closet. 'There's your slut clothes,' he
said."

What Charlene described was typical of the accounts
she'd heard from emotionally and physically abused
women.

"Did he ever hit you?" she whispered.

"No, never. But sometimes I'd wish he had. After
years of listening to Mama about my behavior, I tried to
make it work. Everyone said how lucky I was to have
such a kind and steady husband. And they all talked
about how good he was with you."

"So you turned to John Mandeville again," Andrea
said in a strained voice, trying to comprehend.

"I was so lonely. I hated being in that house with
him." Charlene looked at Andrea. "A lot of people might
not believe this, but John can be a sweet, thoughtful
man."

"Was Daddy anything like I remember him?" Andrea
asked. Every memory seemed to be built on lies and secrets.

"Yes, baby." Charlene put an arm around her and
hugged her close. "Louis loved making you toys and
taking you fishing. I really think those were the only
times he was truly happy."

Andrea hugged her mother back. "Why did you let
me put all the blame on you?" she asked, her voice
shaking with emotion.

"Because I was guilty in a way. I didn't try to understand Louis." Charlene spoke in a wise, serious voice
very unlike her usual self. "Looking back, I can see that
I used Louis. I married him because it made life easier
for me."

"I'm sorry, Mother," Andrea said quietly.

Charlene's eyes filled with tears. She brushed her fingers through Andrea's dark curls. "That's all right, sweetie pie."

Andrea had never felt this close to Charlene. A barrier had been broken down between them. Terrible as it was, Andrea was not devastated by the truth. Charlene pulled back. She took a tissue from her purse and dabbed at her eyes.

"Whew! I haven't been this emotional since Oprah did that show on people reunited with their lost puppies or something."

"Oh, Charlene!" Andrea sniffed and laughed at the same time.

"It's true. Those talk shows are tearjerkers." Charlene breathed in and out, then smoothed down the white cotton shirt she wore. "Am I too wrinkled?"

Andrea gazed at her with affection. "You're absolutely beautiful," she said.

Charlene blushed with pleasure. "Well, I suppose you want to hear more about Louis. What would you like to know?"

"As much as possible. Let's pull all the skeletons out of the closet."

With the worst secret now revealed, Charlene was a veritable fountain of information. Andrea listened for hours, interrupting only a few times to ask questions.

"Hi. I'm back," Andrea called out as she entered the clinic.

"Hi," Troylyn answered from the reception room. She was now at ease in her duties at the clinic. "Everything's going fine."

"We even handled three patients without help," Lisa piped up. The two student nurses grinned with pride.

"Wonderful. Keep up the good work," Andrea called back. With a wave to Terri, she headed for her office.

As she walked down the hall, every nerve ending was on edge. She had to be prepared to meet Denny or Lee. Two days had passed and no word from Lee. There was only a cryptic message on her voice mail at home. She listened to his voice for any hint of how things were going. All he said was that everything was going as planned and that they should not talk at the clinic. He'd call her later. Their exchanges, the few times they met, were no more than brief greetings. She tried to solve the puzzle of what it all meant. Thoughts of Lee, Denny, and the gang never left. They were like constant background noise. It was driving her nuts.

"Now for an even bigger challenge, concentrate on work," she muttered as she took off her jacket.

"Hey, Miss Andrea," Denny said.

Andrea looked up sharply. He shuffled his feet as though he wanted to run at the slightest provocation. "Hi, Denny."

"Uh, looks like you're really busy." Denny stared at her. "I don't mean to bother you. I was just saying hello."

It was obvious he wanted to talk. Andrea remembered Lee's warning. Yet she could not turn him away. He looked lost and forlorn.

"As a matter of fact, I could use a break. How about getting us both a Coke?" Andrea got change out of her desk and handed it to him.

Seconds later Denny came back with two cups and napkins along with the soft drinks.

Andrea nodded to him to sit down. She poured the

cola in her cup and took a drink. "Thanks. I needed that." She grinned at him.

Denny smiled, but it faded quickly. "Uh, so how are things going with you?"

"Good." Andrea was quiet for a moment. "And you?"

"Okay, I guess. Folks back of the bayou always sayin' how much better the clinic is since you took over."

Andrea pictured the poor community where he lived. The gang had its roots there, from what Lee had told her. "I'm glad they're pleased."

"Yeah, yeah. They say the clinic is being run right for the first time since it opened." Denny toyed with the cup in his hands. "Guess it means a lot to them."

"I think we've done a lot to help people. That includes you, Denny. Your work supports us so we can spend more time with the patients."

"Nah, not me." Denny shifted in his chair. "Half the time I was fooling around." He would not meet her gaze.

"Yeah, I had to get your attention a few times." Andrea lifted a shoulder.

"More than a few," Denny said.

"But you've done a good job overall. I know changing old habits is hard, but you've come a long way."

"That means a lot to me," he said in a quiet voice. "I'm used to hearing how much trouble I am. They're right, too. I'm always messing up no matter how hard I try. But I really liked working here, Miss Andrea. I want you to know that." Denny blinked rapidly and cleared his throat.

A lump rose in her throat. She wanted to tell him it would be okay. "I like working with you, too, Denny. But you talk like you're going somewhere."

"No, I, uh, just wanted to say . . ." Denny stood.

"You're a good person, Miss Andrea. I'll always try to do right by you. I gotta go."

Denny hurried off and closed the door behind him before Andrea could reply. She debated whether to follow him, but decided it was best not to. Minutes later there was a knock on the door.

Andrea composed herself, half-expecting Denny to come in and pour out a confession. "Come in."

Lee walked in instead. His dark eyebrows were drawn together. "I was looking for Denny and saw him come out of here. Anything you need to tell me?"

"He didn't say anything directly. But I had the feeling he was telling me good-bye. God, I wish I could do something!" Andrea stood and paced in front of the window.

"I'm going to protect him, Andrea," Lee said fiercely. "I promise you."

"He's on the edge, Lee. I can feel it. I'm afraid he's going to do something desperate."

Andrea turned to him, searching for the reassurance that could only be found in his arms. Lee had already crossed the few feet between them. He wrapped her in his strong embrace and she leaned against him, drawing on his strength. The scent of spice and mint on his skin was a balm to her frayed nerves. Andrea took a deep breath and put her arms around him. Her hands caressed the solid muscles of his back.

"Listen to me, baby," Lee whispered as he lifted her face to his. "I know he's under pressure. Sure, he's pissed about working with the cops, but he wants to get Ty'Rance off his back."

"What if . . ." Andrea trembled with desire when he pressed a finger to her lips. She snuggled against him.

"Don't drive yourself crazy thinking about it." Lee

stared into her eyes. "I need you to trust me," he whispered.

Andrea felt the power of his request. It went deeper than Denny or the investigation. Her response was a kiss, long and deep. She parted his lips gently with her tongue. Lee moaned, letting her take control. The need to touch and taste him roared inside Andrea like a fire. She moaned as a powerful mixture of pleasure and hunger hit her. Lee summoned the control to pull away first, his breathing hard.

"I better leave. The next few hours are critical," he said.

"Yes." Andrea clung to him for a moment longer, then let go.

"Andrea, I . . . There's so much I want to say about how we met and . . . everything." Lee stroked her thick locks gently with his fingertips. "About me and my life."

"I know." She closed her eyes and savored the sensuous delight of his touch.

"I love you so much," he whispered. His voice shook with emotion.

"You just said the one thing I most wanted to hear."

He brushed his lips across her forehead and backed up. "I'll call you when it's safe to. You might not see us for a while."

She felt cold as he moved away from her and walked toward the door. "Sure, I'll think of something to tell the staff."

" 'Bye, baby. Please don't worry." And then he was gone.

He was gone much too soon. Andrea hugged herself, trying to recapture the exquisite warmth of his body. She would follow his instructions to carry on at the clinic as usual. But she couldn't obey his appeal not to worry.

Twenty-two

The sound of her doorbell woke Andrea from a fitful sleep. She glanced at the digital clock next to her bed. The numbers glowed in red. It was two in the morning. Her heart thumped as she got out of bed and put on her robe. Andrea tiptoed to the front door and peered through the peephole. Lee stood outside. She unlocked the door quickly and yanked it open.

"I've been driving around for hours. I just wanted to see you," he said. "Are you okay?"

"Sure." Andrea stared at his haggard expression. "What's wrong?" she said.

Lee came in and waited until she closed the door. "His grandmother called the sheriff's office and reported him missing."

"You think he's run away?"

"That's one possibility," Lee said grimly.

The tone of his voice gave her goose bumps. "Then

we've got to look for him." Andrea headed for her bedroom, but Lee grabbed her arm.

"Forget it, Andrea. You're not getting mixed up in this. Especially not now."

"Don't order me around! You got him into this mess!" Andrea shouted.

Lee let go of her. "You're right," he said quietly. He wiped a shaky hand over his face. "So it's up to me to get him out of it."

Andrea's heart broke at the anguish in his tone. "Don't listen to me, Lee. My nerves are so shot, I don't know what I'm saying." She hugged him and let his head rest on her shoulder.

"I never should have asked him to inform on Ty'Rance."

"Denny set this all in motion by stealing for the gang. There were no good choices for him after that. You know that."

Lee straightened and stepped back. "I'm going to find him." His anguished expression gave way to one of determination.

"He could be in another state by now if he's run away." Andrea shivered with fear. "Lord, I hope he's run away."

"Promise you won't go looking for him, Andrea," Lee insisted.

"Okay, okay. But call me, *please*."

"I will." Lee kissed her and left.

Andrea listened to his car start up and the sound of it fade as he drove away. She paced for a few minutes, trying to sort through her tangled thoughts. Her thoughts raced as she reviewed every possibility, none of them good. Finally she glanced at the clock. It was now three-thirty. She went back to bed but lay staring at the ceiling for another hour. The phone next to her bed rang and she snatched the receiver from its cradle.

"Hello?"

"Miss Andrea, it's me, Denny."

Andrea gripped the cordless phone tightly. "Your grandmother is worried about you, Denny. Where are you? I'll come get you right now."

"No, you can't do that. I'm leaving. I just wanted to say I'm sorry. I lied to you and—"

"That doesn't matter now. Just tell me where you are. We can still work this out." Andrea fought to keep her voice calm. Her whole body tensed with the fear that he would hang up.

"No. It's not safe where I am. Did you know about Jamal?"

She quickly considered what to say and decided on the truth. "He finally told me about two weeks ago, Denny. The board hired him without telling me. They didn't know who was stealing from the clinic."

"So he fooled you, too. You picked the wrong boyfriend and I picked the wrong friend," Denny said, his voice laced with bitterness.

Andrea chose not to talk about Lee but to focus on Denny instead. "Listen to me, Denny. If you don't finish this thing, the sheriff can't charge Ty'Rance with anything. He'll be free to hunt you down. And you know he will! He's connected to gang leaders all over this state." She took a stab at the arguments she thought Lee would use.

"I can't stay here, awright?" Denny said in a taut voice. "I got a gun. If anybody tries to screw with me, I'll—"

"No, no, no! Don't make another big mistake!" Andrea stood and paced as she talked. "What will you do for money? Your grandmother is barely making it on her pension. You can't expect her to help."

"I'll find a job that pays cash. I'll go someplace nobody would expect to look."

"Okay, so maybe I can give you a little cash. Let's meet somewhere."

"No," Denny said promptly. "Maybe you're in with the sheriff now. You want me arrested because of what I did."

"I promised your grandmother I'd help you. That's what I'm trying to do," Andrea said with intensity. "I want to keep my promise. Please tell me where to meet you."

She stood rooted to the floor with her eyes closed, praying. He was silent. All she could hear was heavy breathing for what seemed like an eternity.

"Okay. Meet me at the Waffle Shack on Fourth Street in Houma."

Andrea sat down hard on the bed, her legs weak with relief. "You've made the right choice."

"And don't bring anybody with you. I'll sit where I can see you come in the parking lot," he warned.

She swore silently before answering. "I won't." There was a click and he was gone.

Andrea yanked clothes aside in her closet until she found a pair of jeans and a Grambling University T-shirt. She laced up her sneakers, grabbed her keys and raced out the door. She paused only to lock the dead bolt. She sped down Highway 20, praying that Denny wouldn't change his mind before she got there. The speedometer needled crept up to eighty-five.

"Careful, careful," she muttered to herself as she eased her foot off the gas pedal.

The last thing she needed was to be stopped for

speeding or have an accident. She suffered through a series of stoplights in the small city. She muttered a curse word and drummed her fingers on the steering wheel.

"Come on! Why does the light stay red so long? They roll up the darn sidewalks when the sun sets."

A police car pulled up beside her on the four-lane highway through the middle of the business district. The officer stared at Andrea with an impassive expression. She stopped talking to herself and avoided his gaze. When the light turned green she waited. The police car did not move. Andrea drove ahead slowly. He followed for two blocks, then turned.

"Thank you, Lord," Andrea whispered. "Now go down one more light. There it is."

She was able to park near the door. At this hour, only one waitress and one customer were in the restaurant. Huge glass windows dominated three walls of the Waffle Shack. Andrea looked around, but did not see Denny's car outside or Denny inside. She suspected he was not far away. The waitress stood pouring coffee in a brown mug for the customer.

"Sit anywhere, baby. I'll be right with ya," the woman called out.

"A cup of decaf, please," Andrea said, and chose a booth not visible from the street.

Five minutes later the waitress plunked a brown mug on the table. "Wanna order now or waitin' for somebody?" Her name tag read MARGIE.

Andrea's stomach rumbled at the possibility of food. She had not eaten dinner the night before. "Bring me a bagel and fat-free cream cheese."

Margie giggled and handed her a menu. "Sugar, this is the original greasy spoon. We ain't got no bagels and ain't nothin' fat-free."

Andrea could not help but smile. "At least you have decaf. Bring me a doughnut."

"You got it." Margie winked at her and flounced off. "What you want, baby?" she asked the man seated at the counter.

The man rumbled his order low. Andrea turned her attention back to the expanse of glass. The privacy of her booth was a trade-off since she could not easily watch who approached from outside. She strained to see the small corner of parking lot still visible from her position. Ten minutes later, headlights flashed as a car swung into the parking lot. The lights winked out and a car door slammed seconds later. Tension knotted the muscles in her back as she watched the door.

"Please let it be him," Andrea whispered between clenched teeth.

The glass door swung open. Andrea gasped in surprise when Lee walked in. His gaze swept the entire restaurant. His jaw tightened when he saw Andrea, but he still did not move. She squirmed nervously when his dark eyes narrowed with anger. The male customer turned his head around. He gave Lee only a brief glance before he looked away again. Lee studied the man for a beat, then headed for Andrea. His long-legged stride exuded restrained power, as though he could spring to action if needed. There was an animalistic grace in his every moved. This man had been a cop, but had easily passed for a ruthless gang member. Which side ruled tonight, good guy or bad boy? Her body tingled at the possible answer.

"What the *hell* are you doing out here?" Lee said harshly, his deep voice low and urgent. "I told you to stay home."

"I couldn't do that," Andrea said with just as much

intensity, then lowered her voice to a whisper. "I heard from him. Did you follow me?"

"I went back to your apartment to make sure nobody suspicious was hanging around. Ty'Rance has had his gang watching the clinic. I had to make sure you were all right."

"Thanks." Andrea smiled weakly, then sobered when he didn't smile back.

"And I was going to warn you not to do anything silly." Lee's eyes narrowed. "Like go off on your own to meet him."

"I was going to call you once I talked to him," Andrea said. "I swear!" she added at his skeptical frown.

"You should have called me before you did anything, Andrea."

"He was watching to see if I was followed." Andrea groaned. "He's probably running off as we speak, thanks to you."

"I'm in a Ford Explorer, so he wouldn't recognize that. Besides, I checked out the area for five blocks around. Denny's not here yet unless he's invisible." Lee glanced at the other customer. "I'll wait with you."

"No! He'll take off for sure then. Slip out before he sees you. I can talk him into coming with me." Andrea leaned across the pockmarked table.

"Forget it, Andrea. I'm not going to leave you out here exposed." Lee scanned the restaurant for a third time.

"Don't play superhero! There's nobody here." Andrea chafed with frustration at the stubborn set to his jaw. "I'll be okay."

"No."

"I've got my cell phone. I'll call you the minute—"

"No," Lee said again in a level tone.

"That's right, play the big, strong PI," she muttered. "I'm in this whether you like it or not. I was your number one suspect, remember?"

"And for that I owe you?" Lee's full lips lifted at one corner. "Nice try." He settled back in the booth.

Andrea pressed her lips together and crossed her arms. They sat across from each other without speaking for another ten minutes. Andrea glared at him. Lee gazed back at her with an implacable expression. She jumped when his cell phone rang. Lee calmly pressed the call button and answered.

"Yeah? Where? How the hell am I— Right, right. I'll be there." Lee ended the call and frowned.

"Has the sheriff found him?" Andrea leaned forward.

"Go home, baby. Denny isn't coming." Lee started to get up, but stopped when Andrea clutched his arm.

"I'm not going anywhere until you tell me what's happened." Andrea tightened her hold.

"That was Ty'Rance. They've got Denny and won't let him go unless I deliver the drugs from the clinic." Lee tapped a forefinger on the table, a restless beat to help him think. "It's a test. They'll kill him if I get the sheriff involved. The bastard!"

Andrea now held on to him with both hands. His expression had turned cold and deadly. "You can't do it alone." She put everything into speaking with calm, persuasive force.

"Just go home. I'll handle it."

"How? You've got to give them something and you can't get into the clinic without me." Andrea raised her eyebrows. "You don't know the code for the security system."

"Then give it to me," Lee said sharply.

"No, and that slightly insane ex-cop look doesn't scare me," she said stubbornly, crossing her arms.

"Damn it!" Lee slapped the table so hard it wobbled.

"Don't waste time on temper tantrums," she tossed at him. "Let's go." She stood.

Lee stood with her. "You let me in, then leave," he said, and pointed his finger at her nose.

Andrea pushed her hair from her eyes. "Agreed. You can call Sheriff Boudreaux on the way," she whispered back, then spun around and walked off.

Lee trotted a few steps before he caught up with her. "So now you're an expert at this?" he said close to her ear.

"No, but you are," she said over her shoulder. "I know that's what you would do anyway."

"I hadn't decided. It might not be such a good idea until I know more," Lee said gruffly.

Andrea pushed through the door. Lee came out right on her heels. "You call him or I will. Good cops understand you can't hotdog. You need backup."

"You've been watching too much TV," Lee mumbled.

Andrea did not rise to his taunt. "You know I'm right."

They both got into their separate cars. With a taut frown, he motioned for her to lead the way. Andrea peeled off. The drive back to Bayou Blue did not take long. Traffic was sparse at four in the morning. Pushing eighty-five miles an hour most of the way on the two-lane highway helped. They arrived downtown fifteen minutes later. Andrea drove into the parking lot of the clinic first, with Lee close behind. Lee jumped out of his car and strode toward her.

"You can still give me the keys and the code." He held out a large hand, palm up.

Andrea ignored him and opened the door. She went to the keypad. Lights on the panel flashed rapidly and a high-pitched beep sounded. Both stopped once she entered the code.

"I know exactly what they want," she called over her shoulder as she ran down the hall. "This stuff will get them really excited."

He locked the door and came up fast behind her. "I don't want them excited, I want them pounded into the dirt."

Andrea stopped at the locked pharmacy door but did not open it. "Did you call the sheriff?"

He put both hands on his waist. "Open the door."

"Did you? I don't want you in this alone, Lee."

"Yes, now come on!" Lee yelled.

"Good." Andrea unlocked the back door within seconds.

"Damn it, woman. I've been on the street since I was fifteen. I can take care of business—"

"Right, big, strong secret agent man," Andrea cut him off. She looked around inside at the shelves. "Hmm, painkillers and muscle relaxants. Those should satisfy that scum." She helped him stack six boxes on a small wheeled cart.

Andrea followed him as he pushed the cart down the hall and out the back door. They loaded the boxes into the trunk of his car. Lee waited while Andrea put the cart back inside the clinic and locked up.

Lee grabbed her by the shoulders. "Now, go home, Andrea. I mean it this time. It's the best way you can help."

Andrea wrapped her arms around him and squeezed for a moment. "Okay. Please be careful."

Lee kissed her forehead. "Don't worry. I want to come back to you."

Then she felt something hard and cool. Andrea reached down to his brown leather belt. Lee had a small automatic pistol hooked to it. The gun was hidden beneath the light cotton jacket he wore.

"Good Lord," she whispered, and gazed up at him.

Just then a car pulled up, the sudden glare of the headlights momentarily blinding them. Three men got out of a Chevy Blazer. Andrea blinked against the glare at the dark figures. Then her vision cleared and her heart froze at what she saw. One of the men had Denny by the arm with one hand as he pointed an automatic pistol at Denny's temple with the other. A big man with a toothy grin that lacked humor strode forward. Lee tried to push Andrea behind him. She held on to him, her arms still around his waist.

"Ain't this sweet. Sorry we gotta interrupt such a warm moment."

"What's up with this, Ty? I thought you wanted me to meet you," Lee said, forcing a casual tone. He used his body to shield Andrea.

"Yeah, well, I changed my mind. I'm like that, ya know? Especially when I been lied to." The mean grin turned menacing. "Your boy spilled his damn guts."

"Hold up—"

"No, you hold up!" Ty'Rance snarled. "Good thing I had my boys watchin' him. We caught him tryin' to run out on our deal."

"Don't do something stupid," Lee said.

"Uh-uh, not me. Y'all stupid for thinkin' you could

play me! Gonna take it all for yourselves, huh? You, him, and your woman had it all figured out."

Andrea felt Lee stiffen. Denny had used his street smarts to give them as much time as he could. Ty'Rance thought they were going to steal the drugs and cut him out. She gazed at Denny. No doubt he knew Ty'Rance would understand being double-crossed by another criminal and would come after them. That kept Denny alive a few hours more. Far safer than if Ty'Rance knew the real story. But they were still in serious trouble. Andrea gazed up at Lee. Lee stared at Denny, then looked at Ty'Rance.

"Well, punk?" Ty'Rance barked.

Lee broke free of Andrea's grasp. He pointed at Denny. "You lying little piece of shit! I don't know anything about it."

"Blow it out your ass, Jamal!" Denny screamed back. "It was his idea, Ty! All of it. He told me he had connections with Li'l Bootsie in New Orleans."

"I don't know any dude named Bootsie in New Orleans," Lee yelled. "You can't trust Denny, man."

"Yeah, go ahead, Jamal," Denny shot back. "Try to sell that cheap-ass talk. Ain't nobody buyin' it, though."

"So he should listen to you? Denny, man, you know damn well if it wasn't for me—"

"If it wasn't for you, I wouldn't have no gun in my face, punk!"

Andrea shivered in fear at the dangerous game. She knew he and Denny were playing off each other. The lies were being spun fast and furious. They were improvising like two rap musicians, making it up as they went along. Ty'Rance watched them, his lifeless eyes narrowed to reptilian slits.

"Let's pop all of 'em, Ty!" The man holding the gun on Denny looked wired. Denny grunted when he jammed it hard against his head. "Then we can get the goods without all this hassle."

"Everybody just shut up!" Ty'Rance roared. He paced in a circle for several minutes. He stopped and hitched up his pants in a gesture of machismo. "This is how it's gonna be. I want my stuff. Where is it?"

"In my trunk. All the stuff you wanted. I was gonna deliver it to you, man." Lee pointed to his car.

"Open it," Ty'Rance said.

"I was just slippin' off to see my lady, Ty. I was comin' back. I want money same as you." Denny spoke carefully. "There's lots more where that came from. But we gotta order it."

Lee opened the trunk with his remote. He did not move until Ty'Rance walked over and opened it wide. Then he started toward the car. "That's the only thing he's not lying about, man. You need us."

Ty'Rance held up one hand to indicate Lee should come no closer. He took out a switchblade and cut open the thick cardboard of one box and examined the contents. He turned around to face them again.

"Yeah. Good stuff."

"Like I told you," Lee said.

"Not you. I set it up," Denny complained.

Suddenly, Ty'Rance turned and looked at Andrea. He raked her with a gaze that left her feeling soiled. "Hey, pretty lady. We ain't been introduced."

"She's out of it," Lee said quickly.

"That ain't what Denny told me. Damn, she's fine, too." He slowly took her in from head to toe again. "I'll let you boys go. The dope and the woman are mine."

"Hell no!" Lee took a step forward. He stopped when

the man pointing the gun at Denny aimed at him instead.

"I didn't ask, I'm tellin' you," Ty'Rance said in a flat, cold tone. "This is part payment for all the trouble you caused me. Keep deliverin' the goods and you'll both keep on livin'."

"She's not part of the deal we had, Ty." Lee's deep voice thundered with rage.

"Keep on, fool, and I'll kill you right here, right now. Don't matter to me," the man with the gun said.

Ty'Rance crossed to Andrea and grabbed her arm. "C'mon, baby. I got more of what you need than either of these tired-ass punks."

He yanked her against his body and Andrea recoiled at the scent of sweat, cigarette smoke, and too much cologne. "Take your greasy, stinking hands off me."

Ty'Rance laughed and rolled his pelvis suggestively. "You gonna scream for more."

Lee tackled Ty'Rance low and knocked him to the ground with lightning speed. Andrea went down with them. She struggled to keep both of the heavy men from rolling on her. Ty'Rance held on to her with an iron grip. Andrea bit down with all her might on the meaty hand. Ty'Rance screamed in pain and she bit harder. She rammed her knee in his side for good measure.

"Cut it out or I'll shoot your ass!" The man with the gun swung it wildly. He held on to Denny, but jumped around as he watched the tangle of arms and legs.

"Oh shit, it's the sheriff!" Denny pointed at a dark car in the distance. He jerked on the man. "Let's get outta here. They catch us with those drugs, it's twenty years."

"Ty'Rance, c'mon, man. It's the cops," the man croaked. His eyes were glassy with panic as his gaze darted in every direction.

Denny jerked free and sprinted off into the dark. The man fired a shot at him. Denny stumbled but tried to keep moving. He dragged his left leg. The man fired again. Denny went down and did not get up.

"No, no!" Andrea shrieked at the sight of him crumpled on the pavement.

Another shot rang out behind her. She turned to find Lee and Ty'Rance struggling to control Ty'Rance's gun. Andrea started toward Denny just as another shot exploded. Suddenly a swirl of red and blue lights washed over the scene.

"Get down, Andrea," Lee shouted. His fist smashed into Ty'Rance's chin. The gang leader's head snapped back and his eyes lost focus.

"Drop that weapon!" A voice ordered.

Crouching on the rough pavement, Andrea turned in the direction of the command. A tall, black sheriff's deputy aimed his gun at the man who'd shot Denny. Lee continued to pound Ty'Rance. Through a haze, Andrea recognized Sheriff Boudreaux.

"Hey, hey! You made your point, son." Sheriff Boudreaux and another deputy pried Lee off Ty'Rance. The young deputy handcuffed Ty'Rance.

Lee stood slowly, still panting from exertion. "Had a little change of plans," he gasped to the sheriff.

"So I see," Sheriff Boudreaux quipped. He walked over to where Ty'Rance sat on the concrete with his hands bound behind him. "Guess you done figured this out, but you under arrest, son. Read 'em their rights, then get 'em down to the jail."

Andrea ran toward Denny. "He's hurt, Lee."

When she got to him, his blue T-shirt was stained with blood and dirt. His eyes were half-open. Andrea checked his pulse and touched his skin. It was clammy. "He's going into shock."

"Paramedics on the way, ma'am," a deputy told her.

Andrea shouted orders to the men to help her. She located a flesh wound to his thigh and a ragged bullet wound in his right side. While they turned him over, Andrea dashed into the clinic and got latex gloves, a sheet to cover him, and bandages to stop the flow of blood. The wail of sirens was a welcome sound. A female paramedic rushed from the emergency vehicle as Andrea rushed back outside. They worked together to clean and wrap the wounds. Denny was placed on a gurney by a male paramedic with help from two deputies. Seconds later, they drove away. Andrea watched the white and red lights disappear, listening to sirens fade into the distance. Lee was at her side.

"He'll be okay?" he asked, putting one around her shoulder.

"I don't know," she mumbled, and sagged against his hip. "I'm going to dispose of these and lock up." She held up her gloved hands.

Lee told Sheriff Boudreaux he'd be right back and accompanied her into the clinic. She went to the first examining room, stripped off the gloves, and washed her hands thoroughly in the sink.

"Did you get hurt?" Andrea said over her shoulder.

"Fine time to ask," Lee teased. He leaned against the exam table.

Andrea tore a paper towel from the dispenser, then faced him. She smiled tiredly. "You were beating the hell out of the guy. I figured you didn't need my help."

Lee rubbed his chin. His face was pinched with fatigue. "God, what a night."

"You mean morning. Five-fifteen to be exact." Andrea pointed to a round clock on the wall in the hallway.

"I better call Denny's grandmother," he said.

Andrea gazed at him. Lee looked as though he would collapse at any moment. He must have gone without much rest for days. "I can do it. You look kinda whipped yourself, Matthews."

"No, she should hear it from me. Like you said, I got him into this." He pushed himself away from the table. "I'm going to the hospital after I talk to her."

"Me, too. And I'll be with you when you call her." Andrea enfolded him in her arms. They swayed together for a few seconds, his face buried in her hair. Then they walked out together. Lee waited while she locked the clinic one last time.

Two days later, they were all at Andrea's apartment. Gran had insisted on preparing them a special dinner. Lee and Andrea still moved around gingerly, both bruised from the struggle with Ty'Rance. They sat in the living room after eating Gran's famous peach crunch for dessert. Gran clucked at them and shook her head. "Y'all young people think you're indestructible. Look at ya." She shook her head again.

"It only hurts when we laugh," Lee joked.

"I told y'all what to do. Tante Rosalie's salve works wonders." Gran held up a dark blue glass jar and took off the metal cap. Andrea and Lee gasped at the strong smell.

"Oh Lord! Put that stuff up before we pass out." Andrea waved a hand in front of her face. "Lord have mercy."

"Whew!" Lee blinked. "I won't have a stuffy nose for another ten years."

"Couple of big babies. Suppose you think modern medicine has all the answers." Gran put the lid back on the jar. She stuffed it in her huge purse. "All those miracle cures came from herbs. The old folks used 'em years ago. And they didn't need no prescriptions."

"Went right into the woods when they needed something," Andrea and Lee said together, then laughed. They had heard the speech at least ten times in the past two days.

"All right, smarties. One day you'll need the Fontenot family remedies." Gran shook a finger at them. Then she smiled with affection. "I'm just happy you rascals can still clown around. Hope Denny will be all right."

"Don't worry, Gran. He's responding well after the surgery. It will take a while, but he should be okay," Andrea said.

"At least the bullets didn't hit any major organs or sever an artery. Man, there was so much blood." Lee brushed Andrea's hair with one hand. "You saved him, baby."

"I had help. He's going to need physical therapy, but the prognosis is pretty positive." Andrea sighed.

Denny had emergency surgery that very night. Andrea had been there to explain it all to his frightened grandmother. The doctor had assured them that youth and good health were in his favor. He proved right. It had been touch and go for a while, but Denny had come through.

"And thank goodness that hoodlum is going to jail," Gran said.

"Ty'Rance won't be planning crime waves in Lafourche Parish for a good long time." Lee put a protective arm around Andrea.

Gran stood. "Well, children, I'm going home."

"Don't rush off, sweetie." Andrea stood and nuzzled Gran's cheek. "We want to hear more stories from the old days."

"I'm not young and these old bones need rest. Besides, y'all want to be alone. You both got that sparkle in your eyes." Gran winked at them.

"Give me some sugar before you go." Lee kissed her forehead. "Thanks, Gran."

"Pooh-ya! You don't need to thank family, son." Gran gave him a big hug. "Now, I got to get plenty of rest before tomorrow night."

"What's going on tomorrow night?" Andrea said. She and Lee walked with her to the door.

"Senior citizens dance. Mr. Walter swears we're gonna boogie all night." Gran giggled and waved goodbye.

Lee held Andrea against him as they watched Gran drive away. "She was right. I've got a sparkle in my eye for you," he murmured.

Andrea wiggled in his arms. "So prove it."

Lee pulled her inside the door and closed it. "Can you put up with a guy like me? I'm not always levelheaded or conventional. I know how you hate drama. As for my job, being a private investigator is . . ."

"Not exactly conventional sometimes," she finished for him. "And you don't always tell the truth to do it." Andrea raised her eyebrows at him.

"Not lies . . . exactly." He grinned for a moment, then became serious. "There's a lot about me you don't know. I—"

Andrea pushed him down on the sofa and covered his body with hers. She caressed his thighs as she spoke. "I look forward to probing your secrets," she whispered huskily. His reply was a moan and a long, passionate kiss.

Coming Next . . .

CRAZY THING CALLED LOVE

BY CINDI LOUIS

August 2001

The following is a sneak peek . . .

Irene Newman had warned Jayda that the first-floor apartment at the rear of Paradise was small—and it was—but it had all the character of the old lady herself. There were two fireplaces with Italian tile, fourteen-foot ceilings that gave the impression of spaciousness, and stained-glass windows that surveyed the rear gardens, from where Pleasure Pier could be seen. She took one look and she was in love.

In spite of the size of the place, however, it took the rest of the day to arrange and rearrange the furniture and get everything where she thought she wanted it. Muscles she hadn't known she had ached, and all she wanted to do was take a hot shower and crawl into bed. But she couldn't do that until she found some sheets and towels.

Jayda was bent over headfirst in a large cardboard box, searching for her linens, when a loud *thump* from upstairs caused her to straighten in surprise. Glancing up, she frowned as something hit the floor so hard in the apartment directly above hers that it shook the old-fashioned light fixture suspended from her ceiling. Before she could blink, it happened again . . . then again.

What in the world was going on up there? she wondered, frowning. It sounded as though whoever lived upstairs was dropping blocks of concrete on the floor. And if they kept it up, her light fixture was going to shake loose and come crashing down on her head.

Jayda wasn't a woman who lost her temper easily—she couldn't do so and still maintain control of a court-room with any degree of decorum. So when she started up the stairs to the second floor nearly twenty minutes later, she was calm and cool and more than willing to be friendly.

But when she knocked on the door to apartment 2A and her new neighbor came to see who was calling at nearly ten-thirty at night, the friendly smile that hovered at the corners of her mouth abruptly disappeared. Stunned, she stared in disbelief at Jason McNeal.

Far from impressed with his boyish grin and wicked gray eyes, Jayda didn't even blink. She knew all about the infamous Mr. McNeal and his way with women. Rumor had it that he'd never been turned down for a date, and she could believe it. Good-looking didn't begin to describe the man.

His smooth peanut butter-colored skin and dove-gray eyes weren't the only things that caught Jayda's attention. There was also his square jaw, his sensuous mouth bracketed by deep dimples, and his black, wavy hair cut conservatively short, in addition to well-built, all-hard muscles. That's why he should have been in Hollywood giving Denzel a run for his money instead of trying to knock a hole in her ceiling.

He'd been lifting weights. Behind him in the living room a set of barbells rested on the floor where he'd dropped them, and somewhere in the back of her head Jayda realized that the repeated *thud* she'd heard in her apartment was his weights hitting the floor. That thought, however, barely registered as her widened eyes took him in from head to toe. Her gaze traveled back up his long, hairy legs, stopping at his narrow hips and again at his washboard stomach, but his chest, wide and hairy, made her realize she was still a woman.

Good Lord, the man was big! Who could have guessed that beneath his Armani suits was a lean, rangy body that looked as though it belonged on the cover of *Ebony Man*?

Her mouth dry and her heart thundering, she couldn't keep her eyes from wandering from his bare feet all the way up the long, magnificent length of him. He had to be at least six feet, three inches. She'd heard the gossip about him, seen the way women, including her own clerk, sighed over him whenever he strode down the courthouse corridors, and had never understood what all the fuss was about.

Granted, with his chiseled jaw, sensuous mouth, and dimples, he was drop-dead gorgeous, but no more so than several other good-looking attorneys in town. But now, as her brown eyes lifted to his gray ones and she saw the self-directed humor there, she understood why females of every age tended to make fools of themselves over Jason McNeal. And here she was ogling him like a schoolgirl who'd just stumbled across the captain of the football team.

Furious with herself, she stiffened like a poker, the neighborly little speech she'd planned flying right out of her head. "Do you have any idea what time it is, counselor?"

Propping a shoulder against the doorjamb, he grinned. "I've had women knock on my door to borrow a cup of sugar, but this is the first time one has asked me for the time. I believe it's going on ten-thirty. Do I know you, sweetheart?"

Check these sizzlers from sisters who deliver!

Skin Deep
by Kathleen Cross   0-380-81130-8/$6.99 US/$8.99 Can

Homecourt Advantage
by Rita Ewing and Crystal McCrary
                                    0-380-79901-4/$6.99 US/$8.99 Can

Shoe's on the Otha' Foot
by Hunter Hayes   0-06-101466-4/$6.50 US/$8.99 Can

Wishin' on a Star
by Eboni Snoe   0-380-81395-5/$5.99 US/$7.99 Can

A Chance on Lovin' You
by Eboni Snoe   0-380-79563-9/$5.99 US/$7.99 Can

Tell Me I'm Dreamin'
by Eboni Snoe   0-380-79562-0/$5.99 US/$7.99 Can

Ain't Nobody's Business If I Do
by Valerie Wilson Wesley
                                    0-380-80304-6/$6.99 US/$9.99 Can

If You Want Me
by Kayla Perrin   0-380-81378-5/$5.99 US/$7.99 Can

From best-selling author
Beverly Jenkins
books you will never forget

NIGHT SONG
0-380-77658-8/$5.99 US/$7.99 Can

TOPAZ
0-380-78660-5/$5.99 US/$7.99 Can

THROUGH THE STORM
0-380-79864-6/$7.99 US/$9.99 Can

THE TAMING OF JESSI ROSE
0-380-79865-4/$5.99 US/$7.99 Can

ALWAYS AND FOREVER
0-380-81374-2/$5.99 US/$7.99 Can

0-380-80714-9/$6.99 US/$9.99 Can

A man who doesn't believe in love and a woman who
doesn't trust it find out just how wrong they can be . . .

And Don't Miss

BABY, DON'T GO

0-380-80712-2/$6.50 US/$8.99 Can
"[A] madcap and humorous romp . . ."
Romantic Times

BE MY BABY

0-380-79512-4/$6.50 US/$8.99 Can
"Sexy humor and smoldering passion . . .
Don't miss out!"
Romantic Times

BABY, I'M YOURS

0-380-79511-6/$6.50 US/$8.99 Can
"Sassy, snappy, and sizzling hot!"
Janet Evanovich

Available wherever books are sold or please call 1-800-331-3761
to order.
SA 0101